KT-417-345

Praise for John Sandford

'Sometimes Sandford takes you to places you'd rather not be. But the sheer quality of the writing makes him unmissable' *Literary Review*

'In a crowded market, Sandford shines at the quality end' *Daily Telegraph*

'Delivers twists to the very last sentence' *Daily Mail*

'A series writer who reads like a breath of fresh air' *Daily Mirror*

'Sandford is a cunning writer. He constantly avoids the routine or expected with intelligent and surprising new wrinkles' *Washington Post*

'An exciting and superbly elegant demonstration of intelligent crime writing' *Guardian*

'His effortlessly fluid writing and plotting really impress and his pithy characterization is often sensational' *London Lite*

Pulitzer-prize winning journalist John Sandford is the author of eighteen PREY novels, four KIDD novels and the stand-alone thriller, DEAD WATCH. He lives in Minnesota.

Visit www.johnsandford.org

Also by John Sandford

Winter Prey
Sudden Prey
Secret Prey
Certain Prey
Easy Prey
Chosen Prey
Mortal Prey
Naked Prey
Mind Prey
Hidden Prey
Broken Prey
Invisible Prey
Phantom Prey

Dead Watch
The Night Crew

Kidd Novels

The Fool's Run
The Empress File
The Devil's Code
The Hanged Man's Song

Published by Pocket Books

DARK
OF THE
MOON

JOHN SANDFORD

POCKET
BOOKS

LONDON · SYDNEY · NEW YORK · TORONTO

First published in Great Britain by Pocket Books, 2008
An imprint of Simon & Schuster UK Ltd
A CBS COMPANY

Copyright © John Sandford, 2007

This book is copyright under the Berne Convention.
No reproduction without permission.
® and © 1997 Simon & Schuster Inc. All rights reserved.
Pocket Books & Design is a registered trademark of Simon & Schuster Inc.

The right of John Sandford to be identified as author of this work
has been asserted by him in accordance with sections 77 and 78
of the Copyright, Designs and Patents Act, 1988.

1 3 5 7 9 10 8 6 4 2

Simon & Schuster UK Ltd
1st Floor
222 Gray's Inn Road
London WC1X 8HB

www.simonsays.co.uk

Simon & Schuster Australia
Sydney

A CIP catalogue record for this book
is available from the British Library

ISBN 978-1-84739-185-8

This book is a work of fiction. Names, characters, places and
incidents are either a product of the author's imagination or are used
fictitiously. Any resemblance to actual people living or dead,
events or locales is entirely coincidental.

Typeset in Dante by M Rules

Printed by CPI Cox & Wyman, Reading, Berkshire RG1 8EX

For Benjamin Curtis: Happy Birthday, 2007

Acknowledgment

This book was written in cooperation with my friend Larry Millett, an architectural writer (*The Curve of the Arch, Lost Twin Cities*), local historian (*Strange Days, Dangerous Nights*), and occasional novelist (*Sherlock Holmes and the Red Demon* and four other tales featuring Holmes and Irish barkeep Shadwell Rafferty). Millett was recently described in a general-circulation magazine as "handsome," which threw me into paroxysms of jealousy, but which, in the end, did not deflect us from our appointed deadline. . . .

—JOHN SANDFORD

1

SIX GARBAGE BAGS full of red cedar shavings, purchased two at a time for a dollar a bag, at midnight, at the self-serve shed at Dunstead & Daughter Custom Furniture, serving your fine cabinetry needs since 1986. No cameras, no lights, no attendant, no theft, no problem.

Moonie stacked the bags in the basement, Cross Canadian Ragweed pounding through the iPod ear-buds, singing about those dead-red lips; then up the stairs, pulling the ear-buds, to where the old man lay facedown on the rug, shaking, kicking, crying, trying to get free. Tied with cheap hemp rope, but no matter. The old man was so old and so feeble that string would have worked as well as rope.

"Please," he groaned, "don't hurt me."

Moonie laughed, a long singing rock 'n' roll laugh, and at the end of it, said, "I'm not going to *hurt* you. I'm going to *kill* you."

"What do you want? I can tell you where the money is."

"The money's not what I want. I've got what I want."

Moonie gripped the rope between the old man's ankles and dragged him to the basement stairs, and then down the stairs, the old man's face banging down each tread as they went.

"Oh my Jesus, help me," the old man wept through his bloody lips, his fractured face. "Help me, Jesus."

Thump! Thump! Thump! Nine times.

"Jesus isn't going to help," Moonie said.

The old man pulled it together for a second. "He can send you to hell," he snarled.

"Where do you think I am, old man?"

"You . . ."

"Shut up. I'm working."

GETTING THE OLD MAN onto the bags was the hardest part. Moonie first threw him facedown on the topmost bag, then heaved his feet up. The old man was tall, but frail; eighty-two years old and sedentary and semi-senile, though not so senile that he didn't know what was happening now. He sank down into the bags of wood shavings and thrashed there, got halfway off, then sank down between them, thrashed some more, then quit. Wood shavings made for the most intense fire, and left no obvious residue; or so the arson fans theorized on the Internet.

Moonie got busy with the first five-gallon can of gasoline, pouring it around the basement, around the bags, soaking the old man with it, the unused wooden canning racks, the seldom used workbench, the stack of aging wooden lawn chairs, and then up the stairs. The old man began thrashing again. Moaning, "Please . . ."

The first few splashes of gasoline smelled good, like the shot you got when you were pumping gas into your car; but down in the enclosed space, five gallons of gas, the fumes got stiff in a hurry.

"Don't die on me. Wait for the fire," Moonie called, backing up the stairs, splashing gas along the steps. The second can was poured more judiciously around the first floor, soaking into the Persian carpets, leaking around the legs of the Steinway grand piano, flowing into the closets. When two-thirds of it was gone, Moonie backed through the kitchen, where the first can, now empty, waited. Moonie would take them. No point in making the arson obvious, though the police would probably figure it out soon enough.

A driving rain beat against the kitchen windows. Ideally, Moonie would have preferred to trail the gas out into the yard, and to touch it off from a distance. With the rain, though, that would be difficult. The rain would wash the gas away as quickly as it was poured. So it would have to be kept inside. A small risk . . . the fumes boiled unseen around the killer's ankles, flowing into every nook and cranny.

At the kitchen door, Moonie splashed out a final pool of gas; stopped and looked into the house. The place was huge, expensive, and a wreck. The old man's housekeeper came in twice a week, did some dishes, washed some clothes; but she didn't do carpentry, wiring, or plumbing, and the house needed all of it, along with a wide-spectrum exterminator. There were bugs in the basement and bats in the belfry, the killer thought, and then, giggling now, a nut in the kitchen.

The old man cried a last time, faintly audible against the sound of the rain and wind . . .

"Please, God help me . . ."

Good to know he was still alive—the old man would get the full experience.

Moonie stepped through the kitchen door onto the back porch, took out a book of matches, scratched one, used that one to set off the entire book. The book cover caught, and Moonie played with it, enjoying the liquid flow of the flame, getting it right, then threw the book toward the pool of gas in the kitchen, turned, and ran out into the rain.

The fire popped to the top of the pool of gasoline, flickered across it, snaked one way into the living room, under the shambles of the once grand piano, and the other way, like a living thing, down the stairs into the basement.

The fumes in the basement were not quite thick enough for a real explosion. The old man, surrounded by bags of wood shavings, heard a *whump* and felt the sudden searing heat of a blowtorch that burned away all feeling in an instant, and killed in the next.

That was all for him.

2

Coming Up on Midnight

THE RAIN WAS POUNDING down from a wedge of thunderstorms, and Virgil Flowers was running west on I-90, trying to hold the truck against the angling wind. He'd been due in Bluestem before the courthouse closed, but he'd had a deposition with a defense attorney in Mankato. The attorney, a month out of law school with his first criminal case, had left no stone unturned and no verb unconjugated. Not that Virgil blamed him. The guy was trying to do right by his client.

Yes, the gun had been found in *that* dumpster. The dumpster had *not* been hauled before Wednesday, June 30, even though it was normally dumped on Tuesday, but everything had been pushed back by Memorial Day. The pizza guy had seen the defendant on the 29th, and not the 28th, because the pizza parlor, as patriotic as any Italian-food outlet anywhere, had been closed on Memorial Day, and the pizza guy hadn't been working.

Three hours of it: Blah, blah, blah . . .

By the time he got out of the lawyer's office it was five o'clock, too late to get to Bluestem while the courthouse

was open. Walking along with Lannie McCoy, the prosecutor in the case, they'd decided that the wise course
would be to get sandwiches and beer at Cat's Cradle, a
downtown bar.

They did that, and some cops showed up and that all
turned into an enjoyable nachos, cheeseburger, and beer
snack. One of the cops was very good-looking, and at one
juncture, had rested her hand on Virgil's thigh; perfect, if
her wedding ring hadn't shown up so well in the bar light.

A sad country song.

HE LEFT the Cradle at six-thirty, went home, dumped a
load of laundry in the washing machine. With the washer
rattling in the background, he sat on a rocking chair in his
bedroom and finished sewing a torn seam on a photography vest. Sat in a cone of light from his bedside reading
lamp, sewing, and wondering about the married cop who'd
come on to him; thinking a bit about loyalty and its implications, and the trouble it could bring you.

Feeling a little lonely. He liked women, and it had been
some time since the last one.

When he finished with the vest, he hung it in his gear
closet—guns, bows, fishing and photography equipment—
took a shotgun and two boxes of shells out of his gun safe,
laid them beside an empty duffel bag. He half filled the
duffel bag with underwear, socks, and T-shirts, three pairs
of jeans. Still waiting for the washer to quit, he went out
on the Internet, looking for a letter from a magazine

publisher. A letter was supposed to be waiting for him, but was not.

He pulled up a half-finished article on bow hunting for wild turkeys, dinked with it until the washer finished the spin cycle, then closed down the computer, threw the wet clothes in the dryer, and took a nap. The clock woke him. After a shower, as he was brushing his teeth, he heard the dryer stop running. His timing was exquisite.

He took the clothes out of the dryer, folded them, put some of them away, and some of them in the duffel bag. He threw the bag in the back of his truck, locked the shotgun in a toolbox, stuck a .40-caliber Smith & Wesson semiautomatic pistol under the front seat, and at ten minutes after ten o'clock, he was out of town, headed southwest down Highway 60.

An hour out of town, he could see the clouds bunching up in the west, lightning jumping around the horizon, while a new crescent moon still showed in his rearview mirror. He hit Windom as the wind front from the first squall line skittered through town, throwing up scrap paper and dead leaves. July was the second-best time on the prairie, right after August; the world began to smell of grain and the harvest to come.

He stopped at a convenience store for coffee. The long-haired clerk said, "Gonna rain like a cow pissin' on a flat rock," and Virgil said, "You betcha." He took a leak himself, got back in the truck as the first fat drops of rain hit the windshield, still moving southwest. He cut I-90 at Worthington, got another cup of coffee, and headed west.

Into the Old West, he thought.

The *real* Old West. The Old West of the Sioux, of the high, dry prairie, of the range, of horse and buffalo country, got started somewhere between Worthington and Bluestem. By the time he got there, to the Old West, the rain was thrashing the 4Runner; another deluge in what was already a record-wet summer.

There weren't many lights this far out, but with the storm, I-90 closed down to a tunnel, nothing ahead, only a dim set of headlights behind him, and an occasional car or truck in the eastbound lane. He kept one eye on the white line on the right, aimed the car into his headlights, and hoped he didn't run off the road.

Listening to satellite radio, Outlaw Country. Switched over to jazz, rotated into hard rock, and then back to country.

THINKING ABOUT IT LATER, he didn't really know when he first became aware of the spark.

The spark started as a mote in his eye, above the right headlight, deep in the rain. Then it took on a more graphic quality, and he noticed it, and noticed at the same time that it had been out there for a while. The spark was a bright, golden hue, and unmoving. Another three miles and he identified it: a fire. A big one. He'd seen a few of them at night, but this was up in the *sky*.

How could it be up in the sky, and not move?

He flashed by an overpass, then caught, a half mile to

his right, the red lights of the Jesus Christ radio station: a five-hundred-foot tower—they build them low on the prairie—with red lights that blinked *Jesus*, then went black, then *Christ*, and then black, and then quickly, *JesusChrist-JesusChrist-JesusChrist.*

If he was at Jesus Christ radio, Virgil thought, the spark wasn't in the sky—it was six miles ahead, north of Bluestem on Buffalo Ridge. There was only one thing that could make a spark that big, from this far away, on Buffalo Ridge: Bill Judd's house. The most expensive house for a hundred and fifty miles around, and it was burning like a barn full of hay.

"That's not something you see every night," he said to Marta Gomez, who was singing "The Circle" on the satellite radio.

He got off at the Highway 75 exit, the rain still pounding down, and went straight past the Holiday Inn, following the line of the highway toward the fire up on the ridge.

BUFFALO RIDGE was a geological curiosity, a rock-strewn quartzite plateau rising three hundred feet above the surrounding landscape. Too rocky to farm, the mound had kept its mantle of virgin prairie, the last wild ground in Stark County.

Sometime in the early sixties, Virgil had been told, Judd built his house on the eastern slope of the mound, most of which later became a state park. Judd was all by himself out there, after his wife died, and his son moved out.

He was sexually predatory, if not a sexual predator. There were rumors of local women making a little on the side, rumors of strange women from big cities, and of races not normally encountered in the countryside; rumors of midnight orgies and screams in the dark—rumors of a Dracula's castle amid the big bluestem.

They were the rumors that might follow any rich man who stayed to himself, Virgil thought, and who at the same time was thoroughly hated.

JUDD HAD STARTED as a civil lawyer, representing the big grain dealers in local lawsuits. Then he'd branched into commodities trading, real estate development, and banking. He'd made his first million before he was thirty.

In the early eighties, already rich, when most men would have been thinking of retirement, he'd been a promoter of the Jerusalem artichoke. Not actually an artichoke, but a variety of sunflower, the plant was hustled to desperate farmers as an endless wonder: a food stock like a potato, a source of ethanol as a biofuel, and best of all, a weedlike plant that would grow anywhere.

It might have been all of that, but the early-eighties fad, promoted by Judd and others, basically had been an intricate pyramid scheme, leveraged through the commodities markets. Farmers would grow seed tubers and sell them to other farmers, who'd grow seed tubers and sell them to more farmers, and eventually somebody, somewhere, would make them into fuel.

They ran out of farmers before they got to the fuel makers; and it turned out that oil would have to cost more than $50 a barrel for fuel makers to break even, and in the early eighties, oil was running at half that. The people who'd staked their futures on the Jerusalem artichoke lost their futures.

Judd was more prosperous than ever.

BUT HATED.

Hated enough, even, to be murdered. Nobody knew where the Jerusalem artichoke money had gone—Judd said it all went for lobbying, for getting bills passed in St. Paul and Washington, for preliminary planning and architectural work on an ethanol plant, and loan service—but most people thought that it went into speculative stocks, and then a bank account somewhere, probably with a number on it, rather than a name.

The Stark County sheriff at the time, a man named Russell Copes, had been elected on a ticket of putting Judd in jail. He hadn't gotten the job done, and had shortly thereafter moved to Montana. The state attorney general took a halfhearted run at Judd, on the evidence developed by Copes, and there'd been a trial in St. Paul. Judd had been acquitted by a confused jury, and had moved back to his house on Buffalo Ridge.

That was a greater mystery than even the Jerusalem artichoke business: why did he stay?

Stark County was a raw, windy corner of the Great Plains

that had been losing population for half a century, bitterly cold in winter, hot and dry in the summer, with nothing much in the way of diversion for a rich man.

Now his mansion was burning down.

Everybody in town would know about the fire; even with the thunderstorm coming through, a half-hundred souls had come out to take a look at it.

When Buffalo Ridge became a state park, Judd had donated two hundred acres of prairie, which had been expansively appraised and provided a nice tax deduction. As part of the deal, the state built an approach road to the top of the hill, where an observation platform was built, so tourists could look at the park's buffalo herd. Judd's driveway came off the road. The way the locals figured it, he not only got a tax deduction for donating two hundred acres of unfarmable rock, he also got the state to maintain his driveway, and plow it in the winter.

Virgil had been to the park a dozen times, and knew his way in, threading past a line of cars and trucks pulled to the edge of County Road 8. A sheriff's squad car blocked the park road up the hill, and a crowd of gawkers stood just below it. Even from a half mile away, the fire looked enormous. He eased the truck past the rubberneckers and up to the squad. A cop in a slicker walked up and Virgil rolled down the window and said, "Virgil Flowers, BCA. Is Stryker up there?"

"Hey, heard you were coming," the cop said. "I'm Little Curly. Yeah, he's up there. Let me get my car out of the way."

"What about Judd?"

Little Curly shook his head: "From what I hear, they can't find him. His housekeeper says he was up there this afternoon. He's senile and don't drive himself anymore . . . so he might still be in there."

"Burning pretty good," Virgil observed.

"It's a fuckin' tornado," Little Curly said. He walked back to his car, climbed into the driver's seat, and pulled it through the fence. A woman with a beer can in her hand flipped back her rain-suit hood and peered through the driver's-side window at Virgil. She was dark-haired, dark-eyed, and good-looking, and she grinned at him and twiddled the fingers on her beer-free hand. Virgil grinned back, gave her a thumbs-up, and went on by Little Curly's car and followed the blacktop up the hill.

At the house, the first thing he noticed was that the fire-fighters weren't fighting the fire. No point. The rain meant that the fire wasn't going anywhere, and when Little Curly called it a tornado, he hadn't been joking. Throwing a few tons of foam on the burning house would have been a waste of good foam.

The cop cars were parked behind the fire trucks, and Virgil moved into last place. He unbelted, knelt on the seat, and dug his rain suit out of the gear bag in the back. The suit had been made for October muskie fishing and New England sailing; not much got through it. He pulled it on, climbed out of the truck.

The sheriff's name was Jimmy Stryker, whom Virgil had more or less known since Stryker had pitched for the

Bluestem Whippets in high school; but everybody on the hill was an anonymous clump of waterproofed nylon, and Virgil had to ask three times before he found him.

"THAT YOU, JIMMY?"

Stryker turned. He was a tall man, square-chinned, with pale hair and hard jade-green eyes. Like most prairie males, he was weather-burnt and wore cowboy boots. "That you, Virgil?"

"Yeah. What happened?"

Stryker turned back to the fire. "Don't know. I was down in my house, and one minute I looked out the window and didn't see anything, and the next minute, I heard the siren going, looked out the window, and there it was. We got a guy who was driving through town, saw it happen: he said it just exploded."

"What about Judd?"

Stryker nodded at the house. "I could be wrong, but I do believe he's in there."

Up closer to the fire, a man in a trench coat, carrying an umbrella, was standing with three firemen, waving his free hand at the fire, and at the trucks, jabbing a finger. In the light of the flames, Virgil could see his mouth working, but couldn't hear what he was saying.

Strkyer said, "That's Bill Judd Jr. He's pissed because they're not putting out the fire."

"The New York City Fire Department couldn't put that out," Virgil said. The heat came through the rain, hot as a hair dryer, even at fifty yards. "That thing is burning a hole in the storm."

"Tell that to Junior."

The fire stank: of burning fabrics and old wood and insulation and water and linoleum and oil and everything else that gets stuck in a house, and maybe a little flesh. They watched for another moment, feeling the heat on the fire side, the cool rain spattering off the hoods on their rain suits, down their backs and necks. Virgil asked, "Think he was smoking in bed?"

Stryker's features were harsh in the firelight, and the corners of his mouth turned down at Virgil's question. "Bill Parker, he's a guy lives up in Lismore, was coming into town on Highway Eight. He saw the fire, mmm, must've been a few minutes after it started. He was driving toward it when a truck went by, moving fast. He figures it was going eighty, ninety miles an hour. And it was raining to beat the band. It took the turn on Highway Three, headed down to Ninety."

"He see what kind of truck?"

"Nope. Not even sure it was a pickup. Might've been an SUV," Stryker said. "All he could see was, the lights was set up high."

They looked at the fire some more and then Virgil said, "Lot of people hated him."

"Yup." A few locals sidled past, grinning, hiding beer cans, having snuck past the cops below. Small town, you took care of yourself: Stryker told them, "You folks stay back out of the way."

They watched for another minute, then Virgil yawned. "Well, good luck to you, Jimmy. I'm heading down to the Holiday Inn."

"Why'd you come up?"

"Just rubbernecking," Virgil said. "Saw the fire when I was coming down Ninety. Knew what it must be."

"Goddamnedest thing," Stryker said, peering into the flames. "I hope that old sonofabitch was dead before the fire got to him. Nobody needs to be burned to death."

"If he did."

"If he did." Stryker frowned suddenly, again turned his green eyes to Virgil. "You don't think he might've faked it? Skipped out to wherever he put that money?"

"I think the money might be a legend, is what I think," Virgil said. He slapped Stryker on the shoulder. "You take it easy, Jimmy. I'll see you tomorrow."

"Not too early. I'll be out here awhile." As Virgil walked away, Stryker called, "That money wasn't no legend, Virgil. He's burnin' because of that money."

Behind him, up closer to the fire, Bill Judd Jr. was still screaming at the firemen, looking like he was one step from a heart attack.

THE HOLIDAY INN was smoke free, and Strictly No Pets, but Virgil's room smelled of smoke and pets anyway—snuck cigarettes and cats in the night—as well as whatever kind of chemical they sprayed in the air to kill the smell of smoke and cat pee. You got two beds whether you wanted them or not. Virgil tossed his bag on one of them, pulled off the rain suit, and hung it over the showerhead to drip-dry.

He was a medium-tall man with blond hair and gray eyes, a half inch over six feet, lean, broad shouldered, long armed with big hands; his hair was way too long for a cop's, but fell short of his shoulders. He'd played the big-three sports in high school, had lettered in all of them, a wide receiver in football, a guard in basketball, a third baseman in baseball. He wasn't big enough or fast enough for college football, he was too short for basketball, and had the arm for college baseball, but couldn't hit the pitching.

He drifted through a degree in ecological science, with a minor in creative writing, because it was easy and interesting and he liked the outdoors, the botany, and the girls in the writing classes. He joined the Army after graduation, got semicoerced into the military police, saw some trouble, but never fired his weapon in anger.

He came back home, found that there was no huge demand for bachelor-degree ecologists, and went off to the Police Academy. Got married, got divorced, got married, got divorced, got married, got divorced, and at the end of a five-year round of silliness, decided he didn't want to be a four-time loser, so he stopped getting married.

He was working for the City of St. Paul as an investigator—eight years on the force, getting bored—when he was borrowed by a Bureau of Criminal Apprehension (BCA) unit looking into a home-invasion ring. One thing led to another, and he moved to the BCA. There, he fell into the orbit of a political appointee named Lucas Davenport who made him an offer he couldn't refuse: "We'll only give you the hard stuff."

HE'D BEEN DOING the hard stuff for three years, with a personal side-venture as an outdoor writer. He had credits at most of the magazines that still took freelance stuff, but he wasn't going to make a living at it; not unless he got a staff job, and magazines weren't looking real healthy.

Didn't know if he wanted to, anyway.

Davenport had told him that smart crooks were the most interesting game, and Virgil sometimes agreed.

VIRGIL WORE native dress out on the prairie: faded jeans and scuffed cowboy boots and musical T-shirts, and because he was a cop, a sport coat. In the sun, in the summer, he wore a straw hat and sunglasses. He usually didn't wear a gun, unless he was in St. Paul, where Davenport might see him. The law required him to go armed, but in Virgil's opinion, handguns were just too god-damned heavy and uncomfortable, so he kept his under the seat of the car, or in his briefcase.

After hanging his rain suit in the shower, he got a laptop out of his briefcase, went online. In his personal e-mail, he found the note from *Black Horizon*, a Canadian outdoor magazine, that he'd been expecting for a couple of days. They were working late in Thunder Bay: "Virg, I had to

take a couple graphs out of the section on the portage—
nothing I could do about it, it's all about the space. I tried
not to hack it up too bad. Anyway, it works for us if it works
for you. Get back to us, and I'll stick a check in the mail."

He was pleased. This was his third piece in *BH*. He was
becoming a regular. He opened the attached Word document, looked through the edited section.

Good enough. He closed the document and sent a note to
the editor: "Thanks, Henry. It's fine. I'll look for the
check. Virgil."

Whistling now, he went to the National Weather Service,
typed in the zip code for Bluestem, got the week's forecast:
thunderstorms tonight—no shit—with fair skies and warm
weather the next three or four days, thunderstorms possible
in the afternoons. He checked Google News to make sure
London hadn't been nuked since he left Mankato; it hadn't.

He shut down the computer, got undressed, shook the
little remaining water off his rain suit, got in the shower,
cranked the heat until he couldn't stand it anymore, then
turned it up one more notch. He got out, scalded half to
death, crawled into bed, and thought about Bill Judd roasting
like a bratwurst in the embers of his own home, and a truck
speeding away in the night. *That* would be an interesting murder.

THEN HE THOUGHT about God for a while, as he did
most nights.

The son of a Presbyterian minister and a professor of

engineering, who saw in God the Great Engineer and
believed as devoutly as her husband, Virgil had gotten
down on his knees every night of his life, to pray before
bed, until the first night he'd spent in the dorm at the
University of Minnesota. That night, embarrassed, he
hadn't gotten down on his knees, and he'd shivered and
shaken in fear that the world would end because he hadn't
said his prayers.

By Christmas, like most freshmen, he was done with
religion, and he mooched around campus with a copy of
The Stranger under his arm, hoping to impress women with
long dark hair and mysteries that needed to be solved.

He'd never gotten back to religion, but he had gotten
back some faith. It came all at once, in a bull session in an
Army bachelor-officers' quarters, when one of the guys
professed to being an atheist. Another one, and one who
wasn't too bright, in Virgil's estimation, had said, urgently,
"Oh, but you're wrong: look at all the wonders of the
world. There are too many wonders."

Virgil, having grown up in the countryside, where there
were wonders, and having studied ecology, where he found
even more, had been stricken by the correctness of that
statement from the not-too-bright believer: there *were* too
many wonders. Atheists, he came to believe, generally
worked in man-made cubes, with blackboards and computers and fast food. They didn't believe in wonders
because they never saw any.

So faith came back, but a strange one, with a God his
father wouldn't have recognized. Virgil thought about Him

almost every night, about his sense of humor, and the apparent fact that He'd made rules that even He couldn't bend . . .

Then at one o'clock in the morning, having thought of God, Virgil drifted off to sleep, and dreamt of men sitting in motel rooms, in the dark, secretly smoking Marlboros, watching their cats ghosting illegally around their rooms.

3

Tuesday Morning

THE OLD TOWN of Bluestem, named for a prairie grass, lay almost a mile north of I-90. Over the years, the space between the old town had filled up with the standard franchise places—McDonald's, Subway, Country Kitchen, Pizza Hut, Taco John's; a Holiday Inn, a Comfort Inn, a Motel 6; four or five gas stations with convenience stores, the Ford dealership and two used-car lots. There were also a half-dozen farm and truck service shops, with worn tires stacked outside and muddy-yellow driveway puddles from the overnight rain.

The old town was prettier. The residential areas were dominated by early-twentieth-century homes, each one different than the next, and big, with porches and yards with swings. The shopping district, on Main Street, was four blocks long, yellow-brick two- and three-story buildings, including a prewar movie theater that still showed movies, and all the businesses left over after you took out a Wal-Mart: law firms, insurance agencies, too many gift shops and antique stores, a couple of small clothing stores, four restaurants, a drugstore.

The courthouse was built two blocks back from Main, and was still used as a courthouse. In most small towns, the old courthouses had been retired, to be replaced by anonymous county government buildings and law-enforcement centers built outside town.

VIRGIL PARKED in the courthouse lot, walked past the war memorial—thirteen Stark County boys lost in World Wars I and II, Korea, Vietnam, and Iraq—and inside, down the long hall to the sheriff's office.

Stryker's secretary was a heavyset fiftyish woman with an elaborate pearly-blond hairdo, accented and bias-cut with a couple of tentative spikes sticking out the back like porcupine quills. She squinted at Virgil, took in the sunglasses and the Sheryl Crow T-shirt with the carp on the front, and asked, abruptly, "Who're you?"

"Virgil Flowers. BCA."

She looked him over again: "Really?"

"Yup."

"Sheriff said for you to go on back." She half turned and gestured toward the back wall, which had a frosted-glass window set in a door that said SHERIFF JAMES J. STRYKER. Virgil nodded, and started past, and she asked, "How many times did you shoot at that man in Fairmont?"

Virgil paused. "Fourteen," he said.

She looked pleased: "That's what I heard. You never hit him?"

"Wasn't particularly trying to," Virgil said, though he'd just about given up on this argument.

"They say he was shooting at you," she said.

"Ah, he didn't want to hurt me," Virgil said. "He was letting off some hot air, because he was pissed about being caught. Wasn't really a bad guy, except for the fact that he held up gas stations. Had eight kids and a wife to feed."

"Sort of his job, huh?"

"That was about it," Virgil said. "Now he's gonna be making snowplow blades for six years."

"Huh," she said. "Well, I think most of the boys around here would have shot him."

"Must be pretty goddamn hard-hearted boys," Virgil said, not liking her; and he went on back to Stryker's office.

STRYKER WAS on the phone. Virgil knocked and Stryker called, "Come in," and he waved Virgil to a chair and said into the phone, "I gotta go, but the first minute you find a toenail, I want to hear about it." He rang off and shook his head and said, "Can't find him. Judd."

Virgil eased into the chair. "Nothing in the house?"

"I'll tell you something. When most people build houses, there's a whole bunch of stuff in it that just don't burn too well," Stryker said. He tapped his fingers on his desktop; anxiety. "Judd's house was all wood—floors, paneling, bookcases—and a good amount of it was pine. Dry as a broom straw. There was nothing left up there this morning but the basement and a few pieces of metal and rock—refrigerator, stove, furnace, and even those are melted down into lumps. We think he was in there. But we haven't found a thing."

"Huh."

"I'll tell you, Virgil. If we don't find something, this is gonna plague me," Stryker said. "And everybody in the county, for that matter. We won't know if he went up in smoke, or if he's down on some French island someplace. We won't know if that truck last night didn't have Bill Judd in it, heading for the West Indies."

"Jesus, Jimmy, the guy's what? Eighty?" Virgil said. "They were saying down at the Holiday that he'd been pretty sick. In and out of the hospital. Why in the hell would he sit here for eighty years, and then with six months to live, take off for the West Indies?"

"Probably because he'd think it was funny, fuckin' everybody up one last time," Stryker said. He was unsettled, mumbled, "Sonofabitch," then sighed, looked at two fat file folders on his desktop, and pushed them across at Virgil.

"This is it. Everything we got. There's also a DVD in there, all the same stuff, if you'd rather use a computer. You need Adobe Reader."

"All right," Virgil said. "But boil it down for me. What'd you get, and what are you looking at now?"

VIRGIL WASN'T in Bluestem for Bill Judd, though.

He was there for the Gleasons.

Russell Gleason had been a town doctor for fifty years,

retired for ten. He and his wife, Anna, lived in an affluent enclave of businessmen and professionals on a hillock above the Stark River reservoir, a mile east of downtown and handy to the Bluestem Country Club. Anna had been a nurse for a while, when she was younger, and then had gotten elected to the county commission, where she served six terms and then retired for good. They had three children, but the children had gone, two to the Twin Cities, one to Sioux Falls.

Both were in their eighties and in good health. Russell still played nine holes a day at the club, in good weather, and Anna had her women's groups. They had a house-keeper, a Mexican illegal named Mayahuel Diaz who was well liked by most everyone who knew her, and who came in on weekdays.

Three weeks and four days before Virgil came to town, Russell had played a round of golf on a Friday afternoon, the round cut short by rain. He had a few drinks with his golfing pals, then hooked up with his wife. They'd gone to the Holiday Inn for dinner. On the way back home, they stopped at a SuperAmerica—a credit card said it was twelve minutes after nine when they paid for the gas.

At eleven o'clock that rainy night, a neighbor had been sent to town by his wife to get a quart of milk. As he came past the Gleason place, he saw what looked like a strange sculpture, like a dummy or a scarecrow, sitting in the Gleasons' backyard, bathed in yard lights.

He got a quart of milk and came back up the hill, drove past the Gleasons' house, saw the scarecrow or whatever it was, got as far as his driveway, then said, the hell with it, that scarecrow was too strange. He'd just stop and ask if everything was okay.

It wasn't.

The scarecrow was Russell Gleason, propped up with a stick, his eyes shot out.

THE SHOOTINGS had happened inside the house. Anna had been shot to death as she sat on a couch in the living room; shot once in the heart. Russell had been shot three times, once in the lower back, and once in each eye. Then his body had been dragged outside and propped up, staring gap mouthed and blank eyed into the dark.

"It looked like he tried to run, but he couldn't," Stryker said. "That the sequence was, that he was standing up, and Anna was sitting down. The killer shot her in the heart and Russell turned to run, and the killer shot him in the spine, from the back, just as he got to the dining room."

"How far was that? How far did he run?"

"About three steps. I'll get you the key to the house, on the way out the door, we've got a couple in evidence," Stryker said. "Anyway, the dining room is connected to the living room, and it looks like he was shot as he started into the dining room. He went down, and rolled on his back, and the killer stood over him and shot him twice, once in each eye. Goddamnedest thing."

The slugs were .357 hollow points, and exited the back

of Gleason's head into the floor, and were recovered, though in fragments.

"The eye thing, propping him up in the yard, in the lights—a ritual of some kind," Virgil said.

"Looks like something, but I don't know what," Stryker said, shaking his head. "The second shot was a waste of good ammunition, I can tell you that. And the shooter took a risk—the Gleasons' house is three hundred fifty feet from the nearest neighbor, and it was raining, so the houses were closed up with air-conditioning. Still, a .357 makes a damn loud bang. If somebody had been walking by . . . the third shot was an extra risk."

"Excitement? I've seen that," Virgil said. "Guy starts pulling the trigger and can't stop."

"One in each eye? He had to take his time," Stryker said. "I mean, he fired from two feet away, straight down, but you still have to take your time to put it right through an eye."

"So he's nuts. A ritual, a revenge thing . . . Maybe a warning?"

Stryker sighed. "What the whole situation hints at, when you boil it down, is that it's somebody from here, that we all know. Somebody who went to that specific house, at that specific time, to do the killing. Somebody that they let into the house. No sign of struggle by the entrance. There was a glass of water by Anna's hand, on an end table, like she'd been sitting there awhile."

"Was it dark?"

"Probably. We can't nail it down exactly, but they were

wearing the clothes that they wore Friday. Russell was still in his golf slacks with a fresh grass stain on the cuff. So, sometime after they got gas at nine-twelve—take them five minutes to get out to the house after paying—and before they'd changed clothes to go to bed."

"Nobody saw any cars?"

"No. I think the killer—I feel like it's one guy—came up the Stark River on foot, and then around to the front of the house. If he stayed down in the river cut, in the rain, hell, nobody would see him. A guy who knows his way around could walk downtown, almost, without being seen, on a dark night."

"So tell me what you think," Virgil said. "Who did it? Who might've done it?"

Stryker was shaking his head. "I don't know. This is too cold, for around here. There might be guys here who could do it, but it'd be hot. Lots of anger. Then they'd probably turn themselves in, or shoot themselves, or run for it. Or *something*. So, I don't know. You'll hear that all over town—that I don't know. But nobody else does, either."

"All right," Virgil said. "Give me the rest of the day to look at the paper, and I'll talk to you tonight. I'll be down at the Holiday, you got my cell number if you need me."

"Get you that key on the way out," Stryker said. "When you're done with the house, I'll probably let the Gleason kids have it. They want to get it cleaned out and set up for a sale."

"Nobody's touched it?"

"We've been through it, but we haven't taken anything out. Everything's like it was, but maybe a little ruffled."

THE EVIDENCE ROOM was a closet with a fire door and steel sides. Stryker unlocked it, pulled out a basket, sorted through a dozen Ziploc bags, got the key, and handed it to Virgil. They walked along together to the courthouse door, past a guy painting woodwork.

When they were out of earshot, Stryker said, "Listen, you know how it is in a sheriff's office. Half the guys working for me would like a shot at my job. If they smell a weakness . . . I'll be in trouble. So. You do what it takes. You need anything from me—*anything*—you let me know. Any of my people drag their feet, anybody in the courthouse gives you trouble, I want to hear about it."

"I'll talk to you," Virgil said.

THEY STEPPED OUTSIDE, into the sunshine. A woman was going by on the sidewalk, fifty feet away, slender, pretty, small features, white-blond hair on her shoulders. Maybe early thirties? He was too far away to be sure, but Virgil thought her eyes might be green. She lifted a hand to Stryker and he lifted one back, and her eyes caught Virgil's for a beat—an extra beat—and then she went along toward the corner.

"Another thing," Stryker said. "We've got this newspaper

here and the editor thinks he's the *New York Times*. His name is Williamson. He's investigating my investigation, and he says I'm screwing it up. Just a heads-up in case he calls you—and he will."

Virgil nodded, then said, quietly, "Not to step on your train of thought, there, Jimmy, but look at the ass on that woman. My God, where do the genes come from? I mean, that's an artwork. That's the *Venus de Milo*, and you're a bunch of goddamned Germans."

"Yeah," Stryker said, a noncommittal note in his voice.

Virgil looked at him: "What? She's married to the mayor? You don't even look at her ass?"

"No, I don't, really," Stryker said. "And she's not married. She's been divorced since February. Folks figure she's about ripe for the pluckin'."

"Have you asked her out?"

"Nope," Stryker said.

They both looked after her as she crossed the street and went on down the sidewalk toward Main. Virgil said, "You're divorced, Jimmy. I know you're not hung up on your ex, because she's in Chicago and you hate her. I mean, *I* hate her, and I only met her once. So here's the woman with the fourth-best ass in the state of Minnesota, right in your hometown, and not a bad set of cupcakes, either, from what I could see . . . I mean, pardon me for asking, and not that it matters at all, but you're not queer, or something?"

Stryker grinned. "Nope."

The woman tossed her white-blond hair as she stepped

up on the far curb, and might have glanced back at them—as all women would, she knew they were talking about her—and then Virgil turned to Stryker, about to continue his analysis of her better points, and noticed that Stryker had precisely the same white-blond hair as the woman; and Stryker had those jade-green eyes.

A thought crossed Virgil's mind.

He said, "That's your sister, isn't it?"

"Yup."

They both looked down the street, but the woman had disappeared behind a hedge, at a crooked place in the sidewalk. Virgil said, "Listen, Jimmy, that whole thing about her ass and all . . ."

"Never mind about that," Stryker said. "Joanie can take care of herself. You just take care of this cocksucker who's killing my people."

4

AT THE HOLIDAY INN, Virgil spread the Gleason murder files across the bed and the small desk, isolating names and scratching out a time line on a yellow legal pad.

The sheriff himself had served as the case manager, with a deputy named Larry Jensen as lead investigator. A woman named Margo Carr was the crime-scene tech, and a variety of other deputies provided backup. The medical examiner was based in Worthington and covered an eight-county area of southwest Minnesota. The pathology looked competent, but didn't reveal much more than the first cop figured out when he got to the scene: four shots, two dead.

Carr, the crime-scene tech, had recovered all four slugs, but they were so distorted that their use in identifying the weapon would be problematic. The .357 was almost certainly a revolver—Desert Eagle semiautos, made in Israel, were chambered for .357, but that would be a rare specimen out on the prairie. The fact that no brass was found at the scene also suggested a revolver, or a very careful killer.

A heavy-load .357 was not a particularly pleasant gun to

shoot, because of recoil. A lot of samples passed through the hands of lawmen, who were more interested in effect than in pleasant shooting. A .357 would reliably penetrate a door panel on a car, which made them popular with highway patrolmen and sheriffs' deputies, who were often working in car-related crime.

Something to think about.

JENSEN AND CARR both mentioned in their reports the possibility that the break-in had been drug related, an attempt to find prescription drugs in the doctor's house. Two aspects militated against the possibility: Gleason had been retired for years, and anybody who had known where to find him would have known that; and Carr had found several tabs of OxyContin in a prescription bottle in a medicine cabinet, left over from a knee-replacement operation on Anna. A junkie would not have missed them.

Russell Gleason still had a hundred and forty-three dollars in his wallet. Anna had seventy-six dollars in her purse. Junkies wouldn't have missed that, either. The money hadn't been missed, Virgil thought. The killer simply wasn't interested.

THE COPS HAD INTERVIEWED fifty people in the case, including the housekeeper, and all the neighbors, friends, relatives, business associates, members of the golf club. There were some people who had disliked the Gleasons, but in a small-town way. You might go to a different doctor, or you might have voted against Anna when she was running for the county commission, but you wouldn't shoot them.

One question popped out at him: why the lights on the body? The body would have been discovered the next morning, at the latest, sitting, as it was, so close to the street. If the killer had left the body in the dark, he'd have been certain of more time to get away. Was it possible that he didn't need more time, that he'd come from *very* close by?

VIRGIL GOT A MAP at the front desk and asked the clerk about the Gleason house. The clerk was happy to put an ink dot on its precise location: "You go up this little rise here, and you come around to the right, I think, or is it left? No, right. Anyways, you'll see a mailbox down on the street that says Gleason, and the house is reddish-colored and modern-looking."

"Thank you."

"Folks say you're with the BCA," the clerk said. He was young and ginger haired and weathered, and looked a little like Billy the Kid.

"Yup. We've been asked to look in on the Gleason case, bring a new point of view," Virgil said.

"Seen anything yet?"

"Got a couple of things going," Virgil said. He smiled and wrinkled his nose: "Can't talk about them, though. You know, though, *you* could give me a little help . . ."

"Me?"

"I've had one too many meals here. They're fine, but you know what I mean. Could you recommend another restaurant . . . ?"

THE PRAIRIE LANDS around Bluestem were not exactly flat; more a collection of tilted planes, with small creeks or farm ditches where the planes intersected, the water lines marked by clumps of willow and cottonwood and wild plum. The creeks and ditches eventually collected into larger streams, usually a snaky line of oxbows cut a few dozen feet deep in the soil; and sometimes into marshes or shallow lakes. Sticking out of the planes were isolated ridges and bumps, with outcrops of red rock, much of the rock covered with green lichen.

The Gleasons lived on one of the bumps.

Virgil took a left out of the hotel parking lot, drove five or six blocks north into town, took a right on Main Street through the business district, and headed east. He could see the Gleasons' neighborhood as soon as he turned: straight ahead, a wooded slope, with a hint of glass and shingles. He crossed the murky Stark River and drove up the hill, past a couple of well-kept suburban ranch houses and split-levels, with decks facing west toward the river. Up on top, coming around to the right, he saw the Gleason mailbox right where the motel clerk said it would be.

The Gleason house was built of redwood and glass, with the requisite deck. He pulled up to the garage door, climbed out, remembered what Davenport told him about going into strange houses without his gun, thought, *Fuck it, life is too short*, and ambled once around the house, looking at it from the outside.

Nice house.

Single living level, with a basement, a dozen maple trees on an acre of land, reasonably healthy-looking lawn, a garden shed in a cluster of lilacs at the back. The deck looked both west and south over the river, toward town, and out toward the interstate, a mile away. It'd be pretty at night, Virgil thought, but the way the house sat up high, it'd be colder'n a bitch in the winter. The northwest wind would blow right up into the garage door.

He could see how somebody could walk in with near-invisibility, especially in a rainstorm. Park on any of the streets near the edge of town, jog across the bridge and drop down into the Stark River cut, and follow it right around to the Gleason house. Climb the bank, a matter of a hundred yards in distance and fifty feet in height, and there you were. Back out the same way. There'd probably be enough light from the houses along the edges of the slope, and coming in from town, that you wouldn't even need a flashlight.

Huh.

HE FINISHED his circuit of the house, took the key out of his pocket, unlocked the front door, and stepped inside. The inside smelled like a crime scene: like whatever was used to clean up blood, some kind of enzyme. He stepped into the stillness, to the sense of dustiness, and walked through the entry, past the entrance to the kitchen, into the living room.

The couch where Anna was shot was in a semicircular niche off the living room, designed as a small theater, and aimed at a wide-screen television. The bullet hole was in the far left back-cushion, next to an end table with a TV remote and several magazines, a crossword-puzzle book, a wood cup with a selection of pens and pencils, and a couple of books. That was, he thought, Anna's regular spot, because Russell's regular spot was in a leather recliner at the other end of the couch, under a reading light. The bloodstain on the seat and back of the couch had been doused with the blood-eating enzyme.

The other scrubbed-out stain was in the entrance to the dining room. There were three dug-out bullet holes in the carpet. Standing there, in the quiet, Virgil saw how it must have happened. They knew the killer—Anna was comfortable in her regular spot, and hadn't bothered to get up. Russell and the killer had both been standing, and fairly close to each other. The killer pulled the gun, if it wasn't already out, and leaned into Anna and fired once. She hadn't made a move to get off the couch. Russell turned, got three steps, and was shot in the back.

But they *knew* the killer, Virgil thought: they must have. Anna was facing the TV, as though she might not even have been part of the conversation. If she'd been ordered to sit down, or forced to sit, she would have been facing into the room, where the killer was; she wouldn't have been facing the TV.

He quickly checked the end table for any possible effort by Anna to leave something behind—a scribbled name, anything. Felt foolish doing it, but would have felt more foolish if he hadn't, and something was found later. Nothing. The books were a novel by Martha Grimes and a slender volume titled *Revelation*, which turned out to be, indeed, the book of Revelation.

Virgil muttered, to nobody but the ghosts, "And I saw, and behold, a pale horse, and its rider's name was Death, and Hades followed him . . ."

HE CHECKED the table by Russell's reading light; nothing interesting. Drifted out of the shooting area, through the rest of the place. A den opened off the dining room, with file cabinets and an older computer. A hallway next to the den led to a big bathroom, but without a tub or shower—the public bath—and three large bedrooms, each with a full bath.

He walked through the master bedroom, looking, not touching, and into the kitchen. He was in the kitchen when he heard the sound of a vehicle outside. He went back to the front door, and found a sheriff's patrol car stopped behind his, and a deputy looking at his license plate.

He stepped out on the porch, and the deputy's hand drifted to his hip, and Virgil called, "Virgil Flowers, BCA." Across the way, at the next house down the ridge, he could see a man standing in his backyard, watching them with binoculars.

The deputy said, "Larry Jensen. I'm the lead investigator for the sheriff."

Jensen was another of the tall, thin types, burned and dry, sandy hair, slacks and cowboy boots, sunglasses. They shook hands and Jensen asked, "See anything in there?"

"Nope. I'd like to come back later and go through those file cabinets."

"You're welcome to . . ." Jensen turned and waved at the man in the next yard, who waved back. "That's the guy who ratted you out."

"Too bad he wasn't watching the night the Gleasons were killed," Virgil said.

"Got that right."

Jensen was easy enough, took him in the house, told him how he thought the killings must have happened, and his reconstruction jibed with Virgil's. They walked through the rest of the house, including the basement, and on the way back up, Jensen said, "I have the feeling . . ." He hesitated.

"Yeah?"

"I have the feeling that this was something that stewed for a long time. I went through every scrap of business dealings that the Gleasons had in the last ten years, I talked to about every single person that they knew, interviewed the kids and the kids' spouses. I have the feeling that this goes back to something we don't know about. I'm thinking, Russell was a doctor. What if he did something *bad* to somebody. You know, malpractice. What if back there somewhere, years ago, he killed somebody, or maybe didn't save somebody, a wife or somebody's daddy, and they just stewed and stewed and now they snapped? I mean, Russell dealt with a lot of death in his time—he was the county coroner for years—and what if it goes back to something that just . . . happened? Like happens to all doctors?"

Virgil nodded. "That's a whole deep pit . . ."

Jensen nodded. "When I worked through it, I decided that it meant everybody in the county would be a suspect. So it's meaningless."

Virgil said, "I've got a question for you, but I don't want you to take offense."

"Go ahead."

"Did your office ever issue .357s? To your deputies?"

"Yeah, you could of gone all day without asking me that," Jensen said. "We did, but years ago. We went to high-capacity .40s when the FBI did."

"What happened to the .357s?"

"That was before my time. As I understand it, guys were allowed to buy them at a discount. Some did, some didn't. Tell you the truth, some went away, we don't know where. Record keeping wasn't what it should have been. This was two sheriffs ago, so it doesn't have anything to do with Jim."

"But you thought of that," Virgil said.

"Sure."

THEY TALKED for another fifteen minutes, and Jensen said that he was looking through medical records at the partnership that had taken over Gleason's practice, and also at the regional hospital. "It's buried back there somewhere.

Maybe the same guy killed Bill Judd, if Judd is really dead. He and Gleason were almost exactly the same age, so there's gotta be a tie. Maybe this killer-guy is waiting to go after somebody else, sitting out there thinking about it."

"Could have gone all day without saying that," Virgil said.

VIRGIL FOLLOWED JENSEN back into town, cut away when Jensen turned north toward the courthouse. The motel clerk had recommended two lunch spots, Ernhardt's Café and Johnnie's Pizza, both on Main Street. Virgil decided Italian might be too much, and checked out Ernhardt's.

The café turned out to be a combination German deli and bakery, cold meat, fresh-baked potato bread, pickles, and sauerkraut. Virgil got a roast beef on rye with rough mustard, a pickle, and a half pound of bright yellow potato salad, and took it to one of the low-backed booths that lined the wall opposite the ordering counter.

A minute or so after he sat down, the sheriff's sister stepped in, blinked in the dimmer light, said hello to the woman behind the counter, ordered a salad and coffee, spotted Virgil in the back booth and nodded to him. He nodded back, and a moment later, she carried her lunch tray over and slid into the seat on the other side of the booth.

"Are you going to save Jimmy's job?" she asked.

She was not perfectly good looking—her eyebrows might have down sloped a little too much, her mouth might have been a quarter-inch too wide—but she was *very* good-looking, and certainly knew it. She was smiling when she asked her question, but her green eyes were serious.

"Does it need saving?" Virgil asked.

"Maybe," she said. And, "My name's Joan Carson. Jimmy said you had some nice things to say about my ass."

"Jimmy's job just got in deeper trouble," Virgil said, but she was still smiling and that wasn't bad. "Tell me about that, though. His job."

She shrugged, dug into her salad. "This is his second term. Most sheriffs have to get over the third-election hump. That's just the way it is, I guess. You've pissed off enough people to get fired, if they're not so impressed that they feel obligated to vote for you."

"They're not impressed?"

"They were, until the murders," she said. "Jimmy runs a good office, he's fair with his deputies. Now, he's got these murders and he's not catching who did it."

"Did he tell you that?" Virgil asked.

"Common knowledge," she said. She picked a raw onion ring out of her salad and crunched half of it, and pointed the crescent-moon remainder at Virgil. "Everybody knows everybody, and the deputies talk. Nobody's got any idea who did the shooting."

"Who do *you* think did it?"

"It's just a goddamn mystery, that's what it is," she said. "I know every single person in this town, and most of the relationships between them, and I can't think of anybody who'd do something like that. Just can't think of *anybody*. Maybe . . ." She trailed off.

"Maybe . . ."

She fluffed her hair, like women do sometimes when they think they're about to say something silly. "This is really unfair. The newspaper editor, Todd Williamson, has only been here for three or four years, so I know him less than I know other people. So maybe, before he came here, there was some knot in his brain that we can't see because we didn't grow up with him."

"That's it?" Virgil asked.

"That's it," she said.

"That's nothing," Virgil said.

"That's why I said it's unfair. But I lie in bed at night, going through everybody in town over the age of ten, figuring out who could have done this. Maybe . . ."

"What?"

"Could we have some little crazy thrill-killer in the high school? Maybe somebody who had some kind of fantasy of killing somebody, and for some reason picked out the Gleasons? You read about that kind of thing . . ."

"I hope so," Virgil said. "If it's like that, I'll get him. He'll have told his friends about it, and they'll rat him out."

Virgil's cell phone rang, and he slipped it out of his pocket and she said, "I hate it when that happens during lunch," and Virgil said, "Yeah." The call was coming in from a local number, and he opened the phone and said, "Hello?"

"Virgil, Jim Stryker. You know that Bill Judd had a heart bypass fifteen years ago, and also had some work done on his lumbar spine?"

"Yeah?"

"My crime-scene girl found a coil of stainless-steel wire in the basement of Judd's house, and she swears it's what they used to close up his breastbone after the bypass. And eight inches away, she found a couple of titanium screws and a steel rod that she says came out of Judd's spine. She says there should be X-rays up at the medical center, and she can check, but she thinks that's what she's got. She also thinks she found the back part of a skull, looks like a little saucer, pieces of two kneecaps and maybe some wrist and ankle bones."

"So he's dead," Virgil said.

"I believe so—DNA will tell, if they can get some out of the bone marrow. The arson investigator says that there was an accelerant, probably ten or twenty gallons of gasoline, because he says the fire did a broad lateral flash through the house, instead of burning up," Stryker said. "He means it spread laterally much faster than up, and with all this wood, it should have gone *up* faster."

"How can he tell?"

"Beats me. That's what he said—so, we've got another murder."

"Huh," Virgil said.

"What's that mean?" Stryker asked.

"You up there? At the Judds'?" Virgil asked.

"I am. I'll be here for a while."

"See you in a bit," Virgil said.

JOAN POINTED her fork at him. "Bill Judd?"

"Yeah." Virgil dabbed his lips with a napkin. "They think they might have found some remains. I gotta go."

"If I was a forensic anthropologist, I'd come up and help," she said. "Unfortunately, I don't know anything about forensics or anthropology and I don't much care for bodies."

"What do you do?" Virgil asked.

"Run the family farm," she said. "Twelve hundred and eighty acres of corn and soybeans north of town."

"That's a mighty big farm for such a pretty little woman," Virgil said.

"Bite me," she said.

"Thank you, ma'am. You want to go into Worthington tonight?" Virgil asked. "Tijuana Jack's ain't too bad."

"Maybe," she said. "Give me your cell number. I have to drive over to Sioux Falls for some parts. If I get back in time . . . Mexican'd be okay."

VIRGIL, pleased with himself, went back through town, up to Buffalo Ridge, through the park gates, and around the corner of the hill to the Judd house. He was astonished when he saw what was left. In most fires, a corner of a house will burn, and at least a wall or two will survive. Of the Judd mansion, nothing was left but the foundation, cracked and charred, and a pit full of twisted metal, stone, and ash.

Stryker and one of his deputies, an older fat man with blond curly hair, were talking to a third man, who had a reporter's notebook. A man in a suit was peering into the pit, and three people scuffled around the bottom like diggers on an archaeological site.

Virgil walked up, looked in the hole: picked out duct-work and air conditioners, two furnaces, the crumbled remains of what must have been a first-floor fireplace, three hot-water tanks, a couple of sinks, three toilets, a twisted mass of pipes. The diggers in the bottom were working next to the wreck of a wheelchair; the guy in the suit, Virgil realized, was Bill Judd Jr.

VIRGIL WALKED OVER to Stryker: "How'n the hell they find *anything* in there?"

Stryker said, "This is Todd Williamson, he's editor of the *Bluestem Record*; and Big Curly Anderson." A warning to watch his mouth.

"I met a Little Curly the other night . . ." Virgil said, shaking hands with the two men. Big Curly's hands were small and soft, like a woman's. Williamson's, on the other hand, were hard and calloused, as though he ran his own printing press.

"That's my boy," Big Curly said.

Stryker: "To answer your question, it was pretty much luck. They saw the wheelchair down there and started digging around, looking for a body, and they found that coil of surgical wire. Now they're trying to figure out how the wheelchair got on top of all that trash and the ash, and the body was *under* it. They're starting to think that Judd was in the basement, and the wheelchair was upstairs, on the second or third floor, and dropped down when the fire burned through the floor."

"Coincidence?"

"Seems like. I don't know what else it could be," Stryker said.

"You gonna take this case?" Williamson asked.

"I'm working the Gleason investigation," Virgil said. "Our contact with the press either runs through the local sheriff or the BCA spokesman in St. Paul. I can't talk to you about it."

"That's not the way we do things out here," Williamson said.

"They must've changed then, because I'm from out here," Virgil said. "I played high school baseball against Jimmy here, and kicked his ass three years running."

"You were seven and two, and three of those wins were pure luck," Stryker said. "People still talk about it. Haven't ever seen a run of luck like it, not after all these years."

"Bite me," Virgil said.

"You've been talking to Joan," Stryker said.

VIRGIL TIPPED his head toward the burn pit, and asked, "That's Judd, right?"

Stryker said, "Yup. I gave him a call, he came right up."

Big Curly said, "Probably been down at the bank, reading the old man's will."

Williamson said quietly, "He's about to inherit my newspaper. That won't be good. I'm job hunting, if any of you guys own a printing press."

THEY ALL LOOKED at Judd for a few seconds, then Virgil asked Big Curly, "What's this about a will?"

Big Curly shrugged: "I don't know. I was jokin'."

Virgil to Stryker: "The will's an idea, though. Have you looked for a will?"

Stryker shook his head: "I imagine it's in the bank. Or Bob Turner's got it. Turner was the old man's attorney."

"We ought to take a look at it," Virgil said. "Get a writ to open his safe-deposit box, get his attorney and his kid to go with us. Could be something in it."

Williamson said, "What if he left all of his money to George Feur?"

Stryker cracked a smile. "That'd give old Junior a major case of the red ass, you betcha."

Virgil: "Who's George Feur?"

"Nutcase preacher, found Jesus in prison," Stryker said. "He's got a so-called religious compound over by the Dakota line. He was trying his best to save Bill Judd's soul, according to the local gossip."

"He's nuts?"

Williamson said, "He believes in the purity of the white race and that Jesus was a Roman, and thinks blacks were stuck in Africa because of the curse of Cain, and they should all be shipped back there so they can properly suffer the righteous wrath of God, instead of polluting white women and gettin' all the good jobs at Target. Once a month or so, he and a bunch of people get some signs and go march somewhere, and say all of that. Here, Worthington, Sioux Falls."

Little Curly: "He says Indians are the Lost Tribes of Israel, and they're Jews, and they should all go back to Israel so we can get the Second Coming. Had a few fights with Indians."

Virgil: "And he was converting Judd?" He was thinking of the book of Revelation on the Gleasons' end table.

"He needs rich recruits," Williamson said. "How else is he gonna get the money to buy guns to overthrow the godless Democrats and ship the blacks back to Africa?"

"Ah."

"And the Mexicans back to Mexico, and the Chinese back to China, and the Indians to Israel, and so on and so forth," Williamson said. "I wrote a long feature on him, got picked up by the Associated Press."

"HERE COMES TROUBLE," Big Curly muttered.

Virgil looked and Bill Judd Jr. was headed toward them. Judd was a heavy man, with a turkey-wattle neck under a fat face, thinning hair, and small black eyes. He must have been close to sixty, Virgil thought.

Judd nodded at Williamson, glanced at Virgil, and asked Stryker, "What're you going to do about this, Jim? If that's Dad down there, and if that boy from the state fire marshal was right, then it's murder. What're you going to do?"

"Investigate it," Stryker said.

"Like you're investigating the Gleasons?" Judd shook his head, his wattles swinging under his chin. "Give me a break, Jim. You bring in the BCA or . . . Goddamnit, you bring in the BCA."

Stryker tipped his head toward Virgil. "Meet Virgil Flowers, Minnesota Bureau of Criminal Apprehension."

Judd's face snapped toward Virgil. He examined him for a moment, checked the T-shirt, then said, "You don't look like much."

Virgil smiled. "I'm not easily insulted by suspects," he said. "There been too many of them over the years."

"What the fuck's that supposed to mean?" Judd asked.

"Well, you're pretty much the only suspect we've got at the moment," Virgil said. "In a situation like this, you always ask, 'Who inherits?' The answer, as I understand it, is *you*."

Judd looked at Virgil for a long three seconds, then turned to Williamson. "You keep that out of the newspaper."

Williamson shook his head. "I don't work for you, Bill. I worked for your father, and now I work for your father's estate. When the estate passes to you, I'll be out of here like a hot desert breeze. Until then, I'm working for the estate."

"You better find a job by the end of next week, then," Judd said.

VIRGIL SAID TO JUDD: "We need to look at your father's will. We assume it's in a safe-deposit box. We're gonna get a writ to open it, since it could be material for this investigation. Also because we'd like to see what else is in the safe."

Judd nodded: "That's fine with me. Let's get Bob Turner and go talk to the judge and crack the box. Get things moving."

"Can I come?" Williamson asked.

Stryker said, "No."

Williamson grinned: "No harm in asking. Goddamn, it's hot out here."

ON THE WAY back to their vehicles, they stopped at the burn pit and Stryker called down, "Anything new?"

A chubby woman in a yellow protective suit and face mask stood up, used a paper towel to wipe sweat off her face, put the towel in a trash bag, and said, "I'm dying of heat prostitution."

They all grinned down at her and she added, "Nothing else, really. But we've got the carpals and they're intact; they were under a piece of sheet steel and that must've given them some protection, so I think we're good for DNA. And with Bill Jr. to provide us a sample, we can be sure on the ID."

"Get it done," Stryker said.

On the way down the hill, Big Curly said, "I'd like to cut me off a piece of that," meaning the woman in the yellow suit.

Stryker nodded. "I'll mention it to Mrs. Curly."

ONE OF the best things and one of the worst things about a small town was that everybody knew everything that was going on. The judge knew about as much of the Judd case as Virgil did, and pounded out a writ on his secretary's computer, and printed it.

"Good to go," he said, and handed the paper to Stryker.

Stryker called the Wells Fargo branch and talked to the manager, who said he'd be waiting. Judd's attorney said he'd walk over.

"So let's go," Stryker said.

"GO" MEANT WALKING—the bank was three blocks away, two blocks through an older residential area, cutting the business district about halfway down Main Street. They walked past the drugstore, which gave out a whiff of popcorn, and Judd trotted back and went inside and then caught up, carrying a paper sleeve of it, munching at it like a starving man; and past the newspaper, which shared a building with an office that said JUDD ENTERPRISES, and one that said WILLIAM JUDD JR., INVESTMENTS, then on down the street past a combination barbershop and beauty salon.

The bank's time-and-temperature sign said eighty-seven degrees when they walked under it, and into the lobby. The banker was a white-haired man with a neat mustache, and the lawyer was a white-haired man with a neat mustache; a Mexican-looking guy in jeans and a T-shirt, and a black mustache, stood off to one side with a toolbox. Stryker was becoming a white-haired man with a neat mustache. Should Virgil grow a mustache, he'd look like everybody else, Virgil thought: a monoculture of German-Scandinavian white people, now getting a little salsa poured on it, to the great relief of everyone.

The banker took the writ, and led the way into the vault, explained that since Judd had the necessary keys, which hadn't been found in the burnt-out house, they'd have to drill the box, and would charge the estate for it later. Drilling the box took three minutes, the banker gave the Mexican guy a twenty, and the guy took his tools and left.

The box was one of the bigger sizes; big enough, say, to hold three roasted chickens. The banker carried it to a privacy carrel, but since they weren't being private, they all crowded around when they popped the lid.

Judd said, with some reverence, "Holy shit."

The box was filled with paper. The top two layers were paper money. "Not as much as you might think," the banker said, earnestly, but his eyes had a light in them. "Hundred-dollar bills, ten-thousand-dollar bundles . . .

fifteen, eighteen, twenty. Two hundred thousand in cash."

"Why would he have two hundred thousand in cash?" Virgil asked Judd.

Judd said, "Don't want to get caught short."

They stacked it to one side and Judd pulled up a plastic chair and sat down, staring at the money, while the banker and lawyer dug into the rest of the paper, insurance policies, deeds, photographs, a couple boxes of jewelry.

THAT WAS in the afternoon, in which some other things happened, but none that turned out to be important.

IN THE EVENING, Joan Carson sat in the candlelight at Tijuana Jack's and looked terrific. She wore a cotton summer-knit dress the color of raw linen, with a necklace of marble-sized jade beads that perfectly matched her eyes. She had a scattering of faint freckles across her short nose, and Virgil noticed for the first time that she had a chipped tooth, which gave her a tomboyish vibration.

She leaned toward him, her dress opening just enough to reveal the tops of her breasts, though Virgil looked resolutely into her eyes, and she whispered, "Motherfucker?"

Virgil whispered, "That's what the man said." He laughed, a low, chuckling laugh, and said, "Junior Judd's sitting down, staring at the money, two hundred thousand dollars on the table, three inches from his nose. He's absolutely drooling on it. Then the lawyer says—Turner says—like it's a big mystery, 'I don't see the will here.' And Judd jumps up and screams, 'Motherfucker!' "

She giggled, and rubbed her nose, her eyes bright with amusement.

Virgil continued: "I thought we were gonna have to club him down to his knees, to keep him off Turner's throat. Turner keeps saying, 'It wasn't me, it wasn't me,' and Judd's walking around saying, 'Motherfucker! Motherfucker!' and the bank guy pulls all the receipts and it turns out old man Judd went into the box a week ago. We talked to the vault lady, and she says when Judd went into it, he told her he didn't want one of those privacy booths, he just wanted to get out a document. She saw it, and it was in a beige legal envelope, and we all think it was the one-and-only will."

"Motherfucker!" she said. "I would have given a hundred dollars to see that. What else was in the box?"

"Legal papers, deeds, insurance. The house was insured for eight hundred thousand with another two hundred thousand on the contents, so Junior'll get all of that. That's a million, all by itself, including the cash in the box."

"The old man owned a block of the downtown."

"Where the newspaper is."

"Yes, and he's got several parcels of good land down south of here, that'll be a nice chunk of cash," she said.

"What's Junior own? On his own?"

"He's been in and out of a few businesses, hasn't done so well. Right now he's got three or four Subways in the small towns around, and he's got a little land along the river that he's been talking about developing . . . but to tell you the truth, there hasn't been a big call for housing development around here. Why?"

"He seemed pretty damn excited about that cash," Virgil said. "And pretty upset when it turned out he wasn't going to get it in the next two weeks. I mean, he'll have it in a month or two, but they'll have to run it through probate. So what's the difference, two weeks or two months? But he was pretty upset."

"Huh. He's a jerk, but he wouldn't kill his dad, if that's what you're thinking," Joan said. "I've seen them have some pretty friendly conversations."

"Okay. Just trying to nail down stuff I can look into," Virgil said.

"But I think I can tell you about why he reacted the way he did . . ."

"Yeah?"

"The Judds worship money. They made it a stand-in for all the other qualities of life. If you can be nice, or have money, take the money. If you can be brave, or have money, take the money. If you can have friends or have money, take the money. They're like that. They don't even hide it. Take the money. Pulling two hundred thousand dollars in cash, out of a safe-deposit box, in front of Bill Judd Jr., would be like pulling Jesus Christ out of a box, in front of the Pope."

"Not a nice thing to say about someone," Virgil said. "Especially the Pope."

"It's the truth, though," she said. Her eyes narrowed: "Can I tell all my friends about all this?"

"Well, let me think," Virgil said. "The only witnesses were me, your brother, the lawyer, the banker, Judd, and the vault lady. What are the chances that they all kept their mouths shut?"

"Zero."

"Right. Just don't quote me, okay?" Virgil said. "You could get me or your brother in trouble. Maybe you could hear it from one of the wives first?"

"I know both of them, banker and lawyer," she said. "One of them'll spill the beans, and then I can add everything you gave me."

"Sounds good," Virgil said. "Did I mention I like your dress?"

"Really? I sewed it myself. Ordered the material out of Des Moines."

"Seriously?"

"Try not to be stupid, Virgil," she said. "I bought it at Neiman Marcus, in the Cities."

VIRGIL HAD GROWN UP in Marshall, Minnesota, sixty miles north of Bluestem, as the crow flies, or eighty miles, if the crow were driving a pickup. His father had the biggest Presbyterian church in town, until he retired, and his mother taught engineering and survey at Southwest Minnesota State University, until she retired. They were both still alive and played golf all summer, and had a condo in Fort Myers so they could play golf all winter.

Joan's father had been a farmer. He'd been involved with Bill Judd's drive to make a commodity out of the Jerusalem artichoke.

"I don't remember all this, because I was too young at the time, but Dad thought that nothing good was going to happen with corn and bean prices. There was too much low-priced competition around the world. He thought if we could come up with a new crop, that could replace oil . . . well, I guess back in the seventies and eighties there were all these predictions that oil might run out any minute, and then we'd all be screwed."

"Like now."

"Like now, with ethanol and four-dollar corn. Anyway, if you could *grow* oil . . . I guess he figured they couldn't lose. But it was all bullshit. It was a scam right from the start, cooked up by a bunch of commodities people in Chicago and some outlanders like Bill Judd. When it all went bust, Bill Judd didn't care. He was a sociopath if you've ever seen one. But people who were tied into him, like my dad, *did* care . . ."

She sighed and shook her head. "Lot of people thought my dad was right there in with Judd. But Dad lost half his land. He was farming more than two thousand acres back then. He sold off the land at way-depressed prices, right into a big farm depression in the middle eighties, paid off all his debts, and then he got this .45 that he had, and killed himself. Out in the backyard, one Saturday afternoon. I can still remember people screaming, and I can remember Mom sitting in the front room looking like *she'd* died. That's what I remember most: not Dad, but Mom's eyes."

"Jimmy was pretty hurt, I guess? Boys and fathers?"

"He was." Her eyes came up to meet his. "You don't think Jim had anything to do with Judd's murder?"

He shook his head: "Of course not . . . Were the Gleasons tied in with Judd?"

"They were friendly," Joan said. "There was a tight little group of richer folks, like in most small towns. Doctors, lawyers, bankers, real estate dealers. People say that Judd helped some of them with investments . . . but the Gleasons didn't have anything to do with the Jerusalem artichoke scam. Everyone would have known—it all came out in the lawsuits . . ."

He leaned toward her again, pitching his voice down: "I'll tell you what, Joanie. Jim and I and Larry Jensen, we all think that the Gleason murders and the Judd murder are tied together. Three murders in three weeks, all by somebody who knew what he was doing; where to go and when to go. Even did it under the same conditions, in the rain, in the dark. And that's after you haven't had any murders in twenty-two years."

"What about George Feur? The preacher?"

"I heard of him . . ."

"He's somebody to look at—I even asked Jim about him," she said. "Jim says he's got an alibi. There was a prayer meeting that Friday night, and a lot of people stayed the weekend. There's somebody who'll say that Feur was there every minute of that time. Jim and Larry decided that it *would* have been hard for him to sneak away . . ."

"How long would he have to be gone?"

"Well, if he . . ." She looked up at the ceiling, her lips moving as she figured. "Well, if he drove in and out, half an hour? Probably longer than that, if he walked part of it, or if they talked. But that's not very long, really."

"It's not long if there are lots of people around, and everybody thinks you're talking with somebody else, and you're seen here and there . . . you might get away for half an hour."

"And maybe one of his goofy converts would have been willing to do him a favor. But: if you think the same person killed the Gleasons and Bill Judd . . . I understand that Feur was trying to save Judd's soul, and that they got along. So that doesn't seem to fit."

"It's a connection, though."

"It is . . ." she said. "Feur's a violent man. He was violent when he was a boy—his old man abused him—and he'd go around robbing stores and maybe even banks, when he was in his twenties. Jim tracked him down after a robbery up in Little America. Arrested him out at his aunt's place. He went to prison, got Jesus and all the other crap, too—the white supremacy, and that. Went out west, someplace, studied for the ministry, got a license in Idaho. When his aunt died, he came back here and took over the farm. We'd thought we'd seen the last of him."

"He ever shoot anybody? Ever suspected of it?" Virgil asked.

"Not as far as I know. I do know he used a gun in the robberies."

ON THE WAY BACK to Bluestem, out on I-90, Joan said, "You are very talkative for a cop. I've known every cop in Bluestem and a few from Worthington; some of them were pretty old friends, and none of them have been as talkative as you—telling me all about the case, and so on."

"A PERSONALITY FAULT," Virgil offered.

"Really? I started to wonder, 'Did this man take me out to a fancy Tex-Mex restaurant, and tell me all of this, because he figures I'll blab it all over the place, and that'll stir everything up?' "

"I'm shocked that you'd even think that," Virgil said.

"You don't sound shocked," she said.

"Well, you know," he said. He glanced at her in the dark, and said, "One thing—you're a little smarter than I was prepared for."

She laughed and they went on down the highway.

LATE THAT NIGHT, Virgil turned on his laptop, flexed his fingers, and began writing his story, a little fact, and a lot of fiction. Fiction was different than outdoor writing.

Different because you had to think about it, make it up, rather than simply report an experience. He stared at the computer screen for a moment, and began:

The killer climbed out of the river valley, stumbling in the dark, slipping on the wet grass; paused at the edge of the yard, then crossed quickly to the sliding glass door at the back of the house. He'd seen the Gleasons arrive, their headlights carving up the hillside through the night; you could see them from a half mile away.

Now, through the wet glass, he saw Russell Gleason standing in the living room, hands in his pockets, looking at the television. His wife, Anna, came out of the kitchen, carrying a glass of water, sat on the couch. They were talking, but with the rain beating off the hood of his jacket, the killer couldn't hear what was being said.

The killer touched the gun in his pocket: .357, always ready. No safety, no spring to get soft, every chamber loaded. Inside, Gleason laughed at something: a last time for everything, the killer thought.

The killer stepped back in the dark, walked around the house to the front door. Gleason had been involved in it, right up to his chin: he and Judd would have to pay. He rang the bell . . .

Virgil touched his chin, reading down the electronic document. He was already cheating: he kept writing "the killer," repetitively, which clanked in his writer's ear. He needed a workable synonym. He couldn't use the pronouns "he" or "she," because he wasn't sure which was correct. And Gleason *had* been involved in whatever it was, with Judd, right up to his chin—but what was it?

He had no idea.

But there would be, he thought, a link.

Before he finished the story, though, he'd need a lot of other answers. Where did the killer come from? Where did the gun come from? Where did he/she learn to use the gun? Why was the body dragged to the yard, why were the lights turned on? Had the killer known about the lights on the exterior, and where the switch was, suggesting a familiarity with the house, or had the act been spontaneous? Why the shots in the eyes?

Why then, at that exact moment, had the killer come to the Gleasons?

Why hadn't Stryker mentioned that his father had killed himself because of the Jerusalem artichoke scandal, and his relationship with Judd? How had he, Virgil, managed to get picked up by Stryker's sister on his first day in town? Why had she steered him toward Todd Williamson and George Feur?

Things you had to know, for a decent piece of fiction.

5

FOUR FAT GUYS in short-sleeved shirts, standing outside the courthouse, stopped talking and stared at Virgil inside. Virgil gave the high sign to the secretary, who took in his antique Stones/Paris T-shirt, and shook her head and sighed as though a great weight were sitting on her soul.

He ambled past her desk and stuck his head in Stryker's office. Stryker was sitting with his feet up on his desk and a stunned look on his face. He pointed Virgil at a chair and rubbed his face with his hands and said, "Ah, shit."

Virgil sat. "What?"

Stryker dropped his feet to the floor, turned his chair around, opened a two-six-pack-sized office refrigerator, and took out a bottle of Coke. "You wanna Coke?"

"No, thanks . . ."

"Got the goddamnedest telephone call," Stryker said, twisting the top off the bottle. He tossed the bottle top at a wastebasket, sank the shot. "There's a woman lives out in Roche—you know where that is?"

"Yeah. Other side of Dunn."

"That's it. Town the size of my dick. Her name is

Margaret Laymon and she called me up, about five minutes ago. Says her daughter, Jessica, is the natural daughter of William Judd. She wants to make sure that her daughter gets her rights. As she put it."

They sat staring for a moment, then Virgil said, "Jesus. If there's no will, and she can prove it . . ."

Stryker nodded: "Bill Jr. is gonna have a stroke."

"Wonder if there are any more little Judds running around?"

"That's an interesting question, but I don't know how you'd find out," Stryker said. "Unless they call you up and tell you."

"Huh. You gonna tell Junior?"

"Not up to me," Stryker said. "I told Margaret to hire a lawyer, real quick. She's going to do that. I suppose, what? She'd file something with the court?"

"I don't know. There'd be some DNA tests to do . . ."

"She says that's not a problem. But I'll tell you what *is* a problem." He turned his chair around again, a full circle, thinking, and then said, "Of all the women I ever wanted in my entire life, Jesse Laymon is right at the top of the list. We even went out twice, but not three times. She wants somebody with more of an edge. A ramblin' gamblin' man."

"A bad country song," Virgil said. The second he'd found in so many days. The prairie was full of them.

"But it's true," Stryker said. He took a hit on the Coke. "I get my heart in my mouth every time I see her, but the fact is, what she wants is one of those black-eyed dope-dealing rascals who drinks too much and drives too fast and dances good. That's not me."

"Well, hell."

"Yeah."

THEY SAT for a minute, thinking it over, then Virgil said, "Maybe it's because your dick is the size of Roche."

Stryker had been taking another sip of Coke, and he choked, sputtering, laughed, said, "Come to speak of it, what were you and Joanie doing on her front porch last night about ten o'clock?"

Virgil laughed, but not hard, touched by a finger of guilt. So much apparent friendship, and he was sitting here smiling, and thinking that the Strykers would be suspects in the Judd killing, on any rational list . . .

VIRGIL SAID, "I'm gonna go talk to Todd Williamson, see if he'll let me look in his files, if he's got any. Then I'm heading out to see George Feur."

Stryker's eyebrows went up. "You got something?"

"Not exactly. I want to talk to him, look him over, push him a little," Virgil said.

"When you say, 'Not exactly' . . ."

"Feur's a Bible beater and he's an asshole and he was working on Judd," Virgil said. "Bible beaters don't beat anything harder than the book of Revelation. I noticed when I was up at the Gleasons' yesterday, that Anna

Gleason had a book of Revelation right under her hand when she was shot. A pretty new one, it looked like."

"She did?" Stryker frowned and leaned forward. "Why didn't I know that?"

Virgil shrugged. "Maybe nobody noticed. This was before Judd was killed, and Feur's name didn't really come up until the fire."

"Hell of a thing not to notice, though," Stryker said. "I'll have to talk to Larry and Margo about this. They should have seen it. At least had it in the back of their minds."

Virgil didn't disagree. "Maybe they should have," he said. "Especially for a guy with Feur's history."

"You know about him and me, right?" Stryker asked. "I busted him for robbery, when I was a deputy? He went to Stillwater. Claims I railroaded him."

"Nothing to that, though," Virgil offered.

"No. He was caught on a liquor store camera," Stryker said. "He had a hat pulled down low, but I knew him the minute I saw the tape. Went and dug him out of his hole, got his gun, too. The gun did it as much as anything—it was an old piece with a nine-inch barrel, and that, you see perfectly, on the tape."

"So it was a good bust."

"Yup. It was, and still is."

VIRGIL SAID, "Another thing—if this all somehow involves Judd's money, then your friend Jesse might be in trouble, could be a target for somebody."

"You think?"

"Maybe. Or maybe not." Virgil scratched his ear. "If she's got one of those ramblin' gamblin' guys around, who figured she might become a millionairess, under the right circumstances . . ."

"Man, that hadn't occurred to me," Stryker said. He sat back in his chair, rocking.

"Could Jesse or Margaret set something up?" Virgil asked.

Stryker rubbed his chin. "Not Margaret. Don't see that. Jesse wouldn't do it on purpose. I *could* see her sitting around, suckin' a little smoke, bullshitting with somebody, dreaming about all the money . . . and she wakes up in a world of hurt, when her pal goes off and does something about it."

"A concept to consider," Virgil said.

"I will," Stryker said.

"And if she doesn't have anything to do with it, hell, maybe she'll need her body guarded."

Stryker stood up. "I'm heading out there. You want to look at her, or go see Feur?"

"I'll go after Feur," Virgil said. Stryker had been looking for an excuse to go out. "You can tell me what you get from Jesse and maybe I'll talk to her later in the day."

"Good enough," Stryker said. "You take care."

THE DAY LOOKED like the day before, sunny, a touch of wind, about as nice a July day that you could hope for; four kids, two boys and two girls, were dancing along the sidewalk ahead of him, boys in dropped-crotch pants, the girls with pierced ears and noses, but there was a small-town innocence about it; testing their chops, and sometimes, forgetting, they'd hold hands. They all looked back at him a couple of times, knowing him for a cop.

Nice a day as it was, there was too much humidity hanging around, and thunderstorms would be popping by late afternoon. If it got hot enough, some of them could be bad. Nothing to do about it.

Virgil walked down to the *Record*, stopping at the drugstore for a sleeve of popcorn, and at the newspaper, found Williamson putting the last bit of the next day's newspaper together.

Williamson lit up as soon as Virgil walked through the front door. "I was hoping I'd see you this morning. I called down to the motel and they said you were gone already."

Virgil nodded. "I was hoping to poke through your library, if you've got one. Clippings, and such."

"We can do that. But it'd be pretty damn ungrateful of you, if you didn't answer a couple of questions."

"You can ask," Virgil said.

"You took a different attitude yesterday . . ."

"Well, I was in public. I'll talk to you, but the deal is this: I talk off-the-record, and you write it like it came from God," he said. "I might not tell you everything, but I won't lie to you."

"Deal," Williamson said. He punched a couple of keys on his computer, switched out of his compositing program into a word processor, and asked, "Do you think the .357 used in the murders was one of the guns issued to the sheriff's office years ago?"

"I have no idea," Virgil said. Williamson opened his mouth to object, but Virgil held up a hand. "I'm not avoiding the question. I really don't have any idea. They're not a commonly bought weapon anymore. Most people go for automatics, because they're on TV, and if you're looking for hunting power in a revolver, you might go for a .44 mag or a .454 Casul. The .357s were a cop's gun, at one time, and that's the only reason anybody ever talked about the idea. There were a bunch of them in the sheriff's office, and they all went away, and maybe . . . who knows?"

"All right," Williamson said. "Second question: Do you think the killer is local?"

"Yes," Virgil said.

"You want to expand on that?" Williamson asked.

"No."

"Any suspects?"

"Not at the moment."

Williamson said, "I'm not getting much for my clips."

Virgil: "What time do you have to finish putting the paper together? It's out tomorrow morning, right?"

"Can't push it past three o'clock. I download it to the printing plant—it's over in Sioux Falls—and pick it up at eleven," he said. "If I push it one minute past three, they won't give it to me until midnight or one o'clock, just to fuck with me."

"All right. At two o'clock, you call me on my cell

phone," Virgil said. "You might have the story by then, but maybe not. But it would be . . . your lead story."

Williamson's eyebrows went up. "The Judd fire is the lead story."

"Two days old. Everybody knows it," Virgil said. "This other story is known by damn few, and you'd sure as hell wake up the town tomorrow morning, if you printed it. But if you give me up as the source, you'll never get a word from me for the rest of the investigation."

"Another story from God, huh?" Williamson's tongue touched his lower lip: he wanted the story. "Let me show you the morgue. We still call it that, here."

THE MORGUE was the size of a suburban bedroom, painted a color that was a combination of dirt green and dirt brown. The walls were lined with oak library chests, with hundreds of six-inch-high, six-inch-wide, two-foot-deep drawers, surrounding a desk with an aging Dell computer. Williamson knocked on one of the cabinets. "We file by name and subject. Before 1999, if the subject is something with a hundred names in it, we file the five most important names to the story, and cross-reference to the subject. So if you're showing a goat at FFA, and you're thirty-third on the list, somebody would have to look under FFA to find your name, because we didn't put it in the name file. After 1999, we stopped clipping, and put everything on CDs, cross-referenced by a reference service. You'll find all names and subjects after 1999."

"Even if you're thirty-third on the list?"

"With a goat," Williamson said. "I'd sit here and show you how to use the computer, but you can figure it out in five minutes and I'm on deadline. Instructions are Scotch-taped on the desk on the left side. Have at it."

HE STEPPED AWAY, but lingered, like he had another question, so Virgil asked, "Another question?"

"How're you getting along with Jim Stryker?"

"Good. We've known each other for a while," Virgil said.

"Yeah . . . the baseball. But the word out of the sheriff's shop is that they really had to stuff you down his throat," Williamson said.

"Is that right?"

Williamson nodded: "Could just be office politics, but the word was, you could show off the sheriff's . . . inade-quacies."

"I work on eight or ten murders a year," Virgil said. "You guys go decades without one. I'm a specialist. No harm in calling in a specialist."

Williamson chuckled. "That wasn't how they were skin-ning the cat at the courthouse."

WHEN WILLIAMSON was gone, Virgil wandered around, looking at yellowed labels on the drawers, fig-ured out the system, names over here, subjects over there. The tall files were photos, mostly eight-by-ten originals, which stopped entirely in 2002; must have bought a digital camera, Virgil thought. The photos still smelled of developer and stop bath; the clips smelled of old cigarette smoke and pulp paper gone sour.

The Judd photo files showed Judd in every decade starting in the 1940s, as a young man in a pale suit, but even then with bleak, black eyes.

The pre-1999 Judd clipping files took up four drawers, hundreds of crumbling clippings entangled in small gray envelopes. Judd Jr. had several packets of his own, but they occupied only half a drawer. The measure of a couple of lives, Virgil thought.

The file envelopes had an average of eight to ten articles each, and the bulk of the Judd Sr. clips, amounting to several stories a week, came in the 1980s, during the Jerusalem artichoke controversy.

Judd was eventually accused of thirty-two counts of fraud by the Minnesota attorney general, based on evidence partly local and partly developed out of St. Paul. The assistant AG who prosecuted, and who apparently didn't understand his own evidence, was torn to pieces by Judd's defense attorneys in a trial in St. Paul. The local county attorney and the local sheriff were both defeated in the next election, by pissed-off voters.

After the trial, there was further wrangling over federal and state taxes. The fight dragged through the courts for years, and in 1995, the *Record* reported that attorneys for both sides had agreed to settle the case, the settlement being confidential as a matter of tax law.

The Judd envelopes not involving the Jerusalem artichoke controversy were generally business news: mortgages given and taken, buildings and land bought and sold, the house being built on Buffalo Ridge—for a rumored five hundred and fifty thousand dollars in 1960, with five baths—and lawsuits filed and settled. Except for the Jerusalem artichoke controversy, it might have been the life record of any greedy, grasping, sociopathic businessman.

Judd Jr. was more of the same, without the scandal, and in a minor key: he was portrayed as a greedy, grasping, and largely unsuccessful sociopath.

Virgil read about the suicide of Mark Stryker, which happened after a family picnic, a detail nobody had mentioned. The story did mention that Stryker had been involved in the Jerusalem artichoke scandal, and had sold 1,280 acres of the family farm to pay off associated debts.

ANNA GLEASON was the headliner in her family, as the result of sixteen years on the county commission, and with her own drawer of stories. Judd was mentioned in several of them, but most were routine appearances before the county commission to discuss zoning changes or drainage problems. Russell Gleason had a few envelopes, mostly from when he worked as a coroner in the seventies and eighties, before the medical examiner system was adopted; and in most of those clips, he was simply the voice that pronounced somebody dead.

He read the clips on both Jim Stryker and Joan Carson. Joan's divorce attracted three six-inch articles, which noted only that the marriage was irretrievably broken after five years, and that the judge approved the agreement worked out by the private attorneys. All the good stuff had been left out.

She was described as an "affluent farmer" with residences both in Bluestem and at the family farm. Virgil knew where her town home was, having stood on her front porch the night before, trying for a gentle, sensitive, yet promising good-night kiss, while simultaneously trying to cop a feel.

He looked and finally found the Laymons. Nothing about Margaret, but Jesse had been busted once in Worthington for possession of a minor amount of marijuana, and was cited as a witness in a fight in a Bluestem bar, in which a man had all of his teeth broken out. The man sued, but the suit never went to trial.

Finally, George Feur. He showed up only on the computer, but there were fifteen hits, including an article by Williamson that must have been five thousand words long.

He was, Virgil thought, reading through the computer files, a brass-plated asshole.

VIRGIL LEFT the newspaper office, rolling out of town, back on I-90, heading west. I-94, I-90, I-80, I-40, I-20, and I-10 stretched across the heart of the country like guitar strings, holding the East Coast to the West Coast, with the

Rocky Mountains as the bridge. I-90 shared much of its length with other interstates, but was on its own from Tomah, Wisconsin, to Billings, Montana. Virgil had driven all of it, and more than once.

Some people found it deadly boring, but having been raised on the prairie, Virgil liked it, like sailors enjoy the ocean. The prairie rolled in waves, with small towns coming up and falling behind, and farmhouses and pickups and people riding horses, and buffalo and antelope and prairie dogs. And towns, like freshwater pearls, small, all different, and all the same.

NOT THAT he was going far; just an exit or two.

Feur lived a mile east of the South Dakota line, ten miles north of I-90, in a compound of four steel buildings and one old white clapboard four-square farmhouse, a Corn Belt cube, that tilted slightly to the southeast, and badly needed a coat of paint. The buildings were set in a grove of bur oaks, box elders, and cottonwoods, surrounded by rocky pasture.

The driveway crossed a ditch with a thread of water in the bottom, past a sign that said GOD'S FORTY ACRES, and beneath that, NO TRESPASSING. As he pulled into the dirt roundabout in front of the house, a young man came out on the front porch with a shotgun.

Virgil said, "Ah, man." He was still far enough away that he could do it without being obvious, and he reached down under the seat for his pistol, and put it on the seat next to him. As he stopped and parked, he picked up the weapon, as if picking up a pen or a book, and slipped it into his jacket pocket.

When he climbed out of the truck, the man with the gun called, "Who're you?"

"Virgil Flowers, Minnesota Bureau of Criminal Apprehension. I need to see Reverend Feur."

"You got an appointment?" the man asked. He was maybe twenty-five, and had the foxy look of somebody who'd grown up hungry.

"Nope."

"Maybe you could come back some other time. He's pretty busy," the man said.

"I'd rather talk now," Virgil said. "If I've got to drag my ass all the way back to Bluestem, then when I come back, I'll come back with a search warrant and five deputies and we'll tear this place apart."

"You ain't got no cause." The shotgun was there, but the man hadn't twitched it in any direction: it was simply there.

"You think a Stark County judge would give a shit?" Virgil asked.

The man stared at him for a moment, as if calculating the inclinations of every judge he'd ever met, then said, "Wait here."

IT HADN'T BEEN obvious from the road, but Feur's house and the outbuildings were actually sitting on the slope, which continued back to the east, but flattened out across the road to the west. To the north and south, you could see forever: and they'd been able to see Virgil's dust trail from virtually the time he rolled off the tarmac county road and onto the gravel, five miles away.

Looking around, Virgil noticed the heavy tracking on the dirt sideyard, and the crushed grass around the perimeter of the dirt; it reminded him of the grass ad hoc parking at a county fair. There'd been a bunch of cars and trucks in the yard, all at once. A prayer meeting? The shop building off to his left was a leftover Quonset hut from the Korean War era, made out of steel. Wouldn't defeat a rifle, maybe, but a pistol shot would bounce right off.

A wooden Jesus, carved out of a cottonwood stump by somebody moderately handy with a chain saw, peered across the yard at him, one arm raised, as though blessing Feur's enterprise.

THE MAN with the gun—now gunless—came out on the porch. "Come in," he said.

"Thank you." Virgil nodded at him, climbed the three steps to the porch, said, "After you," and followed the man into the house.

Feur was sitting in a wooden rocker at the corner of the parlor, smoking, and drinking what looked like tea out of a china cup. A small man with black eyes, black beard, and a chiseled, sunburned nose, he was dressed all in black, and wore shiny black leather boots; in a movie, he would have played Mr. Scratch. There were two pictures on the walls, both of a black-haired, black-eyed Jesus, one on the cross.

Feur said, "Mr. Flower? Do you have some identification?"

Virgil nodded, took his ID out of his breast pocket, and held it out. Feur peered at it without touching, said, "Flowers," then nodded at a couch and said, "Have a seat. You wouldn't be related to Rusty Flowers, would you?"

"No. I don't know the name," Virgil said. He sat down, lifting his jacket enough that he didn't pin the gun under his leg.

"Not even sure it's a real name," Feur said. He was younger than Virgil had expected—probably the same age as Stryker, in his middle thirties, but his lined face made him look, at first glance, as though he were ten years older. "I was standing on a bridge at Dubuque, Iowa, one time, and I saw a towboat named *Rusty Flowers*. Often wondered if it was a man, or just something that somebody made up."

They shared a few seconds of silence, then Feur asked, "So what do you want?"

"You've probably heard that Bill Judd got burned up," Virgil said.

"That's what I heard," Feur said. He sighed, blew some smoke, tamped out the cigarette in an aluminum ashtray. "He was a bad man, but he was moving toward the Lord at the end. Too late, though. He hadn't accepted Jesus last time I saw him; he was unwilling to take the step. I suspect Mr. Judd's house fire was only a preliminary introduction to the flames he's feeling right now."

"I wouldn't know about that," Virgil said.

"I *do* know about that," Feur said, and his black eyes glittered with what might have been humor. "What does Mr. Judd's death have to do with me?"

"I was hoping for a Revelation," Virgil said.

"You think I could give you one?"

"If you wanted to," Virgil said. "People say you hand them out in the streets."

"A *book* of Revelation. Of course." He looked past Virgil at the man with the shotgun, and said, "Trevor, could you get a book for Mr. Flowers?" And to Virgil, "Happy to see a man of the law reading the good book."

Virgil, when the gunman was gone, asked, "Trevor?"

Feur shrugged: "What can you do? Your mother gives you a name, and you wear it."

THEY WAITED, and Virgil asked, conversationally, "What's this whole thing with the shotgun?"

"Some people don't like what we have to say. Some of them would like me dead. We are prepared to exercise our right to common, ordinary self-defense," Feur said.

"I understand you have a problem with Jim Stryker," Virgil said.

"We've had our differences. He put me in prison for robbing, and I don't say I didn't do it. But I'll tell you something:

he's a man with a lot of hate, a lot of violence in him. You don't see it, but it's there. If it hadn't been for this other killing, the Gleasons, if it'd only been Judd, I would have said that Stryker would be your number-one suspect. Still might be—but I can't see him doing the Gleasons. Don't know what that would be about."

TREVOR CAME BACK and handed a red-bound volume to Feur, who looked at it and asked, "Who is worthy to open the book, and loose the seals thereof?"

He handed the book to Virgil, who asked, "How many of these have you given away?"

"Few hundred, I suppose. We also publish other books. We find that with most folks, the Bible goes down easier in small chunks," Feur said. "But you didn't come out here to get a book, Mr. Flowers. What do you want?"

"The book, actually," Virgil said, turning it in his hands. It was identical to the one he'd seen at the Gleasons'. "I came here to investigate the Gleason murders, not Judd's, but now I'm doing both. I've only found one connection to both crimes."

Feur's eyebrows went up. "You're going to tell me?"

"Yeah. It's you."

"Me?" Feur's eyes pinched together. "Are you serious?"

"You were known to have been talking to Judd. You just told me so yourself. When I went into the Gleasons' house to look around, what should I find at Mrs. Gleason's right hand, but a copy of your Revelation? So what I need to know is, how close were you to the Gleasons? And how close to Judd, and what is your connection with the two of them?"

Feur sat back in his chair, spread his hands. He had small, feminine hands, but hard and cracked. "I spoke occasionally to Mr. Judd. He shared some beliefs with us, but not all. We were hoping to bring him to the true Lord, and also, to be honest, we were hoping he might provide some financial support. He hadn't done that at the time of his death. His son, as close as I can tell, is useless as tits on a boar. So that is my connection with Mr. Judd. For the Gleasons, I don't believe I ever met them, or were in their presence. I have no idea how they got one of our Revelations. Unless the sheriff put it there. The sheriff doesn't like me. He doesn't like any of us. He is a politician to his bones, and politicians no longer wish to hear the truth."

"Yeah, well." Virgil peered at him for a second, then turned to the other man and said, "Trevor. Get us a Bible, will you?"

Trevor looked at Feur, who nodded. Trevor stepped into what must have been the dining room, and was back a second later with a leather-bound Bible. Virgil passed it to Feur, and said, "Put your hand on it and swear you didn't have anything to do with the death of Judd or the Gleasons."

Feur said, "You're very close to pissing me off, Mr. Flowers."

"Why?"

"Because you don't strike me as a believer, and this is a cynical way to twist me up," Feur said.

"You'd be wrong. I am a believer," Virgil said. "Not quite your kind, but a believer. Now, if you don't want to put your hand on the Bible . . ."

Feur grasped the Bible between his small hands and said, his eyes turned to the ceiling, "I swear on this book, and on my everlasting soul, that I had nothing to do with the murders of Bill Judd or Mr. and Mrs. Gleason. I swear that I play no word games here, that there are no prevarications, that I did not do these murders, killings, and I did not cause them to be done." He looked at Virgil: "Amen."

"Amen," Virgil said. He pushed himself out of the chair. "I guess I'll be going."

"That's it?"

"Maybe. I'd still like to figure out where the Revelation came from. When I find out, I could be back."

"And you'll be judged according to your works," Feur said.

"Revelation 20:12," Virgil said.

Feur cocked his head: "Are you born-again?"

"I'm a preacher's son," Virgil said. "I talked the Bible at supper every night of my life until I went to college, Mr. Feur. You don't get that kind of an education at Stillwater."

"Maybe not," Feur said. "But I kept one book in my cell, the King James. When we were locked down, I had that one book to read; and I read it twenty hours a day.

When we weren't locked down, I read it four hours a night, every night for three and a half years, there among the sodomites and catamites and child molesters. You didn't get *that* kind of education."

Virgil sat back: "Revelation is your text?"

"It is . . ." Feur's eyes went to the light coming through the window, playing on the floor . . . "It is the most powerful thing I've ever read. It *was* a Revelation."

"My personal belief is that Job is the key book in the Bible," Virgil said. "The question of why God allows evil to exist."

Feur leaned forward, intent on the point: "Job talks of the world as it is. Revelation tells us what is coming. I'm not entirely of this world, Mr. Flowers; not entirely. Some of this world has been burned out of me."

Virgil said, "We're all entirely of this world, Reverend. You're just like anybody else, going to and fro on the earth, and walking up and down on it."

Feur was smiling at him, then shook his head once and said to Trevor, "Show Mr. Flowers to the door. And give him one of our booklets about the niggers."

On the way back to town, Virgil's cell phone rang. He glanced at the dashboard: one minute after two. Williamson from the newspaper. He flipped open the phone and said, "Yes?"

"Todd Williamson. You had some news for me."

"This comes from the sky, from nowhere. You can get

confirmation of the rumor from a Mrs. Margaret Laymon or her daughter, Jesse. Jesse, we are being told, is the natural daughter of Bill Judd Sr."

After a moment of silence, Williamson said, "Fuck me with a barbed-wire fence," which Virgil thought was pretty prairie-like of him.

6

WHEN HE'D GOTTEN off the phone with Williamson, Virgil punched up Stryker's cell-phone number, thought about it for a moment, then tapped it. Stryker came up five seconds later. From the background rush, Virgil could tell that he was in his truck.

"Did you talk to the Laymons?" Virgil asked.

"Yeah: sex and money on the low plains," Stryker said. "They're telling the truth. They've talked to an attorney over in Worthington, and they're going to petition the district court for a part in the probate process. Margaret says Jesse will stand up to a DNA test."

"Where're you at now?" Virgil asked.

"Heading back to the office."

"Got your heart in your mouth?"

"I wish I hadn't told you about that," Stryker said. "You gonna spread it all over town. On the other hand, I've got Joanie to hold over your head."

"Listen. I'm just coming up to I-90 after talking to Feur. Not much to report there. So: tell me how to find the Laymons. And give me their phone number."

GEORGE FEUR'S readiness to swear on the Bible, and in a comprehensive way, had impressed Virgil. Feur had the stink of fanaticism about him, and fanatics, whatever else you might say about them, didn't take the Word lightly. Interesting, though, that he'd denied knowing the Gleasons. That was something that could be falsified . . .

The town of Roche once had a bar and a combination grocery–gas station. Now it had two empty and unsalable old commercial buildings slowly sinking back into the earth, and a dozen houses, some neatly kept, some not: flower gardens here, untrimmed lawns there; grape arbors and old wire fences, rusting swing sets and a brand-new tree house, a collapsed chicken house, abandoned farm equipment from the first half of the twentieth century, all gathered on the banks of the Billie Coulee, a seasonal creek that ran down to the Stark River.

A white dog with floppy ears was sitting in the middle of the street when Virgil got there, twenty minutes after talking to Stryker. The dog examined the front of Virgil's truck, realized that it didn't belong to anybody in town, and so ambled off to the side, keeping an eye out for trouble.

The Laymons' house was on the left side of the main street, a white-clapboard story-and-a-half with a brooding dark roof and a brick chimney at one end, a narrow front porch with a white-painted railing. Orange earthenware pots of geraniums sat on the railing, and hollyhocks grew next to the steps. A huge cottonwood stood in back, towering over two smaller apple trees.

A side yard was occupied by a vegetable garden, neatly laid out, tilled and weeded. The sweet-corn leaves were showing brown edges, the corn silk brown, the ears ready to eat. Four rows of potato plants marched along at eighteen-inch intervals, and cucumber and squash vines sprawled around the corn. The whole thing was edged with marigolds, which, Virgil thought, were intended to ward off some kind of rootworm.

In any case, his parents still did the same thing: grew an annual vegetable garden, and edged it with marigolds.

Virgil parked and got out and the white dog barked at him, but only once, and then tentatively wagged his tail. Virgil grinned at him: a watchdog, but not an armed-response dog. At the house, a blond woman came out on the porch. She was dressed for an office in black slacks and a white blouse. She said, "You're Mr. Flowers."

MOTHER AND DAUGHTER didn't look much alike. Margaret, the woman who'd met him on the porch, was in her mid-fifties, Virgil thought, and dressed from Target or Penney's, standard office wear. She was about five-six, a bit too heavy, and busty, with short, heavily frosted hair, plastic-rimmed glasses, and the lined face of a woman who'd been long out in the wind. She'd been pretty; still was, for her age.

Her daughter was almost her opposite: long dark hair,

eyes that were almost black, slender, with high cheekbones and a square chin. She was wearing jeans, cowboy boots, and a plain white T-shirt. She had pierced ears, and was wearing silver crescent-moon earrings. She was waiting in the living room, standing next to an old upright piano. An electric guitar was propped next to it, with a practice amp; the window ledges were lined with pots of African violets.

Virgil stood in the living room for a moment, blinking in the dim light, and Jesse asked, "Ooo. Do you like to rock 'n' roll?"

"I do," he said. He recognized her. She'd been at Bill Judd Sr.'s house, the night of the fire. She'd had a beer can in her hand.

Jesse, to her mother: "He looks like a surfer dude, doesn't he?"

"He's a police officer," her mother said dryly. "You probably should remember that."

"Police officers gotta fuck," Jesse said, flopping back on a worn couch, smiling up at him. "If they didn't, where'd we get all those goobers who go to monster truck rallies?"

"Jesse!" her mother said.

"Thank you," Virgil said. Jesse teased her mother with the f-word, and her mother pretended to be shocked, but wasn't; it looked like an old mother-daughter game. "If I ever have any little goobers, I'll name one of them Jesse."

She laughed, and said, "Want a Pepsi?"

"No thanks, I just want to chat," Virgil said.

"Might as well. The newspaper just called, and every single soul from Fairmont to Sioux Falls will know about it tomorrow morning . . ."

HER MOTHER had been at work when the Judd mansion burned down, and had no idea where she'd been when the Gleasons were killed. Jesse had been on her way to a bar in Bluestem, and saw the fire on the ridge, and trucks pulling out of the bar's parking lot, heading up the hill.

"That good enough?" Jesse asked.

"If you hadn't been to the bar, where'd you get that beer? The one you had at the parking lot?"

She tipped her head toward the kitchen: "Out of the refrigerator."

"So you just went up to the fire to look at it?"

"Of course," she said. "What do you think? You ever lived in a small town?"

"I have, and I know what you mean," he said.

"THESE PEOPLE who got killed, the Gleasons and Judd. They were the same age, and friendly, at least," Virgil said, turning to Margaret. "I'm wondering if there's something way back that's only coming out now. Something that really pissed somebody off, thirty or forty years ago, and winds up in these murders."

Jesse looked at her mother, and Margaret shrugged. "I had a pretty hot affair with Bill Judd, but the only thing I came out of it with was that girl . . ." She nodded at Jesse. "I loved her from day one. For the first eighteen years, Bill sent me a check every month to cover her upbringing, so I don't have any complaints that way, either."

"Don't have any complaints that he didn't marry you?"

"He never asked, which would have been polite, but I wouldn't have done it, anyway," Margaret said. "He could be a good time, but he was twenty-five years older than me, and he could be a mean jerk. I mean really, violent, beat-your-face-in mean."

"How long did you date him?"

"Oh . . . a year or so. But it wasn't exclusive, on his part. He'd screw anything he could get his hands on." She smiled, then tilted her head and asked, "Have you talked to his sister-in-law? She might be able to tell you about those days."

"I didn't know about a sister-in-law. What's her name?"

"Betsy Carlson," Margaret said. "Sister to his wife. She's been in a rest home over in Sioux Falls for, gosh, twenty-five or thirty years now. Think Bill was paying for that, too."

Virgil said, "You sort of linked screwing, with his sister-in-law. Was there something going on there?"

"Yeah." She said it flatly, her voice like flat rocks smacking together.

"Before his wife died, or after?" Virgil asked.

"If you want my opinion, I'd say before he married his wife, during, and after," Margaret said.

"How'd his wife die?"

"Heart attack," she said. "Thirty-two years old."

"Sure it was a heart attack? You say he was beat-your-face-in mean . . ."

"This was before the thing with Jerusalem artichokes, and before everybody hated him, so there wasn't that mean talk you would have heard later. All the official stuff said it was a myocardial infarction, so I guess that's what it was."

"Huh." Virgil said, and he thought, *Russell Gleason was the coroner.*

HE TURNED BACK to Jesse. "How long have you known that Bill Judd was your father?"

Her tongue peeked out, and she rubbed it on her upper lip, thinking. "Mmm, for sure, since the day after the fire. Mom sat me down and told me. But I thought he might be, from one thing or another that she said over the years. I knew it was somebody from around here. She'd start talking about being responsible even when you're having fun, and his name came up a couple of times. And I kind of look like a Judd."

"So, you've sorta known for a while."

"Yeah, but I didn't really care," she said. "Everybody said he was a jerk, and he looked like a jerk, and his son was a jerk, so why would I care? I wouldn't even have thought about it when he died, if Mom hadn't said that I should be practical."

"You mean, get a chunk of the estate," Virgil said.

"That's what it comes down to," Jesse said, and smiled.

"Do you know George Feur?"

"Know who he is, never met him," Jesse said. Margaret shook her head.

"Tell me," Virgil said to Margaret, "what was it like back then, when Judd was on the loose? There are all these rumors . . ."

JUDD HAD SLEPT with an untold number of local women, Margaret said—untold being the literal word, since nobody knew how many. But many. "He liked to go three at a time, when he could find the girls willing to do it. The word was, he liked to do one of the girls, then watch them do each other, and then he could get it up to do another one. And around and around . . ."

"Mom!" Jesse said, maybe really shocked.

Margaret shrugged. "That's the way it was, honey. I didn't get involved in any groups; I was strictly one-on-one. But you know, on the right night, if I'd had a couple of drinks, might have gone for a roll with a couple of the girls. I mean, we were rock 'n' rollers—everything was getting loose, the Stones, the Beatles, the war, smoking dope." She reached out toward his chest, and the Stones T-shirt: "We old people *lived* that T-shirt."

"Were there any other guys involved?" Virgil asked.

"Never heard of any—but there could have been, I guess," she said. "Is that relevant?"

"Somebody had to drag old man Judd down to his basement to kill him," Virgil said. His eyelids dropped, and he looked Jesse over. "Seems more likely to be male than female. Could have been a strong woman."

Margaret said to Jesse, "See—looks like a surfer, thinks like a cop."

"Do you know any other of the local women?" Virgil asked.

"One was Betsy Carlson. I know two more, but . . . I think I'll only tell you one. Michelle Garber, who lives in Worthington, now. She's in the book."

Virgil wrote the name in his notebook. "Why won't you tell me the other?"

"Because she's got a happy marriage and I don't want to mess it up. And it would, if it got out," Margaret said.

"What if her husband found out, and he's the killer?" Virgil asked.

"He isn't," Margaret said coolly. "I know for sure that he doesn't know. And I won't tell who it is."

Jesse's mouth hung open for a moment, and then she said to her mother, "You gotta be kidding me."

Virgil to Jesse: "You know who it is?"

"I just guessed," she said.

"You shush," Margaret said.

"If it turns out to be that man, I'll do my best to put you two in jail," Virgil said. His voice had gone cool, and Jesse sat back. "You gotta understand that."

"It's not him," Margaret said.

Jesse bobbed her head and said, "It really isn't."

WHEN MARGARET suggested there had been a lot of local women, Virgil wondered, did that also imply non-local women?

"There were professionals from Minneapolis," Margaret

said. "That was the rumor. Supposedly one of the local women . . . came down with something that we wouldn't get around here. Supposedly it came from a woman he got at a striptease place up in Minneapolis, on Hennepin Avenue."

Virgil thought, *She'd need a doctor, like Gleason.* "Was this Garber who came down with it?" He looked back in his notebook. "Michelle Garber?"

"No, no . . . I don't know who it was, if there was anybody. Just a rumor. Michelle might know, though. She spent more time with Bill than I did, and she was quite a bit wilder than I was. She might be able to give you more names. Group names."

Virgil tapped his notebook against his chin, looking at Margaret, and said, "Sounds like Judd was out of control."

"If you were ever going to look for one sentence for Bill Judd's tombstone, 'Out of Control' might be it," she said. "He never had enough money, enough land, enough power, enough women. He was an animal."

"He was my daddy," Jesse said thoughtfully.

"Well, there's something to be said for animals," Margaret said. "He certainly could get me going. For a while, anyway."

WHEN THEY were done, Margaret excused herself, said she had to run off to the bathroom. Jesse took him out the front door and they looked at the dog on the street, and Jesse said, "That's Righteous . . ." and then she touched him on the chest, on the old Stones shirt, and asked, "You really like music?"

"Yes, I do," Virgil said. "I'm a damn good dancer, too."

"Who do you like?"

"You know, some old, some new. Kind of like alternative; used to listen to some rap, but it got pretty commercial . . ."

"Music's the only thing that ever moved me, aside from sex," she said. She whistled sharply, and Righteous heaved himself to his feet and started toward them. "I wish Jimmy Stryker liked that stuff. He wants me so bad that he gets little drops of blood on his forehead, every time we talk. But he's . . . so *straight*. He listens to old funky country, Bocephus, Pre-Cephus and Re-Cephus, or whatever they call them."

"He's a good guy, Jim is. And I don't think you'd be bored." Virgil gave her a small smile. "You might be a little too busy for the first, oh, ten years or so, to think much about his music."

"Huh." The dog came up and sat on the porch step and Jesse scratched him on the top of the head, between the floppy ears. "Maybe I'll give him a try. Or maybe not, now that I'm a rich woman."

"You ain't rich yet, honey," Virgil said. "Even if you do get rich, it'll be a while before it happens. Might as well fill up the space with Jimmy. You could find out something good."

"I already know something bad, though," she said.

"Yeah?"

"One time, this was five or six years ago, before he was sheriff, he was a deputy. There was a fight down at Bad Boy's, and he came to break it up. One of the guys in the fight gave him a shove, a little punch, maybe, and Jim . . . I mean, he just beat the hell out of this guy. I mean, beat the hell out of him. Cuffed him, dragged him out to the patrol wagon, banged his head off the ground, banged his head into the car. He was way, way rough."

"Two things," Virgil said, not smiling. "Cops hate to get hit, especially in a crowd of drunks. You can get mobbed if you don't move fast. You get punched, you take the guy down, put him on the floor, put your hand on your gun butt, look at faces in the crowd like you're looking for somebody to shoot. Face them down, right then. Sober them up."

"Still . . . what was the second thing? You said there were two."

"Maybe he was showing off for somebody in the crowd," Virgil said. "Some guys think the tough stuff impresses women. Hope it does."

She nodded. "I've seen that. Just didn't think about it with Jim." Thought about it a second, then said, "It did make me a little hot."

VIRGIL GOT Judd Jr.'s office on the phone as he drove back to I-90, and the woman who answered said Judd was just going out the door and she'd try to catch him. Judd came up a minute later: "What?"

"You have an aunt in a nursing home in Sioux Falls," Virgil said. "I'm out that way, I thought I'd stop and see her. Could you tell me which one it is?"

"Why do you want to see her?" Judd asked.

"Well, we've had three murders. All three people were elderly, and I'm starting to wonder if maybe the cause isn't back years ago," Virgil said. "So, I'm talking to people who knew your father and the Gleasons back when."

Judd seemed to think a minute, and then said, grudgingly, "That's an idea. It's the Grunewald rest home. It's actually north of Sioux Falls, north of I-90 . . ."

Virgil memorized the instructions and when he'd gotten off the phone, decided the news of Jesse Laymon's claim hadn't yet gotten to Judd. He'd been entirely too calm and matter-of-fact. He wondered if Williamson, working on borrowed time, now, was planning to break it on him like a rotten egg. Let him wander around, unknowing, until somebody said, "Uh, Bill . . ."

THE GRUNEWALD REST HOME sat on one of two nearly identical hills a mile north of I-90, ten miles west of the Minnesota line, with a county highway running through the groove between the two hills. Both hills were nicely wooded, with broad lawns beneath the trees. The one on the right showed the Grunewald, a wide brick box, three stories tall, with white trim. The one on the left showed neat rows of white stone; a cemetery.

Nice, Virgil thought. The Grunewald residents could

look out the windows every day and see their future. Virgil pulled into a visitor's slot in front of the home, and walked inside.

The Grunewald was run like a hospital or a hotel, with a front reception desk and lobby with soft chairs. A tiny gift niche was built to one side of the reception desk, and was stocked with candy, soft drinks, women's and family magazines, and ice cream. A tall black woman in Somali dress was working behind the desk.

She nodded at Virgil and he took out his ID, showed it to her, and asked to see Betsy Carlson. The woman's eyebrows went up, and she said, "She doesn't have many visitors . . . You'll have to ask Dr. Burke."

Burke was a busy bald man in a corner office down the hall from the desk. He listened to Virgil's story and then shrugged, and said, "Sure. Go ahead."

"What kind of shape is she in?"

"She is . . . damaged. Hard to tell why. Could be genetics, bad wiring, or she might have taken some drugs and had a bad reaction, or even environmental poisoning. She grew up on a farm. Lots of bad chemicals on a farm when she grew up—they used to spray DDT around like it was rainwater. So, it's hard to know. She's not crazy, she just goes away. Her memories are screwed up, but she has a lot of them. She's never been active and she's gotten less active, so her legs don't work very well anymore . . . So. She is what she is."

On that note, Burke called back to the Somali woman at the front desk, told her to get somebody to escort Virgil into the home, smiled, and wished Virgil good luck.

Virgil's escort was a middle-aged but still apple-cheeked nurse carrying a plastic garbage bag full of something Virgil didn't ask about. They went through a set of locked doors and Virgil asked, "Everybody's locked in?"

"No. We have a locked area for Alzheimer's victims, because they tend to wander and the younger ones can be pretty aggressive. But those doors"—she jabbed a thumb back over her shoulder, at the doors they'd just come through—"they're only locked one-way, to keep people out. Years ago, before we started locking the doors, we had a very nice man as a visitor. He'd visit every couple of days. It turns out he was molesting some of our residents."

"Nice guy."

"When we started to suspect something was going on, we set up some video cameras and caught him at it." She smiled cheerfully at Virgil. "A couple of our Alzheimer's orderlies escorted him to the lobby so the police could pick him up. He resisted on the way, tried to fight, and was somewhat beaten up before they got him to the lobby. He won't come back here, even when he gets out of prison."

"Hate it when they resist," Virgil said.

"It's a bad idea," she agreed.

THE NURSE SPOTTED Betsy Carlson in a chair facing a television that was showing a man chopping up onions and cabbage with the world's sharpest knives, guaranteed not to get dull. "There she is," the nurse said. She put a hand on Virgil's sleeve and said, "She can be a little difficult, so it's best to be sweet with her. If you push too hard, she gets stubborn."

"Dr. Burke said her memory is messed up."

"Yes, but the memories that go back . . . those generally tend to be better. She can't remember what day it is, but she can tell you what she was doing in 1962. And she likes telling you. Another thing, though, is that she sometimes gets . . . she has . . . hallucinations. She sees bugs in her food."

"And there aren't any?"

"*Please*. Not only bugs, she sees people. She sees people's faces in the knots in wood. We're scared to death that someday she's going to see the Virgin Mary in a rust stain and we'll wind up with ten thousand pilgrims on the lawn." She paused, and then said, "She'll be happy to see you—but she'll forget your name all the time, and ask for it."

BETSY CARLSON was tucked into her chair with an afghan. She was the ruin of a beautiful woman, with high cheekbones, an elegant, oval face, and what must have been fine, delicate skin, now furrowed with thousands of tiny wrinkles. Her hair was cut short, and her hazel eyes were glassy and placid. She smiled reflexively when Virgil pulled up next to her.

The nurse said, "Betsy, you have a visitor."

She stared at Virgil for a moment, uncomprehending, then frowned, and asked, "Who are you?"

"Virgil Flowers. I'm a police officer from Minnesota."

"I haven't done anything," she said. "I've been here."

"We know," Virgil said. The nurse nodded at him and drifted away with her garbage bag. "I need to talk to you about Bluestem and some things that have been going on there."

"Bluestem. Founded in 1886 by the Chicago and Northwestern Railway. My great-grandfather was among the first settlers. Amos Carlson. His father fought the Indians in the Great Uprising. My father owned six hundred and forty acres in Stafford Township, the best land in Stark County. He was killed in an automobile accident on County 16 in a blizzard. His skull was crushed. I was born the very next day. My mama always said I was a special child, God's gift. There was a death in the family, and then new life, all at the same time. What did you say your name was again?"

Virgil reintroduced himself, and then began pulling out memories of Bluestem, and Bill Judd and her sister, the days after her sister's heart attack.

She remembered the day of the heart attack: "My sister drank too much, and then she'd fight with Bill; you could hear them screaming all over the house. Usually, about money—he had it, but he hated to spend it. The day she had the heart attack, she was drinking, but she wasn't fighting. She started feeling sick in the morning, and thought maybe she'd drunk too much the night before. Anyway, she decided to move some furniture around in the living room, and we were dragging couches here and chairs over there, and pushing this old upright piano around, and we were just about done when she cries out, 'Lord almighty,' and she falls down. I ask her what's wrong, and she says, 'I hurt so bad, Betsy, I hurt so bad. Go get the doc, go get the doc.' So I ran and got the doctor . . ."

"Dr. Gleason?"

Her eyes faded a bit, and she seemed confused, and then said, "I don't think Dr. Gleason. I don't think we went to Dr. Gleason then. We went to him later."

"Do you remember the doctor?"

"I did. But then, you said Gleason, and that got me sidetracked . . . I, uh, I can't remember."

She did remember about manure spreaders and the funny things that might happen with them; about canning tomatoes, and how everything changed when freezers came in; she remembered playing the piano with her sister, and her sister's wedding to Bill Judd.

"Christ Lutheran Church. I was maid of honor. All the maids wore yellow and carried bouquets of yellow roses. But Bill Judd . . . He was a bad man. He was even bad when he was a boy. He used to steal, and then he'd lie about it, and get other children in trouble. You know what he'd steal?"

"No, I don't," Virgil said.

"Money. He wasn't like other children, who might steal somebody's toy or candy or something. You'd have him to your house and he'd always be looking around for loose change. My mother used to keep a sharp eye on him, after she figured it out. He was bad right from the beginning."

Tears trickled down her cheeks and she said, "After my sister died, there was all kinds of trouble. Bill didn't care about anything, then. She used to hold him back, but after she died, nothing could hold him back."

She began to weep, and a nurse stepped toward them with a question on her face.

"Are you okay?" Virgil asked.

"Bill did bad things, bad things," she said. Her eyes cleared a bit and she said, "Men are no damn good."

"I don't want to get you upset," Virgil said, "but I'm trying to figure out who might have started hating Bill Judd back then. And Russell Gleason . . ."

The nurse asked, "Everything okay?"

Virgil said, "She's a little upset."

"She's late for her nap," the nurse said.

Carlson looked at Virgil and said, "Russell Gleason was there for the man in the moon. That was the thing. The man in the moon. Bill did a terrible thing, and we all knew. Russell knew, too. So did Jerry. Jerry knew about it."

"Who's Jerry?"

She broke into choking sobs, and her whole body trembled. The nurse said, "I think you should stop talking to her. This is not good."

"I just . . ."

"You're really messing her up, is what you're doing," the nurse said. To Carlson she said, "It's okay, Betsy. The man is going away. It's okay. Let's get a Milky Way and then get a nap. Let's get you a Milky Way."

"Not the Milky Way," Carlson said to Virgil, ignoring

the nurse. "It was the man in the moon: and he's here. The man in the moon is here. I've seen him."

She began sobbing again, and the nurse glared at Virgil and said, "Take a hike."

Virgil nodded, tried one last time: "Betsy? Do you know the name of the man in the moon?"

She looked up and asked, "What? Who are you?"

ON THE WAY OUT, Virgil stopped and asked the woman at the front desk if they required anybody to sign in.

"Nope. Not yet. That's probably next."

"Do you remember anybody visiting Betsy Carlson?"

"You know, I think I do. But I couldn't tell you who it was, or even what he looked like. I just remember that she had a visitor, because it was so unusual. This must've been . . . oh, years ago."

"I'm looking into a murder over in Bluestem," Virgil said. "A guy named Bill Judd, who was Betsy's brother-in-law. Do you know if Judd was paying for her care?"

The woman shook her head. "You should ask Dr. Burke that. But as I understand it—just between you and me— Betsy inherited some property from her parents, and when she was admitted here, it was put in trust. I think that's all she's got."

7

WORTHINGTON WAS thirty miles east of Bluestem, another node on I-90. On the way, Virgil dialed Joan Carson's cell number. Wherever she was, she was out of range, so he left a message: "This is Virgil. Gonna be back around six, I hope, if you've got time for a bite. Like to see you tonight. Uh, thought we got off to a pretty good start . . . anyway, let me know." He should have sent flowers, he thought.

In Worthington, he stopped at a coffee shop, got out his laptop, bought a cup of coffee, signed onto the Internet, and brought up a map. The town was twice as big as Bluestem, but it still only took a minute to orient himself and pick out Evening Street.

He took the coffee out to the car and rolled over to the west side, cut Evening, guessed left, guessed correctly, and spotted Michelle Garber's house, a postwar Cape Cod painted pale yellow, with green shutters on the windows and two dormers above the front door. A flat-roofed one-car garage had been attached, later, to the left side of the house, giving it a lopsided look; but better lopsided, in a Minnesota winter, than no garage at all.

Garber, Margaret Laymon had said, was divorced. And yes, Virgil could use Margaret's name when he introduced himself.

GARBER'S HOUSE felt empty. Virgil parked in front, knocked on the door, got no answer, and looked at his watch. Hoped she wasn't in France. The house next door had a bicycle parked off the front step, so he went there, knocked. A sleepy teenaged boy came to the door, scratching his ribs. "Yeah?"

"Hi. Do you know if Miz Garber, next door, is she around? I mean, there's nobody home, but she's not on vacation?"

"Naw. She teaches summer school." The kid turned, leaned back into his house, apparently looking at a clock, turned back and said, "She oughta be coming down the sidewalk in ten or twenty minutes. She walks."

Virgil went back to the truck, brought up the computer to see if he might link into an open network somewhere, got nothing, fished his camera bag out of the back, and started working through the Nikon handbook.

The damn things were computers with lenses; but the ability to take decent photographs was a selling point with his articles. An even bigger selling point would have been drawings, or paintings. Painted illustrations were hot with the tonier hook-and-bullet rags. He'd taken a course in botanical illustration in college, and had thought about signing up for art classes in Mankato, thinking he might learn something valuable. Even if he didn't, he'd get to look at naked women a couple of times a week.

His mind drifted off the Nikon handbook to Joan Carson. That could turn into something, even if it didn't last long . . .

He was getting himself a little flustered when he saw Garber turn the corner at the end of the street. She wore black pants and a white blouse with a round collar, and carried a canvas shoulder bag. With short dark hair and narrow shoulders, she didn't look like an orgy queen.

"Hell," Virgil asked himself out loud, "what's an orgy queen look like?"

GARBER WAS LOOKING at him as she came down the street and he put the camera on the floor of the passenger side of the truck and got out to meet her. "Miz Garber? I'm Virgil Flowers. I'm an investigator with the Minnesota Bureau of Criminal Apprehension. I need to speak with you for a few moments."

She stopped in the middle of the sidewalk: "About what?"

"About Bill Judd. You've probably heard that he died in a fire a couple of days ago."

"I heard that," she said.

"We believe he was murdered," Virgil said. "And because of a couple of other murders . . ."

"The Gleasons . . ."

"Yes. Because of those, we're beginning to wonder if

the . . . genesis . . . of the whole situation might lie in Judd's past," Virgil said. "They're all older people, so we're checking with old friends of Judd."

She looked at him for a moment, the sharp skeptical eyes of a sparrow, then asked, "Where'd you get my name?"

"Margaret Laymon. She said I could use her name."

Garber showed an unhappy smile, then said, "Well. You better come in. Would you like some coffee? All I've got is instant . . ."

Virgil declined: "I just had a big cup and I've been sitting in my truck. In fact, if I could use your bathroom for a moment . . ."

COP TRICK, Virgil thought as he stood in the bathroom. He didn't really need to go that bad, but once somebody'd let you pee in her bathroom, she'd talk to you.

THEY SAT in the living room, dim light behind linen-colored drapes, Virgil on the couch, Garber in an easy chair that faced the television. She looked at him a bit sideways, and said, "If you got here through Margaret, I guess you know about us running around with Bill."

"Yeah, she was pretty specific," Virgil said. "I'm not taking notes on it—the specifics. I don't want anybody to get hurt. But I've got to know if anything happened back then, that might surface all this time later. Violence, sexual activity, blackmail, money, power issues . . . something that could go underground for years and pop up later. It'd have to be something corrosive, something that involved both Judd and the Gleasons."

"How many names did she give you?" Garber asked.

"Only yours, but she said she knew one more—she wouldn't give it to me, because she said if I asked questions, I could break up a marriage."

"You just let it go?" she asked.

"Well, unfortunately, we're not allowed to torture witnesses yet," Virgil said.

She nodded and said, "Listen, I don't usually have coffee when I get back from school. I usually have a glass of wine. Would you like a glass? I know you're on duty . . ."

"The heck with duty," Virgil said. "I'd like a glass."

Garber went out in the kitchen and rattled around for a moment, then came back with two wineglasses and a half-full bottle of sauvignon blanc. She pulled out a rubber vacuum stop, poured a glass for Virgil and the rest of the bottle in her own glass.

"I can think of one thing, that's all," Garber said, as she went through the pouring ritual. "Bill started tearing around the country after his wife died—though there were stories that he used to go up to Minneapolis, even when she was alive, and buy sex."

"So . . . what's the one thing?" Virgil took a sip of the wine, which was so mild as to be almost tasteless.

"Abortion," Garber said.

"Abortion?"

"It didn't come in until, when, the seventies? Bill's wife must've died sometime in the early sixties. I think that's right," she said. "Anyway, he wasn't a big one for condoms, or prophylactics, as we called them back then. It wasn't so easy to get abortions around here. There were stories that Russell Gleason helped some people out. Including Bill."

"Huh. I don't see exactly how that would lead to murder. I mean, we're talking about the absence of a person, a child, not a presence. Unless . . ."

"Unless the antiabortion folks got to someone, who's been sitting there brooding about it all these years, thinking about her lost child," Garber said. "Maybe she got pushed into it by Judd, maybe Gleason did it . . . maybe she's just been sitting out on a farm somewhere, no kids, thinking about the one she aborted."

Virgil sat back: "Maybe you ought to be a cop. That's the best idea I've heard."

"Well, if it's something that goes way back," she said. "If my father had known some of the things I got up to, he might have done something about it. At the time, anyway. But we're all older now, the girls that hung out with Bill, our parents most are gone or too old to do something like murder." She took a hefty gulp of the wine, in a quick hungry way that made Virgil think she might have a problem with alcohol.

"Margaret told me that there were sometimes group . . . encounters . . . at the Judd place," Virgil said, chasing around for the right word. *Encounters*, say, as opposed to *gang fucking*. "She said she didn't know the people involved, because she went one-on-one with Judd. Could you tell me if these group get-togethers, if there were any other males involved other than Judd? Particularly married younger males? I mean, did he bring in any couples, as opposed to just single women? I'm thinking somebody who might be looking back at that time, feeling abused, feeling badly used."

She looked at Virgil for a moment, and then said, "If you get into the details of the whole thing, it sounds bad. But you know, at the time it just seemed kind of exciting and . . . dirty, but in a good way. I'd get almost sick to my stomach on the way over there, but I couldn't wait to get there."

"So there were guys?"

"One guy, at least. Barry Johnson. He was there a lot." She took another gulp of the wine, nearly finishing it. "He was the postmaster in Bluestem. You never would have thought of it, to see him in the post office. Bill got him appointed to the job, through the congressman."

"Were he and Judd involved in a homosexual way?"

"Oh, no, no. Most of the time there were just two women and the two guys, and we'd lay around and drink and sometimes somebody would have some marijuana, but that was about it," she said. "Sometimes there were three women, and us women would, you know, do things with each other, and the guys liked to watch, but they didn't, they weren't—they didn't do anything gay with each other."

"Where's Johnson now?"

She cocked her head and said, "I ought to know that. But I don't." Finished the wine and said, "I think he left here sometime in the middle eighties. This was when Bill was getting older and the whole scene at his place was over. I heard that Barry went to California. Or maybe Florida. Maybe somebody at the Bluestem post office could tell you."

Again, she said, "Excuse me for another minute." She went back into the kitchen, rattled around some more, and then after a moment of silence, Virgil heard a faint pop. A moment later, she returned with another bottle of the sauvignon blanc, and poured herself another glass.

"Here's a question for you," she said. "What could possibly have happened back then—think of the worst possible thing—that would have brought Barry back here to kill people? And something else: How could Barry even get around town without being seen? Hundreds of people there know him by sight, and him coming back, everybody would be talking about it. He'd have to be an invisible man, if he's doing this."

Virgil nodded. "That's a point. But the main thing is, we don't really know what it might be. What if he and Judd had done something really ugly, killed somebody . . . ?"

"But Bill was going to die anyway. Soon. Probably weeks. Why wait all this time and then come back and kill him?" She shook her head. "You know, it doesn't sound to me like a cover-up. It sounds to me like revenge. And it's revenge by somebody you don't see, because everybody can see him. You know what I mean? He's just an everyday guy. He's there all the time, so nobody notices him."

SHE GAVE HIM the names of three more women involved with Judd. Two of them no longer lived in the area—one had moved to St. Paul, and the other had gone north to Fargo. The third one lived in Bluestem, but was divorced and had gone very fat. "I can't see her managing to kill anyone. She can hardly walk a block."

"Huh. Let me ask this: have you ever heard of a character called the man in the moon?"

She looked puzzled, and shook her head: "No. Who's that?"

"I don't know. But I'd like to."

They talked a few more minutes, and then Virgil said, "Is that it?"

She took a third glass of wine; was half drunk and wasn't putting the bottle back in the refrigerator. "Are you working with Jim Stryker?"

"Yes, I am."

She eyed him for a moment, and then said, "I heard one time . . . long time ago . . . that his mother, Laura, might have been sleeping with Bill Judd. And this would have been after she was married. Mark Stryker—Jim's father—was one of those odd guys that you could push around, and people did. I'm not saying there's anything to it, but when Mark killed himself, there were rumors that it was more than losing some land. That he found out that Laura was sleeping with Bill and wasn't planning to stop."

"Is that right?"

"That's what I heard. I don't know how the Gleasons would fit into that. Anyway . . ." Her eyes slid toward the bottle.

"Thank you. You've been a help," Virgil said, standing up.

"If I could go back to those days . . ." Her voice trailed away.

"Yeah?"

"I'd do it in a minute," she said. Virgil realized that she was seriously loaded. "I'd jump right back in the pile. That was the most fun I ever had in my whole damn life."

A BLEAK REALIZATION for a fiftyish schoolteacher, Virgil thought on his way back to Bluestem. Would it lead to something? A commune for elderly rockers on the West Coast? Hitting on a high-school jock? More alcohol?

HE PICKED UP Joan Carson at her house and took her to the McDonald's for dinner—Big Macs, fries, shakes, and fried pies, and she said, "I can feel the cholesterol coagulating in my heart. I'm gonna drop dead in the parking lot." But she didn't stop eating.

"Ah, it's good for you," Virgil said, shoving more fries

into his face. "Eat this until you're forty and then nothing but vegetables for the rest of your life."

"Makes for a short evening, though," she said.

"I was hoping you'd take me out to the farm," Virgil said.

She looked at him: "What for?"

"You know . . . to see what you do."

She shrugged. "Okay with me. You know anything about farms?"

"Worked on one, up in Marshall," Virgil said. "One of the big corporate places owned by Hostess. Harvest time, I'd be out picking Ding Dongs and Ho Hos—we didn't do Twinkies; those were mostly up along the Red River. We'd box them up, ship them off to the 7-Elevens. Hard work, but honest. I used the money to buy BBs, so I could feed my family. Most of the local workers have been pushed out by illegals, now."

She eyed him for ten seconds and then said, "You do have a remarkable capacity for bullshit."

THE STRYKER FARMSTEAD was an archaeological dig in waiting: a crumbling homestead, a woodlot full of abandoned farm machinery and a couple of wrecked cars, a windmill without a prop. The farm was built a quarter mile off a gravel road, in a grove of cotton-woods, at the base of a steep hill. Red-rock outcrops stuck out of the hill, while below it, all around the farm buildings, all the way to Bluestem, and really, all the way to Kansas City, was nothing but the darkest of black dirt, a sea of corn, beans, and wheat.

Among the wrecked buildings, the barn was the exception, and was still substantial. "Don't have animals in it, but we keep it up for the machinery," Joan said. "One of the neighbors—you can't see his place, he's a mile down the way—rents out the loft, sticks his extra hay up there."

The house, a hundred feet across a muddy parking circle from the barn, was little more than a shed. Originally one of the plain, upright, porchless, clapboard farmhouses built on the plains in the late nineteenth and early twentieth centuries, with a coal- and wood-burning furnace and a hand pump in the backyard, it had been converted to a farm office and lounge.

The second level, never fully heated, had been blocked off with insulation and plywood to eliminate heat loss in the winter, Joan said. The utilities had been moved out of the basement to the old back bedroom, and the basement was nothing more than a hole with some rotting shelves holding empty canning jars.

"Probably could get twenty dollars each for those jars, on eBay," Joan said.

"Why don't you?"

"I don't need four hundred dollars."

THE FIRST FLOOR had a barely functioning kitchen with a countertop hot plate, a microwave, and a sink, with a table and six chairs; an electric pump fed the sink. Two ruined couches occupied the living room, with mud circles on the floor where the farmhands had tracked through. An aging computer sat on a table in the former dining room, with a Hewlett-Packard printer next to it, and a couple of four-drawer file cabinets pushed against the lathe-and-plaster wall.

"After the roads got better, it never made much sense to actually live out here," Joan said, as she showed him through the place. "Everything had to be brought out, and you were living out here in isolation. Most of the time, if you didn't have animals, there wasn't much to do. In the winter you did maintenance, in the summer you'd do some spraying and mowing . . . but basically, you were watching the corn grow, or the wheat, or the beans. By the time I was a kid, we had all that Star Wars machinery, a farm wife could sit up on a Deere in an air-conditioned cab with a cassette deck and listen to rock 'n' roll and do the harvest by herself. Ninety percent of it was pushing buttons and pulling levers. No need for a house. I mean, it wasn't *that* simple . . . but it almost was."

"So you moved to town," Virgil said.

"Well, look around," she said, waving at the horizon. "If you look right over there, you can see one other house, but nobody lives in it. It's lonely as hell out here. And Dad killed himself right out back, which still gives me the creeps if I'm out here on a winter night."

"Nice now, though," Virgil said. The sun was slanting down toward the horizon, and a few wispy clouds streaked the pale blue sky; there was just enough breeze to stir the leaves on an endless ocean of corn.

"C'mon," she said. "I'll show you why the house is so far from the road. We have to hurry, before it gets too dark. Bring your camera."

VIRGIL GOT the Nikon out of the truck, with a long image-stabilized zoom, and tagged along past the end of the barn and the rotten timbers of what might once have been a hog pen, past an old pear tree, and a couple of apples, angling downhill to a creek. A footpath, maintained by feet, led along the banks of the creek up toward the hillside. As they got closer, Virgil could see that the creek came out of a crack in the hill, feeding into a broad, shallow stock tank. Overflow from the tank fed the creek.

"This is about as much water as we ever get," she said. "We're a little drier here than farther east. C'mon."

She led him straight into the crack in the hillside, a narrow, rocky cleft that widened to twenty feet, slightly climbing, with the water pounding downhill. The spray caught him a couple of times, a cooling sprinkle on the face and hands.

"Keep coming . . ."

AT THE TOP of the canyon, two hundred yards into the hillside, was a natural rock pool fifty or sixty feet across, fed from a spring that fell down the back wall of the canyon. A few small trees struggled to stay alive in the thin dirt, and cattails rimmed what must've been a muddier flat on the far side. "Cool," Virgil said.

"Called the Stryker Dell on the geological surveys," she said. "Us kids used to come up here and swim. It's good in the evenings, when the sun's coming down the canyon. It's a little gloomy in morning, and cold."

Virgil stepped down to the water, stuck his hand in. Cool, but not frigid, and he said so.

"Because the water's trickling down that rock in the sunshine," Joan said. "This spring will go mostly dry in the fall, it'll just be a stain on the rock. The pond never goes dry, because it's too deep—twenty feet, right below our feet—but sometimes, no water runs out of it. There used to be a pipe up here, that'd feed the stock tank down below. Anyway, it's why the farm was here: year-round water without much work, just by siphoning. If it wasn't for this, my great-grandfather probably would have built out by the road."

Virgil took a picture of her standing on a rock on the edge of the pond, said, "Must've been a great place to come when you were a kid."

"It was; if only there'd been more people around, it would have been perfect."

THEY SAT on the rock, in the sunshine, and Virgil showed her how the Nikon worked. A red-winged blackbird showed up and did some stunts on the cattails, and he took a couple of shots. They compared small-town childhoods, and chatted about college years, dope-smoking and rock 'n' roll, the price of corn-ethanol, about their parents. "My mom lives one street over, and one block down from me," she said. "By now, she knows about your trying to feel me up last night."

"Only teenagers get felt up," Virgil said. "I was expressing a physical affection."

"Huh. *Seemed* like getting felt up," she said.

"I'd like to dedicate some time to do it right," Virgil said. "But this Gleason case, Judd . . ."

So they talked about the case, and he worked the conversation around: "So your mom and dad were good friends with Judd? You think your mom would know something that went on back then? There's gotta be something. Who the hell is the man in the moon?"

"Maybe if we took my mom over to see Betsy Carlson, she could find out," Joan said.

"We could do that," Virgil said. "Think she'd go along?"

"If they let you back in. They might not be too happy to see you, if you had Betsy all freaked out when you left." She stood up and brushed off her seat and yawned. "We oughta get back before dark. I've got my payroll to put together for tomorrow."

HE LEFT HER at her house, in town, after spending another two minutes on her porch. She offered him a cup of coffee, but he had some online research to do, and she had her payroll. "Will you have time tomorrow night?"

Virgil asked. "Maybe we could run up to Marshall, go to a place that has candles and wine."

"I'd like that."

"Call your mom," Virgil said. "Ask if she could run over to Sioux Falls to see Betsy."

"Yeah." She looked out at the coming night, the houses with big backyards, a kid's voice not far away, laughing, and the first of the lightning bugs. "What a great night," she said. "If it were July in Minnesota all the time, you'd have to put up fences to keep people out."

VIRGIL WROTE a little more fiction that night, and invented characters named Joan and Jim Stryker, and himself, whom he called Homer. Homer was terrifically good-looking, and certainly well hung, which might possibly come up later in the story. He smiled in the glow of the computer screen, thinking about it. Had to be funny, however he put it . . .

He wrote,

> Homer felt as though he were being pointed at the Strykers. But if the Strykers had been involved in the murders, why would they call in Homer? They had to know about Homer's clearance record on murders. If Jim Stryker remained in charge, he might take a risk of losing an election, but that was better than dong thirty years in Bayport max.
>
> The abortion thing was out there—and abortion would be a major matter for Feur, of course. Godless commie feminists

with their coat hangers, gong after our virgins. Would it be possible that some local disciple of George Feur had killed the Gleasons, and then somehow, in the Feur group's dealings with Bill Judd, let it slip? Had said something that led Judd to an inference, or even an accusation? If so, how would Homer ever find that person, given the lack of direct evidence?

Homer lay on his bed, his hands behind his head, all four pillows thrown to the floor, and wondered about the man in the moon. And who Jerry was? Jerry had been there for the man in the moon . . . And about the sex. Given the fact that the ex-postmaster wasn't creeping around town, was is possible that one of the other sex partners had slipped over the edge? Again, it could be a religious thing, inspired by Feur.

Anna Gleason . . . What had she been dong all those years ago? Sleeping with Feur? They were of the same age . . .

Goddamn laptop keyboard. Kept missing an *i* when he typed *doing* or *going*, which then came out *dong* and *gong*—could be an embarrassing typo if it happened in the wrong place.

He shut it down, went to bed, spent his two minutes thinking about God, and another ten seconds thinking about dongs and gongs, and finding a new keyboard in a small town, and then fell fast asleep.

8

MOONIE LAY BACK with a little weed, in a little weed—
out in the backyard—and blew smoke at the sky and
watched the Big Dipper rolling around, under the glow of
the Milky Way, and considered the question.

THE NUMBER of necessary killings was growing. There
was no emotional problem there, but the risk had
increased. Moonie recognized risk.

Two of the remaining killings, Jerry Johnstone and
Roman Schmidt, were matters of honor, simple as that. They
were essential and inescapable and had already been delayed
too long. If not done now, the targets might escape forever.

Moonie blew some more smoke at the sky.

Once the honor killings were done, and the reality had
soaked in—the completion of his task, the pleasure of the
memories—there'd be time to rest. Sleep had never come
easily—four good hours were hard to find, and after thirty-
plus years of sleep deprivation, Moonie had built up a
great crankiness.

Or maybe insanity.
Whatever.
Made no difference.

TWO MORE KILLINGS were business necessities. A third, that of Virgil Flowers, might become necessary, because of the way Flowers was deliberately roiling the town. People were closing down, locking doors, talking from behind chains.

Maybe . . . maybe, Moonie thought, the dope wasn't helping. The tactics of the killings had been fine, but the strategy now seemed wrong. Judd should have been last. Could have been last. Moonie had killed him simply because the urge had no longer been containable. And because the old man's brain had been going. No good killing him, if he didn't know why he was dying.

Not an easy thing to manage, multiple murder.

SO WHAT about Flowers?

Flowers would be purely business: he was too competent, a danger.

Flowers also seemed to have a kind of karmic presence: he'd come into Bluestem in the middle of a thunderstorm, had virtually driven into the Judd killing. Then, instead of pushing, probing, demanding, investigating, he'd sort of . . . bullshitted his way around town, not to put too fine a point on it. Gone around talking to everybody, telling lies, telling stories: had taken even the clerk at the Holiday Inn into his confidence.

And in bullshitting his way around town, he'd caused a disturbance. Waves from the disturbance were washing around the county. Instead of waiting for something official to be done, for cop cars and crime-scene crews, people were asking questions, and some were looking backward . . .

Too soon for that.

SO THE QUESTION Moonie was here to decide, after work, out in the backyard on a blanket with a little help from some friendly smoke and the Milky Way, was whether to kill Flowers now, and then go onto Jerry Johnstone or Roman Schmidt, or do Johnstone and Schmidt, and only do Flowers if it was absolutely necessary.

An attempt on Flowers would be huge. Hard to tell where he'd be at any given moment, which meant that the killing ground couldn't be scouted ahead of time. You couldn't simply follow him: if he didn't see it, somebody else would.

Couldn't invite him over and do it, somebody would know about the invitation. That was the trouble with a small town like Bluestem: there were eyes and ears everywhere. You couldn't hang out without people noticing, and worse, knowing who you were, and wondering why you were hanging out. Walk down the street, and you could see the drapes moving, the eyes pressing out of the houses, following behind you; the dogs watching from behind fences, witnessing your intrusion.

There was an old joke about a small town: a real small town meant that you didn't have to use the turn signals on your car, because anybody behind you already knew where you were going . . .

FLOWERS.

Flowers could be taken at the motel. Watch for the light in his room, wait for it to go out, throw some gravel against the sliding glass door, and when he looked out, hit him with a shotgun.

The problem then, would be getting away. Okay—run across the parking lot, behind the Dairy Queen, which would be closed at that time of night, up the alley behind the downtown businesses, out of sight in the dark.

Maybe . . . there was that one streetlight. Take it out ahead of time with a .22? That could be done. But if anybody saw you, even just a glimpse, there was a chance that they'd recognize the build, the stride, the way of running . . . People here knew *everything* about you.

Perhaps Flowers could be lured out somewhere: it'd have to be indirect. He'd have to think he was sneaking up on somebody, and then, when he stepped in the trap, *boom*. And then, and then . . . there'd be a cop frenzy. The BCA would flood the town with investigators.

Have to think about it.

JOHNSTONE and Roman were different.

If they weren't done, Moonie would never get any rest. Their deaths were a basic requirement of life. Johnstone wouldn't be any harder than it was with Judd: Johnstone was an old man, with an old man's neck. A rope would be enough to do it. A knife. A hammer. Wouldn't actually have to shoot out his eyes—a knife would take them out, though he enjoyed the resonance of the gun. Go over to Johnstone's place after dark, knock quietly on the side door. He'd open it. But would he turn on the porch light first? Maybe unscrew the bulb.

Johnstone lived near the Gleasons' house. Sneaking was easy with the Gleasons, but now, in the changed atmosphere, it might not be so easy. Anybody caught sneaking anywhere in Bluestem would be put under a microscope. And if Moonie were put under a microscope, there wouldn't be a single person in town who could provide an alibi, who would say, "Yup, we were out together looking at the fire," or whatever.

If you didn't have an alibi, they'd pick you apart.

Schmidt would be easier in some ways, harder in others. He lived outside of town, for one thing. Make sure the Schmidts were home, pull into the yard, past the yard light, park by the kitchen garden. Take Roman out, then the wife; she was old and slow.

But Roman carried a gun and he was tough, even at his age, and he had to be killed quickly, without suspecting what was coming.

Though it'd be nice to chat with him for a few minutes, when he knew he was dying, when he knew his wife was already dead, to see the hate in his fading eyes.

And then . . .

IF HE HIT SCHMIDT, then Johnstone, who was already a tough target, would get tougher. Everybody would be on edge. But Johnstone had to go; there were only two weeks left before the moon rolled around again.

THEN IT'D BE possible, bearable, after Johnstone and Schmidt, to lie low for a while, and do the business killings, one at a time . . . even let some time pass. Maybe come up with something complicated, so they'd seem like accidental deaths.

When all the necessary killings were done, would it be possible to stop? Maybe not: but if it were necessary to feed the hunger, purely for recreational reasons and psychological comfort, that could be done in other places, as time allowed. Minneapolis, Des Moines, Omaha. Kill and go . . .

HUH.

THE MARIJUANA wasn't helping the thought process, though it was a wonderful thing in its own right: mellowed out the experience, gave life to the stars.

Had to focus. Tactics. Strategy.

Blew a little smoke into the sky and watched the Big Dipper rolling by, watched the lightning bugs blinking out their passions, and Moonie thought, and thought, and finally plucked a flower out of the overgrown jumble of the backyard, and in the shaft of light that came out the bedroom window onto the lawn, plucked the petals one by one, letting God decide.

Johnstone, Flowers, Roman; Johnstone, Flowers, Roman . . .

The flower had quite a few petals, but offered only one conclusion.

ROMAN SCHMIDT was sound asleep when the car pulled into the driveway, and that popped his eyes open. He was far enough out of town that, late at night, several times a year, somebody would use his driveway to turn around, and go back toward town.

The car headlights would sweep through the house, cutting across the bedroom shades, and that would pop him awake. When he was sheriff, lights like that usually meant somebody bringing bad news, and he'd never gotten over that instantly awake reaction.

But now he was an old man, and sleep didn't come that easy anymore. He treasured what he could get, and it pissed him off when he was unnecessarily poked out of a decent sleep.

Unlike most of the cars that did it, this one didn't

turn around. It kept coming, and quickly, and he could tell by the crunch of tires on gravel that it had pulled into the parking place back by the kitchen door. He reached out, touched his clock: 1:30 in the morning.

Who in the hell?

His wife groaned and he said, "I'll go see," but she didn't say anything and he suspected she'd never really awakened. He reached into the bottom drawer of his bedside table, groped around, found the .357, held it next to his leg, and walked through the dark out to the back door in his shorts and T-shirt.

Knock at the door. Bad news. Bad news always knocks quietly. He thought of his son in Minneapolis, his daughters in Albert Lea and Santa Fe. God help him, he'd die of a heart attack if he looked out the window and saw a deputy standing there, looking grim. He'd die of a fuckin' heart attack . . .

Another knock. He snapped on the porch light, took in the familiar face, felt the fluttering of his heart, opened the door and asked, the anxiety riding right to the surface, "What happened?"

"This," said Moonie. The gun came up. Schmidt said, "No," and Moonie shot him in the heart.

GLORIA SCHMIDT screamed, "Rome! Rome!" and groped for the bedside light, and found it just in time to see the muzzle of the gun and the face behind it.

"Not you," she said.

Moonie shot her once in the forehead, and she flopped back on the bed, stone dead.

SCHMIDT WAS FLAT on his back, dead, but he'd still have eyes in the spirit world. Moonie closed the kitchen door to muffle the sound as much as possible, leaned sideways and fired two more shots, through Schmidt's half-open eyes, then opened the kitchen door again, and listened.

Crickets and frogs.

Nothing more. There was time to do this right.

9

VIRGIL LOVED the early-morning hours in the high summer, when there was a cold cut to the morning air, but you could feel the heat coming over the horizon. The perfect time to fish. The perfect time to do anything out-of-doors.

He was up a couple of minutes after five-thirty, peeked out through the curtains across the parking lot, saw the orange upper limb of the sun coming over the horizon. Blue sky. Not a cloud in sight. Excellent.

He sat down, knocked off fifty sit-ups, did fifty push-ups, pulled on a T-shirt and shorts, gym shoes, and headed for the door. Sometimes, in Mankato, he'd plug in an iPod and run to old classic rock, like Aerosmith. The trouble to running with music was, he couldn't think while he was listening to it. Sometimes, that was okay. This morning, he needed to think.

Had things to do, places to go, plans to execute.

Get back to Sioux Falls and see Betsy Carlson at the nursing home. Take along Laura Stryker, Joan's mother, if she'd go . . . do a sneaky interrogation of the elder Stryker, see what she knew about Judd and his love life. See if she'd talk about her husband's suicide, and the effect it might have had on Jim and Joan.

And that made him feel a little bad, but he was a cop, so not *too* bad.

HE RAN UP through town, and back and forth along residential streets, until his watch told him it was 6:15, and that he'd run five miles, more or less. He turned back toward the motel, picked up the pace for the last two blocks, and got to the lobby sweating hard.

He had a further list: historical research at the paper; look up the fat woman that Michelle Garber, the drinking schoolteacher, said had been in bed with Judd. Plot some kind of excuse, as rotten and underhanded as it might be, to get Joan back to the family farm, and up in that hayloft. To that end, steal the extra blanket in the Holiday Inn closet, and hope it got all stuck up with hay.

Garber had mentioned the postmaster who'd shared a bed with Judd and the girls, and had made a point: nobody could really come in from the outside and do this. A persistent stranger would be noticed; even a car seen too often. And a man coming back after years away—or a woman coming back, for that matter—would be noticed instantly, and remembered, and commented upon. He might be missing something, but he believed that he was standing within a half mile of the killer . . .

The shower was perfect. Even the breakfast was good.

Might have been the start of a perfect day, if his cell phone hadn't rung at 6:45, with two syrup-drenched link sausages still on the plate.

STRYKER, BREATHING HARD: "Ah, Jesus Christ, Virgil, we got another one. Two."

"Who?"

"Roman Schmidt and his wife," Stryker groaned. "You gotta get over here."

"Wait, wait, slow down. Roman Schmidt. I know the name . . ."

"He was the sheriff, three before me. Thirty years. Jesus, people are going to be rioting in the streets."

"What's the body look like?" Virgil asked.

"Just like the other one. Propped up on a tree branch, this time. It's just . . . fuckin' . . . nasty."

Virgil got directions to the Schmidt house, threw fifteen dollars on his plate. As he went by the pale-faced night clerk, the clerk blurted, "Have you heard?"

"Ah, man . . ."

OUT THE DOOR, into his truck. He opened his cell phone, scanned down through the directory, punched the call button. A minute later, Lucas Davenport, his boss, said into the phone, "This better be good. You better not be in a fuckin' fishing boat."

"Listen, we got two more down here," Virgil said.

"Oh, boy . . ." Davenport was in bed, in St. Paul. "Same guy?"

"Yes. There's display on the body. Worse than that. It's Roman Schmidt, a former sheriff and his wife. Stryker says that townspeople are gonna be in the street. And since this makes five, we'll start getting heavy-duty media heat."

There was a moment of silence, and then Davenport said, "And?"

"And? And what?"

"What does this have to do with me, when it's not even seven o'clock in the morning?" Davenport asked.

"I thought you'd like to know," Virgil said.

"I would have, I guess, at nine-thirty," Davenport said. "But at seven o'clock—before seven o'clock—it's your problem."

"Thanks," Virgil said. "Listen, does that Sandy chick still work for you?"

"Part-time."

"Can I call her?" Virgil asked. "Get her to carry some water for me?"

"Yeah. Call me after nine, and I'll get you her cell number," Davenport said. "She goes to school in the morning."

"What about the media? What do I do about them?"

Davenport said, "Wear a fresh shirt, tell them that you're following up a number of leads but you're not able to talk about them for security reasons, that all state and local authorities are cooperating, and, uh, you expect a quick resolution to the case."

"Thanks, boss."

"Virgil, I didn't send you out there to be stupid. Handle it, handle the press, get back to me when you've got it figured out," Davenport said. "I'll monitor your activities on Channel Three."

IF VIRGIL was having a bad morning, it was nothing in comparison to Roman Schmidt's. The killer had pushed a forked stick into the dirt of the driveway and had pushed the fork rudely beneath Schmidt's ears, one tine of the fork on either side of his neck. It was enough to hold the sightless body upright, but the down pressure of the body, pulling on the stick, had forced his tongue out. Flies were crawling around his face, into the eye sockets and his mouth.

His legs were splayed, and his penis peeked out of the fly of his boxer shorts.

"That is brutal," Virgil said, standing with his hands in his jeans pockets. "The family here yet?"

"Not much family, not that we know of—maybe some cousins. They never had children."

Virgil and Stryker were fifteen feet from the body and Virgil could see heel grooves in the dew-soft soil of the parking area, where the body had been dragged from the house. "Where was he killed?" Virgil asked.

"Right at the back door," Stryker said. "The first shot took him low in the heart, out a little higher in back. It looks like somebody knocked on the door, was standing on the step, Roman opened the door and *bam!* He's dead. We know he opened the door because the slug didn't go through it. Gloria was in the bedroom. Looks like they'd been asleep awhile. Then, whoever did it, came and put the last two shots through his eyes. There are holes in the kitchen floor, inside the door."

The body was found by the newspaper deliveryman. Virgil was the fifth cop there: the two guys on the night patrol had come in first, Big Curly right behind him, because he lived only a mile away, and heard the call on his scanner, and then Stryker and Virgil. Now more cops were showing up, blocking off the yard, waving traffic through on the county highway. Crime scene running a bit late, but expected in the next several minutes.

"Any sign of resistance?"

"No, but that's not a sure thing. We cleared the house and then I got everybody outside, so's not to mess the place up," Stryker said.

Big Curly came over. "I barfed," he said.

"You okay?" Virgil asked.

"I knew them my whole life," Big Curly said. "They lived three doors down when I was growing up. I said hello to Roman or Gloria every day for fifty years."

"Maybe take a seat, get some coffee," Virgil said. "Not much to do until crime scene gets here."

"Okay," Big Curly said. He took a step, then turned, and said, "You know, Jim, Rome liked his guns. That drawer was open on his bedside table. I bet there was a weapon in there. If somebody came in late, while he was asleep, I bet he took his gun to the door with him. The killer might have picked it up."

Stryker nodded and Virgil said, "Good eye."

Curly went away and Virgil said, "You've been assuming that the killer is a guy—male."

"You think it's a woman?" Stryker's eyebrows went up.

"I had an open mind on the issue. These guys are old, and don't weigh much, but they were dragged. I'm thinking, now, Curly's right—it's a guy."

"Uh . . ."

"A strong woman could have dragged them, as long as she didn't worry about hurting them, which she wouldn't, because they were dead. But: take a guy from Schmidt's generation. He's up, he's got his gun, he goes to the door, sees who it is—recognizes him—and opens the door. Gets shot."

Stryker was puzzled. "A woman couldn't do that?"

"A woman could—but Roman wouldn't have opened the door with his dick sticking out of his shorts. He would have said, 'Hang on, let me get some pants on,' and he would have put something on, and then he would have opened the door."

Stryker looked at him for a minute, and then said, "Sometimes I suspect you're smarter than I am."

"Better ballplayer, too," Virgil said. "But where that leaves us, is right back at what you were assuming anyway. Not a major advance."

"SPEAKING OF major advances," Virgil said, "have you heard from Jesse?"

For a moment, the issue of Roman Schmidt flicked out

of Stryker's eyes: "You sonofabitch, you've been messing with my love life."

"And . . ." Like Davenport.

"I appreciate it." Stryker started to laugh, remembered where he was, and choked it off. "She called me up last night and she said, 'Jimmy, you want a chance with me?' I said, 'Yes,' or something like that. I actually mumbled a lot, but the basic bottom line is, I was gonna take her to Tijuana Jack's tonight."

"It's off?"

"Of course it's off," Stryker said, looking sideways at Schmidt. "If I took her out tonight, and somebody from town saw me, I'd be dead meat, politically. That'd be the end of my job. They'll want me out there twenty-four / seven, driving the back roads, looking for Roman's killer."

Virgil looked around, making sure nobody would over-hear them: "That's horseshit, Jim. Not that they wouldn't think it, but you're not gonna find the killer driving the back roads. You want some advice?"

Stryker shrugged. "Depends on what it is."

"Take her to Brookings. Or Marshall. That's what, an hour? Give you time to talk. Tell her straight out what's going on, why you've got to go so far. She seems pretty bright; she'll understand it. She'll understand that you're taking a risk for her."

"Gotta think about it," Stryker said.

"Just don't be too nice," Virgil said. "She likes *edge*. Mix up *nice*, with a little law-enforcement *edge*."

"That what you're doing with Joanie?"

"Joanie and I are operating on a higher level," Virgil said. "You're not. So do what I tell you." He looked back at Schmidt, sitting in the dirt, with the fork under his ears. "Isn't this the most fucked-up thing you've ever seen?"

"When I get this cocksucker, I'm gonna kill him," Stryker said.

"Atta boy," Virgil said. "Feel the burn."

A WHILE LATER, Virgil said, "I'm going back to town. As soon as your crime-scene people will let me inside, I want to know. Something in there might tell us what's going on. It'll be on paper, if there's anything. I don't think this guy is leaving any DNA behind."

"What's in town?"

"Historical research," Virgil said.

He drove back to town, parked, got his briefcase out of the car with his laptop, went to the newspaper office, and found a scrawled note Scotch-taped to the window: "Out on story, back later." The note looked like it had been written in a rush. He'd probably passed Williamson as the newspaperman headed to Schmidts', and he was coming in.

Frustrated, he rattled the doorknob, and to his surprise, it turned under his hand. He had a quick snapshot vision of Williamson lying on the floor, with two black holes where his eyes should be. He pushed in: the place was empty. He really needed to look at the files . . .

He reached back, pulled the taped note off the window, and let it fall to the floor. Hey, he never saw it, and the door was open. On the counter inside was a fresh stack of papers, with a coin box. The lead story was headlined NEW CLAIM FOR JUDD FORTUNE.

That would sell a couple papers, he thought.

Back in the morgue, he pulled clip files on every name he had in town: the Judds, the Gleasons, the Schmidts, the Stryker family, the Laymons, George Feur.

Judd's wife had been named Linda—and when she died, in 1966, the story must've been the biggest one in the paper that week, with a seventy-two-point headline. She'd been rushed to the hospital, the story said, but had been declared dead on arrival by a doctor named Long. An autopsy had been done, and found the cause of death to be an aortic aneurysm. The clip on the autopsy said that the coroner, Thomas McNally, declared that "once the aneurysm tore open, there was no possibility of survival. She bled to death within a minute or two."

Judd was characterized as "distraught."

That was not quite the story he'd gotten from Margaret Laymon, who remembered it as a heart attack, but it was close enough.

HE READ FORWARD in the Judd files, but after Linda Judd's death, it appeared to be mostly business news, and then the Jerusalem artichoke scandal.

He went back, looking through the huge collection of

clips on Roman Schmidt, who had even more than Judd
Sr., and found a few intersections with Russell Gleason.
Gleason was occasionally cited as the coroner, apparently
alternating with Thomas McNally. That hadn't been
uncommon in country towns, Virgil knew, where local
doctors took turns doing an unpaid extra duty.

Roman Schmidt and Gleason were cited together in fifteen or twenty highway accidents, an accidental gunshot
death during deer season, a man who was killed by a deer,
old people found dead at home, several drownings and
infant deaths, one "miracle baby," a kid who'd stuck his
arm in a corn picker and had bled to death, and several
more gruesome farm accidents, including a man who'd
been cut in half by an in-gear tractor tire, after the tractor
rolled on him.

But Virgil couldn't find Judd's name in any of them.

The Laymon files he'd already seen, but there was
nothing to indicate that Margaret Laymon had had a
romance with Judd. Garber, the alcoholic schoolteacher,
had no file at all; to his surprise, neither did Betsy Carlson,
Judd's sister-in-law. Shouldn't there be a story at the time
of the sister-in-law's death, since she was the witness? Or
maybe, like Williamson had said, they only filed the most
important names, and she just wasn't important enough.
Have to ask, but it seemed strange.

The Stryker files were large: Mark Stryker's suicide was
covered extensively, but most of the story detailed the
family history before Mark. Laura Stryker was mentioned
as working as an office manager at State Farm. Virgil

checked files under "State Farm Insurance," and found that the local agency was owned by Bill Judd Sr.

Huh. Nobody had mentioned that. No way to tell from the clips when she began working there, or when she left . . .

THE ROOM WAS close and warm, and after a while, Virgil leaned back in the chair and closed his eyes. Let Homer out: worked on a little fiction.

Laura Stryker rolled away from Bill Judd, both covered with a sheen of sweat, gasping from the sex, and dropped her feet to the floor. No doubt about it: she was missing life with Mark. Nice guy, but not what she needed. "I'm going to tell him," she said, pulling up her underpants.

"Aw, don't do that. You know that we're not long for this. We're just fooling around, honey."

"Doesn't necessarily have everything to do with you, Bill. Has to do with me: and I'm telling him . . ."

Try again.

Mark Stryker, trembling with anger, rigid there in the kitchen, shaking: "I won't put up with it. I put up with shit all of my life, and I won't put up with this. I'll tell the kids, I'll tell your folks, I'll talk to anybody who'll listen. You're not leaving me, you're leaving Bluestem. You won't be able to walk down the street . . ."

"I wanted to be civilized . . ."

"Civilized, kiss my ass," Mark Stryker said, his voice rising, shrill. "This is the last time you'll ever see the kids. I'm not letting some whore come around to the farm . . ."

He turned and went outside, shouted back at her, "I knew what you were doing, whore. I knew . . ."

Laura, the anger rising in her, with the fear, hadn't thought about the kids; Mark was outside, looking up at the screen over the sink, still there, shouting. The gun was there, in the kitchen drawer, behind the towels, the clip in the next drawer, took only a second to slam the clip into the butt, jack a round into the chamber . . . the gun right there in her hand, hot, Mark in the yard . . .

"I killed him . . . I'm freaking out here, I killed him in the yard."

"Jesus Christ, Laura . . ."

"You fix this." Not weeping, but out of control. "You tell them it's suicide. I'm not going to lose the kids . . ."

"Jesus Christ, Laura . . ."

"You call Russ Gleason . . . you tell him . . . I know about his little abortion mill. You tell him that Mark committed suicide . . ."

Virgil yawned and opened his eyes. Fiction. But a story was going there, beginning to feel like something—at least he was pulling the dead people together.

And then he thought, what if this wasn't about the men? What if it was about the wives? What if Gloria

Schmidt and Anna Gleason had been in bed with Judd, and now somebody was killing them, and the shooting of their husbands, through the eyes, was symbolic of some kind of blindness, or a looking-away . . .

What if Laura Stryker wasn't the perpetrator, but was the next target?

HE SAT in the morgue for two hours, altogether, typing notes into his laptop, thinking. Every few minutes, the outer door would rattle, he'd hear change go into the coin box, and the door would close again. Once, there'd been no change, and he'd been tempted to peek and see who it was, stealing a newspaper; but he stayed with the clips.

When he was finished, he knew a lot more than when he'd started, but nothing that seemed to connect with the murders. Everybody in town may have known that Judd was sleeping with local women, and sometimes in a pile of them, but it never got into the newspaper.

He took ten minutes to get the clips back in their envelopes, close down his computer. He walked back through the newspaper office, picked up the note on the floor, taped it back on the window, and went to his truck.

Laura Stryker.

HE CALLED JOAN: "Did you hear about Roman Schmidt?"

"I did." Her voice was hushed. "Virgil, this is god-awful.

Completely aside from the fact that Jim is going to lose his job—it's god-awful all on its own."

"Well, if we catch the guy, Jim could still pull out of it," Virgil said.

"Gotta be soon," she said. "Do you have any ideas?"

"We were talking about going to Sioux Falls with your mom. Think I could take her right now?"

"I'll call her. Do you want me to come?"

He hesitated, then: "If you want."

"I'll call her. I'll get back to you in two minutes."

LAURA WAS happy to go. Virgil drove to Joan's house, rang the doorbell, and she waved him inside: "I just got here, I was out at the farm," she said. "I have to change into something that doesn't smell like dirt. Maybe take a really fast shower. I told Mom we'd be there in twenty minutes."

"Happy to wash your back," Virgil said.

"I need that," she said. "There's always that one spot right in the middle, it's been dirty for eight years now."

"What happened eight years ago?"

"That was the year before I got married," she said.

SHE WENT OFF down the hall to the back bedroom, yelled, "There's Coke in the refrigerator, there's instant coffee, you could make it in the microwave." He stirred around in the kitchen, looking it over, checking the refrigerator. She wasn't a foodie, that was for sure. She had about three knives, and most of the stuff in the refrigerator looked like it had been there for weeks.

A door in back closed: the bathroom? He got a Coke, went into the living room. An open door led into what might have been a small dining room, or television room, now converted to an office, with a desk, computer, and file cabinets. He saw a wall of family photos, stepped into the room and looked at them: found the same thin man in plaid pants in two of them, thought it might be her father.

But she and Jim must take after Laura, because Mark Stryker really was a slight figure, except that he had the same white-blond hair of his son and daughter . . .

Slid open a drawer in a file cabinet, listening for her, for a footstep, looked at some tabs—business and taxes—and pushed it shut.

Just being snoopy now, he thought. No good could come of it. He eased back into the living room, heard a door open: "Hey. Are you going to wash my back, or what?"

ALMOST STOPPED HIS HEART.

He put the Coke down and headed back down the hall; saw her damp face and hair at the end of it, and then she pulled back inside the bathroom. And by the time he'd gotten to the bathroom, she was back inside the shower.

He opened the shower door, and there she was, her back to him, as well as the third-greatest—he gave her an instant promotion—ass in Minnesota, and maybe on the entire Great Plains. "Oh, my God," he said.

"Just the back."

"Just the back, my sweet . . ."

"Just the back," she said. "You offered, I'm accepting."

"If you . . ."

"Don't you get in this shower, Virgil Flowers," she said. "You'll get all wet and we have to be at my mom's in fifteen minutes and she'll know that we've been up here fooling around."

"Gimme the soap and back up," he said.

He washed her water-slick back, and the third-greatest ass, and then, squatting, her legs, one at a time, working upward, and by the time he was getting done, she was hanging on to the faucet handles, and when he *was* done, he snatched her out of the shower and turned her around and kissed her and said, "Fuck your mama."

"Not my mama," she said. "Not my mama."

THEY WERE twenty minutes late getting to Laura Stryker's, driving over with all the truck windows down. Joan wanted to get the smell of sex off them, she said.

"Not as late as I might have hoped," Joan said.

"You weren't complaining twelve minutes ago," Virgil said, "unless that was your way of screaming for help."

"Don't be too proud of yourself," she said. "I'd been waiting for a long time. Bill Judd Junior could have gotten to me after all that time."

Virgil leaned close to her: "The fact of the matter is, you've gotten hold of something far beyond your simple country experience."

That made her laugh, and she pushed him away and said, "Next time, though, we're going for the *slow* hand."

WHEN THEY GOT out of the truck, Joan said, "Stay here, but leave the doors open. Mom might smell something if we don't air it out a little more."

"Jesus, Joanie, you're an adult . . ."

"It's my *mom*."

So he left the doors open and the engine running, and stood out in the sunlight and worked up a little sweat while Joan collected Laura. In two or three minutes they were on the front porch, Laura carefully locking the door behind her.

Laura was a handsome woman for her age, slender as her daughter, with carefully cut and tinted hair. If you were checking out mothers to see what a daughter would look like in twenty-five years, you would have taken the daughter. She got into the backseat, said, "Pleased to meet you, Virgil," and Joan hopped into the front passenger seat and said, "That's the first time I ever saw you lock the front door."

"Everybody's locking doors now. If Janet came over after dark, and knocked, I might hide out and not answer, not until this killer's caught," she said.

Joan to Virgil: "Janet's her best friend," and to Laura: "I don't think you have to worry about Janet."

"The word is, the murdered people probably knew the killer. What do you think, Virgil?"

Virgil nodded. "I think that's right."

THEY RAN DOWN to I-90, and up the ramp, heading west, and talked over the murders. Virgil filled them in on the Roman Schmidt killing, the killer's tendency toward display.

"So what are they looking at?" Laura asked. "They must be looking at something."

"Gleason was looking at his backyard and up the hill, Schmidt was looking straight down his driveway at the road. Nothing in particular," Virgil said.

A minute later, Laura asked, "What direction were they facing? If he was facing down his driveway, Roman was facing east, and if Russell was looking up the hill, he was facing east. Would that be right?"

Virgil thought for a moment, orienting himself, and then said, "Yeah, that's right."

"They were killed at night—so maybe toward the sunrise," Laura said.

Joan asked, "But what would that tell you? That you're dealing with a religious nut?"

"That Feur person," Laura said. "Jesus was resurrected at sunrise. Maybe that has something to do with it. And in the Bible, east is the most important direction."

Virgil said, "Huh. Well, Judd was burned to death. What does that mean? Hellfire?"

"We're talking about a crazy person," Joan said. "I don't think you're gonna figure out anything from that kind of stuff. He's doing it because he's crazy."

"Interesting to talk about, though," Laura said.

They talked about the Laymons. The story was all over town five minutes after the first person picked up a newspaper. "Margaret Laymon. I didn't know it was Bill that did it, but it doesn't surprise me," Laura said. "Margaret was a hell-raiser when she was young. Somebody was going to do it, sooner or later."

"They didn't have the pill yet?"

"Yes, but . . . I don't know. Maybe she wanted to have a baby, and wanted Bill to be the daddy. Women get strange, sometimes."

"You being one, I'll take your word for it," Virgil said. "I hadn't noticed, myself."

CROSSING THE BORDER into South Dakota, Virgil asked, "Was Betsy Carlson prominent in any way? I mean, before she came here?"

"Oh, lord, yes. Her parents were very well-off early settlers, owned a good chunk of land along the railroad, one of the banks, at least for a while. Betsy was the life of the party when she was young," Laura said. "Everybody was a little surprised when Bill Judd married her sister, instead of her."

"There were rumors that he didn't actually have to marry her, to get what he wanted," Virgil said. "The old 'Why buy the cow if you're getting the milk for free?'"

"Could be some truth to that," Laura said. "Back then, people tended to look the other way . . . Have you been talking to other people . . . mmm . . . related to Bill Judd?"

"A couple," Virgil said. "Margaret Laymon, of course. A woman who now lives somewhere else—I've got a list I'm working down."

"Well, cough up the names," Joan said.

"Ah, you don't want to know," Virgil said. "Besides, I couldn't tell you if I wanted. I scrawled them all down in my notebook, and it's back at the motel. He apparently got around town, though."

His eyes caught Laura's in the rearview mirror. She was watching him with just a hint of a smile on her face.

Virgil added, "The question I was working up to, was, why wouldn't there be any press clippings about Betsy Carlson? I was looking in the newspaper files today, and there's not a single one."

After a moment of silence, Laura said, "Well, that's ridiculous. She was in every club in town, she was president of most of them, at one time or another. There should have been a hundred stories about her."

THE FLOOR NURSE at Grunewald rest home was not happy to see Virgil again, and got in his face. "Betsy was very agitated after you left. She still hasn't recovered. She tries to walk, but she's too weak. We're here to protect our clients, and you could be hurting her."

"I'm sorry about that," Virgil said, with not much

contrition. "But we've got a fairly desperate situation over in Bluestem. There were two more people killed this morning, and we believe they involve something that started in Betsy's time. So: we've got to talk to her."

The nurse let her disapproval show, but when she took them to see Carlson, the old woman showed no sign of recognizing Virgil. Instead she squinted at Laura Stryker and when Laura said, "Hello, Betsy," she quavered, "Laura?"

"Yup, it's me," Laura said.

The three of them pulled up chairs, and with the nurse hovering in the background, Laura started talking to Carlson about the old days in Bluestem, about playing up on Buffalo Ridge. Carlson was older than Laura, so they hadn't run with the same groups, but they'd all known each other.

Carlson's memories wandered, sometimes were sharp, other times, vague. At one point, she blurted, "I remember when Mark died. That was an awful day."

"Most awful day in my life," Laura said. She glanced at Joan. "I was afraid for the kids. Jim was bad, but Joanie . . . I was afraid she might die. Or go crazy . . ." She bit off the sentence, realizing that it might not be the most diplomatic thing to say, given whom they were visiting.

Carlson's head bobbed, and then her eyes drifted away, and then she looked at Virgil and said, "Did you find the man in the moon?"

Virgil smiled and said, "I looked, but I couldn't find anything. I could find him if I had a better name."

She shook her head and Virgil could feel her drifting again: "Doesn't have a name. Not that I knew, anyway. They took him away, but he came back. I saw him." She shook her head and went silent, and then she said, "You can't look at all his face. Just look from his eyes to his chin, in this circle." She moved a trembling hand to her face, and traced a circle from the middle of her forehead, past the end of an eyebrow, down across a cheekbone, around and under her mouth, and back up the other side to her forehead again. "You can only see him if you look in there. The man in the moon."

"Do you know anybody who'd like to hurt Bill?" Joan asked.

The old woman looked at Joan for a moment and then almost giggled. "Who wouldn't, that's the question."

They pushed, but she declined into babble. They waited, to see if she'd recover, and she went to sleep.

"GODDAMNIT," VIRGIL SAID, as they were crossing the parking lot. "Doesn't know the name, but she knows he's here. The man in the moon."

"What're you going to do?" Joan asked.

"Go back to Bluestem. See what's going on at Schmidt's. Maybe . . . maybe go talk to the judge about getting a subpoena to look at Judd's bank records. And Gleason's, and Schmidt's."

"How about the Strykers'?" Laura asked.

"I've ruled out two of the Strykers," Virgil said, as they settled in the truck.

"Which two?" Joan asked.

"That's the tough question," Virgil said.

ON THE WAY BACK, he pushed Laura about sexual and business relationships in town when Gleason and Schmidt overlapped as sheriff and coroner.

"You don't think it's about the Jerusalem artichoke scam?" Joan said. "Around here, that's always a topic of conversation."

"If it weren't for Gleason and Schmidt, maybe. But with those two . . . from what everybody tells me, they were all movers and shakers in town, and friendly, but I don't think anybody would blame Russell Gleason for the artichoke thing." His eyes went up to the rearview. "Do you?" he asked Laura.

She shook her head: "It never occurred to me that he could be involved, and us Strykers knew as much about the artichoke business as anyone. No. I don't think that's it."

"This comes down to craziness, and craziness . . . craziness isn't usually about some long-ago hustle," Virgil said. "There's something else: sex, violence, illegality of some kind . . . some crazy bitterness that got covered up and suppressed, and now is sticking its head out. I was thinking, maybe . . . maybe there'd been a homosexual thing, that Judd pushed it on some kid back then, a kid who wasn't gay but did what he was told to do, or forced to do, and that's made him crazy. But my . . . names . . . say that there wasn't any male-on-male gay stuff."

Laura looked at him through the rearview, but said nothing. At her house, she got out, closed the door, walked around to the front of the truck and made a rolling motion, so that Virgil rolled down the window. "What you want to know about, didn't happen," she said. "Absolutely did not."

"What are you talking about?" Joan asked her mother.

"Virgil knows," Laura said, and she turned away and headed up her front sidewalk.

"WHAT THE HECK was that about?" Joan demanded, as they rolled down toward her house.

"About eliminating Strykers, as suspects."

"What?"

Virgil sighed. "She was telling me that she didn't have an affair with old man Judd, and, as a corollary, that that's not why your father killed himself, and so there's no reason for any Stryker, and in particular, Jim, to have killed him. Or the others."

She stared, aghast. "My God, Virgil. What have you been up to?"

Virgil said, "I've been listening to talk. There's talk that your mother and Judd were involved back around the time of your father's death. She worked in an insurance office that Judd owned. If she says she was not involved, I believe her. I don't think she'd lie, when we've got all these killings

on our hands, not if she thought it might make a difference."

"Of course she wouldn't," Joan said, angry now.

Virgil shook his head. "You can't tell what people will
do, when their reputations are on the line. But: she didn't.
I believe her."

"It's hard to believe that you suspected," Joan said.

"I didn't, really," Virgil said, again, without much contrition. "I'm just investigating."

10

JOAN DIDN'T INVITE him in, when they stopped at her house. Her attitude wasn't exactly frosty, he decided as he pulled away, but she was thinking about him, about her mother, about Jim, and about her father.

After he dropped her off, Virgil called Davenport in St. Paul, got the cell-phone number for Sandy, the researcher, and caught her as she was walking back to her apartment from class at the university.

"I need massive Xeroxes," he told her. "I need income tax returns for a whole bunch of people. Do you have a pencil? Okay: William Judd Sr., William Judd Jr., a whole family named Stryker"—he spelled it for her—"including Mark, Laura, James, and Joan, also a Roman and Gloria Schmidt, husband and wife, Russell and Anna Gleason, husband and wife, Margaret and Jesse Laymon, mother and daughter. They all live in Stark County, most of them in Bluestem, and the Laymons live in the town of Roche. R-O-C-H-E. Can you do that?"

"Yes. Want me to run them through the other agencies—department of public safety, corrections, all that?"

"Everything you can find on them. Put it in a FedEx and see if you can deliver it to the Holiday Inn in Bluestem, tomorrow."

"Never happen," she said. "How far is Bluestem from here?"

"Four hours."

"I'll get it there, one way or another. I'll talk to Lucas," she said.

While he was talking with Sandy, Virgil pulled into the courthouse parking lot. When he closed the phone, he went inside, found the district court judge, told him what he needed, then drove out to the Schmidt house.

The day was turning hot, the leaves on the trees turning over, giving them a silvery look in the breeze; and the corn popped and rustled in the fields along the way out.

Schmidt's body had been removed, but not until after a photographer from the Sioux Falls paper, with a lens two feet long, and a monopod, had skulked into the cornfield across the street, and had taken several shots before he was noticed, and the sight line blocked with a patrol car.

Big Curly wanted to seize the photographer at gunpoint, but Stryker contented himself with having a chat with the editor about good taste and the feelings of relatives, along with possible criminal-trespass charges and a future lack of cooperation if the photos got published.

"A trespass charge wouldn't hold up in Minnesota,"

he told Virgil. "We gotta hope his editors don't know that."

"Ah, newspapers don't print body shots too often," Virgil said. "I hope."

GLORIA SCHMIDT'S BODY was still in the bedroom, but it would be moved as soon as the people from the funeral home got back. Processing of the house was still under way: "Probably won't be done until tomorrow morning," Stryker said.

"I'm itchy to get in there and look at their paper," Virgil said.

"We gotta process. I'm trying to stay out of there myself," Stryker said.

"I know . . . all right. I'll go down to the bank and look at records. Did your guys see a bank safe-deposit key in there anywhere?"

"Not me—I can check," Stryker said. "C'mon around back."

Virgil followed Stryker around the side of the house and in the back door, into a mudroom. "Probably be in the chest of drawers in the bedroom, or a drawer in the home office," Virgil said.

Inside, it was cooler, but with the smell of blood and body gases in the air. Stryker stopped at the mudroom door and called, "Hey, Margo."

"Yeah?" A woman's voice from the front of the house.

"Have you seen anything that looked like a safe-deposit key?"

"Yeah. You want it?"

"Is it a problem?" Stryker called.

"No problem. Under his socks in the bureau. Doesn't look like anybody touched it."

"All right . . ."

Stryker said to Virgil, "We've got media. They're calling. I've set up a press conference for three o'clock in the main courtroom. You gotta be there."

"I will be."

A MOMENT LATER, the redheaded crime-scene tech came out, dressed in paper pants and shirt, and handed a blue cardboard envelope to Stryker, who handed it to Virgil, and said, "Let me know if there's anything."

"Absolutely," Virgil said.

BACK IN TOWN, he went to the courthouse, picked up the subpoenas, stopped at one of Bill Judd Jr.'s Subways and got a sandwich for lunch, then continued on to the bank. The manager first opened the Schmidt box, where Virgil found paper—insurance, deeds, wills, old photographs—and no money. He did find a ring made of solid gold, with a small diamond inset, and the name Vera Schmidt engraved inside. Roman Schmidt's mother?

There were two curiosities.

In a yellow legal envelope he found a photograph of a blond woman, nude, lying faceup on what appeared to be a medical examiner's table. Half of her face was torn and bloody, her mouth was slightly open, and one side of her body was covered with what appeared to be purple bruising. She was clearly dead. Nothing else: no name, no date.

The other was a mortgage, dated 5-11-70, for the house where the Schmidts had been murdered. The mortgage loan came from Bill Judd Sr., for fifteen years, at four percent interest. The mortgage had a retirement paper clipped to it, paid in full in 1985, right on time.

Virgil wasn't sure what the mortgage loan rates were in 1970, but four percent seemed low. The payments were listed as $547 a month, and that seemed high for the time. Maybe there was some land attached to the house, Virgil thought; he'd check.

Was the death of the woman somehow involved with the granting of the mortgage? Schmidt would have been in his first few years as sheriff . . . Had Judd been involved with the death of the woman?

Or Judd Jr.? Virgil didn't know exactly how old Judd Jr. was, but he appeared to be near sixty. If something related to the photograph happened at the time Judd gave Schmidt the mortgage, that would put Junior in his early twenties, prime woman-killing time. Had to think about it.

He went back to the photograph, and looked at it for a long time. The print had started to fade, but the original was carefully done—professionally done. Would a news-paper back then have the ability to shoot color? Might that provide a date? In the corner of the shot, he saw equipment that he thought might not be medical: it might be embalming equipment, but having never seen any mortuary gear, he wasn't sure . . .

The bank had a color Xerox machine. He made two Xeroxes of the photo, rented a new box, got a new key, and locked up everything but the Xeroxes. He'd asked the bank manager if he could use the Xerox privately, without anyone looking over his shoulder; when he was done, and the Schmidt paper was locked up again, the manager asked, "A clue?"

"You wouldn't believe it if I told you," Virgil said. "I think we're finally making some headway."

The manager was openmouthed: Virgil thought, *Spread it around.*

NEXT HE WENT to the safe-deposit box where they put the Judd Sr. papers after drilling out the original box. With the banker looking over his shoulder as a witness, he took out the money, removed all the paper, put the money back, and locked the box again. The paper he took to a carrel, where he began working through it. There was nothing at all about the Schmidts or the Gleasons.

In fact, in all the business papers, the only thing that was clear was that Judd Sr. had given his son at least two million dollars over the years—copies of gift tax reports had been carefully clipped together with other tax papers—and had loaned him another million.

The kid was deeply in debt to his old man . . . but the old man was already dying, so it seemed unlikely that Junior would take the risk of hustling him along, when the estate was about to fall to him anyway.

WHEN VIRGIL had finished with the boxes, the manager moved him to a computer terminal in a vice-president's office, and signed him onto a bank service that kept computer images of checks. "There are images going back to 1959. The early ones can be a little obscure, because they were on microfilm, and got blown up and computerized later . . ."

He looked first at Roman Schmidt's account, and a light went on in his head: from 1970 through 1985, when Schmidt was supposedly paying off a mortgage on his home, he found not a single check that appeared to be a mortgage payment.

That, he thought, was something.

Looking through a half-dozen Judd accounts, he found more than thirty thousand checks, so many that he simply didn't have time to work through them. But there were no incoming checks for $547 between 1970 and 1985; no sign that Roman Schmidt had ever written a check to Judd. Just as interesting, during the whole period of the Jerusalem artichoke scam, he found little variation in Judd's income or outgo. There had to be other accounts that he didn't know about. He'd talk to Sandy, Davenport's research assistant, and see what she could find in the state's corporate filings . . .

AGAIN, the Gleasons were a dry hole.

WHEN VIRGIL WALKED out the door, it was one o'clock in the afternoon, one of the best of the year: very warm, with a touch of breeze, and the smell of August coming up. He got on his cell phone, and called Joanie: "I thought you might be the tiniest bit irritated with me when I dropped you off," he said. "Were you?"

"Somewhat. But I'm over it," she said. "I was surprised, more than anything. After I thought about it, I wasn't surprised anymore."

"Mmm. Would you be interested in going out to the farm this evening? Explore the pond and the waterfall?"

"Maybe, if you play your cards right," she said.

"What cards would those be?"

"Stop at Ernhardt's and buy us a box lunch and a six-pack. Or box dinner. Picnic. Then I won't have to cook anything."

"Deal," Virgil said. "I've got a question. Is there a funeral home in Bluestem?"

"Sure. Johnstone's. Over on the west side, by the cemetery. Go out on Fifth Street, you'll run right into it."

"Do you think they might have records going back to the seventies?"

"Well, Gerald Johnstone's still alive. He must go back to the fifties. His son, Oliver, runs the place now. But Gerald's sharp as a tack, he lives up by the Gleasons. About six houses down the way, on the left. Right on the edge of the coulee. Wife's name is Carol."

"Hmm." Virgil thought: Betsy Carlson, the old woman in the nursing home, said that "Jerry" had been there the night of the man in the moon.

"He sure as heck didn't do it," Joan said. "He's sharp, but I doubt that he could pick up a gallon of milk, much less a body."

"All right . . . What kind of sandwiches?"

VIRGIL WALKED OVER to Ernhardt's Café, ordered a box lunch, roast beef sandwiches on sourdough, with mustard and mild onions, a pound-sized carton of blue-cheese potato salad, a six-pack of Amstel, two plastic plates, and two sets of plastic silverware. The woman behind the counter said he could have it in ten minutes, or he could pick it up anytime before six o'clock. He told her he'd be back at five, borrowed her phone book, and looked up Gerald Johnstone's address.

JOHNSTONE LIVED in a redwood-sided ranch-style house with a walkout basement on the coulee side, a deck looking out at the town, and a three-car garage. A sprinkler system was watering the unnaturally green lawn when

Virgil pulled into the drive. He dodged the overlapping wet spots along the drive and the walk to the front door, ducked under a wind chime, and rang the bell.

A moment later, an elderly man, gray-faced and wary, spoke through a screened window to the side of the porch. "Who are you?"

Virgil held up his ID. "Virgil Flowers, Bureau of Criminal Apprehension. Like to talk to you for a couple of minutes, Mr. Johnstone."

Johnstone unlocked the inner door, pushed open the screen door. He was well into his eighties, Virgil thought, tall, too thin, with shaky hands and blue eyes that seemed to be fading. He was bald on top, with a few strands of silvery white hair combed over the bald spot. "Don't usually have everything all locked up," he said. "My wife is pretty nervous about all these killings. Old people like us."

As he said it, a woman called from the back, "Jerry? Who is it?"

"Police," he called back.

As Virgil stepped across the threshold, she came out of the back of the house holding a stack of neatly folded towels. She was a pink, round, busy woman, fifteen years younger than her husband. She asked, "Are you the Flowers gentleman?"

"Yes, I am," he said. "Pleased to meet you."

THEY TALKED in the living room. The Johnstones didn't know anything about anything, but they were scared to death and were willing to admit it. "He's killing my friends, whoever it is," Johnstone said. "Bill Judd wasn't much of a friend, especially in later years, but I knew him pretty well. Roman and Gloria and Russell and Anna *were* my friends. I'm afraid that . . . you know . . . he might be coming for us."

"Any idea why he might be? What he's doing?" Virgil asked.

"No idea at all. We've been wracking our brains," Johnstone said.

Carol Johnstone said, "In a town like this, everybody has a little spot of trouble with everybody else, sooner or later—we're all too close together. But you get over it, and you're friends again. But who could hate this much . . ." Her voice trailed off. Then, "I'd like to say something, but I wouldn't like it getting around."

"Absolutely," Virgil said.

"George Feur was working on Bill Judd," Carol Johnstone said. "Talking to him about his soul, trying to get some money out of him—and he did get some money out of him, I think. Feur deals in hate, and the people around him are attracted by it. I think that's where the problem might be, but why they would kill old people, I don't know."

"'Cause they're nutcases," Gerald Johnstone said.

Virgil said to Gerald Johnstone, "I'm looking at Reverend Feur. But there's also a possibility—because the victims are somewhat elderly—that something happened way back when," Virgil said. "I'd like you to look at a photograph of a body and tell me if it was in your funeral home."

And to Carol Johnstone: "It's not a pleasant picture, ma'am . . ."

"Pictures of bodies never bothered me," she said. "I worked in the funeral home for thirty years and saw everything you can see."

Virgil nodded, and took out the color Xerox of the woman on the table. He handed it to Gerald Johnstone, who looked at it with his vague eyes, focused, and then seemed to shudder with recognition.

He said, "That looks like our funeral home. This is a funeral home in the picture, and it looks like our dressing table . . . but I can't say that I remember the case. It appears to be an automobile accident, is what I'd say. We had lots of those. Didn't have full funerals—just dress the body and ship it back to wherever they came from. So . . . I can't remember."

Virgil thought, *He's lying.*

Carol was shaking her head: "I'd remember it if I'd seen it, but I never saw it. Where did it come from?"

"I don't know," Virgil said. "I was hoping you could tell me."

She shook her head. "I was there, but I never saw that woman. Must have been a dress-and-ship. Whoever she is, she isn't local."

"Okay," Virgil said. Gerald Johnstone was still peering at the picture, replaying something in his mind, but again he shook his head. "I'm sorry," he said.

Carol Johnstone, Virgil thought, was telling the truth. Gerald Johnstone was lying through his teeth.

HE PUSHED the old man: "It's important that we know if it's your place or not," he said. "Is it your funeral home?"

"It could be," Johnstone said. "But the way the picture is . . . it's too close up. The table is the same kind we had, a stainless-steel Ferno. We don't have it anymore."

Carol Johnstone said, "That *is* our place, Jerry, before the remodel." She tapped one corner of the photo, the corner of an odd machine that looked like an oversized blender. "That's that old Portiboy, remember? I'm sure that's our place."

Gerald Johnstone shook his head: "I think it is, but I don't remember the case. We did hundreds of automobile accidents over the years, and I'm just . . . too old."

Still lying, Virgil thought. "When did you do the remodel?" he asked.

"That was 1981 into 1982. All new equipment by 'eighty-two," Carol Johnstone said. "Whoever that is, had to be killed before that. But the table and the Portiboy go way back. Before our time."

VIRGIL ASKED, "What about the man in the moon?"

Knew he'd taken a misstep. They were both mystified, and showed it. Carol said, "What?"

"Betsy Carlson said something about the man in the moon. That she'd seen the man in the moon. She seemed to think there might be a connection . . ."

Carol shook her head, but again, Virgil thought he saw a spark in Gerald's eye. Virgil said, "She told me, 'Jerry was there for the man in the moon, Jerry knew about it.' "

Carol was shaking her head, but Gerald's eyes drifted away as he said, "It's a complete mystery. What does it mean?"

VIRGIL, LOOKING DIRECTLY at Gerald Johnstone, said, "If you remember *anything*, you let me know. You called this killer a nutcase, and that's the exact truth of the matter. Keep your doors locked—if he thinks you might be involved in whatever is going on, you're both at some risk."

Carol Johnstone said suddenly, "This will sound silly . . ."

"Tell me," Virgil said.

"The night the Gleasons were killed, we weren't here. We're here two hundred fifty nights a year—we have a place in Palm Springs where we go in the winter—but that was one night we weren't. We were in Minneapolis, visiting our daughter, and seeing a show. When we came back the next day, there were police all over the street . . ."

"Ah, this is nothing," Gerald Johnstone said.

"I'd like to hear it anyway," Virgil said.

Carol nodded: "Anyway, we stopped and found out from one of the deputies what happened, and Larry Jensen came over and interviewed us, but we didn't have anything to tell him. We were gone. But when we first came in the door, the welcome mat was moved."

"Oh, Carol," the old man said, rolling his eyes.

"Well, it was," she said. "You know how I like everything neat, and it was off to the side of the door. I thought then that somebody moved it. Well, the Gleasons were killed in the middle of the night, and we were back at one o'clock in the afternoon, so . . . who moved it?"

"You think that whoever killed the Gleasons . . . ?"

She shivered. "They were right there, down the street. We have timers on our lights so it looks like somebody's home, lights going off and on . . . Maybe . . ."

He looked directly at Johnstone: "If you remember anything, you tell me. We don't want somebody else to die."

"I'll think as hard as I can," he said.

"If it turns out you're lying to me, you could spend the rest of your life in prison, as an accomplice."

Carol got hot: "Hey! He's not lying. We'd do anything to catch this . . . monster."

"I'm just saying," Virgil said.

HE LEFT THEM at that—interesting, that Gerald Johnstone should be lying. He needed to track down the photo, and then he needed to come back and pound on Johnstone.

As he got back in the truck, he thought about the welcome mat being moved, sighed, dug his pistol out from under the car seat, and clipped it to his belt. He drove back across the coulee, went to the newspaper, and found Williamson sitting at his computer, writing.

He looked up when Virgil came through the door: "Hell of a story on the Laymons," he said. "I owe you a large one."

"You hear anything new on the Schmidts?"

"No. Damnit, if they were gonna get killed, I wish they hadn't done it on the day the paper comes out. We won't be able to print a word for a week. In the meantime, we're getting eaten alive by the *Globe* and the *Argus-Leader*." The *Globe* and the *Argus-Leader* were the dailies in Worthington and Sioux Falls.

"You can pay me right now, for the one you owe me," Virgil said. He looked at his watch; fifteen minutes to two. "I'd like to see the papers from 1970."

Williamson said, "We don't have them that way. Not whole papers. Back before 1995, they're on microfilm, and they have them at the library. If you have a name, it'd be in the clip file . . . ?"

Virgil shook his head. "No name. I don't even know what I'm doing. Where's the library?"

"Just up the hill . . . Are you going to the press conference?"

"Wouldn't miss it for the world," Virgil said.

"Neither would anybody else in town. I don't know what Stryker's going to do—people are already starting to crowd into the courtroom. Won't be room for the reporters."

VIRGIL HUSTLED UP to the library, a flat red-brick building on the corner of Main Street. Inside, a pale-eyed, blond librarian with the smooth skin of an eighth-grader, took him to a microfilm booth at the back of the stacks. "I'll show you how to thread the microfilm. It can be a trial," she said. She went to a wooden file cabinet with dozens of small drawers, muttered, "Nineteen seventy." She pulled it open, took four boxes of microfilm out, and handed them to Virgil, then went back to the file and said, "Darn it. We're missing a box. Somebody has misfiled it."

He was interested: "Which box?"

She started sorting through them again, explaining, "We don't start a new drawer until the last drawer is full, and when I opened it, it was loose—so there's a box out somewhere. It looks like . . ." She stood on her tiptoes, pushed her glasses up her nose, looking into the drawer, and finally said, "We stop at the middle of May, and start again in September. So one box is missing. We have four months on each roll . . . Darn. I tell people to leave the refiling to us, but they don't listen."

"Could it be misfiled?" Virgil asked.

She pulled open a drawer from the nineties, that was only partially full of microfilm boxes. Checked them, said, "These are right," and then went through a bunch of empty drawers at the bottom of the case. She said, "I think it's been taken by somebody. I'll check these after we close—I have to work the desk—but I think it's been taken."

"I'd appreciate it if you'd check," Virgil said.

THE MISSING BOX intrigued him. The librarian showed him how to thread the film they had, and he looked at four months around Schmidt's mortgage loan, and in the quick review, saw nothing that struck him. No strange women in automobile accidents . . .

Not enough to work with; not yet. And it was possible that Judd had simply *bought* Schmidt, to be used as necessary.

VIRGIL WAS OUT the library door at twenty minutes to three. By ten minutes of three, he'd changed into a pale blue shirt with a necktie, khaki slacks, and a navy blue sport coat. Looking at himself in a mirror, he decided he looked like a greeter at a minor Indian casino.

He got back to the courthouse at one minute to three. Twenty people were standing outside the courthouse door, mostly older, mostly men, mostly deep in conversation. Two television remote trucks were parked on the lawn, cables snaking through the doors of the courthouse.

Inside was chaos. The courtroom might take a hundred people if nobody breathed too hard. In addition to two TV cameramen, who'd rigged lights over an attorney's table that had been dragged in front of the judge's bench, there were two on-camera people, both women; four tired-looking men and two tired-looking women who were probably from newspapers; two guys with tape recorders who might be from radio stations; and about a hundred locals who weren't going anywhere.

Virgil stuck his head inside, took it all in, then headed down the hall to Stryker's office before he attracted any attention. His phone went off, and he pulled it out of his pocket: Stryker. He buzzed past the secretary, stuck his head into Stryker's office and said, "Yo."

Stryker hung up the phone. "Where'n the hell have you been?"

"Running around," Virgil said. "Do you know what you're going to say?"

"Well." Stryker shrugged. "Tell the truth, I guess."

"Jesus, Jim, you can't do that." Virgil looked around, saw the secretary watching, and closed the office door on her. "It'd stop us in our tracks."

"Maybe if you'd been here an hour ago, we could have cooked something up."

"There's no cooking," Virgil said. "You go out there, you give them the gory details of the three scenes—Gleason, Judd, and Schmidt. Everybody local already knows about them, so you're not giving anything away. Talk about them being shot in the eyes. Talk about Judd being burned right down to the anklebones. TV people will like that. Tell them that we've developed information that would suggest that the killer is local, and that we've come up with a number of leads that we can't talk about, but that . . . if they come back in a week or ten days, we believe that we'll have a lot more. That we're rolling."

"Are we?" Stryker asked.

"Kind of."

"Virgil . . ."

"You don't tell them what it is, dummy," Virgil said. "That's the confidential part. We're rolling, but we can't talk about it."

"If I do that, and if I don't come up with something in ten days, I am truly screwed."

"If you go out there and say we ain't got jack-shit, you're truly screwed anyway," Virgil said. "If you go out and say the hounds of hell are on the killer's heels, maybe he'll make a move that we can see."

"Mother of God."

"She ain't here, Jim. It's just you and me."

STRYKER STRAIGHTENED himself out, and as they were about to go out, asked, "How much detail?"

"More than you think you should. The eyes, and the fact that it seems to be a ritual. The stick that propped up Schmidt, facing toward the east. That Gleason was propped up, facing the east. That nothing was left of Judd but his ankle and wrist bones, and the wire from his heart. They'll eat that up . . ."

"I'm gonna need some heart work," Stryker said. "Honest to God, I'm gonna need some heart work."

At the last minute, walking down the hall, Virgil whispered, "You're the grim sheriff of a rural county. You're an honest, upright, tight-jawed, God-fearing cowboy. You don't want to talk about it, but you think you should, because we're in a democracy. You're grim. You don't smile, because the dead people are friends. This guy is killing your people."

"Grim," Stryker said.

HE WAS, and he pulled it off, barely moving his jaws.

Virgil said thirty-two words: "We're working on it hard,

and like the sheriff says, we're rolling. But the BCA's position is that the sheriff runs the operation, and we let him do the talking for us."

A woman from a television station in Sioux Falls liked Stryker a lot, got tight with him, pushed him a little: "What're you gonna do when you catch this guy?" she asked.

"Gonna hope that the sonofabitch fights back," Stryker said, his face like a rock. "Save the state some trial money."

They didn't even cut the *sonofabitch*.

AFTERWARD, in Stryker's office, Virgil told him the truth: "I think you did it."

"So we got ten days or two weeks." He took a turn around his office. "What'd you think about the chick from Sioux Falls?"

"If Jesse doesn't work out, give her a call," Virgil said.

"She had a nice . . . bodice."

Made Virgil laugh.

THE TV PEOPLE were packed up and gone by four-thirty, leaving behind a crowd of locals who were dissipating like the fizz on a hot Coke. Virgil picked up the box lunch at Ernhardt's, and called Joan: "You ready?"

"Not until after the news."

Virgil went back to the motel, peed, put on a cowboy shirt and running shoes, let the shirt hang outside his pants to cover the pistol. On the way to Joan's house, he dialed

Sandy, Davenport's research assistant. "How are we doing with the tax returns?"

"I've got them stacked up to my elbows," she said. "I talked to Lucas, and I'm sending them down there with a messenger. He'll leave here tomorrow at eight, you should have them by noon."

"Terrific. Get me one more set of records, if you can: Carol and Gerald Johnstone, both of Bluestem, owners or former owners of the Johnstone Funeral Home."

"They'll be in the package," she said.

"Also: check with the state historical society, and see if they have copies of the *Bluestem Record* newspaper for the months of May through September, 1969."

"I couldn't do that today—they'll be closed," Sandy said. "Tomorrow I won't be here—and then there's the week-end. I could see if I could find somebody else . . ."

"Ah, boy . . ." Virgil said. "Okay. Monday, first thing?"

"First thing."

He described the dead woman on the table, told her she might have been an auto-accident victim. "If I find anything, I'll fax it to the motel," she said.

"No, no—call me on my cell. You can read it to me. I don't want to give this away."

11

THE NEWS WAS just coming up when Virgil knocked on Joan's front door. She shouted, "Come on in," and he went through into her living room. "Did you see me at the press conference?"

"No . . ."

"I got crushed," Joan said. "I was in the back and this fat guy from the Firestone store, I got welded to his butt. Here we go . . ."

THE PRESS CONFERENCE was the lead story and sucked up four or five minutes of the broadcast. Virgil had been right about the details: they loved it. And the cameras loved Stryker's face, and the tight jaws. "That's my brother," Joan said, delighted, when it was over. "He looked like a movie star."

"He was good," Virgil said.

"You've been holding out on me, too," Joan said. She'd stacked a duffel bag near the front door, and picked it up on the way out. "You never told me that you guys were rolling, you've been all downbeat."

"Yeah, well . . ." he mumbled.

"What?"

"Nothing," Virgil said.

"What'd you say?" They'd just gotten into the truck. "You said something."

He leaned over, kissed her on the cheek, and said, "It's all bullshit. We got nothing."

She was flabbergasted. "Virgil."

"That's the way it is."

"Virgil . . ."

"We got ten days."

He backed out of the driveway, and she didn't say another word until they were out of town. Then, "Did you bring the food?"

"Exactly what you ordered," Virgil said.

"You got nothing?"

"Well. Maybe something."

"Virgil!"

He then fumbled behind the seat, in his briefcase, and hooked out one of the color Xeroxes and passed it to her. She recoiled: "Yuck."

"Any idea who it is? Probably before your time, though . . ."

"No. Where'd you find this?" she asked.

"In Roman Schmidt's safe-deposit box. Nothing but the photograph. No other paper that might suggest what it is. I have a feeling that it's before the middle of 1970."

"Did you look in the paper?"

"The paper's on microfilm, in the library," he said.

"Somebody stole a roll from the middle of 1969, but there's no way to know if that's the one we're looking for."

"Really. Virgil, you may . . ." She hesitated, then: "Does Jim know about this?"

"Not yet. I'm going to tell him when I see him, but I think he might be out of town at the moment," Virgil said.

"Out of town? He can't be," she said. "What else happened?"

He grinned. "I swore I wouldn't tell anyone."

"I don't care—tell me anyway."

Virgil laughed and said, "I think he's taking Jesse Laymon out to dinner. Someplace far away, where nobody'll see him. Because he's supposed to be working the Roman Schmidt case night and day, even if there's nothing to do."

"Oh, my God." She pulled her bottom lip: "Well, I hope he gets laid. And if he does, I hope it's worth it. Because he really is in trouble, here, Virgil. I wouldn't be surprised if one of the Curlys declares that he's running for sheriff, one of these days."

"You think?"

"Big Curly thought he was the natural successor to Roman Schmidt. He might be past it now, but Little Curly would take the job in a minute."

"Neither one of them struck me as a wizard," Virgil said.

"No, but their families have been here forever, they know everyone, they've slapped every back in the county, and, they're fairly good-natured. If Jim really slips, one of them will run."

"Ah, we'll get the guy. Next week or so," Virgil said.

"You think?"

"Yup."

"Will anybody else be killed?" she asked.

He had to think for a minute, then said, "Maybe."

JOAN MADE HIM park the truck in the barn, a gesture toward discretion, and then they walked through the low weeds to the creek, and up the path into the Stryker's Dell. The running shoes made the going easier; cowboy boots weren't made for climbing rocks. At the top, on the left side of the pond, Joan opened the duffel and took out a quilt. "Straight from Wal-Mart; makes the rocks softer," she said.

Virgil unloaded the food and beer, and when he looked up, she was unbuttoning her blouse. He squatted on the rock, watching, as she took it off, slipped out of her shoes, socks and jeans, popped the brassiere, tossed it with the other clothes, and slipped out of her underpants. "See anything you like?"

"Well, yeah," he said.

"Last one in," she said, and she was over the side of the rock, six feet into the water, and Virgil was shedding shoes, shirt and pants as quickly as he could get them off. Fifteen seconds after she went over the side, he followed, the water a bracing slap. When he came up, she was there to push his head back under.

They played around the pool for a few minutes, laughing and sputtering, the water cool but not cold, refreshing in the summer heat; and the stones in the direct light of the setting sun were warm as toast.

The pool's back wall, to the east, where the spring came down, had eroded into a steep ramp. At the top of the ramp was a finger of dirt and grass, and beyond it, a rocky hillside running up to the crest. The pool walls on the north and south sides went straight up forty feet or so, solid red rock. A local kid had once jumped off the top on a dare, Joan said, had landed in not quite the deepest part, and had broken a couple of foot bones when he hit bottom. "That was the end of that," she said. "We had to carry him out."

The west side was the canyon, with the sun setting right in the center of the slot. It did that in May and August, she said, then swung farther north and south, depending on the season.

They were facing each other, blowing water, Virgil working on a new game; he had a handful of her pubic hair, and her two hands were on his chest, and he was about to suggest a different move when he caught the reflection up the hillside, beyond the head of the pool.

He thought it might be water on an eyelash, a refraction off a splash, something else, but then he caught it again and he pushed her head underwater and ducked under himself, caught her arm, and dragged her deeper toward the head of the pool. She struggled against him, but he pulled hard, until he felt the east wall, and then they rose two feet to the surface and she shouted, "Virgil, Virgil, what are you doing . . . ?"

A frightened tone threaded in her voice as she shook water away from her face.

Virgil shoved her against the wall and said, urgently, "There's somebody on the hillside above us. I saw a reflection off glass, off a lens . . ."

She turned to look, but they were out of the line, against the face, "What?"

"Somebody up the hill . . ."

"A camera?"

"Could be a camera," Virgil said.

"What else . . . ?"

"Could be a scope," he said. "When somebody's looking at you with glasses, you can usually see their arms."

She looked at him, shocked, then looked at their clothes. "Oh . . . God."

"Yeah."

"You're sure?" she asked, craning her neck to look overhead.

"I saw it twice." He looked back at their clothes, and then said, "I want you to stay right here. I'm going underwater to that corner right there, I'm going to come out fast. I don't think . . . he's at least a couple of hundred yards away, maybe three hundred. I don't think he can get me if I'm moving fast. Once I'm behind that lip, I can get out to the clothes, get my gun."

"I thought . . ."

"I started carrying it today . . . tell you later. Now. Stay here. I'm going."

He took two deep breaths, then pushed himself straight

down the wall. Had to go deep, because the water was clear. When he hit bottom, he oriented himself, pushed off the wall, kept thinking, stay deep, stay deep, felt the bottom shelving, came up slightly off-line, surged forward with a butterfly stroke, lurching toward a groove in the rock and was almost there, almost in, when there was a slap on the wall to the right. One hand slipped and he went down, lurched again, slipping, and then he was into the groove, hurting, registering the crack of a rifle shot, pushed himself up the groove, skinning his knees, crawled up behind the wall, six feet from his weapon.

Joan shouted, "Virgil, he's shooting, Virgil!"

Not hit, he thought. Everything still working. He looked back at the wall and could see the pockmark where the slug had hit: two feet above where his head had been. Not that close, but close enough to scare him.

He shouted back to Joan, "I'm okay. You stay there." He started counting. One minute, one minute thirty seconds. Joan made a questioning gesture, and he put up a finger: wait. Two minutes . . .

WHEN HE'D HUNT deer up north, and he'd see a buck threading through the trees, he could focus on any given shot for a minute or two. After that, he'd lose precise focus. He'd trained himself to wait until the deer was right down a shooting lane before he even started to focus, because two minutes were a long time to concentrate on a shot. Two minutes, twenty seconds, and he coiled himself against the wall, spotted his pistol, said to himself, go, go, go: and he went.

Six feet out, half a second, get the gun, six feet back. The incoming slug was just that fraction of a second too slow, slapping off the rock a yard wide and again, too high.

He had the gun. He stood, popped his head out for a half second, pulled back. Dropped to his knees, popped his head out again, saw movement: like a bear, somebody in dark clothes near the crest, running toward the crest, away from them. He pulled back, stood, turned around the corner, braced himself on the rock, aimed the pistol five or six feet high and started pulling the trigger, counting out seven shots. He had no idea how much elevation he needed at four hundred yards, but it'd be a lot—the pistol shot almost five inches low at a hundred yards.

If he hit something, the chances of which were vanishingly small, that was all to the good. Mostly he wanted a bunch of slugs flying around the guy like bees.

Because, he thought, the guy couldn't take the slightest chance of getting hit. If he was hit, or even seen, he was done . . .

SO: A STALEMATE. Virgil was down in the pool, without any way of going after the guy. But Virgil was also armed and wary, down among the jumble of rocks, and would be hard to get at.

Virgil stood next to the wall, ready to take cover, and

watched, and watched, and saw nothing more. Finally, he shouted at Joan, "Underwater, just like I did, into that groove. He's not there anymore, but don't take any chances. Get out of there quick."

She nodded, pushed herself under, and a few seconds later, surfaced and crawled into the groove, across the rock, and then stood up next to him.

"Now what?" She shivered. She'd been in the cool water too long.

"Now I do this for a couple more minutes, and then I grab the clothes."

"Virgil . . ."

"I'm about ninety-nine percent sure he's gone. He can't be seen. You can hear that rifle for a mile or more, and it's not hunting season . . . He's got to move. He's got to get out of here."

"Probably go straight north on Holman. There's nothing there, before you hit Highway Seven. Once he's on Seven, he's just another car."

"Then that's probably it," Virgil said, and he thrust himself away from the wall, grabbed the clothes, and was back. He handed her her bra and blouse, then pushed her back against the wall and kissed her and said, "Getting shot at makes me horny."

"And your penis is about a half-inch long. Cold water does it every time. It's sort of a tragedy, isn't it?"

Virgil looked down at himself and said, "That wasn't the cold water, sweetheart. That was fear, pure and simple." He stepped back, looking up the hill. "If he'd been cool about it, he could have slipped up close, we'd be playing in the pool and *bang!* He could have done both of us."

She leaned out from the wall and asked, "I wonder why he didn't?"

"He might have been planning to, but he stopped to look things over with the scope. That's when I saw him. I think he wanted to wait until we were out of the water so he could get a full body shot, but he got impatient and stopped to look us over . . ."

They were dressing as they talked; when they were done, Virgil said, "I'll get the stuff."

"Fuck the stuff," she said.

"He's gone," Virgil said. "He's gone . . . but we stay close to the wall anyway. If there's any other place he'd wait, it'd be while we're coming out of the mouth of the canyon."

VIRGIL POPPED OUT AGAIN, grabbed the food, and jumped back. Then out again, snagged Joan's duffel, and hopped back. Never exposed for more than a second. Time enough for a snap shot, but not a good one, not if the shooter couldn't anticipate the move.

When they were ready, Virgil said, "Squeeze in close to the wall, and when we have to show ourselves, move fast. One at a time. You first."

Fifty feet back into the canyon, they were protected. They stopped and Joan used the quilt to wash the blood off Virgil's face. "You've got five small cuts." She traced them with her index finger, on his temple and cheek. "I don't think stitches, but you could use some Band-Aids."

"Got some in the truck."

At the mouth of the canyon, an obvious ambush spot, they sat, watched, and finally made the move, running one at a time past the stock tank, crouched through the weeds, behind the barn.

Breathing hard, Joan said, "That's a heck of a fourth date. I don't think you've got a reasonable encore."

THE BARN was going dark as the sun went down. Virgil got a box of shells from the truck and reloaded the magazine for the pistol, the shells clicking into place. When he was finished, he opened the back hatch, lifted the concealment cover, took out a shotgun and a box of shells, loaded the shotgun.

Joan said, "It was you he wanted."

"I think so. He's getting tired of my act."

"That's a relief," she said. "At least *I'm* safe."

He laughed. "Yeah. Listen, about that short penis thing . . ."

"It's not your fault."

"It's not that; I just wish you'd use some word other than penis, you know? Sounds too much like peanut." He finished loading the shotgun and pumped a shell into the chamber and put it between the front truck seats. "Why don't you say . . . dick. That'd be good."

"Seems crude."

"Whatever." He stepped away from the truck and looked up at the overhead light. "Does that light come on when the barn door goes up?"

"Yes."

"It'll silhouette us. I'll get it." He took off his shoes and climbed up on the hood of the truck, and then on the roof, reached up and unscrewed the lightbulb, left it hanging by a thread. "Punch the door lift, just enough to turn on the light."

She punched the lift button, and the lightbulb remained dark.

"When I say to lift the door, lift it; then climb in the back-seat, get down low, and hang on. I'm getting out of here."

He climbed into the truck, started the engine, and braced the shotgun, muzzle down, between the passenger-side floor and seat. "Punch the button; get in."

She did, and he watched the door going up, seeming to take an eternity; then he hit the gas and the truck blew through the opening, backward, and he kept it moving, backward, in a circle, around the parking circle, jabbed the brake, jammed the shift into Drive, and tore down the short driveway to the county road, skidded onto the road with a quick brake and another pulse of acceleration, and they were gone.

"We okay?" Joan asked.

"Yeah. He's long gone; but we're so far away from help that we didn't dare take the chance . . ."

He drove past the hill, away from town. "Where're we going?" Joan asked.

"Got some people to talk to." He slowed, pulled over, and said, "Let me get rid of the shotgun, and you can ride up front."

THEY STOPPED at five farms along Highway 7, and spoke to one guy mowing a ditch: Who had they seen on the highway?

Shrugs and shaken heads: nobody in particular.

On the way back to town, Virgil said, "I thought everybody knew everybody else's car."

"Not out here. In town. If it'd been something unusual, like a Toyota or a Mercedes, somebody might have noticed. But a Ford or a Chevy, unless there's a sign on it . . ."

VIRGIL DIDN'T WRITE much that night: he was stuck on story development.

> Homer was pissed off and scared. The killer was coming after him: time to let somebody know about that, file a report.
>
> But: the man in the moon. He spent some time considering it—thought about Jesse Laymon's moon earrings. Those had a man in the moon, but Homer didn't think Betsy would be talking about a symbol. She was talking about a man.
>
> And Homer thought about the new moon coming up as he was driving into the thunderstorm, on the way to Bluestem, the crescent moon in his rearview mirror. Could the moon be triggering this guy? A new moon? Huh. The moon came up in

*the east, just like the sun did. Were Gleason and Schmidt
propped up facing to the east, because that was where the
moon came from? Facing the moon, but not allowed to see it?*

Crazy talk.

*Before going to sleep, Homer thought about the shooting
that afternoon. Scary, but the guy had missed. Could have
gotten a lot closer . . . Did the shooter intend to kill, or only to
frighten? If only to frighten, why?*

Virgil went to sleep hoping that Homer would come up
with an idea; because at this point, Virgil himself had none
at all.

Went to sleep dreaming of Joanie Stryker on the rock at
the dell . . .

12

VIRGIL OPENED his eyes: daylight.

He felt good, but a little stiff from sleeping on the floor.

Worried about the gunman, he'd taken the cushions off the couch, and had thrown them on the floor behind the bed, and put the pistol under the bed next to his hand. He didn't like the idea of sleeping through the night next to a sliding glass door. Joan was at her mother's. No point in taking a chance.

But he *did* feel good. Things were happening, and he was still alive.

Part of it was the absence of sex after the long naked interval in the pool. He'd tried to talk Joan into sneaking through the glass door into the Holiday Inn, but she turned him down: "Everybody in town would know before you got the curtain pulled. It's all right to sneak around and have sex, but it has to be creditably sneaky."

"Ah."

"My place," she said. "You could walk over in half an hour."

"I don't want you going to your place tonight. I was thinking . . . your mother's. You'd be close, but not where you'd have a target on you; he could be waiting for us to get back to your place . . ."

"Well, we're *not* doing anything at Mom's . . ."

So, they called it off.

Hands all over each other, parked three blocks from Mom's, like a couple of teenagers; and he dropped her.

And woke up feeling good. Maybe he could take a break from the hook-and-bullet magazines, and write a piece for *Vanity Fair*: "Violence: The New Aphrodisiac." But that wouldn't be right—it'd always been an aphrodisiac, as far as he could tell. Something primitive there . . .

Maybe, he thought, they should have stayed in the barn for a while, up in the hayloft.

When he was a teenager, there were locker-room fantasy stories—maybe one or two were true—of guys getting the farmer's daughter up in the hayloft. His best friend, Otis Ericson, had claimed to have nailed one of his girl cousins, Shirley, who was in their high school class, and even in eighth grade, had tits out to here.

In what Virgil assumed was nothing more than an effort at verisimilitude, the alleged fuckee warned Virgil against hay cuts, or hay rash: "And you sure as shit don't want to get any hay in her crack. She'll be bitching and moaning for a week. Take a blanket."

The thought that Otis Ericson might have actually

gotten Shirley Ericson naked, in a hayloft, had, at the time, seriously turned him on; still did, a little, though the last time he saw Shirley, she'd sort of spread out.

LYING ON THE FLOOR, he looked at his watch: eight o'clock. Threw the cushions back on the couch, yawned, stretched, did his sit-ups and push-ups, cleaned up, and called Davenport.

"Still too early," Davenport said.

"I was shot at last night," Virgil said.

"Virgil! You okay?"

"Nothing but scared," Virgil said. "The shooter wasn't that good. Scoped rifle, I was up on a friend's farm, missed me by a couple of feet and I wasn't moving that fast."

"Tell me you had your gun," Davenport said.

"I had the gun. Saw him running, fired seven shots at maybe four hundred yards, chances of hitting him were zero . . . but . . . thought I should let you know. I'm pushing something here. I'm going to write some notes and e-mail them to you. Just in case."

"Goddamnit, Virgil, you take care," Davenport said. "You want help?"

"Just get me that paper that Sandy put together."

ON THE WAY to breakfast, the desk clerk said, "You've got mail," fished an envelope out of a desk drawer, and handed it to him. The address was typed; no return address. Mailed yesterday from Bluestem. He went on to the dining room, holding the envelope by its edges, slit it open with a butter knife, and slid the letter out.

You're barking up the wrong tree. Look at Bill Judd Jr.'s debt and think "estate tax." Look at Florence Mills, Inc.

That was it—no signature, of course, and the note was *typed*, not printed. Who'd still have a typewriter? Somebody old, like Gerald Johnstone, the funeral director. The stamp was self-sticking, so there'd be no DNA.

Estate tax? Florence Mills? Sounded like something more for Sandy to do, when she got back.

He finished breakfast, went back to his room for his briefcase, went out to the truck; went back to the room to get his gun, back to the truck; and headed out to the Stryker farm, past the farm, around behind the hill.

The far side of the hill, opposite the dell, had once been pastureland, before the countryside had emptied out, with the red quartzite right on the surface. There were clumps of wild plum and scrubby shrubs, thistle and open spaces with knee-high grass.

Virgil cruised the backside of the hill until he saw the truck tracks leading off-road. He turned off, bounced across a shallow ditch, and then ran parallel to the tracks, up the hill, to a copse of trees and bushes just below the crest of the hill. The tracks swerved around the copse, and ended. This was where the shooter had parked, out of sight from the road. He sat in the car for a minute, watching the road, and saw not another single vehicle; he was alone except for a red-tailed hawk, which circled the slope, looking for voles.

The hawk dropped, hit the ground, out of sight: breakfast. Virgil stepped out of the truck and looked at the tracks made by the shooter's vehicle. There were enough weeds and grass that any tread marks were hidden. He followed one of the tracks back down the hill, and never saw a clear print. Followed the other one back up, found nothing.

From the car park, looking up the hill, with the sun still at his back, he could see disturbed grass where the shooter had been. He got the shotgun out of the back of the truck, loaded it alternately with buckshot and solid slugs, jacked a shell into the chamber, and followed the trail to the top of the hill. A hundred yards over the crest, he could see the front lip of the pool, and the farther down the hill he went, the more of the pool he could see. The trail wasn't straight at this point. It moved between clumps of shrubs, which meant that he and Joan must've already been at the pool.

Another hundred yards, and he found the shooter's stand: a circle of crushed grass next to the broken-off and rotted stump of a small tree. If he'd rested the rifle on the stump, he'd have been able to see two-thirds of the pool. To see more, he would have had to go right up to the lip of the dell, without cover.

He checked around the nest: no brass. The guy had cleaned up after himself.

FROM VIRGIL'S VIEWPOINT, the dell, down below, didn't look like much: a crack in the landscape, with a wider spot, and a pool, near the bottom. He walked down, and when he got right on top of it, the character changed. Down here, the ground seemed to have been hit with a mammoth cleaver, carving a sharp trench right through the quartzite down to the pool.

If the shooter had been cooler, or braver, he could have waited until they were fooling around under the spring, out of sight, and then walked or crawled up to the back wall. From there he would have had them at sixty or seventy yards, and there would have been no place for Virgil and Joan to hide.

On the other hand, if they'd seen him sneaking down, and had gotten back to Virgil's gun and down the canyon, he'd have been screwed. In the folded, broken rocks of the canyon, a guy with a pistol could hold off a small army.

On that thought, Virgil took out his cell phone: he had a signal. You might not down in the dell, but you wouldn't know unless you were down there. Maybe the shooter had taken that into account. He *could not* allow somebody to see him, and walk away . . .

LOT TO THINK ABOUT. The day would be hot again. Another good day for the pool, but he wouldn't be swimming again until the killer was caught, or dead.

Virgil went back to the truck, shucked the shells out of

the shotgun and put it away, and headed back to Roman Schmidt's place. Larry Jensen, Stryker's investigator, was there, with the crime-scene people. Virgil took Jensen aside.

"Where's Jim?"

"At the office. He said you'd probably show up and want to get in. We're just about done. Let me go talk to Margo."

"Okay. I got a note in the mail today, I was wondering if you could check it for fingerprints."

He explained, and gave Jensen the note and envelope, folded into a piece of hotel writing paper. Jensen read it, frowned. "Shoot. That's not a direction we've gone."

"Hardly had time," Virgil said. "Anyway, I'm on it. I've got a researcher up in St. Paul who can pull the corporate information, and I've got some income-tax forms coming in. If you could check this letter . . ."

"Wonder who uses a typewriter?"

"Somebody Roman's age," Virgil said.

MARGO CARR, the crime-scene specialist, showed him Schmidt's home office, a table made out of a wooden door, set across two filing cabinets. A computer, no type-writer. "Everything in here has been worked," she said.

"You think the killer was in here?"

"No. I think the killer shot Roman, shot Gloria, then came and shot Roman twice more, then dragged him out-side and propped him up with a stick he'd already cut. I don't think he went anywhere in the house, off the line of the bedroom."

"Do you think he knew the inside of the house?" Virgil asked.

"Maybe. Or maybe Roman turned on a light in the bedroom and gave it all away."

"Find anything at all?"

"One thing," she said. She went back to a plastic trunk, opened it, and brought back a Ziploc bag with a cigarette filter in it. "Found this right by the back steps. Cigarette butt. I can figure out what kind, I'm sure, but I know it's a menthol— I can smell it. Wasn't rained on, so it's recent. The Schmidts didn't smoke."

He looked at the butt, and then at Carr: "You think?"

"I'm grasping for straws, here. That's what I got."

A MOMENT LATER, he was sitting at Roman's desk, his eyes closed, trying to remember: the pack of cigarettes next to George Feur's elbow, when Virgil interviewed him at his house. Salems? Virgil thought so. His visual image was of a green package, an aqua green . . .

His cell phone rang: Joan.

"How are you doing?" she asked.

"Not bad. I'm confused, but I'm looking pretty good," he said. "I might go out tonight, see if I can pick up some chicks."

"Good luck."

"Yeah. Anyway, I'm at Schmidt's. I've got something for you to think about: how many people, once they figured we were going out to the farm, would have known how to come down that slope to a place where they'd have a free shot at us?"

She thought for a moment, and then said, "Well, probably not everybody."

"Not everybody?"

"It's a fairly famous swimming hole, Virgil. Kids would park up on that hillside, up in the trees, then sneak in past the stock tank and go up the canyon and skinny-dip. I mean, if you didn't do that at least once in high school, and get laid up on that rock, you were *nobody*."

"How often did *you* do it?" he asked.

"We agreed not to talk about our histories," she said.

"No, we didn't."

"We have now," she said.

He offered to take her to the Dairy Queen, having exhausted the fine-dining possibilities at McDonald's.

"I'll order a pizza from Johnnie's," she said. "My place at four o'clock, we'll go back out to the farm. It's a great day. Be careful. And bring a better gun."

"*You* be careful."

VIRGIL DUG THROUGH the Schmidts' filing cabinet, which turned out to be a waste of time. He did learn that they were fairly affluent: Gloria had been an elementary-school teacher in Worthington—a friend of the alcoholic schoolteacher? Probably not, though: Gloria was most of a generation earlier, and would have taught in a different school. Wonder where the money came from? They had half a million dollars in a Vanguard account; but then, they'd had a long time to build it up.

The most interesting material was in Schmidt's computer. He had a dial-up account, and he had e-mail from Big Curly, and they were talking politics. Curly was looking for support for his son to run against Stryker in the next election.

Schmidt was talking, but wasn't eager to side with someone who might be a loser. "We better wait until we are close to the time, have a better idea of what the opportunities are," he wrote back in one of the notes. But he didn't say no.

Sitting there, looking at the Schmidt material, Virgil started thinking about the letter he'd given to Larry Jensen. How many people knew what tree he was barking up? The banker, of course, and anyone he might have gossiped with.

And the Johnstones.

"That damn picture," he said aloud. Had the photograph somehow generated the note?

STYMIED at the Schmidts'—there was nothing right on the surface, and a full analysis of all the Schmidts' financial transactions would take a lot of time. He heard people knocking around in the back of the house, and gave up. Back another day, if nothing else popped up.

He went out through the kitchen, saw Big Curly, Little Curly, and a deputy he didn't know, standing in the yard with Jensen. He waved and said, "I'm outa here."

"Anything?" Jensen asked.

"We need an accountant," Virgil said.

"Yeah . . ."

He'd be back to Schmidts', Virgil thought, to see if somebody erased that e-mail about the election . . . if somebody would mess with evidence at a murder scene. Be an interesting thing to know.

ON THE WAY into town, he saw another hawk circling, like the one he'd seen out at the farm, and that made him think of the shooting, and the slope, and the farm, and skinny-dipping, and the whole question of why the shooter hadn't come closer and taken the sure shot.

And how he'd missed by two feet at three hundred yards. Of course, it wasn't that hard to miss by two feet. But if you had the rifle sitting on a stump, the shot should have been closer than that.

He thought about that for a minute and then slowed, pulled to the side of the road, and called up the Laymon place. Jesse picked up the phone: "Hello?"

She did have a nice whiskey voice, Virgil decided. "This is Virgil," he said. "I'm calling on behalf of Jim's sister, who's reluctant to gossip with you. But did we see you guys up in Marshall last night? About seven? We had to dodge a restaurant because she was sure it was you guys."

"Not us. We went over to Sioux Falls," Jesse said.

"Ah, shoot. So I ate pizza while you guys were doing surf 'n' turf. You pay? Being a rich woman?"

She laughed, and said, "No, I didn't. And really, why are you calling? You're sneaking up on something."

"I am not," Virgil said cheerfully. "Honest to God, this is nothing but the purest gossip. I personally took his beautiful sister up to the Stryker Dell late last night. You guys coulda come along."

"I don't think so," she said. "Skinny-dipping with your sister? Jim's waaaaayyy too straight for that."

"Didn't think of that," Virgil said. "I'd be, too, if I had a sister . . . So'd you have a good time?"

"Yes, I did. He's just like a puppy," Jesse said. "But he pays *attention* to me."

"Told you, that you might like it," Virgil said. "I was afraid he wasn't going to make it at all, with the Schmidt case. I couldn't see how he'd be out of there before eight o'clock, and everything around here closes up at nine."

"No problem," she said. "He just dumped what he was doing and came over; that's what he said, anyway. We were in Sioux Falls by eight-thirty."

"Ah, well . . . so now I come to the *real* reason I called," Virgil said.

"I knew it . . ."

"I haven't been able to catch him this morning," Virgil said. "He isn't there, is he?"

"*Virgil!*"

"Sorry, honey, I need to find him."

"I don't sleep with guys on the first date," she said. "Not at home. Most of the time, anyway."

"Suppose that leaves something for him to look forward to," Virgil said. "Don't tell him I called and asked you this, or he'd probably beat the snot out of me."

THEY CHATTED for another minute, then he closed the phone. All right: if they'd been in Sioux Falls at eight-thirty, Stryker picked her up at eight, and would have been available to do the shooting. Why? That was another question, but knowing who was available was a step in the right direction.

Though he really, really didn't think Stryker had anything to do with it.

Really.

HE STOPPED AT the courthouse, found Stryker leaning in the window at the assessor's, chatting with a clerk. He straightened when he saw Virgil, and Virgil asked, "You got a minute?"

"Yup." As they walked away from the assessor's desk, Stryker said, "Larry called me, said you got a letter this morning . . ."

They went into Stryker's office and closed the door, and Virgil sat in a visitor's chair and grinned and said, "I don't know how to exactly approach this particular report . . ."

"Spit it out."

"A friend of mine from here in town . . ."

"Joanie . . ."

". . . and I decided to go for a swim last night, and she knew this famous local swimming hole . . ."

Stryker's eyebrows went up. "You went skinny-dipping up at the dell? With my baby sister?"

"Yeah."

"Do any good?"

"Somebody with a rifle ambushed us," Virgil said.

He was watching Stryker's face, and Stryker's smile died so naturally that it seemed impossible that he already knew. "*What!*"

"Two shots, from up on that hillside. Trying to hit me, not Joanie," Virgil said.

"Virgil . . ."

"I hit a nerve someplace," Virgil said.

"Holy shit, man." Stryker bucked up in his chair, the wheels skittering over the plastic floor-protecter. "You gotta stay away from Joanie until this is over. Jesus, he coulda killed both of you. Like shooting sitting ducks, down in there . . ."

"Yeah. I've been trying to figure out why he missed. Maybe just a bad shot," Virgil said.

They talked about it for a couple of minutes, then Virgil said, "They're not after Joanie, whoever it is. I think . . . I gotta run down the letter from this morning. Are you looking at prints?"

"Yeah, they're doing the glue thing right now . . ."

"All right." Virgil pushed out of his chair. "I got one more thing—I tell you because you're a friend. I was going through Roman Schmidt's e-mail this morning. Big Curly was trying to get Schmidt to support Little Curly in a run against you this fall. They were talking back and forth, going over the possibilities."

Stryker rubbed his chin with his forefinger: "Doesn't surprise me," he said. "What'd Roman have to say?"

"He suggested that they don't do anything until they get closer to the election, see which way the wind is blowing. Didn't say no."

VIRGIL WAS WALKING back to his car when a tall, older man in a white straw hat yelled at him. "Hey! Mr. Flowers . . ."

Virgil waited by his truck as the man cut across the street and came up to him. He was gray haired, weathered, wiry, in jeans and a golf shirt. "I'm Andy Clay, I live up by the Johnstones? And, you know, where the Gleasons used to live?"

"Yeah, how are you?"

"Fine. Well, maybe not," Clay said. "I want to tell you something, just between you and me, and maybe ask a question."

"No problem."

"I saw you at the Johnstones' yesterday. Everybody in town knows who you are, now," Clay said. "Anyway, later on, I was down at the gas station, getting gas for my mower, and Carol pulls up in their Lexus truck. She doesn't even say 'hi,' she just starts filling it up and washing the windshield and she looks like she's in a hurry. So I went on back up the hill, and I'm gassing up the mower and here comes Carol in the Lexus. She parks in the driveway instead of the garage, and then here comes Gerald out the front door with a big bag, and he throws it in the truck. Then they both go back inside and then they come out with a couple more bags—I'm mowing the lawn by this time—and then she locks the door, and they take off."

"Take off?" Virgil asked. "You mean, like getting out of town?"

"Unless they were donating a bunch of suitcases to the Goodwill," Clay said. "The thing is, they've got these timer lights, that turn the lights on and off when they're gone? Well, everybody up there knows about them, and they were going last night. One comes on here, another goes off there. Then the first one goes off, and the second one comes on. You know. It's almost like a signal: *The Johnstones are gone.*"

"Huh," Virgil said. He thought about it for a moment, then said, "So what's the question?"

"We were talking about it last night, up on the hill," Clay said. "Should we *all* get out?"

THE FUCKIN' JOHNSTONES, Virgil thought as he went back to the motel.

Too late to get the highway patrol to drag them back. Gerald Johnstone knew something about the picture of the dead woman, and Virgil needed to know what it was.

Time for threats, now—if he could find them. Didn't

they say something about visiting a daughter in Minneapolis?

He called Davenport. "I got a couple of people who may be running. Not the killers, but they know something. If Jenkins and Shrake are sitting on their asses . . ."

He explained and told Davenport that he didn't know the daughter's name. "We can probably find it in the vital records," Davenport said. "I'll get the guys on it. They've been restless."

"Well, Jesus, don't let them beat these people up," Virgil said. "These are old people."

"You mean, we should only beat up young people?" Davenport asked. "There are as many old assholes as there are young ones. Especially since the boomers got old."

"Yeah, well . . . I'd just as soon my witnesses didn't die of a heart attack. Tell them to take it easy. No kicking."

"I thought you wanted them scared," Davenport said.

"A little scared," Virgil said. "Not *too* scared."

AT THE MOTEL, the desk clerk had three cardboard boxes, sealed with tape, stashed behind the counter: "A guy brought them in a half hour ago. He said they were from St. Paul."

They felt like boxes of bricks. Virgil hauled them to his room and unloaded the stacks of paper. Too much stuff, but it had to be looked at. Some of it, anyway.

Before he started on it, he called Davenport again, got a name, called a guy at the secretary of state's office, and found that he could look at all current corporate records, online, including the confidential files, if he had a password. "I'll set you up with a temporary password: chuzzlewit," said the guy, whose name was Martin. He spelled the password. "That'll be good through next Wednesday. If you need another one, call me up again."

"What's a chuzzlewit?"

"It's a word unlikely to be figured out by some little hacker-geek between now and Wednesday," Martin said.

So Virgil, reluctant to start on the pile of paper, pulled out his laptop, stared at it for a moment. A problem had been pecking at the back of his mind for a day or so, and he put in the disk that Stryker had given him on the first day, the one with the paperwork on the Gleason killing. Included with everything else were a couple of hundred jpg photographs of the crime scene. He combed over them for a half hour, then, satisfied, said, "Huh."

No Revelation, as far as he could see.

Then he went online with the secretary of state's office and searched for Florence Mills, Inc.

Florence Mills, according to the information in the original filing, had been created three years earlier to "build, buy, or lease facilities for the production of corn-based and switchgrass-based ethanol as a renewable fuel," a joint venture between Arno Partners, a limited liability company registered in Delaware, and St. John Ventures, of Coeur d'Alene, Idaho.

Not much there. He had a feeling that the Delaware company would be hard to check. Delaware was an easy place to set up a corporation, requiring minimal information, and a stickler for legal procedures when you wanted to mine their corporate records.

Idaho, he thought, might be easier, and it was: called the Idaho secretary of state's office, was told how to look at online public records, and with a certain sense of what he'd find, looked up St. John Ventures: George Feur, chief executive officer and chairman.

He called Stryker: "What happened with Judd Sr.'s office? Did you seal it up, or what?"

"Yup. Couldn't say for sure that Junior didn't get in there, though. They're right next to each other. If there was a big pot of cash or something . . ."

"I need to get in," Virgil said. "Right now."

"I'll walk down. Meet you there in ten."

JUDD'S OFFICE included a small outer waiting room with a secretary's desk, a side room with a Xerox machine, a printer and a half-dozen file cabinets, and a large inner office with leather chairs, dark-wood paneling, and a new wide-screen television sitting on top of a bar. The newspaper office was on one side, and Judd Jr.'s office on the other; they hadn't seen either the newspaper editor or Junior when they unlocked Judd Sr.'s office.

Stryker locked the door behind them and Virgil said, "Not too much light. Just the inner office and the file room. I'd just as soon that not everybody in town knows that we're here."

"Probably know anyway," Stryker said, gloomily. He was discouraged by the results of the Schmidt investigation: "Nothing's coming up, man. What about you? Anything working?"

"The letter this morning implied that Bill Judd Jr. has money problems, and mentioned Florence Mills," Virgil said. "It supposedly was set up to make ethanol out of corn and switchgrass—and it's half owned by George Feur."

"Feur?"

"Yeah. I can't find out who owns the other half, because that half is owned by a Delaware corporation. We could probably find out next week, but it's too late today. We're gonna need some papers, and it's already two o'clock on the East Coast. I'm thinking that if the Judds are involved with Feur, and . . . I don't know. There's something going on there."

"Ethanol? Shoot, it could be another goddamn Jerusalem artichoke scam. There's the same kind of gold-rush thing going on . . . the people who got killed weren't only old, they were mostly pretty well-off. Could have been investors in another scam."

"Yeah. Even the Schmidts. They had half a million in Vanguard." Virgil thought for a second, and then asked, "Is Larry Jensen still out there?"

"Yeah."

"Get him to check the Vanguard statements. There should be monthly statements, like with a checking account. See if there've been any big withdrawals in the past three years. Not like for a car . . . bigger than that."

"I'll call now."

While he went to call, Virgil began going through Judd's files, looking for anything involving Arno Partners or Florence Mills. Stryker came back: "Larry'll check. What are we looking for?"

"Arno Partners, A-R-N-O, or Florence Mills. If you could crack open his computer, run a search on either name . . ."

"Why don't I do the files, you do the computer. You gotta be better at computers than I am . . ."

JUDD'S COMPUTER wasn't password-protected and had almost nothing on it other than Microsoft Word, with automatic formatting of letters and envelopes with Judd's return address and a letterhead. Nothing at all in the doc-uments file. The e-mail file hadn't even been set up. A fancy typewriter, Virgil thought.

He was closing it down when he caught sight of the secretary's machine in the outer office: non-networked, both freestanding.

"Judd still have a secretary?" he asked Stryker, who was sitting on the floor of the file room.

"Yup. Amy Sweet. We told her to go on home and to send the probate lawyer a bill for her last week of work."

"Gotta talk to her," Virgil said. He dropped behind the secretary's desk, booted up the computer. More files, this time. He ran a search on Arno and one on Florence Mills, and the Florence Mills search kicked out a half-dozen documents.

"Got Florence Mills," he called to Stryker. He opened the documents, one at a time: payments to High Plains Ag & Fleet Supply, in Madison, South Dakota. Stryker came to look over his shoulder: "Sonofabitch," he said, reaching past Virgil to tap the screen, a payment for one thousand gallons of Bernhard Brand AA. "Look at this."

"I don't know what that is," Virgil said.

"Anhydrous ammonia. They've got an ethanol plant somewhere, and they're buying AA. I mean, it could be legitimate if they're growing, as well as cooking, but I'll tell you what I think: I think they're manufacturing methamphetamine, bigger than life."

"Ah, man," Virgil said.

Stryker: "I checked Feur with the NCIC. He's had some run-ins with the law, since he got out, but they were all bullshit. You know, disorderly conduct for protests, that sort of thing. Nothing hard, like dope."

"Sit tight," Virgil said. He got on his phone, called Davenport. "You told me once if I ever needed anything really bad from the federal government, you've got a guy high enough up to get anything."

"Maybe," Davenport said. "I'd hate to burn up a favor on an errand, though."

"Call him. Tell him to go to the DEA and see if there's

anything on a George Feur—any possible connection to methamphetamine distribution through one of those fascist white supremacist convict groups. I need it just as fast as you can get it."

"You break it?"

"Maybe; not what I thought, though," Virgil said.

"I'll have him dump it to your e-mail, if there's anything," Davenport said.

VIRGIL TO STRYKER: "Do you know any accountants that you can trust, who don't work for Judd?"

"One . . ."

CHRIS OLAFSON ran a bookkeeping, financial planning, and accounting service out of a converted house on the west side of town. Stryker swore her to secrecy: "This is about the murder investigation," he said. "Virgil has a hypothetical question for you . . ."

"Go ahead." She was a bright-eyed, busy, overweight woman, of the kind that drip efficiency.

"If you had a rich father—a millionaire, I don't know how many millions—and you borrowed a lot of money from him, over the years, how would that complicate your inheritance?" Virgil asked.

She knitted her fingers together and said, "That depends. Did the father gift any money to Junior . . . to his son?"

They all smiled at each other, acknowledging the fact

that she knew who they were talking about, and Virgil said, "I don't know. What do you mean, gift?"

She gave them a short course in the estate tax. When she was done, she asked, "So, hypothetically, how bad is Junior screwed?"

Virgil rubbed his head. "We'd have to get down some exact numbers to know that," he said. "I've got some tax records down at the motel . . . but they're all bureaucratic bullshit. So . . . I don't know if he's screwed at all."

"He's not a real good businessman," Olafson said brightly. "They should have had an estate plan. Does anybody even know where all of Judd's money is? Was it in trusts, or what? Did the killer burn down the house to get rid of planning documents?"

"We don't know any of that stuff," Stryker said.

"Maybe I ought to run for sheriff," she said.

"Get in early, avoid the rush," Stryker said.

THEY BOTH STOOD, and Olafson said, "Sit back down for a minute. Would you like Cokes? I want to give you *my* hypothetical."

"We're in a bit of a hurry," Virgil said.

"Take you five minutes," she said. "Cokes?"

They both took a Coke, and Olafson said, "Suppose Bill Judd had a big tank of money somewhere, that nobody knew about but his son. Like money and interest from the Jerusalem artichoke scam."

Stryker started to say something, but she held up a finger.

"Suppose Judd Senior starts to fail, first mentally, and then physically, and it looks like he's about to die. Once he's dead, any money taken from the account could only be taken by fraud. And the fraud would be pretty visible: the bank says money was taken out on August first, but lo, Judd was dead three weeks before that. Even Junior's smarter than that.

"In the meantime, the son goes to his accountants, and they say, 'It's really bad. You've been gifted right up to the limit, so the whole estate is exposed to taxes. Plus, you're so far in debt to him that you're going to *owe* money to the state and federal government and they are going to foreclose you. You can't even go bankrupt, because bankruptcy doesn't wipe out back taxes.' So what do you do?"

Virgil shrugged: "It's your hypothetical."

"So the old man is failing mentally, and you're down there in his business office, and you know about this big tank of money. You know the codes, or you have the checkbooks, that you need to transfer money to the old man's bank account . . . and the old man is so far gone mentally, he won't see it. You couldn't give it to yourself, because that would either be fraud, or more debt, and it would all be on paper. But if you were willing to forge his signature, if you gave that money to a business that the old man supposedly owned—even if he was too far gone to know that he owned it—and if you had a way to take that money back out of his business, whatever it was, say, for services that were never performed . . ."

"You're saying he was embezzling from his old man."

"I'm not saying that. I'm saying that if I'm elected sheriff this fall, I'll look into it."

"Suppose he was pouring money into a corn-ethanol plant?" Virgil said.

She shook her head: "The government would take the plant, and any profits should show up in tax filings. You have to remember: you have all this paper—checks and banks, purchases and sales. The government won't believe you, if you say that you lost it."

"Suppose the profits coming out of the plant were hidden?"

"What I'm trying to tell you is, *you can't hide it*. Not very well. The feds would do the books," she said. "They're good at books."

"Suppose the plant was making two products. The above-ground books worked out to the penny. The under-ground stuff, there were no books at all. You know, like they make a hundred thousand gallons of ethanol, sell ninety thousand, claim they only made ninety thousand, and sold the other ten thousand gallons as over-the-bar vodka, two bucks a quart, underground."

"Then, if nobody gave you up, you'd make some money," she said. "But the distribution network, the low unit value of the product, would hardly make it worth the risk. Somebody would talk, and there you are on tax evasion."

VIRGIL TOOK STRYKER outside and asked, "You think she can be seriously trusted? No gossip?"

"She's been an accountant here for twenty years, since she got out of school—you couldn't get one word out of her about how anybody spent a nickel," Stryker said. "And nobody'll get a word out of her about what we were talking about. She's like a Swiss bank."

Virgil said, "I got a lot of paper in from St. Paul. Tax records, corporate stuff, stuff I took out of the bank. It really needs an accountant—somebody who can work it overnight."

"Ask her," Stryker said. "You'll have to pay her—but there's no question about trusting her."

"We can pay her. We need the analysis."

THEY WENT BACK to Olafson, and she agreed to do it: "Too many people dead. Of course I'll do it. I'll even give you my state rate—overtime, of course, rush job."

"And that would be . . ."

"Hundred and ten dollars an hour," she said.

Sounded like a lot, but then, it was only for eight or ten hours: "It's a deal. I'll go get the paper, you type up an agreement and I'll sign it."

BACK OUT ON the sidewalk, Stryker said, "If you're supposedly developing an ethanol plant, but what you're really doing is using the plant to buy bulk chemicals to manufacture methamphetamine—I mean, we're not talking about a coffeepot on a stove somewhere; we're talking about tons of it. The profits wouldn't be two dollars a quart. The profits would be astronomical. You'd need quite a bit of up-front money . . ."

"From the Judd money bin. And you'd need a distribution network."

"From Feur, if he's really involved in it."

They looked at each other, and Virgil said, "Let's check back at the hotel. Maybe Davenport's guy got me something."

DAVENPORT'S GUY WAS Louis Mallard, who was something large in the FBI. He sent along a single paragraph: "A Rev. George Feur of the first Archangelus Church of the Revelation was one of a number of people under surveillance in Salt Lake City and in Coeur d'Alene for his association with extremist antigovernment groups like the Corps. The Corps was known to distribute drugs, including cocaine and methamphetamine, to finance its activities and for the purchase of weapons. Surveillance was terminated after three months with no evidence of Feur's involvement in illegal activities, although he had extensive connections with people who were involved in illegal activities."

"That's it," Stryker said. "He's involved. He's got the connections."

"What about Roman Schmidt and the Gleasons?" Virgil asked.

"I don't know about the Gleasons—except that they had some contact with Feur. There was that Book of Revelation. Maybe they were investors. Roman . . ."

"What?"

"Roman was pals with Big and Little Curly," Stryker said. "Guess who patrols west county?"

"Big and Little Curly?"

"That's their country out there," Stryker said. "They know it like nobody else. If you were moving a lot of meth around, it'd be useful to have a lookout with the sheriff's department."

"Hate to think it," Virgil said.

"So would I," Stryker said. "I'd rather lose the election than find that out."

THEY SAT STARING at the laptop screen for a couple of minutes, then Virgil asked, "What're you doing tonight?"

"Thought I'd go see Jesse," Stryker said. "I've got something going, there. I don't know . . . but the case comes first. What do you have in mind?"

"I don't want to talk to the Curlys. I'm thinking we might want to do some trespassing. Feur and Judd have the ethanol plant over in SoDak, so what's his farm all about? What I'm thinking is, it's the distribution center. He's way out in the countryside, he has those religious services, there are strangers coming and going from all over the place, not unexpected with that kind of church . . . might be when they move the stuff. Lots of guys in trucks."

"If we're gonna do it, best to do it late," Stryker said, looking at his watch. "It's almost four, now."

"I wouldn't ask, but I'd be a little worried going out there without some backup," Virgil said.

"Wait until the town goes to sleep . . . and move," Stryker said. "Meet me at my place at one in the morning?"

"See you then. You might bring some serious hardware," Virgil said.

Stryker nodded. "I'll do that. Feur's boys have some heavy weapons out there."

"One good thing," Virgil said, after another minute.

"What's that."

"You'll still get to see Jesse."

"She's got me if she wants me," Stryker said. He seemed puzzled by it all. "I looked in her eyes last night, in that candlelight, and I thought my heart was gonna explode."

"Where're you going tonight?" Virgil asked.

Stryker shrugged: "I don't know. Jesus, thinking of someplace interesting just about kills you. I can't take her out to the club. I'm afraid to go to Tijuana Jack's or anyplace in Worthington—it's just too close, and I really don't want to be seen out on the town. Not yet."

"Life sucks, then you die."

"Easy on the die stuff," Stryker said. "I'm a little nervous about sneaking up on Feur."

13

VIRGIL WAS STUCK. With the accountant working the records, he had nothing to do until four, and then he had a date—and the date wasn't going to help with the investigation. On the other hand, wandering around town wouldn't help much, either.

Time to talk to Judd? And look at other names in his notebook? Suzanne Reynolds, the overweight ex–sex groupie?

Judd first.

HE WENT DOWNTOWN; a guy at the SuperAmerica, gassing his truck, waved at him, and Virgil waved back. Parked in front of the Great Plains Bank & Trust, looked at a Red Wing jug in the window of an antique shop, and strolled down to Judd Jr.'s office.

His office was a mirror image of his old man's: same dark wood generating financial gloom, a secretary at a desk behind a railing, two wooden chairs for visitors to wait in.

The secretary said, "Mr. Flowers. Let me see if Mr. Judd is available." The door to Judd's office was open, and she stuck her head inside and said, "Mr. Flowers is here."

Judd said, "Send him in."

JUDD WAS WEARING half-frame reading glasses, looking at a printed-out spreadsheet that he folded and pushed to one side of his desk. He pointed at a chair and asked, "You getting anywhere?"

"Somewhere," Virgil said. "I can't tell you how I know it, but I can tell you for sure that I've upset somebody. . ."

"That's good," Judd said. "That's something."

"I've got a question for you. I don't know how far you've gotten in working through your father's estate . . ."

"The Jesse Laymon deal is going to hose me off pretty good, I can tell you," Judd said.

"That's something else . . ."

"Well, I think there's a question of whether she might have wanted the old man to disappear," Judd said.

"That's being looked into."

"By the sheriff, personally, is what I hear."

"By me," Virgil said. "Anyway: where'd your old man stick the money from the Jerusalem artichoke business?"

Judd looked at him for a minute, then barked; he'd laughed, Virgil thought. "Virgil, there is no money. There is no secret account. As far as I know, there wasn't much to begin with, and believe me, some very sharp investigators from the state and from the IRS tore up everything they could find. It does not exist."

"You're sure."

Judd tapped his desk a few times, then sighed. "Look, how can you be sure? My dad grew up poor, and he was a hard-nosed sonofabitch. Came out of the Depression, and made his own way. So he might have hid some money, if there was any. But if there was, he never would have told a soul. I mean, if he had it, it was a *crime,* and he wouldn't have taken any chances with that."

"But then the money just would have been lost . . ."

Judd wagged a finger at him. "Not lost if someday you needed it. Like with anybody who dies with money. Say he had an account in Panama or somewhere, invested it in overseas securities. The investment would grow, and if he ever needed it, he could get it. He never needed it."

"You're sure."

"It's not that I'm sure—I'm not sure about any of this. What I believe is, there never was any money. You're wasting your time looking for it, and if somebody killed him trying to get it, then the murder was a waste of time. There is no Uncle Scrooge's money bin."

THEY TALKED for a couple of more minutes, then Virgil was back on the street. Looked in his notebook, found the address for Suzanne Reynolds, and headed that way, in the truck. Thinking about Judd: and who the heck was Uncle Scrooge?

REYNOLDS CAME to the door of her house, blinking in the sunlight: she'd either been dozing, or watching TV, and her heavy face was clouded with sleep.

She opened the door and said, "You're Mr. Flowers?"

"Yes, I am," Virgil said, holding up his ID.

"Michelle said you might be coming," she said. She pushed open the door.

VIRGIL FOLLOWED HER past the kitchen into the tiny living room. Reynolds wasn't overweight, but rather was morbidly obese. Virgil thought she must weigh three hundred pounds, though she was no more than five-four. The house stank of starch and fat, and doors and windows not opened. In the living room, a plate with three cold surviving French fries sat next to an open jar of mayonnaise. She picked up one of the French fries, dipped it in mayonnaise, pointed it at a plush-magenta La-Z-Boy, said, "Sit down," and ate the fry.

Virgil sat down and said, "I'm talking to people who had relationships with Bill Judd Sr. back in the late sixties and seventies. I'm not trying to mess anybody up, I'm trying to figure out if there was anything back then that could have led to these murders. All the people were of the same age . . ."

"Seems like you're a generation too late, then. They're all twenty years older than us girls were."

"Yeah, but you're what I got," Virgil said. "Let me ask you this, privately between the two of us. Did the Gleasons or the Schmidts or the Johnstones have anything to do with . . . this whole relationship thing with Judd?"

She was taken aback: "The Johnstones? Are the Johnstones dead?"

"No, no. I should have made that clear. It's just that they were people of this age who might have been involved in something that would snap back—we're thinking it had to be serious. Revenge, something that festered. Since Gleason was a doctor, and a coroner sometimes, and Schmidt was the sheriff, and Johnstone was the under-taker . . ."

"I see where you're going," she said. She thought about it, and then said, "The only things I can think of, are the Jerusalem artichoke business, and then the sex. Maybe somebody's husband just found out about the sex and couldn't stand the thought, but this was a *looonngg* time ago. People get over stuff like sex: it's just a little squirt in the dark. No big deal."

"Some people think of it as a little more than that," Virgil said. "Michelle told me that it might have been the best part of her life. The most fun, anyway."

A wrinkle spread across the lower part of Reynolds' face, and Virgil realized that she was smiling. "She was a crazy one," Reynolds said. "She liked everything: boys, girls, front, back, upside down." She shook a finger at

Virgil: "Here's something. Polaroids were a big deal back then, and Bill used to take some pictures. You know, home-made porno. You could even get Polaroid slide film, and take pictures and develop them yourself, and then have slide shows . . ."

Virgil was getting uncomfortable. "You think some of those pictures . . ."

"Well, suppose somebody's daddy or brother or husband got a picture of some guys getting his little girl airtight. That could set something off," she said.

Airtight. He'd Google it later. "Michelle said she only knew of one other guy who . . . took part. The post-master . . ."

"There were more'n that," she said. "Two or three more, but not all from right here. Not all the girls were from here, either, there were some that came down from Minneapolis, one used to come down from Fargo. But: like I said, those things fade away. Who cares, when you're fifty-five and fat? If I were you, I'd be looking at the Jerusalem artichoke scam. That's what I'd do."

"You think that might be more combustible . . . ?"

She shook her finger at him again. "Listen. You're not from here. That thing . . . you had to be here. There were old men crying in the streets. People lost every-thing they had: borrowed money against their homes and farms . . . lost every damn dime of it. Lots of people. If you lost your farm in the eighties, you wound up working in a meat-cutting plant somewhere, or going up to the Cities and working the night shift in an assembly plant, five dollars an hour. Can't even feed your kids. That's what could come back on you. That's what could come back."

"You think?"

She nodded. "Us girls . . . we were playing. It was in the sixties, and everybody was playing. But the artichoke thing . . . that was real, screaming, insane hate. There were people who would have hanged Judd if they could have gotten away with it, and I'm not fooling. He was lucky to live through it: you'd hear people talking about taking their deer rifle out, and shooting him down. Talking out in the open, in the café." She stopped talking for a moment, and Virgil watched her, and then she said, "And what made it worse was, Bill was laughing at them. His attitude was 'too bad, losers.' He was laughing at them, and there was little kids eating lard sandwiches. *Lard sandwiches.*"

AT THREE-THIRTY, he was back at the motel; got cleaned up, thinking about Reynolds in her dark living room, with her French fries, and lard sandwiches. She'd once been a pretty girl, he'd been told.

He met Joan at four o'clock. They stopped at Johnnie's Pizza, found that they agreed on sausage, mushroom, and pepperoni, and the inherent evilness of anchovies. "Little spooky going back to the farm," Virgil said, as they rolled out of town. "Keep an eye out the back. See if there's anybody trailing us."

"You don't have to trail anybody out here," she said. "If you see Joan Carson heading out of town on this road, it's ninety-five percent that she's going out to the farm. There's not much else out here."

"Didn't think of that," he said.

"Besides, we're not going to the farm," she said. "We're going up the hill behind it—that's as nice as the dell in its own way, and I want to see where that guy was when he was shooting at us."

"I was already up there," Virgil said. "First thing this morning."

"You were?"

"It was a *shooting* site, Joanie. I had to go up and look around," Virgil said. "Didn't find a thing."

"Did you go to the flat rock?" she asked.

"What flat rock?"

"Ah—didn't go to the flat rock." She was being mysterious about it.

THEY WENT PAST the farm, followed the road around behind the hill, cut into the hillside where the shooter had gotten off, and where Virgil was that morning. Joan looked over the spot where the shooter had hidden his truck. Then Virgil got the shotgun out of the back of the 4Runner, and walked her along the now-faint track through the weeds to the stump where the shooter had made his nest. The day had turned hot, the humidity climbing, and far down to the southwest, they could see the puffy white tops of clouds that would become thunderheads; the world smelled of warm prairie weed.

"He might not have known the hillside that well," Joan said, when she saw the shooting nest. She pointed far down to her left. "There's a spot down there where you can come in—that's where kids come in when they're sneaking out to the dell. Good hidden place to park, too. Then, you'd come up from the side of the dell, where there's a really sharp break. We never would have seen him. He would have been right over our heads."

"So he messed up in a couple of ways," Virgil said. "I was wondering if he meant to miss us . . . but I can't see why he would. And he wasn't that far off. If he meant to miss us, he was playing a dangerous game."

They probed around some more, then headed back to the truck. Joanie pointed him west, to a clump of shrubs where they left the car, out of the sun. "Ground's too broken up above here, you can screw up a tire," she said. "Get the pizza. I'll get the blanket and cooler."

She led the way up the hill to a formation that almost looked like an eroded castle, a natural amphitheater in the red quartzite, at the very summit of the hill. They found a spot with shorter grass, in the shade of a clump of wild plum trees, and put down the blanket. Virgil braced the shotgun against one of the trees.

"I need pizza," Virgil said. "Beer. Hot out here."

"Get a beer. I'll show you the flat rock. Put the pizza on the rock in the sun, it'll stay warm . . ."

HE FOLLOWED HER across the hillside to a narrow bed of flat red rock, twenty feet long, six or eight feet wide, sloping just a few degrees to the south. When he saw it, Virgil thought, "Blackboard," and Joan said, "Look."

He looked, but he didn't see for a moment. Then he saw a handprint, a small hand, the size of a woman's. Then another, and another, and then a cartoon arrow with a tip and fletching, and a turtle and a man with horns, and then more hands, and circles and squares of things that he didn't recognize.

"Petroglyphs," Joan said. "Chipped out of the rock. Pecked out with another stone. Something between three hundred and a thousand years old. There are older ones at Jeffers, but these are pretty old."

"Jeez . . . Joanie." Virgil was fascinated. He got down on his hands and knees, crawling around the rock. "How many people know about these things?"

"The Historical Society people, and folks who are interested in petroglyphs and who won't mess them up. My grandfather told a reporter that there used to be a circle of stones here, not this red quartzite, they looked like glacial rocks, or river rocks. They were arranged around the flat rock like a clock, and each stone had a symbol on it. People stole them over the years. Nobody knows where they are now—probably some big museum, or Manhattan decorator shop or something."

"Look at this . . ." He was pointing. "That looks like an elk. Did they have elk here?"

"That's what they say. There are three buffalo over in the corner up here."

"THERE'S A MAGAZINE article in this," Virgil said, eventually. "Something about plains hunting in the Indian days . . . take a lot of photographs, mess them around in Photoshop, make a story out of it."

"Leave them alone," Joan said, shaking her head. "It's nice to know that they're out here. That they have nothing to do with magazines or television."

SO THEY SAT under the plum trees and talked, ate pizza, drank beer, and watched the thunderheads grow from white globes into pink anvils, as the sun slid down in the sky. Joan gave him a talk:

"I was thinking about us last night, and I don't think this is a real relationship. You're my transition guy. You're the guy who gets me back into life, and then goes away."

"Why am I gonna go away?" Virgil was feeling lazy, lying back on the blanket, fingers knitted behind his head as a pillow; and he didn't disagree.

"Because you are," she said. "We'd be serious about as long as one of your marriages was serious. You're a good guy, but you've got your problems, Virgil. You manipulate. I can feel you doing it, even if I can't figure out what you're doing. That would drive me crazy after a while. And I have the feeling you're pretty happy when you're alone."

"That doesn't sound so good," he said.

"Well, you're gonna have to figure yourself out," she said. "Anyway, I'm not giving you the gate. I'm just saying . . ."

". . . we're not for all eternity."

"We are not," she agreed. "But the sex has been grand. I didn't even remember how much I used to like it. My husband . . . I don't know. It just got tiresome. He was more interested in playing golf than playing house, that's for sure."

"Good player?" Virgil asked.

"Not bad, I guess. The last year we were married, one of the most intimate things we'd do is lay in bed, and he'd tell me about every one of seventy-seven shots on the golf course that day—the club, the ball flight, what happened when it landed, bad breaks, good breaks, what he was thinking when he putted. But you know . . . someday, you just gotta grow up."

"Why'd you marry him in the first place?" Virgil asked.

"He was good-looking, hard worker, available," she said.

"There are worse things in the world."

"Yeah, but he just didn't flip my switch," she said. She plucked a long grass stem and nibbled on the butt end. "I thought we'd grow into it, but we didn't."

"A lot of women think men are like raw lumber—something that you can build a house out of, with a lot of hard work," Virgil said. "But some guys, you know, they're going to do what they're going to do. Can't work with them. They're not good lumber."

"Is that what happened with your wives?"

"Oh . . . no. I just married them because they were hot and I was stupid. Actually, all of us were stupid. Didn't know what we were doing. Somebody had to work. Couldn't go dancing all the time . . ."

THEY WERE STILL talking about it, watching the birds, arguing about whether the thunderheads were coming in or would slide to the south, eating pizza . . .

And a slice of a woman's laughter slid over the hillside like a butterfly, fragile, attractive, and definitely there.

"Who's that?" Joan asked, sitting up.

Virgil shrugged. "I haven't seen anyone . . ."

"Somebody in the dell," Joan said. "Come on. Let's sneak up on them."

Virgil thought: *Oh, no. Stryker.* "Joan, maybe it'd be better, you know, let it go."

"Don't be retarded," she said. "C'mon. We're missing something."

"Joan, I think it might be Jim. And Jesse."

She looked at him for a moment, a wrinkle appearing between her eyes, then, amused, she said, "So what? Let's go, you sissy." And she was off across the hillside, using the scrub brush as cover, moving through the weeds in a crouch, a country-girl sneak. Instead of approaching the dell from the top, she led the way around to the north side, and then got down on her hands and knees as she crawled up to the edge of the bluff, where they could look down into the pool.

When Virgil eased up beside her, she whispered, "Oh, my. I never suspected Jim even knew about that."

Stryker and Jesse were on an air mattress on the same rock where Virgil and Joan had left their clothes and bags. Jesse was naked, on her back, her hands on Stryker's head, which was between her thighs. "That's disgusting," Virgil said. "They're like a couple of animals."

"Shhh, they'll hear you. Did you tell Jim about doing this? Or did he think it up on his own? I'd hate to think you were sharing our little secrets."

"Believe me, I'm not sharing our little secrets," Virgil said.

Joan said, "Whoops, here we go. Main event."

Stryker was moving over Jesse, stopped at her navel, her breasts. Joan pulled at Virgil's belt buckle. "Get your pants off, Virgil. Jeez, come on, hurry up."

"Joan, this is terrible . . ."

"C'mon . . ." She was slipping out of her jeans. "This is really good . . ."

What could a guy do, Virgil wondered, as he slid out of his jeans, but try to be polite?

ON THE WAY HOME, Joan said, "I've known Jim every day of my life—I've got a picture of him holding me, I'm all wrapped in a baby blanket, when I was a newborn. He's

always been . . . guarded. Quiet. Reticent. One of those
guys with muscles in his jaws. I couldn't even imagine him
letting it out like that."

"He let it out," Virgil agreed. "He's also a smart guy, and
sooner or later you could let it slip that we were up there.
That could ruin something for them."

She considered that for a second, and then said, "I will
never say another word about this to anybody.
Including you."

"Are you planning to think about it? When you're in
bed with somebody?"

"Think about what?" But he glanced at her a few seconds later, and caught her smiling. She said, "Shut up."

He said, "Incest. That's what it is. One of those
Greek things."

VIRGIL HAD MOVED to the second floor of the motel,
so he could sleep on the bed. He brought up his laptop and
checked the National Weather Service radar out of Sioux
Falls. The line of thunderstorms that he and Joan had seen
brewing to the southwest was about to roll into Sioux Falls,
slow moving at ten miles an hour or so; getting stronger.

No talk of tornadoes, but there was a severe thunderstorm alert for parts of northwest Iowa, southwest
Minnesota, and southeastern South Dakota. Could be raining when they got to Feur's. Which might not be bad. Rain
and wind would cover movement, and scent: Virgil wasn't
worried so much about electronic sensors as dogs . . .

He hit the lights and climbed in bed, looking for two hours of sleep before he met Stryker. A lot going on. He hadn't fully digested the Feur–Judd involvement, and all its implications. He and Stryker had made some leaps in their assessment. Maybe they'd find out more tonight, and maybe the accountant would have more in the morning . . .

The killings could easily have been carried out by a crank freak. The shit stirred people's brains around. Take one of those grim, abused country kids you see from time to time, that thousand-yard stare, mix in some nutcake religion, a convict's point of view taken from the Corps, plus a little methamphetamine, and you could grow yourself a genuine monster.

But that photograph of the dead woman, that he'd taken from Schmidt's safe-deposit box . . . that came from way back, when Feur would have been a kid. What was that all about?

And then, of course, there was Joan's assessment of his, Virgil's, personality . . . a lot to think about.

AS HE WAS DRIFTING OFF to sleep, his alter ego, Homer, popped up in his mind:

The shooter humped over the hill, moving low through the weeds. A hundred yards down the slope, he could see Homer and Joan in the pool, naked as jaybirds, chasing each other around. He eased down behind a stump to look them over with the scope; variable power, two-to-eight, and he took a

minute to crank it all the way up to eight. That narrowed his
scope picture, but he could see their faces clearly enough.

He'd become aware that he wasn't quite in the right spot.
If he'd come in from the side, if he'd hidden his car in that
grove of trees down to the right . . .

Virgil's unconscious writer hesitated. Why hadn't the
shooter parked down there, in that grove?

Then he was asleep.

14

THE ALARM KICKED him out of bed at 12:30. He sat up, yawning, jumped in the shower, brushed his teeth, dug a tab of Modafinil out of his dopp kit, popped it, dressed, and was out in his truck at five to one.

The streets were still dry, but the lightning was close, off to the west, and the moon passed in and out of ragged fingers of cloud.

He was at Stryker's by one o'clock, a cool breeze slipping down the streets, the leaves on the trees beginning to stir. He parked in the street, and saw Stryker moving behind a dark picture window at the front of his house. A moment later, his garage door started up. Virgil got the shotgun and his pistol, a bottle of water, two Snickers bars, a pocket flashlight, his rain suit, and a couple of Ziploc bags full of extra shells.

Stryker backed into the street and Virgil climbed into the passenger seat, and they were halfway up the street before Stryker turned on his headlights and asked, "You bring a rain suit?"

"Yup. You awake?"

"I'm fine." He flicked a finger at the lightning to the west. "Probably won't need the water bottles."

"Looked pretty interesting on the radar," Virgil said. "You know where we're going?"

"Right down to the foot. We'll be walking in from three-quarters of a mile out. Gonna be darker'n a bitch, but we'll be mostly on the road."

"Lightning will help," Virgil said.

"As long as we're not hit." They were clearing the town, the last few lights fading behind them as they took the road north toward the Stryker farm, then turned west toward Feur's. Coming in from the back.

GOOD THING ABOUT rolling out in the night, Virgil thought with a tight smile, was that he could put some talk and time between the afternoon at the dell, and the next time he had to look Stryker in the eyes, in daylight. If he'd had to do that, first thing, Stryker would have known that something had happened, he'd have seen it in Virgil's eyes. He was a good enough cop that he might have figured it out . . .

Stryker said, "After we split up this afternoon, I walked over to the ag extension service to look at their photo set for the county. The photography was six years old, but Feur hasn't built anything new out there. There's the house, where you've been, there's a big garage and shop in the side yard, that would have been on your left as you drove in."

"I saw that Quonset hut. It was in pretty good shape."

"Yes. Then there's the barn out back, that was remodeled into a meeting room, and people who've been inside say it's pretty open. They have meetings on Wednesday and Saturday nights and Sunday mornings, fifty, sixty people, come from a hundred miles around. The sheds next to the barn don't look like much. They must be eighty years old."

"So the places to look are the Quonset hut, the barn, and the house. I've been in the house, one room, anyway, didn't look like much."

"I've been in that. There's a basement . . . haven't seen it. The shed is what I'd like to get a peek at. If they're moving drugs through, in bulk, that's dangerous stuff. They might want to keep it outside the house."

"Are you thinking about going in?" Virgil asked.

"I'm more thinking about watching for a few hours. See if anything isn't right. Look for dogs. See if there's any security stuff. See if we can *smell* anything. Look for any precursors."

"Didn't see any dogs when I was out there," Virgil said.

"That's good; that's the best thing. Most people don't know it, but dogs can see almost as well at night as they can in daylight. Burglar alarm won't hunt you down, like a dog will."

THE DARKNESS DEEPENED as they got away from the lights of town, and as the clouds spread overhead; then they crossed the top of a low hill and Stryker slowed and killed the lights. They were on gravel, creeping along, the lightning nearly overhead, with Stryker staring at a GPS screen. Then he said, quietly, "We're there."

"Can't see a damn thing," Virgil said.

"I left a rock out here," Stryker said. He'd put a couple of strips of black gaffer tape over the interior and door lights, and he said, "Be right back." He shifted into Park, climbed out of the truck, and using a penlight, walked down the road. He was back in fifteen seconds, climbed back in the truck. "We're right there . . ."

He shifted into Drive, rolled forward thirty feet, then hooked through the ditch and powered blindly up a low rise, and then down the other side. He stopped once, got out, walked, flicked the light a couple more times, then pulled ahead and again turned blindly to the left, drove another thirty feet. In the illumination of a lightning stroke, Virgil saw that they were about to plow a stand of sumac. "This is it."

"What is it?"

"Used to be a farmhouse. The Miller place. Abandoned and dangerous. The fire department came out a couple of years ago and burned it down for training, filled in the hole where the root cellar was. But there're still the wind-break trees that used to be around the house. We're back in what used to be the side yard, so there won't be any reflections off the car, if somebody comes down the road."

VIRGIL GOT HIS SHOTGUN, and Stryker popped the back hatch of the truck and took out a long gun of some kind. In another flash of lightning, Virgil saw that it was an

M-16-style rifle, and Stryker had loaded an extra-capacity magazine.

"Is that semiauto? Or full?"

Stryker racked a round into the chamber. "Semiauto's for people who shoot prairie dogs."

USING THE PENLIGHT, they walked back out to the road, and then single file along it. There was enough lightning that they could navigate by the flashes, and Stryker's GPS homed them in on the Feur place. They were making noise, Virgil thought, crunching along on the gravel, and with the *zzzzzi-itttt* sound of their nylon rain suits, as their legs crossed and their arms worked, but it was nothing in the wind.

Four hundred yards out, they crossed the ditch again, and eased over an old barbed-wire fence. Stryker was talking quietly, almost muttering: "Go slow and watch your footing. There's a lot of rock around. This used to be pasturage; the plowing land was on the other side of the road."

And they stumbled a few times, closing in. The wind was coming up, not howling, exactly, but strong, and gusting. There were lights at the house—night-lights, Virgil thought—and a bright sodium vapor light above the loft door on the barn, and another on a pole in front of the machine shed. The pole light shook and trembled in the wind. They found a spot, a hundred yards out, in a cluster of thistles, and sat and watched, fifteen minutes, twenty minutes, half an hour. Nothing changed in the houses or outbuildings.

Then the rain came, spattering through the weeds, and they could hear the change in pitch when the main front hit the road in front of Feur's place, another note when it hit the steel buildings, and a few seconds later, it was on them. A minute after that, a second-floor light came on in the farmhouse, and then another, the second one from a small window directly below the peak of the house. "Taking a leak," Virgil said to Stryker. Another minute, and the bathroom light went out, then the other. Back in bed.

The rain was beating on them now and they sat on their feet, heads down, hands in their side pockets, dry, but not especially warm. Another half hour, and then Stryker nudged Virgil and said, "Might not be a bad time to look at the machine shed."

"Lead the way."

They crawled and duckwalked in, moving quickly between lightning strikes, freezing with every flash. Five minutes after they left their watch post, they came up behind the machine shed. At the side door, Virgil tried the knob. Locked: no give at all. They put their heads together to block as much light as they could, waited for a lightning flash, and then Stryker hit the button on the penlight.

And Virgil said, "Uh-oh." Medeco locks, and almost new. "I didn't even know you could get these things out here."

"What?"

"Medecos. Look at this door," Virgil said. "This thing has got some heft to it; steel, I think."

"We're not getting in?"

"We're not getting in," Virgil said.

"So . . ."

"So let's go sit some more."

THEY MOVED BACK, slowly, a little of the stress leaking away; they couldn't find their original spot, but found another just as wet. "So they got steel doors and great locks. That makes it a little more interesting," Stryker said. Twenty minutes later, sputtering in the rain, he said, "I'm starting to feel like an asshole."

Another twenty minutes, and the main slab of thunderstorm had passed, and the wind had shifted, and they were able to sit with their backs to it.

Stryker said, "We knew it'd probably be a waste of time."

"Yeah, but after you come out here . . . you kinda expect something to happen, because you made the effort."

"Don't work that way, grasshopper," Stryker said.

"Sun comes up at five-thirty, more or less," Virgil said.

"We should be out of here twenty minutes before that."

Virgil looked at his watch: "Not yet three."

"So we sit for two hours. Maybe get some sleep."

"Not gonna sleep out here . . ."

THE RAIN STOPPED, the wind dropped, and the lightning rolled away to the east. Virgil had given up hope of getting anything useful when he saw headlights bouncing

up the road to the south. As far as he knew, Feur's was the
only place out this way. He nudged Stryker, who was head
down, and maybe sleeping. Stryker's head popped up. He
saw the lights and said, "Who's this?"

"Early riser," Virgil said.

They were both stiff, and they stood up, their bodies
obscured by weeds even if somebody had night-vision gog-
gles, and stretched, and watched as a pickup truck slowed,
pulled into Feur's yard, and then slowly backed up to the
machine shed.

The driver got out and walked over to the house, skirt-
ing a puddle in the middle of the drive, and then stood on
the porch, waiting. Lights came up, and a minute later, the
driver was let into the house. "Let's go see who it is,"
Stryker said.

Back through the weeds, on their knees, and duckwalking,
down to the back of the machine shed, then up along the
side. The driver had parked only a couple of feet from
the main door.

"Take a chance?" Virgil asked.

"The lights are on the other side of the house . . . I think
they'd be paying attention over there."

"Cover me, then."

Stryker snuggled down with the machine gun, and
Virgil crawled along the ground next to the door, behind
the truck. Missouri plates. He heard a rattling, and froze.
Nothing. He fumbled in his pocket, found a pen, wrote the
number in the palm of his hand, and then again on his fore-
arm.

He was about to start back when a thought occurred to him. He'd just rewired the lights on his trailer connection, and if this Dodge was anything like his truck . . .

He groped around for a minute, then risked a quick flash with his light, well under the truck bed. Spotted the wires, got a grip on them, and hung on them, all of his weight, yanking until something came free. He risked another flash—hell, the first one had worked—and saw raw copper on two wires.

That should do it, he thought.

Then the dog barked. Once.

A FUCKIN' DOG in the truck. And not a small one.

He said aloud, "I'm coming," and he scuttled back across the face of the building into the dark beside Stryker, and the dog barked again, several times.

"What the hell was that all about?" Stryker whispered, as they duckwalked away. The dog started barking again, but the sound was muffled by the truck cab, and nobody came out of the house. Fifty yards out, they were on their feet, hunched over, and then a hundred yards out, they were upright and moving away. They found their nest, and settled into it.

"Wires," Virgil said. "Whenever we find out who this guy is . . . why, I'm afraid he'll have a moving violation. If we need it."

"A moving violation?" Stryker asked.

"I yanked the wires on a tail-light," Virgil said.

"That'll go on his permanent record," Stryker said.

"Yes, it will."

"When that dog . . . You owe me money for a laundry bill."

NOTHING MORE HAPPENED at the house for half an hour, when the door opened, and three men, one of them Feur, came out, looked around, and then crossed the yard to the machine shed. They were inside for ten minutes, then came out carrying four five-gallon metal gas cans. They loaded them carefully in the truck's camper, moved some things around in the interior of the camper, went back inside the shed, got four more cans. They closed the doors on the camper, talked for a few minutes, and then the driver got back in the truck, waved, and pulled out. The left rear taillight was out.

"Let's go," Stryker said.

They eased away in the dark, and two hundred yards out, tried to cross to the road. Stryker got tangled in the fence and ripped his coat, said, "Damnit, I just bought it this spring," and then they were on the road, jogging. The moon, on its way down, broke through the ragged clouds on the back edge of the squall line, and helped them along.

"We're there," Stryker said, his face a pale oval in the light from his GPS. They cut across the ditch back into the dark, risked a couple of flashes, got the truck, pulled around in a circle, and bumped back onto the road.

"Let's go talk to the computer," he said. "See where this guy is coming from."

"Two possibilities," Virgil said. "The gas cans have something in them besides gas. Maybe, in addition to gas. Get some plastic chemistry flasks, slip them down in there, fill it the rest of the way with gasoline."

"The other possibility . . ." Stryker reached overhead and started pulling gaffer tapes off the internal lights.

"The other possibility is that there really is gas in the cans, but our guy couldn't stop because he couldn't risk being seen. A guy on the run, or being really careful."

"Careful about what?"

"Say he's the shooter," Virgil said. "Coming in from someplace else—Kansas City, most likely, with the Missouri plates. You could get a pretty damn good shooter in Kansas City. So he fills it up just before he leaves town, drives up here, does the job, picks up an extra twenty gallons, and that'll get him all the way back. Never stops at a gas station, nobody ever sees him. He's not on any security tapes . . . How far could you go with a full tank and forty gallons?"

They both thought awhile, and then Stryker said, "At least to Kansas City."

"But then," Virgil asked, "why didn't they just put it in the tank here? Fifteen gallons, anyway."

Stryker said, "There's something else in the cans, Virgil."

"That would be my thought," Virgil said.

Another two miles: "Unless he's just picking up some lawn mower gas," Stryker said.

THERE WAS LIGHT in the east when they pulled into the courthouse. Stryker led the way into the office, where a dispatcher lifted a hand inside his Plexiglas cage and Stryker got on a computer and ran the Missouri plates. They had a return in ten seconds: Dale Donald Evans of Birmingham, Missouri. Birmingham was just outside Kansas City. With his name and birth date, they ran Evans through the NCIC, and came up with six hits.

"Burglary, burglary, burglary, assault, theft, assault. Done two, three, five years, total, all in Missouri," Stryker said.

"Thought they gave you the first three burglaries for free," Virgil said.

"Not in Missouri, apparently. Or maybe he stole something big."

"Or from *somebody* big." Virgil tapped the screen. "You know what he is? He's a trusted small-timer. Did his time, kept his mouth shut. So now, he's a driver. Run up to Minnesota, pick up a load, a few beat-up cans of gas mixed up with some firewood and a chain saw and maybe a generator and some tools . . . nobody gives him a second look."

Stryker leaned back in his chair: "I could use some recommendations, about what to do about all of this."

"We need to take a meeting," Virgil said.

DAVENPORT GROANED into the phone: "Virgil, god-damnit . . ."

"Get your big white ass out of bed and call the DEA," Virgil said. "I need to talk to one of their serious guys, like right now."

"You got something?"

"Biggest meth lab in the history of big meth labs," Virgil said. "Maybe."

He could hear Davenport yawning. "Okay. I can call a guy. But is there some reason that you're calling me at five-thirty in the morning?"

"Yeah. About forty gallons of meth is driving down to Kansas City. We need to get somebody on it, and we figure the feds are as good as anyone."

A DEA AGENT called back twenty minutes later. With Stryker sitting across from him, Virgil gave the agent a précis of the investigation, the killings, the ethanol plant, and what they thought. The DEA man, whose name was Ronald Pirelli, and who said that he was in Chicago, said, "Sit there, at that telephone."

Ten minutes later another DEA man called and said, "Can you brief a team in Mankato in four hours?"

"We could do that," Virgil said. "Why Mankato?"

"Because it's almost halfway between here and there. Ten o'clock at the Days Inn."

"We could be there in two hours," Virgil said.

"Got the big guy flying in from Chicago," the DEA man said. "He can't make it before ten."

VIRGIL HUNG UP and said to Stryker, "We started a prairie fire, boy. You're gonna be a hero."

"Either that, or I'll be a farmer again," Stryker said. But he looked happy enough. "Rather leave that to Joanie, tell you the truth."

Virgil retrieved his car from Stryker's house, drove back to the Holiday Inn, tried to catch an hour's sleep, and failed. Instead, he got caught in a recursive semiwaking dream involving dogs and running in the rain. At seven-thirty, he got up, found a good, clean, conservative Modest Mouse T-shirt, took a shower, and went and got Stryker.

Stryker was wearing a necktie. He looked at Virgil's shirt and said, "That's nothing but cold, deliberate insolence."

On their way to Mankato, the accountant called on Virgil's cell phone: "When can we get together?"

"We've been called to a meeting up in Mankato; we'll be back this afternoon. You got something?"

"A headache and a big bill. And, I have to say, our friend is in worse shape than we thought. I can't prove it, because it doesn't have anything to do with numbers, but he has extra money coming in. Quite a bit of it. I'm going to bed. Call me when you get back."

"Be careful. Keep your mouth shut," Virgil told her.

THE GUY from Chicago was Ronald Pirelli, who'd called that morning. He was a short, dark man wearing a black linen jacket, black slacks, a French-blue shirt, and six-hundred-dollar sunglasses. He had three other agents with him, all casually dressed, and all with the wary look of the DEA.

FBI agents, Virgil thought, usually looked sleek. DEA guys usually looked like they'd just driven a Jeep back from Nogales, with the windows down.

Pirelli had arrived a couple of minutes before Virgil and Stryker. They followed him down to the room rented by another of the agents, and they all introduced themselves and Pirelli asked Virgil, "What's with the T-shirt?"

Virgil said, "I thought my Sheryl Crow shirt might piss you off."

"Hey . . ."

Pirelli was affable, the other agents skeptical, watching Stryker carefully, and Virgil even more carefully: One of them said, "You've got kind of a weird reputation, dude. Everybody in Minneapolis calls you 'that fuckin' Flowers.'"

Stryker laughed and said, "You wanna know something? He's been seeing my sister, and just the other night, honest to God—she's a farmer; she's got no contact with Minneapolis—I asked her what she was doing, and she said, 'Goin' out with that fuckin' Flowers.'"

The agents all laughed, and the skepticism receded a little, and Pirelli said, "Give us what you've got."

WHAT THEY HAD was mostly conjecture, with a few names and background. They sketched in the story of the Jerusalem artichoke scam, and the general belief that Bill Judd Sr. had a hidden account somewhere. That Judd Jr. was in desperate financial straits, and the death of his father would make them worse, not better. That Junior might be embezzling from the hidden fund.

"Why didn't he just keep that money, instead of doing this ethanol thing?" Pirelli asked.

"Maybe a couple of reasons," Virgil said. "First, there might not have been enough money left in the account— not enough to take care of all his debts and provide him with some security. He's getting to be an older guy. Second, it's coming out of a bank account, somewhere. There'll be a paper trail. It's not that easy to do things in cash anymore . . . people want checks and wire transfers and financial controls. The way they did it, it looks like old man Judd put up some starter cash for an ethanol plant. They actually make some ethanol, and sell it, probably, but we think they're also running this little chemical factory on the side."

"I wouldn't be surprised if they own some land around the plant, to grow corn for processing," Stryker said. "Then they'd be on the up-and-up ordering all the chemicals they'd need. The smell of the meth processing could be passed off as just another stink from the ethanol plant."

"But basically, there's no indication whatsoever that this

ethanol plant has anything to do with meth," one of the agents said.

"I suppose that depends on how imaginative you are," Virgil said. "We've got a bunch of dead people. We've got a nutcase preacher who's tied to the Corps. We've got a guy desperate for cash. We've got them buying anhydrous ammonia by the tanker truck, and they're making alcohol by the tanker truck, and we've got hard guys coming and going in the night, with five-gallon cans of gas. These are the same guys who could act as a collecting system for the hard-to-get chemicals. You get one dumb-ass driving around a metro area buying a package of diet pills at every possible store, and you can get pounds of the stuff every day. You get ten dumb-asses driving around doing it, in ten different metro areas, and you can get a ton of it in a week. We know that they're connected into a distribution system, through the Corps. That could also be a collection system for the other stuff they need. I mean, maybe they're selling the ethanol as moonshine at five dollars a quart; but I doubt it."

"So if these are small-town guys, how does he afford an ethanol plant?" another agent asked.

"You ever seen one?" Stryker asked. "Ethanol plant?"

The DEA guy shook his head. "Not that I know of."

"There are some ethanol plants that look like grain elevators. In fact, most of them do. And the newest ones look like little refineries. But some of the older ones, going three-four-five years back, look like a big garage. Basically, an ethanol plant is a still. What they're making is moonshine; that's all it is."

Pirelli said, "For the past two years, there's been an ocean of crank flooding the area between the Mississippi River and the Rockies. Most of it's going down to Dallas–Fort Worth, San Antonio, Houston. Heavy stuff, pure white, not that brown stuff you see out of coffeepots. We've been going crazy trying to find the source. One possibility we have is that it has something to do with the Corps. The guys who are dealing more than a few ounces are all tied in."

"What about Dale Donald Evans?" Stryker asked. "He ought to be home by now."

Pirelli's eyebrows went up. He took a cell phone from his pocket, scrolled, and punched. A minute later he asked, "Get him?" He listened, and then said, "Stay just like that. He didn't take the gas cans out of the truck?" He listened some more and then said, "Call me."

To Stryker: "He got home forty-five minutes ago. Doesn't have a garage. Parked the truck."

"He's got a bad tail-light," Virgil said. "You could stop him on a violation, have the cop check the gas cans . . . It's a little thin, but it'd hold."

"Lucky thing about the tail-light," one of the agents said.

WHEN THEY WERE DONE with the briefing, Pirelli said, "Okay. What we'd really like is, for you two to take the day off. Enjoy your Saturday afternoon, enjoy your Sunday. I'll call you Monday. Or Tuesday."

"Monday," Virgil said.

"Or Tuesday. There's this Sioux Indian guy about to drift into Madison, South Dakota, where his car is gonna break down. He'll be there for a while, watching that plant, talking with the locals. In the meantime, we're gonna be on Dale Donald Evans like yellow on a Chinaman. If this turns out to be what you think it is, we'll give you a call. We appreciate the help of local authorities, and when we take down the Reverend Feur, you'll be right there with us."

Stryker slapped his thighs, and said, "Sounds like a deal." To Virgil, "Sound like a deal to you?"

Virgil said, "Okay with me, if it's okay with everybody."

One of the agents said to Virgil, "You know, Modest Mouse music is really sorta *gay*."

15

ON THE WAY back to Bluestem, Virgil said to Stryker, "I don't want to bring you down, but I don't think Feur killed Schmidt or the Gleasons. Might have killed Judd, using the Gleasons as cover."

"That brings me down," Stryker said.

"Thing is, the Gleasons and the Schmidts . . . that has the smell of craziness about it."

Stryker: "Let me share something with you, Virgil: George Feur is pure, one hundred percent, grade-A high-test bat shit."

"In the wrong way," Virgil said. "If we're right about him, if they've been pumping meth out of that ethanol plant, then you've got a guy who believes in organization and networks and conspiracies. He sets up cover companies. He raises start-up funding. The guy who killed the Gleasons, and the Schmidts . . . this guy believes in chaos and oblivion. He believes he's the only real soul in an ocean of puppets."

"Ah, fuck." Stryker peered out his side window, watching the summer go by. "Ah, fuck me."

"Speaking of fuckin' you, how are things on the Jesse front?"

"Shut up."

THEY WENT STRAIGHT to the house of Chris Olafson, the accountant. Stryker banged on the door off and on for three or four minutes, before she finally came to the door in a dressing robe. "Come in. I'd just finally gotten to sleep."

"We haven't been to sleep yet," Stryker said. "What'd you find?"

She shook her head: "Junior's goose is cooked."

"How cooked?"

"Very cooked."

Junior had gotten all the tax-free gifts he was entitled to, some two million dollars. That meant the total estate was taxable. But the total estate was less than anyone had expected, at a little more than six million, and that included "assets" of two million in loans to Junior.

"The state and federal government are going to want roughly four million. That means that Junior won't get anything. He just won't have to pay off the loans. But the fact is, if Jesse Laymon is entitled to half of the estate, Junior is going to owe her a million. If you look at his earnings from the Subways at face value, he might just be able to do it. However . . ."

"However . . ." Stryker repeated.

"If you look at the tax returns, everything seems okay. But I know the kind of money you make from a fast-food place, because I do all the McDonald's and Burger Kings and Arby's around here. A Subway does *not* do a McDonald's business, but Junior's places do, according to his tax returns. They are selling sandwiches as fast as they can make them—which is strange, because if you go into one of Junior's stores, there's hardly anyone in there."

Virgil said, "He's reporting more than he's earning?"

"Yes. I think so. He's piping in money from somewhere else, running it through the Subways, paying taxes on it—and then it's clean. He's running a money laundry."

"Ah," Stryker said.

"The downside of that is . . ." She hesitated, and then peered over the top of her glasses at Stryker. "The downside is, your friend Jesse Laymon could make a claim for half of the loan assets—half of the Subway franchises—and then find out that there's nothing there. The most successful Subways in Minnesota suddenly can't sell a sandwich."

"So he's broke?"

"Not as long as he keeps running those Subways. But without the extra money . . . he's in trouble."

"Is he sticking it someplace? Like his old man?"

"Can't tell you that," she said. "But I can tell you, he owes taxes and penalties on all his illegal earnings, so after the IRS gets finished with him . . ." She shrugged.

VIRGIL SAID, "Chris, I want all the paper back. I don't want you to mention to anybody that you talked to us. I don't think you're in danger, but I can't promise that you're not. Some people have probably seen us come in here . . ."

". . . I'm sure."

". . . so word will get around town. You want to be very careful for the next couple of days."

"Then what?"

"Then we'll see," Virgil said, grinning at her.

AS THEY were leaving, Virgil asked her, "You mentioned Jim's friend Jesse Laymon. Would you have any more specifics on that friendship?"

She shrugged and smiled at Stryker. "Word was, you were seen heading up toward the dell."

Stryker said, "I'm moving to California."

"She's a very pretty girl," Olafson said. "Too bad about her inheritance."

AT THE COURTHOUSE, Stryker got out of the truck and said, "I'm running out of gas. Too old for this overnight shit."

"Yeah, I'm gonna take a nap," Virgil said. "Gotta call Joanie. Maybe you should call Jesse, the four of us could go out somewhere."

Stryker yawned. "I'll ask Jesse. Give me a call when you get up, but not too early. Like, six-thirty or seven."

JOAN'S CELL PHONE kicked over to the message service. Virgil said, "I'm just going to bed. Jim and I were talking, maybe the four of us could go out tonight, later on . . ."

He took a while going to sleep; went down deep when he did. His cell phone rang five times before he realized what it was. By the time he got to it, it'd stopped ringing. He punched up the number: didn't recognize it, but it was from the Twin Cities. He redialed, and Shrake came up.

"Hey, Flowers. It's me and Jenkins. We're looking at your old guys. You want us to run them in?"

"Jeez, Shrake, where are you?"

"In their living room. Their daughter's living room," Shrake said. "You want us to take her, too?"

"Shrake, what are you doing? Where are you?"

"Okay, then," Shrake said. "We'll leave her. I don't think she'd last too long with all the muffin crunchers down at Ramsey."

"They can hear you," Virgil said. "You're scaring them, right?"

"You got that right," Shrake said, and he laughed.

Virgil said, "Okay. You tell them to glue their asses to the couch and I'll be there in four hours. Tell them if they go anywhere, I honest to God . . . Wait. Let me talk to them. Let me talk to Gerald."

A moment later, Gerald came on the line, and Virgil said, "Gerald, you motherfucker. You know something about that picture. I'm going to put your ass in jail and your wife's ass in jail, for murder, if I don't find out what it is. You sit there: I'm leaving Bluestem right now and I'll be there in four hours. Now: gimme Shrake."

Shrake came back up and said, "Yeah?"

"Take the rest of the day off," Virgil said.

"It's Saturday, dickweed. This was my day off."

"Then take tomorrow off, too. I don't think Gerald's going anywhere. Gimme the address. The daughter's name is, what, Jones?"

"Cornelia Jones, that's correct. DOB six eighteen forty-seven. We're at her house in Apple Valley, get off at Cliff Road . . ."

VIRGIL HAD grille-mounted LED flashers on the 4Runner, and a removable roof-mount flasher that plugged into his cigarette lighter. He'd never used them for criminal inquiries, but occasionally did use them when he felt like driving fast.

He called the highway patrol district office in Marshall, told them that he was making an emergency run back to the Cities east on I-90 and north on I-35, as part of a murder investigation, and asked them to advise the other districts; and told them that he'd be using the flashers.

He got Joanie as he left town. "I didn't think you'd be up yet . . ." she began.

"I'm heading for the Cities in a hurry," Virgil said. "Back tomorrow, I hope."

"What happened?"

"Got the Johnstones and they know some shit. Tell Jim when he gets up—he'll be getting up in an hour or so."

"I will. Be safe, Virgil."

THE 4 RUNNER would do an honest ninety, but at one hundred, it was breathing hard, and starting to move around the road. Virgil backed off to ninety-eight, put it on cruise control, turned on some music, and made it into the south end of the Cities in two and a half hours, got off at the main Apple Valley exit, drove in circles for a while, finally cut Roan Stallion Lane, which was half a block long, and pulled up in the driveway of Cornelia Jones.

The house was suburban-comfortable; its distinguishing characteristic was that the lawn was essentially a field of hosta plants. Thousands of them, like a midget army from *Invasion of the Body Snatchers*.

VIRGIL DRAGGED a rocking chair halfway across the living room so that he could plant his face a foot from Gerald Johnstone's, and said, "Gerald, you are a bad man. You are covering up for a guy who's murdered at least five people. You were lying to me the other day and I knew it and now you've dragged your wife and daughter into it. This is a criminal conspiracy."

Gerald started to blubber, which wasn't attractive in an elderly man. Carol Johnstone patted his thigh and said, "Tell him, Jerry, tell him, and it'll be all right."

The daughter, a stolid woman with a skeptical look on her face, said, "Maybe we ought to get a lawyer. We don't know what we're doing here."

Virgil didn't want any of that, and said to her: "You can call a lawyer. Then we'll all go down to jail, and I'll have them booked for obstruction of justice and abetting a murder after the fact, and you can put up your house as bail, to get them out. Now: I need the information. I'll get it one way or another, but if we screw around for three days and somebody else is murdered while Jerry sits on the information I need to catch the killer, then I'll put his aging ass in prison, and your mother's too, and they'll stay there until they die. All right?"

That got Gerald going again, and Virgil hardened his face, and when Gerald got it under control, he said, "It was the man-on-the-moon party . . ."

Virgil closed his eyes, feeling like he'd just crossed a mountaintop, and said, "Ah, shit. A party, not a man."

ON JULY 20, 1969, the day that Apollo 11 landed the first men on the moon, Johnstone said, Bill Judd Sr. had a party at his house on Buffalo Ridge, to watch the crescent moon come up. The state park had not yet gone in, and the road up to the house was nothing more than a long gravel driveway, coming over the back of the hill, to the back of the house.

The party was right in the heart of the Bill Judd tomcatting days, seven or eight women and four or five men, some of the women local, two or three of them "entertainers" from the Cities.

"I honest to God don't know what happened up there,"

Johnstone said. "All I know is what I heard through the back door. They supposedly had some cocaine, maybe, and plenty of liquor, of course, and were generally up there raising hell. They also had a cookout going.

"So late that night, one of the girls—but maybe not one of the girls, this is what's crazy, because you're not going to get a bunch of guys, you know, having sex relations with a woman who's nine months pregnant. I don't even know if she *could* . . ."

He looked at his wife who said, "It'd be uncomfortable."

Johnstone started to tap-dance. "You hear things, over the years . . . What I'm telling you, could be all wrong . . ."

"Just tell me, Gerald," Virgil said. "I'll sort it out."

"The story was, something happened between this woman and Judd. The other people were out in the yard with a telescope, seeing if they could see the men on the moon. There wasn't any chance, of course, but they had this telescope and they were way up on the ridge and they were drunk . . ."

"Gerald: the pregnant woman."

Johnstone nodded. "So late at night, they're out there, and they see a car that looks like it's come off the driveway. It's going down the hill, away from the party, sort of aimed down this crease in the hillside, and people are going crazy, yelling, they think the woman in it is drunk and lost, and they run down that way . . .

"And damned if she doesn't drive the car right off Buffalo Jump," he said.

"'The bluff.'"

"Right below Judd's house. Supposedly, Indians used to stampede buffalo right off the cliff. So this car goes over the side and people are running around yelling and screaming. Judd comes running out of the house, and then he and a couple of guys jump in a car and they go tearing down the driveway and around to the bottom of the jump . . ."

"And in the meantime, one of the other girls said, 'She's gotta be hurt bad,' so they called the fire department and the fire boys got a rescue truck headed out that way."

"She was killed," Virgil said.

"Yeah, but not right then. She was what we call brain-dead now—she had head injuries, and neck injuries, but her heart was still going when Judd and the other guys pulled her out of the car. Then the fire boys got there and they hauled her over to the hospital. She died in the emergency room, but the doctor . . ."

"Gleason," Virgil said.

Johnstone stared at his daughter for a long time—ten seconds, fifteen—and then he sighed and said, "Yeah. Russell Gleason. Russ delivered the baby. Tough delivery, but the baby lived. There was a story in the paper, called it the 'Miracle Baby.'"

"So why would somebody kill Gleason for delivering the baby?" Virgil asked. "If he was there at the emergency room, he couldn't have been at the party, he had nothing to do with the woman."

"That I can't tell you," Johnstone said. "I can tell you a

rumor, and I can tell you a thought that passed through my mind."

Virgil flicked his fingers at Johnstone, a "gimme" gesture.

Johnstone said, "There was a rumor that the woman hadn't been there for the party. Hadn't been invited. That she came down on her own from the Cities, in her own car, and that she'd been there before the party, and had had a fight with Bill. Bill could be rough as a cob.

"Nobody knows what happened, but there were rumors that he wasn't right there with everybody else when they saw the car rolling down the hill. He came running out of the house a minute or so later. The question was . . . Where was he when the car came off the driveway? Once it came off the driveway, going down that seam in the hill, it was going to go over the bluff. Was the woman committing suicide? Why didn't she turn, or put on the brakes?"

"Or was she dead unconscious when she went in the car?" Virgil asked. "Did somebody else steer it off the driveway?"

Johnstone's head bobbed: "It could have been done. Could have rolled the car down to the seam, let it go, run back over the shoulder of the hill—this was at night, remember—then up and into the house, and then out the front . . ."

"Was there any suggestion of that at the time?" Virgil asked.

Johnstone shook his head. "No."

"Was there an investigation?"

Quick nod.

"Roman Schmidt," Virgil said.

"Yup."

"Jerry, you really messed this up," Virgil said, lying back in the rocker and letting it rock a few times. "God help you if anybody else gets killed in the next couple of days, before I can figure this out." He rocked a few more times, and then remembered: "You said a thought passed through your mind."

"Yeah." Johnstone reached up with both hands and scratched his head above his ears, and then said, "I didn't want to tell you all of this, because I really don't *know* anything. But. I remember when I saw that girl's body, on the dressing table, all bashed up in the accident, cut up in the hospital . . . How'd she get those bruises? Some of the bruises were fresh, but they weren't fifteen *minutes* old. They didn't develop between the time she died and the time she went off Buffalo Jump. They were *hours* old. But the doctor said she died in the accident, the sheriff . . ."

"What happened to the miracle baby?" Virgil asked.

"Adopted out," Johnstone said. "I don't know the details to that. But, the baby was adopted out. Baby boy."

VIRGIL LEFT THEM SCARED: "You stay here. You're at risk, but if it took Shrake and Jenkins a whole day to track you down, I don't think the killer will get you. If you decide you don't want to stay here, if it starts to feel hinky, get out to a motel. You don't have to go far, to be completely lost. If you do that, you let me know. I'll give you my cell phone . . ."

OUT IN HIS CAR, he went through the name file on his computer, called Dr. Joe Klein.

"It's that fuckin' Flowers," Klein said, when he came up. "What do you want?"

"You going out?"

"No. I'm reading Proust, fifty pages a night, all summer," Klein said. "I'm forty-two pages in, on tonight's quota."

"Sounds like a great read, you gotta have a quota," Virgil said. "That's how I read a chemistry book one time."

"Great chatting with you, Virgil," Klein said.

"Just being sociable," Virgil said. "How's the old lady?"

"What do you want?"

"I want to come over to your house and have you look at a photograph," Virgil said.

"Will this be billable?"

"Hell, I don't know. I doubt it."

KLEIN WAS the Hennepin County medical examiner. He gave Virgil directions to his home in Edina, north and west across town, from Apple Valley. Virgil was at his front door in twenty minutes.

Klein's wife, Kate, met him at the door. She was tall, thin, with a sharp nose and gold-rimmed glasses. "Gimme a hug, you big lug," she said.

He did; and she felt kinda good . . .

Klein said, "That's enough of that. What's the picture?"

They took it into his home office. Kate, a pediatrician, looked over their shoulders as Klein inspected it with a magnifying glass. Klein hemmed and hawed a bit, and finally his wife said, "My, God, Joseph, you're not in federal court. Spit it out."

Klein tapped the photo, the woman's rib cage. "Your undertaker is right. If she died in fifteen or twenty minutes, these bruises didn't come from the accident. Besides, I've seen bruises like this before—this is what you get when somebody dies after a bar fight. When somebody gets beat bad with a pool cue, you see this striping effect, if it has time to develop. Say, there's a bar fight, a guy gets beat bad, dies the next day. This is what you see. If he dies right at the scene, you don't see it."

VIRGIL CALLED JOHNSTONE: "Gerald, did you ever go up to Judd's house?"

"Oh, yeah. Several times. I wasn't real popular with him, because I was the mortician and he was sort of superstitious. But I did go a few times."

"Did he have a pool table?"

"Oh, sure. He had everything. Swimming pool, pool room, hot tub . . . he had all that stuff. The joke was, his decorator was *Playboy* magazine."

KATE KLEIN SAID, "Pool room?"

"Yup."

"God, you lead such a neat life," she said. "If only you were a rich doctor, I might have married you."

"You woulda had to get in line," Klein said. "This boy's been married so often he's got rice burns on his face."

16

VIRGIL LEFT THE KLEINS'.

Saturday night, nowhere to go.

He thought about calling Davenport, but he'd been lean-ing on Davenport too hard, and decided to let it go. Instead, he checked into the St. Paul Hotel, put on a fresh pair of jeans, a Flaming Lips T-shirt, buffed up his boots, and headed over to the Minnesota Music Café for a couple of beers.

Bumped into Shrake, who was there with a big-haired sec-retary from the Department of Agriculture; she said she dated him because he had a big gun. Then Shrake wanted to know what happened with the Johnstones, and a couple of St. Paul cops came over, and Virgil danced with a woman who had a butterfly tattoo around her navel. He'd gone back for a third beer when a woman's hand slipped into his back jeans pocket and a familiar voice said, "I'd know that little butt anywhere."

He turned and said, "Goddamn, Jeanie. How've you been?"

She said, "Okay," and to a girlfriend, she said, "This is my first ex-husband, Virgil Flowers. I'm either his second or third ex-wife, I forget which."

"Be nice," Virgil said. He looked her over and she did look okay: prosperous, even. "Still in real estate?"

She rolled her eyes: "Yes. Shouldn't admit it, the way it's fallen out of bed, but . . . nothing like selling a house. Makes me feel good."

So they chatted awhile, and he started remembering some of the better times they'd had, and then she patted him on the chest and said, "Guess what? I might get married again."

"Hey . . . great, man," Virgil said. "Anybody I know?"

"No, no. He's at Wells Fargo, a vice president in the mortgage department. Known him for years."

"And he's available because . . ."

She shrugged. "His marriage broke up. Same old stuff. Everybody works, nobody talks."

"He got kids?" Virgil asked.

"Two; but he'd like a couple more."

"Does he dance?"

She laughed: "Not like you, Virgil. He does, but like a banker."

"Ouch."

Pretty good time, all in all, and he danced with the girl-friend a couple of times, and at one o'clock in the morning, a little drunk, rolled into bed at the hotel, all alone.

Thought about God for a while.

Sunday

NOT EXACTLY HUNGOVER, but a little lonely. He got cleaned up, got breakfast, checked out of the hotel, and drove over to the Historical Society. The library was closed.

He called around, and the duty officer, which was not her title, but what she did, led him to the microfilm machines, and got him the missing roll of microfilm.

He spooled through it, found the paper that came out on July 24, the first one after the man-on-the-moon party, and there it was.

A "miracle baby" was delivered to a twenty-nine-year-old Minneapolis woman moments before she died at the Bluestem Memorial Hospital emergency room Sunday night after an automobile accident on Buffalo Ridge.

Margaret (Maggie) Lane of 604 Washington Avenue, Minneapolis, apparently lost control of her car as she was leaving a "man on the moon" party at the home of William Judd Sr. Witnesses say the car plunged over the Buffalo Jump bluff after leaving the driveway fifty yards below the Judd house.

An autopsy revealed .07 percent blood alcohol, below the legal limit, and Judd said that "Maggie had only a glass of wine or two during the party."

"This is an awful tragedy," Judd said. "She was a warm, interesting woman and nobody ever had a thing bad to say about her."

Stark County sheriff Roman Schmidt said that deputies interviewed all the partygoers, and were satisfied that Lane's death was accidental. "She'd only been to the Judd house a couple of times. She wasn't legally drunk, but she may have had enough that she became confused as she was leaving, and turned the wrong way as she came over the shoulder of the hill," Schmidt said.

*A witness called the volunteer fire department, and a
rescue squad reached the car within ten minutes. Lane was
taken to the emergency room, where Dr. Russell Gleason delivered a healthy 7-pound, 4-ounce full-term baby even as the
boy's mother was dying of extensive and what Gleason called
"surely fatal" brain injuries.*

*The baby will be remanded to the care of Minnesota child-
protective services . . .*

There was one bad photograph of the wrecked car sitting at the base of the bluff. The picture had been taken
with a flash of some kind—were flashbulbs still used by
news photographers in 1969? There were a few white faces
in the background, unrecognizable, and three cops close to
the car. One of them was a young Big Curly.

THE NEXT PAPER came out on July 31, and oddly, Virgil
thought, there was no mention of the Miracle Baby. Not a
single word. In his hometown, he thought, there would
have been recurring stories for a month.

He went to the dailies at Worthington and Sioux Falls,
and found stories similar to that from the *Bluestem Record*.
But the dailies were farther away, and the death happened
the same day of the first manned landing on the moon,
and so was tucked away in the back of the papers.

He thought about it for a while, then called Stryker,
and told him about the story. "You know, I've never heard
that," Stryker said. "You would have thought I'd have

heard it. I mean, it'd be something that people talked about."

"Got drowned out by the noise from the moon landing," Virgil said. "So go over to the hospital, and find out what happened to the kid. I mean, kick somebody's ass off the golf course, and find out where he went."

"I'll do that."

VIRGIL HUNG OUT at the Historical Society for a while, looking at an exhibit on early photography, all those Civil War guys with white eyes and stolid faces. Stryker called back: "Nothing there. I mean, there's something there, but it's nothing. The child was turned over to protective services on August second. That's it. You'll have to work it from that end."

"And it's Sunday."

Stryker: "Wonder what's happening with the DEA?"

"That's what I'm wondering. If I stay up here, and it goes down tomorrow, I could miss it."

"Well . . . get the research chick to work it," Stryker suggested. "Get back here. I've been thinking about it, and it's all Feur. No mystery, no weirdness. Just Feur."

"Give me the logic," Virgil said.

"We've got a series of huge crimes, murders," Stryker said. "Then we find out there's a professional criminal, right in our backyard, selling dope all over the country, and he's been doing it for years. Back at the beginning, he needed seed money to get started, and he needed a way to hide the operation. That's about the time all these little farmer-sponsored ethanol plants were popping up. This crime we know about, with Feur, involves some of the same people involved in the others: the Judds. I don't know how you tie the Gleasons in, but I could see a reason for Roman Schmidt: Schmidt was monitoring the cops through the Curlys. The Curlys might not even have known about the rest of it. You say Schmidt was willing to cover up a murder, take money for it. When you've done it once, you'll do it again. In fact, the Judds might even have pulled him into it."

"I don't know," Virgil said. "If somebody had to kill the Gleasons, they could have done it in a quiet way. Kill them, but don't pose them. Try to make it look like a murder-suicide. Something . . . But the way it was done, was nuts."

"Got your head up your ass, Virgil. It's Feur."

Virgil scratched his nose, made the call: "I'm coming back."

HE WAS BACK by five o'clock, having stopped in Mankato to check his mail, pay bills, and run a load of laundry through the washer and dryer. Before he left home, he went into his closet and took out his third-most-favorite deer rifle, a Browning Lightweight Stalker semiauto in .30-06, an extra magazine, and a box of cartridges. The rifle wasn't as accurate as his best bolt action, but it was as accurate as he was, and could put some heavy metal on a target in a big hurry.

Heading west, into the sun, he could feel some kind of climax just over the horizon: too many things going on, not to have something shake loose.

THAT NIGHT, they went out to Barnet's Supper Club in Sioux Falls, five of them—Stryker and Jesse Laymon, Virgil and Joan, and Laura Stryker. There was one tough moment on the way over, when Laura told Jesse that she should get Stryker to take her up swimming at the dell some hot night.

Jesse giggled and admitted that they'd already been. Then Joan and Virgil had to spontaneously join in teasing Stryker, and they pulled it off. And then the three women began working on Virgil and Stryker. Something was up with the case, they knew, but Virgil and Stryker weren't talking.

Later that evening, Virgil was looking at the jukebox when Laura Stryker came by, on the way back to their table from the women's room, and she stopped and asked, "Are you and Joanie going to get serious? You look like it."

"Not that serious," Virgil said. "She gave me a little talk. I'm not husband material. I'm her transition guy."

"Damn it. I need a grandchild," Laura said. "I want to be around long enough that my grandchild can remember his grandmother."

"You've got a few years," Virgil said.

"*I've* got enough years to be a *great-grandmother,*" Laura said. "But one side of the family stops when Joan's clock runs out. I think Jim and Jesse . . . I think I've got something going there."

They both turned and looked at Joan, who was leaning across their table, making a point to Stryker and Jesse. "She'll be okay," Virgil said. "I'm her transition guy, but I wouldn't be surprised if she has somebody picked out, on the other side of the transition zone."

"I hope so," Laura said, "or I'd suggest that you go ahead and knock her up."

Before they left, Virgil went out in the parking lot and called Sandy, Davenport's researcher, who'd just gotten back from a weekend trip. "Goddamnit, honey, you picked a bad time to go away. I need you to get some stuff for me tomorrow morning, and I need you to rain fire and brimstone on anybody who stands in your way. A woman named Margaret Lane, also known as Maggie, was killed in an auto accident on July 20, 1969 . . ."

He gave her the rest of the details and said, "Find that kid."

Monday

VIRGIL WOKE UP in Joan's bed. She was lying flat on her back, her head cocked off to one side, and a less charitable man might have said that she was snoring, if only softly. She was wearing a T-shirt as a nightgown and had pushed down the sheet. He pulled it up to her chin, then slipped out of his side of the bed, yawned, stretched, did some sit-ups and push-ups, as quietly as he could, then got his clothes and walked naked down the hall to the bathroom. He used her toothpaste, which was a cinnamon-flavored gel, and scrubbed his teeth with his index finger. When he came back down the hall, pulling yesterday's shirt over his head, she cracked her eyes and said, "I'm not getting up yet."

"That's okay." He looked at his watch. "Seven forty-five. I'm heading back to the motel. Call you later?"

"Call me later," she said, and closed her eyes and snuggled into the bed. He pulled on his boots, lifted the sheet, looked at her ass, said, "Masterpiece," and went on out the door. A neighbor was fooling with his sprinkler system, and when Virgil came off her porch, he raised a hand and called, "How're ya doin' Virgil?"

"Doin' good," Virgil said.

"I bet you are," the neighbor said, with cheerful, barefaced envy.

AT THE MOTEL he cleaned up, chose a Decemberists T-shirt, which he saved for days that he felt might be decisive, and called Sandy.

"Jeez, Virgil, I hardly got started. The baby was processed through the Good Hope adoption service, which seems like it might not exist anymore. I'm trying to find out what happened to their records. I'm also working it the other way, through child-protective services."

"Call me the minute you get anything: I want to know every step of the way."

She called back in ten minutes, as Virgil was sitting in the restaurant, eating pancakes and link sausage. "I've got something, but it's not specific yet."

"What is it?"

"It's the list of child-protective-service adoption actions through the district court. I can't get the files themselves, without jumping through my butt—which I'm willing to do, but there are dozens of them, and I've only got one butt."

Virgil was shocked: "Sandy, you don't talk that way."

"I'm a little cranky this morning," she said. "Anyway, what I can get, without permission, is the file headers, which I can pull up on my computer. These are the names of the adoptive parents. They're organized by year, and there are . . . let me see . . . about a hundred and seventy files for 1969. If the adoptions are randomly distributed through the year, and I don't see why they wouldn't be, the adoption of Baby Boy Lane would have taken place in the last half of the year, and probably the last four or five months. I can read the names of the eighty-five adoptive couples and see if anything rings a bell."

"Can you get the file afterward?" Virgil asked.

"We might need to do some legal stuff, but I can get Lucas to do that," she said.

"Read the names . . ."

She started, "Gregory, Nelson, Snyder . . ." He stopped her when she said, "Williamson . . ."

"Williamson?"

"Williamson, David and Louise."

"You gotta be kidding me," Virgil said.

"Yank the file?"

"Yank the file. Call me as soon as you get it."

VIRGIL BLEW PAST Stryker's sullen secretary into his office, shut the door, and leaned across Stryker's desk, Stryker's mouth open, and asked, "What do you know about Todd Williamson?"

Stryker said, "Todd? Came here three years ago, pisses me off, sometimes . . . What're we talking about?"

"He's the Miracle Baby. And after thinking about it, thinking about what Judd's sister-in-law said, about looking at him in the middle of his face . . . I think he might be Judd's natural son. From his eyebrows to his lips, he looks like a Judd."

"Oh . . ." Stryker held his hands up in the air, *what next?* "Jeez."

"Something else occurred to me. He's the dog that didn't bark," Virgil said.

"What?"

"He's at every crime scene—he knows everything. But I didn't see him at the Judd fire. Where the hell was he? The fire trucks went out there with their sirens screaming, where was Williamson?"

Stryker said, "I don't know. Maybe . . . running away from it?"

Virgil nodded: "He's the guy. Bet you a dollar."

THEY WERE TALKING to the judge about a search warrant when Sandy called again: "Lucas screamed at a man at CPS and they won't cough the file without a court order, but the guy confirmed off the record that the kid was Baby Boy Lane."

"I will kiss you on the lips next time I'm up there," Virgil said.

"I'll look forward to it," she said, primly.

THE JUDGE SUGGESTED that there was little evidence to support a search warrant.

Stryker said, "Randy, goddamnit, don't dog us around with some pissant evidence bullshit. It's about fifty percent that Todd is the killer and he's gonna do it again. I want to get all over him before he has a chance."

"What if you don't find anything? He's gonna sue your pants off," the judge said.

"Not my pants, the county's pants," Stryker said. "If I don't solve this case pretty damn quick, I'm gonna lose my job anyway, so why should I care? Sign the warrant."

"Okay, okay, keep your shirt on."

Outside the judge's office, warrant in hand, Virgil said, "Your judicial efficiency is a marvel."

"Out here, you take care of yourself," Stryker said.

They brought in Larry Jensen, the investigator, and four other deputies. Stryker and two of the deputies took the newspaper office. Virgil, Jensen, and two more deputies headed for Williamson's home. "Call me every five minutes, tell me what you got," Stryker said. "Find a .357."

"Find a typewriter," Virgil said.

WILLIAMSON LIVED in a square, flat, single-story white house with a flat-roofed garage set farther back, and a long screen porch on the front, in an old neighborhood on the east side of town. From Williamson's house, Virgil thought, getting to the Gleasons' would have been a snap: Williamson was two blocks from the riverbank.

In the heavy rain the night of the murders, he could have walked over to the bridge across the river, off the far end of the bridge, along the riverbank, and up the slope to Gleason's. After the killings, he could be back home in fifteen minutes. No muss, no fuss, no cars in the night. And that, he thought, was why the killings may have taken place during a thunderstorm. The neighbors wouldn't be out, everybody would have been snuggled up in front of the TV.

Virgil drove over, alone in his truck, because he'd learned that if he went to a crime scene in somebody else's vehicle, he'd need to leave before they did, or after they did. Jensen and the other two cops followed in two sheriff's patrol cars. Virgil stopped in front of the house, and the deputies pulled into the driveway, one car going all the way to the garage, to cover the back door.

They got out, watching the doors, Virgil with a hand on his weapon, Jensen with a hand on his own. The screen door was open and he and Jensen went through, hammered on the front door. No answer. Tried the door: locked.

Jensen said, "Wait one." He went out to his car, brought back a long-shaft Maglite, and used the butt end to knock out a pane of glass in the door. Reaching through, he flipped the lock. "We're in."

THEY CLEARED the place, making sure that Williamson wasn't inside, then started pulling it apart. The furniture was comfortable, but old, as if it had come from a high-end used-furniture place. There were six rooms, all on the first floor: kitchen, small dining room, living room, good-sized bath, a bedroom used as a home office, and the actual bedroom. Exterior doors leading out through the kitchen to the garage; and out the front.

Virgil took the bedroom, Jensen took the office, one of the other deputies did the kitchen. Virgil opened and emptied all the drawers, worked through the closet, checking all the pockets in all the clothes, checked the walls and baseboards for hidey-holes, plugged a lamp into the outlets to make sure they were real, turned and patted the mattress, lifted and turned the box springs, lifted the braided rug.

The only thing he found of even the remotest interest was a half-dozen vintage *Penthouse* magazines, featuring well-thumbed hard-core porn, stashed under the corner of the bed, within easy reach.

Jensen was hung up in the office. "Lot of paper," he said, looking up from the office chair, his lap full of files. "So far, nothing about being adopted. Got job stuff; he was in the Army in Iraq in ninety, in supply . . . No guns at all."

The cop in the kitchen had come up empty, and had then gone out to the garage, gotten a stepladder, and now had his head poked through a hatch that led into a space under the roof. "Lots of insulation," he said. "Lots of dust. Doesn't look like it's been opened in years . . ."

Virgil was working through the living room—found another stash of porn, this on video, behind the DVD player—when he heard the deputy outside calling, "Hey, hey, Todd. Hold it, Todd."

Virgil drew his pistol, felt Jensen moving in the office, and then Williamson came through the screen door and the front door on the run. Virgil, from the corner of his eye, could see through the porch screen that Williamson's car had been dumped in the street, the door still open.

Williamson's hands were empty but he was screaming and came straight at Virgil, and Virgil pushed the weapon back into the holster and when Williamson kept coming, hands up, he took one wrist and turned him, pushed him, and Jensen was there to push him again, and the other cop came in from the kitchen, and the outside deputy ran in the front door, his pistol drawn, and Virgil turned to Williamson and Virgil was shouting, "Hands over head, hands on the wall, on the wall."

Williamson shouted, "What the fuck are you doing, what the fuck is going on . . ." but he put his hands on the wall, and Virgil patted him down.

"What the fuck . . ."

Virgil said, "You can slow down, or we'll have to put some handcuffs on you. Calm down; you can step away from the wall."

Williamson's face was dead red, and he was breathing like a man having a heart attack. "What the hell is going on?"

"We're searching your house. We have a warrant."

Williamson's mouth worked, but nothing came out for a minute, and then Virgil saw him relax, make the small move that meant that he'd gotten it together. Virgil stepped back. "You okay?"

Williamson, still angry, but not uncontrolled: "What . . . are . . . you doing?"

"We're looking for anything that might tie you to the murders of the Gleasons, the Schmidts, and Bill Judd."

"What . . . what?"

"We know about your adoption," Virgil said.

"My adoption? My adoption?" His mouth hung open for a moment, then, "What about my adoption?"

"You were born here in Bluestem when your mother was killed in an automobile accident after a party at Bill Judd's. You're Bill Judd's son."

Williamson actually staggered back away from Virgil. "That's not possible. How is that possible? That's horse-shit."

"You didn't know?" Virgil was skeptical.

"No!" Williamson shouted. "I didn't. I don't believe it. My mother . . ." He reeled away. "My mother got pregnant and gave me up for adoption. Didn't want me. That's what my mom told me. My real mom."

"Your real mom . . . ?"

"My real parents . . ." Williamson's face had gone from red to white, and now was going red again. "David and Louise Williamson. Where did you get this bullshit?" He looked around. "What have you done to my house? What have you done? You motherfuckers are gonna pay for this . . ."

THEY COOLED HIM OFF and Virgil told him, bluntly: "We're going through here inch by inch. Frankly, it's not possible that you wound up here by accident."

"Not by accident. Not by accident," Williamson said. "I was working up in Edina, at the suburban papers, and Bill—it was Bill, not me. My editor met Bill at an editor-and-publisher meeting. My guy came back and said Judd had seen some of my stuff, and wondered if I'd be open to working in a small town."

"So you left Edina and moved to Bluestem?" Virgil's eyebrow went up. "Not a common thing to do."

Williamson looked around and said, "Okay if I sit

down?" Virgil nodded, and he dropped onto a couch, and wiped his sweaty forehead on the sleeve of his shirt. "Look. I was working in the Cities, I was making thirty-eight thousand a year, and it wasn't going to get any better. I learned journalism in the Army; I don't have a college degree. The big papers were losing staff, everything was going in the toilet. So Judd says, come on down to Bluestem, I'll pay you forty thousand a year and vouch for you, so you can get a mortgage."

Williamson looked around the house. "You know how much this place cost?"

Virgil shook his head, but Jensen said, "I think it was up for forty-five thousand?"

"They took forty. I'm paying two hundred a month for a pretty decent house. In the Cities, I lived in a slum apartment that cost me eight hundred a month. The job wasn't going to get any better, either, even if the papers survived. Out here . . ." He shrugged. "I've got my own house, I'm sort of a big shot . . . I like the work."

The anger flooded back: "So go ahead and search, you fuckers. There's nothing here because I had nothing to do with any murders." To Jensen: "You know where I was when the Gleasons were killed? I was at the Firehouse Funder, down at Mitchell's. There were three hundred people there, and I was reporting it, and I gave a talk." He started shouting again. "You think about asking me for an alibi?"

"Take it easy . . ."

Still shouting: "And that stuff about Bill being my

father . . . I want to see some proof. I want to see some DNA. Hey: you got a warrant? Are you searching the office . . ."

WILLIAMSON WAS out in the kitchen, getting a cup of coffee, watched by a deputy, when Jensen said to Virgil, "If that was an act, it was a pretty good act."

"If he did the murders, he's a psycho," Virgil said. "Psychos spend their lives fooling people . . . You want the dining room? I'll take the garage."

17

Monday Afternoon

CUMULUS CLOUDS WERE thick as cotton balls in a hospital room, some of the bottoms turning blue: more thunderstorms coming in. Stryker was sitting at his desk, fingers knitted behind his ear, heels on the corner of his desk, staring out the window across the parking lot. Virgil sat across from him, saying not much.

Finally Stryker yawned, stretched, dropped his feet to the floor, and said, "Well, that was your basic cluster-fuck."

"There's a connection in there. Gotta be," Virgil said. "I will bet you one hundred American dollars that he's the guy."

"It was one dollar this morning."

"One hundred dollars," Virgil repeated.

"Straight up? A hundred dollars?"

Virgil thought about it for a moment, then said, "You'd have to give me two to one."

Stryker tried to laugh, then shook his head, said, "Damnit, he's gonna crucify us Thursday morning."

"Then we need to give him a better story," Virgil said. "I'm thinking about calling Pirelli. See what he has to say for himself."

"You do that, " Stryker said, standing up. "I've got to run over to the jail. If I don't see you later, I'll see you tomorrow."

VIRGIL WANDERED OUT of the office, stopped at the men's room. The second-best place to think, after a shower, was a nice, quiet urinal.

Williamson claimed that Judd found *him*; that he hadn't found Judd. That had a certain straightforward logic to it that appealed to Stryker. If Williamson was Judd's kid, Judd would have known it. Was it possible that as he'd gotten old, and maybe started to think about what was coming, maybe started to read a little Revelation, that he'd softened up, and gathered his children around him? Was that why his will wasn't in the safe-deposit box? Had he been thinking of changing it? Would that have given Junior reason to get rid of the old man?

On the other hand, Williamson's alibi, that he'd been at the Firehouse Funder, was too convenient for Virgil's taste. The fund-raiser had been held at Mitchell's, the local sports bar. Mitchell's back door emptied into an extra parking lot. From the parking lot to the Gleasons' house was a five-minute jog along the railroad tracks, then across the bridge and up the hill. All suitably dark. And by ten o'clock, the eating had been over for two hours, and the drinking had gotten under way. Would anybody have noticed if Todd Williamson, so evident around the place all evening, had slipped away for twenty-five minutes? Had not gone to the john, but out the back door?

As far as Virgil was concerned, the alibi was far short of watertight.

Stryker disagreed.

Fuck him.

HE WAS WASHING his hands when a deputy stepped in, glanced at the two empty toilet booths, then said, "I need a word with you, but I don't want it getting out that I talked to you."

Virgil shrugged: "Sure, but . . ."

"But what?" The deputy's name tag said "Merrill." He was nervous and blunt. He wore gold-rimmed glasses and a brush mustache.

"But this is a murder case," Virgil said. "If you've got something to say, you oughta say it. I can't promise to hold it confidentially."

Merrill rubbed his nose, looked at the door, and then said, "I saw you up to the fire at Judd's."

Virgil nodded: Let the guy talk.

"So . . . this is probably nothing, and that's why I hate to say anything . . . but . . ."

"Say it; I ain't gonna bite," Virgil said.

"Jesse Laymon was there. Drinking beer, rubberneckin'."

"Yeah?"

"Well, she's seeing the sheriff, socially, everybody knows that. The thing is, I know her truck, and I didn't see it come in, and I didn't see it go. I never saw her ride off with any of the other people there. I know about everybody in the county, everybody who was up there, and I've been asking around . . . I can't find anybody who took her, or who brought her in. It was raining like a cow pissing on a flat rock; seems odd to think that she walked in."

"She had a can of beer in her hand when I saw her," Virgil said.

"Yup," Merrill said. "I assumed that she came up with the folks from the bar. But I can't find anybody she rode with."

"You sure you'd know her truck?"

"Man, Jesse is . . . one of the hottest chicks in the county. I know her truck. I wave at her every time I see her."

Virgil looked at him for a minute, then said, "Keep your mouth shut on this."

"You gonna do something about it?"

"I will."

BUFFALO RIDGE was something like the hill at the Stryker farm, but twenty or fifty times as large, covered with knee-high bluestem grass, outcrops of the red rock, with a spring, a stream, and a lake on the north side, and Judd's house and the Buffalo Jump bluff on the south-east. There were park roads both north and south; the south road came off a state highway and curled around the top of the mound; halfway to the top, Judd's driveway broke off to the east to the homesite, now just a hole in the ground.

Virgil took the drive, parked next to the foundation hole. He got out and looked in. The ash had been worked over with rakes. Looking for a safe, Virgil thought; Junior hoping for a will.

Okay. If he were going to kill a man, and set fire to his house, how would he run? Wouldn't run south, because you'd fall over the bluff and kill yourself. Wouldn't go east, because there was nothing there but a lot of hillside, weeds, and rocks. You could break a leg in the dark.

You could run back down the drive, to the park road, then down the park road to the entrance. Would you get to the entrance before the fire department? Must be a mile or more, and the fire department had a couple of first responders on duty all the time. If you were in a car, or a truck, you could get down there in a minute, but running, even with a small flashlight, would take you eight minutes or so.

Or you could go north, climbing the hill, and then circling around. That would be more dangerous, again risking rocks and holes, but you could take it slow in the rain, and work up behind the rubberneckers . . .

He knew the road, so he walked the north route, across the hillside. Came over the top, saw the first of the buffalo. They were far enough away not to be a problem, but he kept an eye on them; and they kept an eye on him. The day was still warm, close to perfect, but the clouds were thickening up. He zigzagged looking for a trail, a break that somebody might have followed through the high grass, but saw nothing in particular.

And the going was rough. He tried walking with his eyes closed, and floundered around like a two-legged goat. Huh.

He looked back at the road. The road was it.

BACK IN BLUESTEM, he walked down to Judd Jr.'s office. His secretary was standing in the door of the inner office, talking, and stopped when Virgil came in. She said, "Mr. Flowers is here."

Judd stepped into Virgil's line of view, cracked a smile: "You got old Todd hung from a light post yet?"

"Not yet," Virgil said. "I need to talk to you for a minute."

Judd pointed at a chair, and said to the secretary, "Run up to Rexall and get me a sleeve of popcorn."

She wanted to stay and listen, but shook her head and shuffled off. Virgil waited until she was gone. Judd said, "I don't need any more family members, Mr. Flowers. I already had one too many."

"Yeah, well, I guess you should have talked to your father about that," Virgil said. He asked, "Who cut your father's lawn? Who cut that piece of short grass out between the house and the bluff? I didn't see any lawn mowers on the garage pad."

Judd was puzzled: "Well, he had all of his yard care done by Stark Gardens. They got a greenhouse and do lawn care and cleanup . . . Why?"

"Trying to nail a few things down—who might have

been coming and going," Virgil said. "The night of the fire, do you have any idea of how long it took the fire department to get up there?"

Judd shook his head—"You could ask them, but I imagine, let me see: Somebody had to call it in, then the guys had to get going . . . had to get through town . . . Doesn't seem long, but I bet it was eight or ten minutes."

"Okay." Virgil stood up. "Thanks."

Judd said, leaning back in his leather chair, "I'd like to know something. Just between you and me. Private."

"Ask," Virgil said.

"You gettin' anywhere?"

Virgil said, "I think so. I feel like things are about to break."

Judd said, "Jesus, I hope. I made some calls up to the Cities, to ask about you. Word was, you're pretty good. I need to stop walking around feeling like there's a crosshairs on my neck."

Virgil thought about Pirelli and his DEA crew: "I can sympathize. You could be excused for feeling a little twitchy right now."

AT THE SHERIFF'S OFFICE, he asked for Margo Carr, the crime-scene tech. She worked the north county as a full-time deputy when she wasn't doing crime-scene work, he was told. He borrowed a radio and called her.

"You keep your crime-scene stuff in your truck?"

"I do," she said.

"Meet me somewhere," he said. "I need to borrow some spy equipment."

There was a moment's silence, then she said, with a smile lurking in her voice, "Mr. Flowers, Agent Flowers . . ."

Flowers said, "Just meet me."

They hooked up five miles out of town. Carr was a red-head, chunky in all of her gear, and not that pretty, but she gave off a distinct vibe, and Virgil had the feeling that there'd never been a shortage of men coming around. He borrowed a metal-detecting wand from her. "When you said 'spy equipment' . . ." she began.

"Between you and me, that was for other listeners," Virgil said. "If other listeners ask me what I borrowed, don't tell them."

THE SUN WAS a red ball, still two hand-widths above the horizon, thunderheads starting to pop up, when Virgil turned off the interstate and headed into Roche. The bad thing was, it was Monday evening, and most people didn't go dancing on Mondays. The good thing was, Roche was tiny. He could park a half mile away, down the back road out of town, on the crest of a hill, and watch the Laymon house with his Zeiss binoculars.

That's what he did. There was a Ford Taurus and a beat-up Ford F-150 parked in the side yard, one for each of the women, he thought. Jesse would be out, or going out. Stryker was all over her, and she did like to move around. Her mother was the question . . .

While he waited, he put through a call to Pirelli. Pirelli was working, he was told, and would probably call back in a minute or two, or maybe never.

Pirelli called back: "Things are moving. Be patient. I won't talk to you about this on a cell phone, but we got to an inside guy, one of the local grain handlers. There's a building out there that they call 'the lab,' and none of the locals are allowed in. We are ninety-nine percent, and after tonight . . . we should be better. So . . ."

"Stay in touch."

STRYKER SHOWED AT 8:30.

Jesse didn't wait for him to come in. As soon as he pulled up, she came out, walked around the front of the truck, and climbed in. Stryker did a U-turn and headed out of town, toward the interstate. They were ten miles from anywhere, so it'd take them twenty minutes to get back, even if they had a fight and called the date off . . .

So there was the second car. Virgil watched for fifteen minutes, half an hour, hoping in the fading light that Margaret Laymon would go for a ride. A few minutes before nine o'clock, she came out to her car. He wasn't precisely sure it was she, but whoever it was got in the Taurus, did a turn, and headed for the interstate.

Virgil started the truck, and rolled in behind her.

Watched her taillights disappear . . .

Was it possible, he wondered, that Jesse, having already

learned from her mother that she was a Judd heir, had also learned there might yet be a third heir? And not knowing that the third heir was already in town, had gone about eliminating any leads to him? Or might there be a conspiracy to set Jesse up with an inheritance?

That, he thought, sounded like a TV show.

So why are you sitting in this truck, Virgil, with a butter knife in your hands, a butter knife that you stole, showing no conscience about it at all, from the poor folks at the Holiday Inn?

Because a butter knife was the perfect thing with which to slip the crappy lock on the Laymons' front door.

HE DIDN'T HIDE. He made sure Margaret was well out of town, then turned back and parked in front of her house. Put the metal wand in a jacket pocket, held the butter knife partly up his coat sleeve, in his right hand. Pushed the doorbell, heard it ring. Pushed it and held it. Dropped the butter knife into his hand. Held the doorbell, looked back toward the interstate. No head-lights.

Slipped the knife into the crack of the door, pushed, felt the lock slip, and pressed the door open with his toe. Stepped inside, into the light. Five minutes to go through the house. Checked a bedroom, found old photos, a made bed, and a framed Doors poster. Had to be Margaret's.

Next bedroom: an iPod on the nightstand, the bed unmade. Jesse's. Now where . . . ?

Virgil looked around, turned on the wand, and began to hunt. He moved through the bedroom quickly, getting metallic pulses from almost everything. But nothing in a wrong spot . . .

And finally got a strong pulse from a pair of knee-high winter boots in the closet, which was the second place he'd looked, after the chest of drawers.

Turned the boot, and the revolver tumbled out into the lamplight.

He didn't touch it immediately, but he smiled. Pretty good. He took a pencil from his pocket, moved the gun around. Smith & Wesson, .357 Magnum. He slipped the pencil down the muzzle, used it to lift the gun and drop it into a Ziploc bag. He put the bag in his pocket, then sat back on his heels, working it through.

After a minute, he moved back through the house, closed the door behind him, heard the lock latch. In the dark, he could see lightning both to the southeast and to the northwest, but could hear no thunder. Those storms would miss Bluestem. Overhead, a million stars twinkled down from the Milky Way.

VIRGIL WAS PARKED on the street in front of Stryker's house when Stryker pulled into his driveway. Virgil got out of the truck, a bad taste in his mouth. Stryker had pulled into his garage, and was standing outside waiting, the garage door rolling down, as Virgil walked up the driveway. Stryker: "Something happen?"

"Maybe," Virgil said. "But I've got a little trouble talking to you about it."

Stryker cocked his head: "What's that mean?"

"I've gotten a tip—won't tell you where from—that Jesse might have been up at Judd's place the night of the fire—that she might have walked back down the hill after it started, instead of coming in from the outside."

"That's goofy," Stryker said. "She was with a bunch of people from the bar."

"Then it shouldn't be a problem," Virgil said. "Everybody knows everybody. All we have to do is track down everybody who was up there, and find who gave her a ride up there. My tip says, she wasn't driving her own truck."

"Well—let's do that. We'll get the guys on the gate, see who was there, see who saw who."

"First thing in the morning?"

"Well—some of the guys who were on duty at the time, should be on duty right now. Let's call Little Curly and George Merrill. They were on the gate. Let's go do it."

Virgil followed him back to the courthouse, and inside. He got Curly and Merrill on the radio, told them to come in, quick. They both acknowledged, and Stryker led the way to his office, sat down, and said, "If you won't tell me where the tip came from, it came from a deputy. I can see the guy's problem, but god-damnit . . ."

"Don't push anything with anybody," Virgil said. "This is tangled up enough, without you starting your re-election campaign. Just keep your mouth shut."

MERRILL GOT BACK FIRST. He came in, thumbs hooked on his belt, looked warily at Virgil and then Stryker: "What's up?"

Stryker: "George, we need the names of everybody you saw down by the gate on the night of the fire . . ."

Merrill said, "Well, you know, the usual guys . . ."

Little Curly came in while they were making the list; Stryker told him what they were doing. He looked at the list, added a name. Virgil asked, "You both saw Jesse Laymon. Did either of you see her truck?"

Merrill and Little Curly glanced at each other, then they both looked at Virgil and shook their heads: "Nope."

"That's what we needed," Virgil said. "Thank you much."

When they were gone, Stryker, who was looking at the list, said, "First thing tomorrow. I'll have these guys run down by ten o'clock."

AT THE MOTEL, Virgil got a beer, carried it up to his room, broke out the laptop, looked at the motley, disconnected collection of paragraphs about Homer and his investigation of the Bluestem murders.

Sat down and wrote,

With the .357 in his hand, Homer rocked back on his heels, and wondered whether somebody was trying to frame Jesse; was trying to screw the investigation; was trying to provide contrary evidence for a later trial; or if Jesse might actually have something to do with the murders.

Whichever it was, somebody had deliberately fed Merrill into the investigation—which was why Homer asked Bill Judd Jr. about the lawn-mowing service. The hole in the ground that used to be Judd's place held no gas-fired engines, as far as Homer could see. No lawn mowers or snowblowers or utility carts. So if Jesse hadn't gone up there with her truck . . . how'd she gotten the gas up there, the gas that was used as the accelerant? Maybe she'd run up a mile-long hill in a thunderstorm with fifty or sixty pounds of gasoline, and carried the empty cans out the same way?

Bullshit, Homer thought. Somebody was setting her up, trying to push Homer into searching her house, where the gun was planted in the second-most-obvious place. Be interesting to see if the .357 was actually the murder weapon . . .

He knew at least one possible suspect who had access to Jesse's bedroom, but it was so obvious that it couldn't be right; couldn't be Stryker. Couldn't be.

Virgil yawned and closed down the laptop.
Who'd fed Merrill to him?
Have to ask.

18

VIRGIL AWOKE to a tapping on the motel-room door. Light was pushing through the drapes, so it had to be morning. He crawled across the bed and looked at the clock: seven A.M. Another knock, more insistent this time.

"Hang on," he called. He got his pistol, checked it, stepped over to the door, not crossing in front of it, reached across, and rattled the chain.

No gunshots. "Who is it?"

"Joan," Her voice quiet.

Virgil popped the chain, opened the door, standing there in his shorts and gun. "What's going on?"

She was dressed in worn jeans and a T-shirt, and had a bandana wrapped around her head, covering her hair. "I was headed out to the farm, I saw Jim on the street, he says you're thinking Jesse. I'd like to hear about it."

"Come on in," Virgil said. She stepped inside and he closed the door and put the gun away, and said, "I might be onto something, but this goddamned town, I'm not telling anybody." He grinned at her, trying to soften it, make it a little jokey.

"Including me." She crossed her arms. Always a bad sign with a woman, Virgil thought. "That'll be a first," she said, "Virgil Flowers keeping his mouth shut."

Virgil said, "I'm gonna shave. You can watch." She trailed him to the bathroom, and Virgil splashed water on his face, and said, "When you come into a small town like this, on a dead case, you have to do something to get things moving again. I talk. It works."

She was skeptical: "You mean, you're a naturally reticent, quiet, bashful, introverted sort of guy, who'd never say anything about anybody, and it's all been a technique to mess with us Bluestemmers?"

Virgil was smearing shaving gel on his face. He stopped under his nose, looked at her in the mirror: "First time I ever heard 'reticent' or 'Bluestemmer' in a spoken sentence."

"So. Are you just fuckin' with me?"

"Joanie, you are a great woman and that's the truth," Virgil said, "but we've got at least five dead people and one psycho. I came here to get him. That's what I'm going to do."

She showed a smile. "So it's not Jesse. You said 'get him.' "

He rinsed the razor under the faucet and said, "That first night we went out, I mentioned that you were smarter than I thought. You just wormed an objective personal pronoun out of me . . . Want to wash my back?"

WHEN JOAN had gone, Virgil went online, checked his mail. Sandy, Davenport's researcher, had shipped him what she could find on Williamson, and it was all fairly routine.

No arrests, three speeding tickets over two decades, three years in the Army, including Iraq in '90. Never married. Adoptive parents not listed in Minnesota directories, hadn't filed income taxes with Minnesota in at least ten years.

He didn't bother checking Jesse: he had Jesse's story.

Judd: he spent an hour crawling through the paper he had on Judd. The accountant, Olafson, had done the numbers, but he was hoping for a name, an event, an association . . .

And did no better than he had with Jesse.

He thought about the .357. Wondered how long he should wait. Sooner or later, he thought, there was a good chance that somebody would suggest searching Jesse's house. He wanted to see where the suggestion came from, but didn't want to wait *too* long.

VIRGIL CAUGHT STRYKER at ten o'clock, as he was talking to a slightly hungover carpenter with a bandage on his nail hand. The carpenter said that he'd ridden up to the fire with a friend named Dick Quinn. Stryker skated around a direct question of whether the carpenter knew how Jesse Laymon got there, but instead showed him a list of the names he had, and checked off who rode with whom, and who drove.

The carpenter had seen Jesse, but didn't know how she got there. When they walked back out to Stryker's truck, Virgil asked, "Anybody see her truck? Or give her a ride?"

Stryker said, "One guy saw her and thought her truck was at the end of the line. But nobody was looking at trucks, they were looking at the fire."

"Want to know what I would do?" Virgil asked.

Stryker shook his head: "After yesterday, I'm not sure."

"I'd have one of your deputies watch Williamson, get one to track Bill Judd, and one to watch Jesse. If two of them look like they're about to collide . . ."

"If I stake them out, everybody in the county will know in fifteen minutes," Stryker said. "Including them."

"Better than piling up more dead people," Virgil said.

"Virgil . . . let me finish this. I only have to find a couple more people. Then we'll talk about a stakeout. Now— what're you doing today?"

"Maybe push Williamson," Virgil said. "Maybe push Jesse. Maybe talk to Judd some more. Somewhere in that triangle, there's an answer."

"You do that, and I'll nail down this list. Then let's talk."

VIRGIL HAD JUST GOTTEN in his truck when his phone rang. He opened it: Pirelli.

"We're getting together at the Holiday Inn, in Worthington," Pirelli said. "There's a rumor going around that we're about to raid the meatpacking plant, looking for illegals. If you and Stryker want in, you need to be here."

"When are you moving?" Virgil tapped his horn at Stryker, who looked back. Virgil waved him over.

"Around noon," Pirelli said. "Feur is on his way back to his farm from Omaha. We've got a guy just loaded fifty gallons of gas into the back of his truck, up at the ethanol plant. He should be getting to the farm a little after Feur, unless one of them stops along the way."

Virgil rolled down his truck window, put his finger over the mouthpiece, and said to Stryker, "Pirelli."

Pirelli was saying, ". . . you need to get briefed, if you want to be in on it."

"We'll be there by eleven," Virgil said. "You need more troops?"

"No. And we want to keep this off the air. We don't want any curious deputies sticking their noses in. We don't need strange guys with guns."

"Give us an hour," Virgil said. He closed the phone.

Stryker: "Today?"

"We're leaving right now for Worthington," Virgil said. "Pirelli wants to keep it off the air. You ought to check out, make up some kind of excuse, and we're rolling."

"Hot dog," Stryker said.

THEY SLAMMED Virgil's gear in the back of Stryker's Ford, and Stryker called dispatch and told them he'd be out of touch for a while. The dispatcher said, after a pause, "Okay, there." Stryker said to Virgil, "He thinks I'm going to Jesse's for a nooner," and he threw back his head and laughed.

Virgil said, "Not a bad idea."

"Tough choice, fuckin' or fightin'," Stryker said. "In the long run, I prefer fuckin', but at any given moment, fightin' can while away the hours."

THEY MADE the run to Worthington in half an hour. The feds had taken over the end of one wing of the Holiday Inn, and Virgil and Stryker were stopped by agents when they tried to walk back. One of the agents spoke into a radio, then nodded at them, and said, "Last room on the right."

THEY FOUND PIRELLI in a meeting room with twenty other agents, all in jeans, short-sleeved shirts, and ball caps. Pirelli was standing next to a pull-down projection screen, and the agents were on folding chairs, facing it, like a kindergarten class with guns. In the middle of them, a computer was sitting on a stand with a PowerPoint projector.

Pirelli said, over the heads of the agents, "You're just in time for the movies," and to the agents, "This is Jim Stryker, sheriff of Stark County, the man with the hat, and Virgil Flowers, Bureau of Criminal Apprehension, with . . . what kind of T-shirt, Virgil?"

Virgil pulled opened his coat to show off the Arcade Fire shirt.

"What the hell is Arcade Fire?" asked a Latino-looking dude with a New York accent.

"World's best hurdy-gurdy band," Virgil said.

PIRELLI SAID, "Guys, you've been briefed, I just want to talk about the territory a bit more, while we're waiting, and now that we have local people here. We've scouted it, we've flown it, we don't anticipate any huge trouble, but we gotta be ready. John Franks and Roger Kiley have long histories . . ." He paused, then said to Virgil and Stryker, "Franks is the guy bringing the stuff down from the ethanol plant; Kiley is at Feur's place now. He and a couple of other guys hang out there, patrolling around. We don't have IDs on the others."

"A guy named Trevor," Virgil said. "Last time I saw him, he had a Remington pump."

Pirelli stepped to the computer and projector, brought up an image on the screen, and did a search for "Trevor." A moment later, a "Trevor Rich" popped up, with a police ID photo from Wichita Falls, Texas.

"That's him," Virgil said, looking into Trevor's blank eyes.

Pirelli pulled up some text and read it for them: "Armed robbery, assault with a deadly weapon, terroristic threats. Ex-wife has been missing for four years; nobody knows where she went . . . he says California. If he goes back inside, he stays."

"He looked like such a nice boy," Virgil said.

"Kiley and Franks are the same deal: guns, trouble, and severely pissed off at the government," Pirelli said. "We've got to get right on top of them."

"How are you going to do that?" Virgil asked.

"That's a little complicated," Pirelli said.

THE COMPLICATION INVOLVED getting both Feur and the dope at the house at the same time. They had an observation plane overhead, watching the dope, along with two cars tracking it on the ground, and an electronic position finder planted on the truck itself.

"We want Feur on the premises. Then we grab the dope before they can do anything with it," Pirelli said. He went back to the computer keyboard and pulled up a satellite view of Feur's farm. "We don't know exactly where they'll move the stuff, but we think it's likely that they'll put it in this shed, rather than in the house," he said, touching the garage/shop with a red dot from a laser pointer. To Virgil and Stryker: "When we met in Mankato, you said that when Dale Donald Evans loaded gas cans, he backed up to the shed. We expect Franks to do the same thing, to unload.

"As soon as Franks is in the yard, we hit them," Pirelli continued, circling the yard with the laser dot. "We can time that right down to the minute, where we come off the interstate. Even if they see us coming over the top of the rise"—he touched a terrain feature on the satellite photo—"they'll have less than a minute of reaction time. If we can catch them in the yard, they're toast. We had a guy go by, take some high-res photos of that shed. It doesn't look like much. If they try to fight from it, we can take them out. The house is even shakier . . ."

"You don't want a massacre," Stryker said.

"Nope. We want to catch them in a helpless condition, so they quit," Pirelli said.

"Are you sure about the meth?" Stryker asked. "That they're bringing meth down from South Dakota?"

"Yes," Pirelli said flatly. "That lab at the ethanol plant; best meth lab any of us have ever seen in the States. They've got some as good down in Mexico, but nothing better."

Virgil piped up: "That shop might be a little harder than you think."

Pirelli raised an eyebrow: "Yeah?"

"It's got new Medeco locks and steel doors. Hardly any point, if the thing has cardboard walls."

"Have you been inside?" Pirelli asked.

"Of course not. That would be illegal, without a warrant," Virgil said.

"We got stuff that'd take down those doors like they were tissue paper," one of the agents said.

"Sure, when you decide to," Virgil said. "But if Franks has ten gas cans in his truck, with twenty gallons in gas and the rest in crank, and if he has time to unload the crank and stir it around in the gas, he could have a nice little campfire in there and run out with his hands over his head . . . Maybe you need to order up a fire truck."

Pirelli said, "We gotta be on top of them before he can unload. We will be less than a minute behind him, and he'll have no reason to hurry. With any luck, he'll want to take a leak before he unloads."

"I hope," Virgil said. "But it worries me."

"With these kinds of deals," Pirelli said, "there's always about a twenty-eight percent chance of a disaster. That's just the way it is. However we have to do it, these guys are worth eliminating." He looked at the satellite picture, then said to Virgil: "But you're right. It's worth worrying about."

THEY STOOD AROUND talking to the agents, then Virgil borrowed Pirelli's laser pointer, and Virgil and Stryker went over the ground around the house—a ditch here, a big rock there, where they could site long guns.

There was a long seam of darker grass extending from the barn area, up the hill, and into a clump of brush southeast of the farmstead. One of the agents asked if it were a ditch that could be used to approach the houses.

"Don't know," Stryker said. "We did our recon on the north side."

Pirelli was on the phone with somebody doing surveillance on the two target cars as they approached Feur's farm. One of them was working the math on a simultaneous arrival, and at twelve-forty, Pirelli said, "North side, take off."

Six agents got up, and walked out.

Pirelli said, "Five minutes, guys. We're on the road in ten. Drivers, fast, but no lights. Keep spaced out right until we're at the exit, then close up tight. You know all this, so let's remember it. Everybody: be careful. We don't want to lose anybody out there, and this is a tough bunch. Virgil, Jim, you hang back a little—not way back, but a little back. We've choreographed the entry, here."

Five minutes later, Pirelli said, "Let's mount up," and they streamed out of the room, no jokes, no talk.

Moving fast.

19

BEFORE THEY SETTLED in the trucks, Virgil and Stryker squeezed into standard-duty body armor. Though it wouldn't stop any heavy loads, it'd be good against shot-guns and pistols. Some of the DEA guys were wearing heavier stuff: they'd be the first in.

Stryker asked Virgil to drive: "I want to be able to work the radios to my guys—just in case."

FROM THE WORTHINGTON on-ramp to the exit nearest Feur's place was thirty-five minutes at legal inter-state speeds, half an hour at the normal illegal driving pace. Pirelli, talking to his outside pacemaker, modulated the speed of the DEA trucks, seven of them, all blacked-out GMC Yukons.

"Keep spaced out, my happy ass," Stryker said, watching the trucks ahead of them. "We look like a Shriner parade."

"As long as Feur doesn't have lookouts on the interstate, we'll be okay," Virgil said. A minute later, "Real purty day, ain't it?"

"Sure is," Stryker said cheerfully. He popped his safety belt, knelt on the seat, dug around in the back, and came up with the M-16. "If you see me firing this into a gopher hole, you just say to yourself, 'Don't bother about that— it's just old Jim popping off a few rounds in an effort to get re-elected.'"

"Gettin' some smoke on your ass."

"That's right," Stryker said.

"I still don't think Feur did the Gleasons, Jimmy. I don't think we're out of the woods on that guy," Virgil said.

"Whatever. I plan to take full credit on the meth lab, at least in the hometown papers," Stryker said. He pulled the magazine out of the M-16, thumbed the cartridges a few times, said, "What have you got back there? Shotgun isn't much use on a house."

"Shotgun, Remington semiauto .30-06."

"That'll knock the corner off a brick," Stryker said, with approval. "FMJs?"

"Yeah."

"I got sixty rounds. Wish I had a couple more clips."

"This is an arrest, not a war," Virgil said.

"Whatever," Stryker said. He slapped the mag back into the rifle, jacked a round into the chamber, clicked on the safety.

"I hope this thing works like Pirelli says," Virgil said. "I can appreciate your needing to get re-elected, but nailing that psycho is more important than keeping a few oil-field workers from taking their vitamin pills."

Ahead, the GMCs slowed, and Virgil slowed with them,

the speed dropping to fifty-five. *We really do look like a Shriner parade,* Virgil thought. *Hope nobody's watching.*

As far as they ever found out, nobody was. They were four miles from the exit when the speed picked up, and Pirelli called Virgil on his cell: "Feur got home fifteen minutes ago. Franks is coming up to the exit. We're going in. You guys hang back a bit."

"'Ten-ninety-six," Virgil said, and shut his phone.

"What does that mean?" Stryker asked. "I never heard of a ten-ninety-six."

"Means, 'Fuck you,' " Virgil said. He closed on the GMCs.

Stryker said, "I'm gonna try to crawl in the backseat. Stupid we're both sitting up front." He pulled the headrest out, tossed it in the back, and crawled awkwardly over the seat. "You want me to uncase the Remington?" he asked.

"Might as well," Virgil said. "Hope to hell we don't need it. There're two magazines in the side sleeve, all set."

FOR THE FIRST MINUTE or so north of the interstate, Virgil thought, it was unlikely that anyone ahead would notice them. Then they hit the gravel road and a plume of dust exploded from under the trucks' wheels, along with a roaring sound, like a nearby train, and everybody behind the first two trucks slowed down. The interval grew, and drivers began to move into the left lane, one truck fishtailing, and Stryker shouted, "Watch that, watch that . . ."

"He can't hear you," Virgil shouted back.

"I can't see a thing . . ." Stryker was holding on to the passenger seat, peering out from the back, into the thickening cloud of road dust.

THEY TOPPED the rise south of Feur's place, and if nobody had seen them yet, they would pretty soon; but they were also less than a minute out, closing fast, and when Virgil moved right to get out of the funnel of road dust, Stryker shouted, "Franks' truck is in the yard, it's in the yard . . ."

THE FIRST TWO DEA trucks hit the yard, and the agents were out, shouting at Franks, who'd just gotten out of his truck. Franks may have said something, and a dog rocketed out of the truck and jumped one of the agents, who went down, rolling with the dog.

The third truck went past the driveway turnoff and set up on the road. The fourth stopped across the driveway, and the fifth stopped short, the agents out in the road. Virgil swerved around the back truck and put the Explorer in the ditch opposite the end of the driveway, and shouted, "Out the left side, left side," and they both got under cover, saw running agents on the road, and then the gunfire.

There were two dogs out, one of them on an agent's face, the other wheeling in the dirt in a fight around Franks' truck, and then the screaming agent, dog on his face, managed to throw it off and another agent shot at it, missed, and the dog went for him, and another agent fired.

Four or five of them were in the yard when a machine gun stuttered from the house and one of the agents went down and the others started screaming and firing at the house, little pecks of paint and dust and wood popping off the front of the house, windows shattering. Franks, who'd been standing hands-over-head, turned toward the shed and hit the front door. The door popped open—unlocked—and Franks disappeared, and two agents were down.

Stryker was on the ground in the ditch, the M-16 to his shoulder, and he opened up on the top row of windows in the house, blowing out most of a magazine in a single hose job.

Virgil scrambled across the street, into the ditch on the far side, keeping a truck between himself and the house, and when he heard another machine gun open behind him, lurched out of the ditch, running toward the first truck in the yard. An agent was on the ground six feet from the truck and Virgil hooked him and dragged him behind it, the agent's M-16 bumping along under his arm, hung on a sling.

The truck had fifty bullet holes in it, broken glass spraying all over, two tires gone. The agent was still alive, but his legs were torn to pieces, and he was fading. A brown-and-white dog, that might have been a pit bull, bleeding from its sides and head, scrambled around the truck, pulling with his front legs, back apparently broken, fixing on Virgil. Virgil loved dogs, but he didn't even think about it and yanked his pistol and shot the dog twice.

HEARD SOMEBODY SCREAMING. Another agent, behind the other entry truck, was shouting at him, and Virgil saw a bloody patch in the dust behind him, but the agent was still operating and he pointed out between the trucks and Virgil saw a third agent down and he shouted back, and the other agent screamed, "You get him, I'll unload on the house, I can't move, I'm hit . . ."

Virgil shouted, "Do it," and the agent rolled and opened up with his M-16, tearing across the windows, and Virgil kicked out from behind the truck's wheel, grabbed the downed agent, and dragged him back, behind a tire. Another dog was coming for them, tongue out, bleeding, picked the agent with the gun, who was reloading, hit him just as he slapped the magazine in. But the dog got a piece of armor, not an arm, and tore at it and the agent found a pistol and put it at the dog's head and fired. The dog lurched and turned and looked at Virgil, a doggy smile on its bloody face, and then it toppled over.

Virgil was behind the truck with two wounded agents, or maybe, he thought, one dead. He looked at the man, caught a breath. No: still alive. He popped open the back door of the truck, lifted the wounded agent inside, and a hail of bullets knocked out the far windows and then went on.

He picked up the second agent, the unconscious one, struggling against the weight, and threw him on top of the first. He threw the first man's weapon on top of them, then crawled into the driver's foot-well, gripped the steering wheel overhead, shifted the truck into reverse, and hit the gas pedal with his hand.

Felt something scratching at him, ignored it, backed straight across the driveway on two and then three rims, heard the volume of fire picking up from the DEA agents to give him cover, never tried to turn, backed entirely across the yard into the field, across the field fifty yards, eighty yards, bumping over rocks and small trees and brush, the truck rocking violently, a hundred yards, and then he hooked into the roadside ditch and hit the brake.

HE CALLED PIRELLI on his cell phone: Pirelli screamed, "How bad, how bad?"

"Two pretty bad," Virgil shouted. "If you got a truck that works, get it down here. You gotta make a run like *right now.*"

"I'm calling the north team in, they're coming right by . . . If you got anything you can fire at the house, hose it down, hose it down . . ."

Virgil got the M-16 in the back of the truck, with two magazines, began popping three-shot bursts at the house as he saw a dust funnel coming down the gravel road from the north, moving fast.

One of the north group was trying to run right past the house. When he got close, Virgil emptied the last of the magazine at the upper windows of the house, where most of the fire seemed to be coming from, dumped the mag, slapped another one in, and as the north truck passed the driveway, hosed the house again.

The north truck slid to a stop in the shelter of the ruined truck. An agent piled out, wild-eyed, and Virgil shouted, "You know where the hospital is?"

"Yes, yes, we scouted it . . ."

They carried the two downed agents to the working truck, and the north guy shouted, "How bad are you hit?"

Virgil looked down at himself: blood, but not his. The agent touched his forehead, and Virgil reached up. More blood, and this time it was his. Didn't feel like much. "You go on," Virgil shouted. "Go on."

The agent took off, chased by a couple of slugs from the house when he broke from the cover of the wrecked truck.

Virgil dug through the back of the wrecked truck, found a box with six mags in it, stuck one in the rifle, stuck the others in his jacket pockets, darted across the road and into the ditch on the west side. From there, he was able to crawl through the swampy water toward Stryker's Ford.

HE COULD HEAR Stryker still firing from behind the Explorer, and he cleared the truck and Stryker turned toward him and said, "Need more ammo."

Virgil tossed him three of the mags he'd gotten from the truck, and Stryker shouted, "I think Pirelli's hit, he's in the ditch on the other side."

"I'll get him if you can dust off the house again," Virgil shouted. "Let me get my kit."

Virgil crawled into the truck and got his first-aid kit, then back out, crouched in the ditch, and shouted, "Anytime . . ."

Stryker popped up and unloaded a clip in one long burst and Virgil vaulted the narrow road, landing in the ditch on the other side, saw Pirelli with an M-16 shooting one-handed, blood soaking through his left shirtsleeve. Virgil crawled up and shouted, "How bad?"

"It hurts. I think it broke my shoulder," Pirelli shouted back. Everybody was shouting. Virgil could hear men screaming all around the house and hundreds of rounds pumping out. The house seemed to be falling apart, but there was still fire incoming.

Virgil pulled a heavy pad and a roll of tape out of his kit, and he and Pirelli eased to the bottom of the ditch, Pirelli on his back. Virgil found a bloody wedge knocked out of Pirelli's shoulder, just below the edge of his body armor. He jammed the pad under Pirelli's shirt and wound two yards of tape around his shoulder, cinching it up tight, shouted, "No artery, don't see any arterial bleeding," and Pirelli nodded and said, "Reload me."

NOW THE FIRING from the house had stopped, and an agent launched himself out of the east-side ditch to the car where the third wounded agent had been lying, the guy who'd covered Virgil while Virgil dragged the dead man's

body. Another burst of fire from the house, but the agent
made it, and the DEA shooters pounded the window
where the burst had come from.

Virgil, down in the ditch, reloaded Pirelli's M-16 and
then heard Stryker scream, "Watch out, watch out!"
and Virgil looked up and saw, at the shed, Franks walking out through the shed door with a long revolver in one
hand. He took three steps and shot at the agents behind
the truck, no effort to cover himself, and the unwounded
agent stumbled back away from the man on the ground,
trying for his gun, and then somebody hit Franks with a
burst, and Virgil could see his shirt shaking, but Franks
stayed on his feet and fired another shot from the pistol
and then he went down.

Distracted by the appearance of Franks, Pirelli had half
risen to his knees, shouting, and now another burst of
gunfire spattered around them and Pirelli went down
again, flapping one arm, and Virgil shouted, "Get down,"
but it was too late; Pirelli had been hit again. Virgil
crawled down to him, and Pirelli sat up and said, "Got
me," and dropped back on the ground. Two holes: one in
a leg and the other in the right arm. The one in the arm
was bleeding hard, but not arterially; the arm was crooked
and surely broken.

Virgil ripped open Pirelli's pant leg: that hit was super-
ficial, ripping away skin and a quarter-inch of meat.

"How bad?" Pirelli groaned.

"You're not dead yet," Virgil said. More tape to put pressure on the wounds; then Virgil said, "This is gonna hurt.

I've gotta move you across the road and up the ditch where we can get you outa here."

"Do it."

He braced himself and grabbed Pirelli's armor at the neckline, cocked himself, and shouted at Stryker, who said, "Ten seconds," and disappeared, crawling down the ditch. Then Stryker flashed a hand, screamed, "Go!" and Virgil ran across the road, dragging Pirelli. Stryker popped up, twenty feet from his previous position, and burned another mag.

Pirelli made no sound at all when they landed in the water on the other side. Virgil kept the motion going, dragging him up the ditch, through the muck, to the wrecked DEA truck. Five minutes, a hundred yards, Pirelli didn't make a sound. They reached the truck, went another ten yards, and stopped. Virgil said, gasping for air: "Somebody'll come and get you."

"That place is bunkered up. We didn't know it, but it's gotta be bunkered up," Pirelli said. His face was pale as a cloud, his eyes unfocused with shock, but he was coherent.

"Something," Virgil said.

AT THAT MOMENT, there was an explosion at the house. Not huge, but big enough. Then another one. A DEA agent had gotten a grenade launcher going, and hit the house with high-explosive rounds, and then with what looked like a gas round. And from behind the hill, to the northeast, where Virgil and Stryker had crawled on their scouting trip, a distinctive single boom. Virgil had never shot one, but he suspected it was a fifty-caliber rifle. The DEA was taking the house out.

Virgil said, "Just lay here; I'll be back," and he crawled back up the ditch. Franks was lying spread-eagled in front of the first DEA truck, obviously dead. Two agents in armor were behind the truck, a third agent on the ground. Stryker was still in the ditch, popping single shots off at the house: not much seemed to be coming out.

One of the first-in agents was squatting behind one of the trucks in the road, all four tires shot out.

"What about the guys behind the truck?" Virgil shouted.

The agent yelled back, "Harmon is gone. Franks shot him right in the head. Two more wounded, not bad; the others are okay. How bad are you?"

"Not bad. We've got four good tires. I'll back out of here if you can get that grenade guy to put in a couple more rounds. Pirelli's hurt pretty bad. I need to make a run to the hospital."

"Soon as you get it fired up, I'll tell him to start putting rounds in. Go like hell."

Virgil got in the foot-well of the Explorer. The passenger-side windows were shot out, glass all over the seats, a few holes, but the tires were good, and intact, and nobody had been shooting at the engine block, where they might've hit electronics.

The truck started, and he shouted, through the broken windows, "I'm ready," and two seconds later, heard the first grenade impact, and he started rolling backward up the ditch, building momentum, afraid he'd bog down in the wet bottom, and then another grenade, and the *boom* from the fifty-cal, and another grenade, and he risked sitting up, looked back over his shoulder, and accelerated onto the road and into the shelter of the damaged DEA truck.

Pirelli was still in the ditch, half sitting now. Virgil ran down to him, and Pirelli asked, "What time is it?"

"Damned if I know," Virgil said, and he grabbed Pirelli by his armor and said, "Hold on, now," and dragged him across the road to the Ford, loaded him through the back door, flat on his back, then got in the truck and backed up another two hundred yards, hearing the grenades pounding Feur's place, then risked stopping, made a U-turn through the ditch and was on his way out. "What time is?" Pirelli called. "What time is it?"

"Time to go," Virgil shouted back, and that seemed satisfactory, and Pirelli stopped talking.

IN THE REARVIEW MIRROR, he could see Feur's house, with smoke—maybe gas?—but no fire. Then he was over the rise and onto the interstate and he didn't bother calling the hospital, and he was moving too fast anyway, and if they had a brain in their head, with two wounded agents already in, they'd be ready for more. A mile from the exit, he saw a DEA-looking truck heading back, saw a shattered window: the guy who'd made the run to the hospital, headed back.

Eight minutes to the Bluestem exit, up and left, accelerating up the hill, then right to the hospital, the big arrow of the emergency room, three cop cars sitting outside of it, deputies looking toward him, flinching at the sound of his wheels, and then he was there, out, shouting, "We got another one, Pirelli, he's hurt. Need a gurney, need a gurney . . ."

The hospital had one full-time surgeon, Virgil learned, with another on his way from Worthington. The one on the job was working back and forth between injured DEA agents and he looked at Pirelli and said to a nurse, "Clean him up," and then he was gone.

The nurses took Pirelli off and Virgil went outside, where a deputy said, "We've got guys heading down to Feur's," and, "The DEA guy went back."

"The doc say anything about the first two guys?"

"They're hurt bad. One of them's right on the edge, the other's better." The deputy's face was pale, anxious. "I need to get down there . . ."

"You need to stay here," Virgil said. "Coordinate. Call your guys, tell them to take it easy going in, because there's a war going on down there. Once they're inside two hundred yards, they could get shot up. Best to hold back, isolate the farmhouse, and let the DEA guys take it down. Block the roads, don't let anybody in or out. Look for people on foot."

"I'll call them," the deputy said, and then Virgil was in his truck and rolling. He was halfway down the highway when an agent named Gomez called: "We've got contact with Feur: he's still inside, he won't talk, says for you to call him."

"I'll be there in three or four minutes, if you can stall him. You could listen in."

DEPUTIES HAD SET UP a roadblock just off the interstate. Virgil went on through, did a U-turn four hundred yards out, backed down to the wrecked DEA truck, and left his truck there. Carrying the M-16 he'd taken from the DEA agent and two mags, he worked his way back down the roadside ditch.

THE HOUSE WAS a ruin. The second floor was gone, part of it falling inside the frame of the house, part of it out in the yard. Popping his head up every few yards, Virgil could see what appeared to be olive-drab sandbags, the kind used by the Corps of Engineers for flood control.

They *had* been bunkered up, he thought, but the pounding from the grenade launcher had knocked out the frame of the house.

As he crawled, he noticed that there was no firing; very little sound at all. A lot of gasoline around, though. Five dead trucks, all shot to pieces, leaking gas; smoke coming out of one of them.

Stryker was no longer in the ditch. He'd moved across the road, and was sitting behind one of the trucks. Virgil heard a grenade hit the house, and made his move, slid in next to Stryker.

Another agent came running over. All he said was, "You ready? It's for you." He had a phone in his hand, and he pushed the "call" button, and handed it to Virgil.

Feur answered a minute later. "What?"

Virgil said, "This is Virgil Flowers. You feel like coming out?"

Feur chuckled. "No, I guess not. I have a question for you, though. Why in the *hell* did you come in shooting? You could have knocked on the door. I could take a couple years inside. But you came in shooting and now there are dead cops, and I'm not gonna sit on death row, waiting for the needle."

"Ah, man," Virgil said. "It was Franks' goddamn dogs. We weren't shooting you. The dogs went after an agent, chewing him up. Somebody shot at the dog, somebody shot back from the house."

"All this happened because of dogs?" Feur didn't seem surprised.

"Well, not exactly. If you hadn't been making a ton of crank, if you hadn't built bunkers inside the house, if you hadn't shot back . . . Was that you, or Trevor, or one of the other guys?"

"Trevor," Feur said. "Silly fool. Always liked those guns too much. He paid for it: he's gone now. There's only two of us left, me'n John. We're both hurt, trying to decide what to do."

"You aren't gonna take any more cops with you," Virgil said. "The DEA is talking about bringing in a tank from the

National Guard. Run that house over like a trash compactor."

After a few seconds of silence, Feur said, "Call me back in two minutes. John's hurt, I need to see what he wants to do."

VIRGIL PUNCHED OFF. He'd been holding the phone close, so the agent could listen in, and the agent said, "Good. If he's talking, he'll quit." Then, "What about our guys?"

Virgil said, "One's real bad, one may be dying. Not dead yet, they're working on both of them at the hospital. Pirelli's got a bunch of holes, but I don't think he's gonna die. What about the others . . . ?"

"We sent two more in; not good, but not terrible." The agent nodded, chewed his lip, said, "Why'd Franks turn those dogs loose?"

"Crazy guy," Virgil said. "A whole house full of crazy guys."

HE LOOKED at the phone, and redialed. Feur answered, and said, "We're quittin'. But we can't get out of here. We're all piled in. We're not gonna shoot, but you'll have to get us out."

"Where are you?"

"Right in the middle of the house, first floor, the whole top floor came down on us. Can't see any cracks, just a lot of lumber. John is hurtin' bad."

Virgil could hear another man talking in the background,

but couldn't make out what he was saying. "Gonna take a while," Virgil said. "I'll tell you what, Reverend. You best not resist. Won't do any good, for one thing, but the other thing is, these boys are pretty pissed. If they toss an incendiary grenade in there, you'll get a little preview of hell."

"We're done," Feur said. "We're done."

"Just in case, you know, something happens," Virgil said. "Why'd you do the Gleasons and the Schmidts?"

Feur said, "I don't lie on the Bible, Virgil. I had nothing to do with that. And look—it wouldn't make any difference to anybody or anything if I came right out and admitted it. Not with those dead cops all over the yard. But I had nothin' to do with it."

THE AGENTS TOOK it slowly: built a commanding view of the house from the loft of the barn, from the top of the shed, then moved in close to the house, pushed some sandbags around, built a strong point that looked right down into the wreckage.

The agent named Harold Gomez had taken charge. Another agent said to him, "We need some chains, maybe a Bobcat. We need to move some big pieces."

Gomez nodded. "Get one. Get two. Get them down here."

ANOTHER SANDBAGGED strongpoint went up at the opposite corner of the house. With an agent there, his gun trained on the wreckage, Virgil and Gomez moved in close to look at the house. To their left, another agent had spread a blanket over the forms of the dead DEA man and Franks.

The wrecked house smelled bad, raw lumber and dust and old paint, the odor of rotten eggs. A couple of other agents moving around the wreckage pointed out parts of a body, blown to pieces, under a portion of the second floor that had collapsed into the yard.

"Direct hit with a grenade," Gomez said.

An agent put down his rifle, walked up the front steps, dragged some siding and two-by-fours to the side, and then a few more pieces. He shouted, "Can you hear us?"

No answer.

"Careful," Gomez said. "Basement could be a problem."

THEY MOVED FARTHER around the house, and Gomez said, "You've got a cut on your scalp."

"Piece of glass or metal," Virgil said. "When I was backing the truck out."

"Goddamnit," Gomez said. "Goddamnit. Ah, Jesus, what do I tell Harmon's wife?"

ANOTHER AGENT HAD PUT on gloves, and was clearing debris from the other side of the house, walking carefully on an exposed piece of floor. "Hey, you in there? Hey?"

To Gomez: "Looks like another body, or pieces of one."

Moved more lumber, but they'd need the Bobcat, Virgil decided. He called Feur on the cell phone. No answer.

"Maybe hurt," Gomez said. Moved a bit more lumber. "I gotta go into town, see my guys . . ." Gomez might be going into shock, Virgil thought.

More rotten eggs.

Virgil sniffed, sniffed again, then said quietly and urgently to the agent on the house, moving lumber, "Get off there. Don't ask me any questions, just get off, right now." And to the agent on the other side—"Quiet. Get off there . . . get back, get those guys out of the sandbags, you guys get back . . ."

He was talking quietly as he could, backing away. Gomez: "What, what?"

Virgil said, "That's propane. That's the rotten-egg smell." He looked around, saw the tank next to the barn. "They're filling the place up with propane. They're gonna blow it up."

"Propane . . ." Gomez was quick. He backed away, turned away, said quietly into his radio, "Guys, everybody get back, keep it quiet, but get the hell back, there's gas, they may be getting ready to blow it . . ."

TEN MINUTES LATER, Virgil was feeling a little stupid, sitting in the ditch across the road. An agent suggested that he run up next to the barn, and turn the propane off, but the barn was too close to the house, too exposed if there was an explosion. "Give it another ten minutes," Virgil said. "Maybe I'm full of shit."

ELEVEN MINUTES AFTER Virgil moved the agents off the house, the place blew. Not like a bomb, but with a hollow *whump*. Five tons of lumber went straight up in the air or sideways with a gout of smoke, curled at the top, like an atomic bomb. Virgil covered his head with his hands, and when nothing landed on him, peeked over the edge of the ditch. A ripple of fire was running through the wreckage: "Now, you need the fire department," he said.

"Holy mackerel," Gomez said. "Holy fuck." A few seconds later a helicopter showed up, and when it turned, they could see the Channel Five logo on the side.

Virgil shook his head. "That's what we needed. That's exactly what we needed. Smile, Harry, you're on TV."

Not done yet.

Gomez made a call, said, "That oughta get rid of the chopper," and with the helicopter still circling, they walked cautiously across the street, to the house. An agent ran out of the field behind the barn to the propane tank, pulled off the valve cover, and Virgil could see him spinning the valve.

Gomez said, "Gonna be another one of them right-wing legends. Last stand at Reverend Feur's."

"Anybody look in Franks' truck yet?"

"Not yet."

They went that way, yanked open the back panel on the

camper, saw the row of gas cans. A couple of other agents drifted over. Gomez turned the cap on one, sniffed, said, "Gas," tipped it into the sun, to see better, then walked away and carefully poured the gasoline into the dirt at the side of the yard. A gallon or so poured out, and then a glass tube fell out, and another. Gomez kept swirling the can until he had them all, twelve tall bottles that might once have contained spices, all full of powder.

"It's all true," he said. To one of the agents: "What am I gonna tell Harmon's wife?"

The agent shook his head, and finally said, "That we killed all those motherfuckers who did it."

THE AGENTS UNLOADED the rest of the gas cans, and all carried glass bottles. They went through the shed, found five more cans, all with bottles. Feur and his friends had been moving meth twenty and thirty pounds at a time. "Been doing it for years," Gomez said.

They walked through the barn, knocked in the doors of the two old Quonset huts, without finding anything more. Looked into the house: the interior had been blown to flinders, and the fire was getting stronger.

"Fire department's coming," one of the agents said. "Not that I care."

THE HELICOPTER WENT AWAY, the maddening thump leaving the place in the silence of insects and birds.

Virgil, Stryker, and Gomez climbed into the barn's loft to look at the house from a high point; amazing, Virgil thought, what gas could do.

They were standing there when the fire truck arrived. The fireman put foam on the fire for three or four minutes, and the fire was gone.

Gomez said, "We're gonna have to say something. Press conference up in Bluestem; we sort of had it set up for tonight. Still gonna have to do something . . ."

"Call Pirelli. He was still talking when I saw him, maybe . . ."

Gomez got on his phone, pushed a button. No answer.

Stryker came over and said, "Get off the phone."

"What?"

"Get off the phone. Look at this—look at this." He led them to the loft door, looking down at the house.

"FEUR WAS a mean, feral asshole," Stryker said. "What's he doing committing suicide? He'd want his day in court, if we'd had him cornered."

Gomez spread his hands: *"What?"*

Stryker pointed up the hillside. "That satellite photo that you had in the motel. One of your guys was looking at a seam that comes down to the house, and he wondered if it was a ditch that we could crawl down. We didn't know. But when we walked around the barn, right over it, I didn't see a thing. Didn't notice it. The only way you can see *anything,* is to get up high. Up here."

"Yeah?" Virgil looked at the hillside, still didn't see much.

"It's that line of greener weeds," Stryker said, pointing down and to the right. "See it? That's what you get when you dig. New weeds. It's a dead straight line. It looks to me like somebody put down a culvert."

"What?" Gomez, eyes wide. "That little line?"

"All you'd need to do is get the pipe, rent a backhoe, run the line straight up the hill to that brush. Then if the cops ever caught you in the house, you get down the basement, light a candle, turn on the gas, and seal the tunnel. Regular old manhole cover with some plastic tape or foam. Then you crawl out the culvert . . . skin your knees up some . . . I keep thinking, he didn't answer the cell phone the last time Virgil called."

"Sonofabitch," Gomez said. They climbed down from the loft, and Gomez got on his radio. A half dozen agents came running.

"THE LINE GOES right into that clump of trees," Stryker said, pointing up the hill. "There's like three clumps coming down the hill, and then the last clump on the bottom, it goes right into that clump."

"They might already be out," Virgil said.

Gomez told his guys, "Armor up. Fast. Let's go, let's go . . ."

Eight of them crossed the field in a long skirmish line, while the two functioning north squad trucks ferried six more agents in an end run to block off the field to the south. The last hundred yards they did on hands and knees, moving two at a time, the DEA agents performing like well-trained infantry. Gomez was working the radio, had the north squad in position, and they tightened the noose on the end of the seam.

And when they got there, they found a depression that had once been a farm dump, two rusted car bodies from the forties and fifties, corroded farm machinery, a half-buried cylindrical washing machine.

One of the agents put his finger to his lips, and pointed urgently. There, on the side of the slope nearest the farmhouse, a piece of corrugated steel, like the kind used in silos, was too conveniently arranged on the slope. The agent eased up to it, listened, peered under the sheet, then put his finger to his lips again, and backed off.

"That's it," he whispered to Gomez. Gomez waved back the troops. They moved back in a loose circle, and Gomez walked away with his radio. Fifty yards out, he stopped, clicked on the radio, and briefed the waiting agents, listening on their headsets.

It'd be a hell of a crawl, Virgil thought, looking down to the farmhouse. The smallest culvert that would take your hips and shoulders, pushing with your toes, bad air . . . Anything more than a two-foot culvert would take a hell of a lot of digging. The seam wasn't that big . . .

THEY WAITED an hour, then started working it in shifts. From the time they'd first jumped Franks, until the house went up, was little more than an hour. They'd figured out the seam a half hour later. Two hours after that, four of the DEA troops and Stryker were watching the sheet of steel, and Gomez was back at the house, watching two agents carefully probing into the basement.

Then Gomez took a radio call: "They can hear them coming."

He and Virgil jogged up the hill, two more agents running along behind. When they got close, an agent near the culvert exit stood up and made a hands-down gesture: *"Quiet."*

The agents on duty had backed into a semicircle, on their stomachs, behind rocks, behind humps in the field, all zeroed in on the sheet steel. The lead agent at the site pointed them toward a red outcrop. They went that way, squatted down, peering through a clump of weeds, and Gomez drew his pistol. "Easy," Virgil breathed.

Stryker eased up next to them and said, whispering, "We could hear them talking. Must be really tight in there."

They waited twenty minutes; the lead agent said once, on the radio, to Gomez, "Patience, patience, they're right there," and Gomez repeated it to Virgil and Stryker.

Twenty minutes, and then the sheet of metal twitched, and then a man's head and shoulders pushed from beneath it. He pulled out a long weapon, looked like another M-16. He knelt for a moment, catching his breath, then turned and snaked up the bank that he'd just emerged from, looking down toward the farmstead. He watched for a second, then slipped back down the slope and pushed the sheet up, said something, and then Feur came out of the ground, sat up, gasping for air, looked around.

The two talked for a few seconds, then Feur pointed up the hill, and they both stood, crouching, weapons hung low in their hands, and then the lead agent shouted, "Freeze. DEA. Put your hands over your head."

Both men froze, then Feur shouted, "Virgil?"

Virgil yelled, "You're good, George, just drop the weapons."

Feur spotted the direction of his voice, yanked the M-16 up. Stryker cut him down, and the rest of the DEA guns tore the two men to pieces. Beside him, Gomez had gotten to his knees, and emptied his pistol at the two.

"Jesus," Virgil said. "Oh, Jesus, stop, man . . ."

THEY WALKED DOWN. Feur and the man he'd called John—Virgil supposed—were six feet outside the end of the culvert, lying on their backs. They'd been hit forty or fifty times. Their weapons were converted M-15s.

Feur didn't look peaceful; he looked like a dead weasel. John didn't look like anything. His face was gone.

One of the armored agents said to Gomez, "They resisted. It was straight up. We did it straight up."

Gomez nodded: "Straight up," he said. "The motherfuckers."

20

A DUCK-BILLED WRECKING machine plucked splin-
tered lumber out of the wreckage of the farmhouse, like a
steel velociraptor; the sun was rolling down below the
horizon, the sky as orange as a bluebird's belly.

Virgil sat in the open door of the barn's hayloft, feet
dangling, eating a bologna sandwich provided by the tax-
payers, two other agents chewing along with him, talking
about the fight, when Gomez walked up on the ground
and called, "Let's go to town. TV is waiting."

"Fuck you," Virgil called back.

"I knew you'd say that. I talked to Davenport, and he
says he wants to see your happy face on all channels, thank-
ing the governor for this opportunity to take crime fighting
into the sticks."

"Fuck Davenport," Virgil said.

"Get your ass down here. I'm too tired to fool around."
Gomez walked away, stopped to talk to Stryker. Virgil
stood up, dusted off the seat of his pants, picked up a half-
drunk bottle of Pepsi, and stepped toward the ladder.

One of the agents, the Latino-looking New Yorker

who'd given Virgil a hard time about his T-shirt, said, "Virgil. We owe you. Puttin' those guys in the truck and taking them out of the yard. We pay. You ever need help on *anything* . . . you call us. No bullshit."

The other agent nodded, said through a mouthful of Wonder Bread and bologna, *"Anything."*

GOMEZ AND STRYKER rode to Bluestem with Virgil, in the shot-up Ford, trailed by two more agents in one of the north-crew trucks. They'd both been back and forth since the killing of Feur. The two badly wounded DEA agents were still alive. One would probably make it, the other probably not; two more, whom Virgil didn't know, were less seriously wounded, and almost everybody was scratched and pitted by rocks, dust, and pieces of metal.

Pirelli was screwed up, but not terminally. A slug had busted up his shoulder joint, and putting that back together would be tough. His broken arm was another problem, and would take a while to heal.

"AND JUDD," Stryker said. "Where is that asshole?"

A DEA arrest team had gone after Judd as the raid on the farm was taking place, but hadn't been able to find him. His car was at his office, the door was unlocked, but there was no sign of Judd.

"This bothers me," Virgil said. "Why would he be gone?"

"Tipped?" Gomez asked.

"By who? One of your guys? When Pirelli called me, Jim and I were together, and we were together every inch of the way. Neither one of us called anyone."

Stryker nodded; Gomez said, "Maybe . . . I don't know."

GOMEZ ASKED, "You got a better shirt than that?"

"And another jacket," Virgil said. "We can stop at the motel."

"Keep the jacket; I don't want you guys washed up," Gomez said. "I want you looking messed up, but the T-shirt is too much. Looks crazy, given all the dead people."

"I got a black AC/DC shirt that should be perfect," Virgil said.

"Virgil."

"I take care of myself," Virgil said. "Stop worrying about it."

They stopped for two minutes at the motel, Virgil pulled on a plain olive-drab T-shirt that gave him a vaguely military look, and Gomez said, "Not bad."

Stryker said, "Hell of a day." He had three little pockmarks on his left cheek, showing blood. He wasn't cleaning that up, either.

A DEA INFORMATION specialist had flown in from the Twin Cities and set up the press conference at the courthouse, the same room where Virgil and Stryker had been after the killing of the Schmidts.

More media this time: a half-dozen trucks, including freelance network feeds going up from satellite trucks parked in the courthouse yard. Too late for the evening news, but the late news would get it, the cable channels, and the morning network shows.

Gomez led the way: gave a terse, five-minute briefing, using the satellite photo of the farm, an outline of the fight, starting with the attack of the dogs—compressed the time a bit between the first shots at the dogs, and the fire from the house—and ending with the shootings of Feur and the man they still called John. He showed off a gas can full of glass tubes of methamphetamine, and allowed the best-looking media lady to handle one of them, holding it up to the lights for the cameras.

While she was doing it, Virgil noticed Joan and Jesse at the back of the room, looking at him and Stryker with deep skepticism. They were standing next to Williamson, who turned repeatedly to Jesse, talking at her, teeth showing.

At the very end, Gomez pulled Virgil and Stryker in front of the cameras and said, "We'd particularly like to thank Sheriff James Stryker, who as you can see was mildly wounded while suppressing the fire from the farmhouse, and Virgil Flowers, of the Minnesota Bureau of Criminal Apprehension, who risked his own life to save the lives of two of our wounded men. Damnedest thing I ever saw, when Virgil backed that truck out of the yard. These are two good guys."

Virgil was genuinely embarrassed, but the media were

happy, given local heroes in what otherwise might have been interpreted as a fuckup, with six or seven people dead, and five in the hospital.

After the briefing, the questions started, a few of them hostile, but Gomez was a pro. He turned the hostility back on the questioners, pointing out that they'd seized enough meth to save several hundred lives, "including that of young men and women; methamphetamine is one of the drugs of choice in our public schools."

Williamson had one question for Virgil: "Is this the end of the murder epidemic in Bluestem? Were the Gleasons, the Schmidts, Bill Judd Sr., were they all killed by Feur and his men? And what was the connection?"

"I'd like to answer that question, but I can't, because I don't know the answer," Virgil said. "As far as I'm concerned, the investigation continues."

Davenport called on Virgil's cell as he was shouldering his way out of the press conference: "You did good," Davenport said. "Now—when are you going to collect the nut job?"

JESSE AND JOAN were waiting on the sidewalk outside, along with Laura Stryker and a dozen people from the town. Joan said, "What the heck were you guys doing out there?"

Stryker snapped at her: "Our job. I'm the sheriff of this county. They didn't hire me to catch a bunch of dogs."

There was a murmur of approval from the crowd,

and Joan said, fists on her hips, "So now there are dead people everywhere and you've got blood all over you . . ."

Jesse was as angry as Joan, and it occurred to Virgil that they'd make good sisters-in-law. Virgil said, "I've got to go," and he walked past them out to his truck, did a U-turn, and drove over to the hospital. A couple of sheriff's cars were still parked outside the emergency entrance, cops on the lookout for any further trouble. Inside, Pirelli was out of it, sound asleep, one arm and shoulder encased in fiberglass, one leg bandaged and elevated.

A DEA guy in the hall said, "Virgil," and Virgil asked, "How are they?"

"Hangin' in there. I think . . . Doug made it this far, I think he's going to hold on."

"Prayin' for them," Virgil said, though he wasn't, because he didn't think prayer would help. He went back to the motel.

JOAN WAS COMING down the hall from the direction of his room, saw him, and asked, "Are you pissed at me?"

"Mildly," he said. "I don't need to take any shit about what happened today. Either to Jim or me or even the dead guys. It just happened—it's nobody's fault but Feur's, and he paid for it."

"We were scared," she said.

"That's okay. I don't want to hear about it. Tomorrow, you can tell me all about being scared."

She touched his hair, with the matted blood. "I could wash your hair out for you. That's going to hurt."

"You could do that," he said.

THEY SNUGGLED UP on the bed, no sex, just snuggling, Virgil full of Aleve, his hair wet, and she said, "In the press conference, when you said you didn't know if the killing was all done . . . what you meant was, it isn't."

"I don't think so. In fact . . ."

"What?"

"We're looking for Bill Judd Junior. Got watches out for him, but he seems to be gone. The thing is, I think he might be dead."

She rolled up on her elbow. "You still think Williamson?"

"The Williamson thing freaks me out. When we braced him . . . I sort of bought it. He seemed as freaked out as I was, when I figured it out. He was screaming at us."

"So . . . ?"

"So I don't know. If you pointed a gun at my head and told me to spit out a name, I'd spit out his. You think a guy, he's in the Cities, he's a newspaperman, wouldn't he know who his real mother was? Just do a search? He says he didn't, he didn't care who she was. And I guess even if he did, he wouldn't necessarily know that Judd was his father."

"If he'd ever gone for a birth certificate, to get a passport or something . . ."

Virgil rolled over on his back, felt the skin pulling around the cuts on his scalp and face. "I got to think about him . . . What was he talking to Jesse about? I saw you guys together in the back of the room."

"Well, he started out by shaking her hand, saying 'long-lost sister,' and then he started pushing her around. Where was she last week? When did she really find out she was Judd's daughter? Where was her mother?"

"Like he thought *she* might be involved?"

"He was unpleasant," Joan said, "But he's never been a real pleasant man."

"I keep trying to think, who else?"

SLEEP PULLED HIM UNDER. He woke up at two o'clock, and Joan was gone. Went to the bathroom, and then back to the bed, went under again, thinking . . . Who else? Nobody had said a thing about the .357 . . .

Of course, Jesse wouldn't; but he didn't think that Jesse was the killer, because that would be aesthetically incongruent. She was just too good-looking.

He smiled, and mentally wrote his little story, in which the best-looking woman would never be the guilty one:

> Homer shook his head. The shoot-out with Feur, the death of Feur, had blocked up a lot of potential information.
>
> Brilliant, though, the way Stryker had picked up that seam in the hillside. Homer would never have seen it. And

thank God for Stryker's reflexes: he cut Feur down before he
had a chance to open up on Homer himself.

  Mmmm . . .

Anyway:

ARCHDUKE FRANZ FERDINAND of Austria got his
ass shot in Sarajevo in 1914, touching off World War I. His
wife was killed at the same time. A little less than ninety
years later, a bunch of guys in Scotland formed a band called
Franz Ferdinand, which was why Virgil was pulling a Franz
Ferdinand T-shirt over his head the next morning at
seven o'clock.

  Find out what happened to the DEA guys. He stopped
at a gas station across the street from the motel and bought
a MoonPie and a Coke: sugar, fat, and caffeine, the breakfast of champions.

  Pirelli was awake in a standard room, Gomez asleep on
a couch under a window. Virgil asked, "How're you
doing?"

  Pirelli said, "I'm hurting. Ah, God."

  "How're your guys?"

  "Both still alive." Pirelli reached out his good hand, and
knocked on the wood-grained plastic of the bedside table.
"I think, I hope . . ."

  "What about Harmon?"

  "I talked to his wife last night," Pirelli said. "She's
coming out today."

"I don't want to be there," Virgil said.

"Neither do I."

They both looked into a corner for a moment, and then Virgil asked, "Was it worth it? If you'd had a good idea somebody was going to be killed . . . ?"

"Fuck no, it wasn't worth it." Pirelli shook his head. "Don't tell anybody I said that. If I'd known what was going to happen, I'd have set up five hundred yards away and hosed down Franks and his trucks and the house and killed the whole bunch of them. But I didn't know."

"So what's next? For you?"

Pirelli shrugged: "Media, today. Docs say I'm gonna be out of work for six months or so. Then back to Chicago. Try to figure out why we're all of a sudden rolling in heroin down in Gary . . . same ol' same ol'."

"Nobody's pissed at you?"

Pirelli shook his head. "DEA guys get killed. It's not like the FBI."

STRYKER CAME IN. "Morning, bright eyes," he said to Pirelli. Gomez sat up on the couch, shaking his head, smacking his lips. Stryker said, "Talked to the doc one minute ago: things aren't looking too bad, but they're gonna move you all to Rochester today. Mayo."

"I don't think I need the Mayo . . ." Pirelli started.

"They say you're gonna need some reconstruction on that shoulder," Stryker said. "A couple of pins. Might as well get the best."

THEY TALKED FOR A WHILE. A DEA team was flying in from Washington to reconstruct the fight, and the house, and do an after-action report. The South Dakota ethanol plant had been taken down without a fight; most of the plant was legit. The lab was not: it was a clean, efficient, meth production line. There was a national stop-and-hold on Bill Judd Jr.

They were talking about that when Stryker took a call, listened for a minute, then said, "Five minutes."

And to Pirelli, Gomez, and Virgil: "Bill Judd. He's dead. Up at his old man's place."

STRYKER AND VIRGIL went together in a county truck. Gomez and another agent followed in one of the blacked-out DEA trucks, out to the main drag, out of town and up the hill to the Buffalo Ridge park entrance, through the park gate, and up the driveway to Judd's.

Four sheriff's cars were parked by the burned-out basement, one deputy leaning on his car, talking on his radio, four more deputies standing in the high grass, north of the house, near the crest of the hill. Virgil and Stryker hopped out of the truck and Stryker raised a hand to the deputy at the car, and then they led Gomez and the other agent through the grass up the hill.

"Hell of a thing," Big Curly said, as they came up.

"What happened to him?"

"The crows were here . . . but it looks like something cracked his skull open. His brains . . . take a look."

Judd was on his back, wearing a suit and dress shoes. He didn't have sightless eyes staring at the sun, because he no longer had any eyes. Crows. The top of his head was misshapen. Not as though he were shot, but more as though his skull had been crushed. Flattened.

"Piece of rebar over here," one of the deputies said. "We're waiting for Margo to come up, but it's got blood on it, and some hair."

Virgil and Stryker went over and looked: a piece of rusty steel that might have been picked out of the burned house. "That would have done it."

No gunshot wounds. "We know one thing," Little Curly said. "It wasn't suicide."

GOMEZ ASKED, "What do you think? Feur?"

"We need a time of death, but I don't think so. It's my other guy," Virgil said.

Gomez grimaced, did a slow three-sixty, looking at the prairie lands stretched out around him forever, said, "Interesting little culture you got going here."

"Gotta be Feur," Stryker said. "Gleasons, Schmidts, the Judds—it's a Feur cleanup operation. They were gonna get out, they weren't gonna leave anything behind."

"I don't know," Virgil said.

Another deputy's car pulled in below them, and Margo

Carr got out, took a gear bag out of the trunk, and trudged up the hill. "Another one," she said, heavily.

"Last one, but maybe one," Virgil said.

"What does that mean?" Stryker asked.

Virgil shrugged.

Down the hill, another truck pulled in, and Todd Williamson got out. The deputy at the truck put out a hand to him, but Williamson jogged straight past him, beat the deputy to the edge of the heavy grass, and pulled away, the deputy still yelling at him.

Big Curly blocked him: "You can't be here."

"Screw that," Williamson said. He poked a finger at Virgil. "If the genius here is right, I'm next of kin. So what happened to my brother?"

VIRGIL HEADED BACK to the motel, with one stop at the accountant's office. Olafson had just gotten up. She raised the shade on her office door, cocked an eyebrow at Virgil, and opened the door.

Virgil stepped inside and asked, "If something happened to Bill Judd Jr., would that change what happens with his father's estate?"

"Is he dead?" she asked.

"Pretty much," Virgil said. He told her about it, and she shook her head and said, "May the Good Lord keep him."

"Estate?"

Olafson made a noise, then said, "I'd have to look up the law, and you might even have to get a special ruling.

But you know what? I think it's possible that Jesse Laymon and Todd Williamson, if they can prove a blood connection to Senior, could stand to get a bigger piece of the estate."

The argument would be complicated, she said, and hung on what the IRS would do about Junior's debt, how it would be counted against the estate. "And with this nut cake running around killing everybody, I'm not sure I'd hang around to make the argument."

Virgil thanked her, and continued on to the hotel. Shut down his cell phone, took off his boots, put the chain on the door, stretched out on the bed. There'd been a thread running through this thing, he thought, right up to the firefight at Feur's place. If he could only find one end of it, and pull it . . .

21

VIRGIL ROLLED OFF THE BED, looked at the clock—he'd been down an hour—brushed his teeth, and stood in the shower. At the end of a case, when the facts were piling up, a nap often worked to clarify his thoughts: instead of being scattered around like crumbs, they tended to clump together.

AND THAT HAD HAPPENED.

ABOUT FEUR: Jim Stryker was at least partly correct. When Virgil thought about it, it seemed unlikely that a town the size of Bluestem would be home to two, separate but simultaneous, very large crimes. Yet Feur had denied the connection, even when it wouldn't make any difference to him. Could he have been protecting someone? Seemed unlikely—seemed unlikely that in Bluestem he could have an unknown relationship so close that he would die protecting it; that he would swear on a Bible.

ABOUT THE OTHER SUSPECTS: Stryker, now, or some other cop—the Curlys, or the Merrill guy, or even Jensen or Carr—or one of the Laymons, or Williamson. Did he, Virgil, have a perceptual problem? Did he come to town and view certain people as suspects because those were the only people he saw, or spoke to, or heard about? He'd gotten all over Williamson. Had he been conditioned to do that, because Joan had mentioned Williamson's name the first time he met her? He thought about it and decided: No. That might have been the case, except for the Revelation . . .

The book of Revelation at the Gleasons', the cigarette butt at the Schmidts', the anonymous note, and the corporate evidence on Judd's secretary's computer, all had pointed him at Feur, or Judd and Feur together. He was being pushed by somebody.

A PASSING THOUGHT: Bill Judd's secretary. Who was she? The evidence for the Judd-Feur connection came right out of her computer. He'd heard her name, but didn't remember it . . .

MORE IDEAS: Could he *clear* anyone? If he could clear Stryker or Williamson, or the Curlys, the Laymons, or the Judds, then he'd know something. Other suspects would come into sharper focus. Was Joan a suspect? She'd gotten close to him by noon on his first day in town. How about Jesse Laymon, or her mother, Margaret? How long had they really been waiting for Judd to die?

ALSO: In one way or another, the killer of the Gleasons and the Schmidts, and probably the Judds, had been in Jesse Laymon's closet. Stryker had been there, he thought. Who else? Technically, her mother, but her mother wouldn't be framing Jesse . . . at least, not for any reason that Virgil knew of. There was the additional problem that the Laymons' house could be entered by any teenager with a stick . . .

HUH.

VIRGIL GOT his gun, clipped it under his jacket, put on his straw hat, and called Stryker.

"When we were in Judd's office, looking at the secretary's computer . . . What was her name again?"

"Amy Sweet. You think we ought to talk to her?"

"No need to bother you. I might stop by and have a chat," Virgil said. "Sort of at loose ends, is what I am. Can't get over Junior getting hit like that."

"Yeah. Still think it was Feur . . . You still think it wasn't?"

"I've moved a few inches in your direction," Virgil said. "But keep your ass down anyway."

AMY SWEET WAS another middle-aged woman, who might have been a rocker at one time, too heavy now, round-shouldered, wrapped in a housecoat with pink curlers in her hair. "I'd be happy to talk to you," she said at the door of her small home, "but I've got to be in Sioux Falls for a job interview at one o'clock."

"Take a couple of minutes," Virgil said.

"What was all the excitement a while ago?" She pushed her face toward him, squinting, nearsighted.

"Uh, there's been another murder."

"Oh, noooo . . ." She stepped across the room, fumbled around on a TV tray, found steel-rimmed glasses, and put them on. "Who?"

"Bill Judd Jr."

"Oh, noooo." Round, Swedish oooo's.

"Miz Sweet, when we were going through Judd Sr.'s office, we found some invoices on your computer, for chemicals that were apparently used in an ethanol plant out in South Dakota . . ."

"I heard about it on TV. That was the same one? The one where they were making drugs?"

"Yes, it was," Virgil said.

"Oh, nooo."

The sound was driving him crazy; she sounded like a bad comedian. "Who in town knew about the ethanol plant?"

She turned her face to one side and put a hand to her lips. "Well, the Judds, of course."

"Both of them?" Virgil asked.

"Well . . . Junior set it up, but Senior knew about it."

He pressed. "Are you sure about that?"

"Well, yes. He signed the checks."

"Did you see him signing the checks?" Virgil asked.

"No, but I saw the checks. It was his signature . . ."

"Do you remember the bank?"

She shook her head. "No, no, I don't." She frowned. "I'm not even sure that the bank name was on the checks."

"Did you ever talk to Junior about that?"

"No. It wasn't my business," she said. "They wanted to keep it quiet, because, you know, when ethanol started, it sounded a little like the Jerusalem artichoke thing. The Judds were involved in that, of course."

"So how quiet did they keep it?" Virgil asked. "Who else knew? Did you tell anybody?"

He saw it coming, the *noooo*. "Oh, noooo . . . Junior told me, don't talk about this, because of my father. So, I didn't."

"Not to anybody?"

Her eyes drifted. She was thinking, which meant that she had. "It's possible . . . my sister, I might have told. I think there might have been some word around town."

"It's really important that you remember . . ."

She put her hand to her temple, as though she were going to move a paper clip with telekinesis, and said, "I might have mentioned it at bridge. At our bridge club. That a plant was being built, and some local people were involved."

"All right," Virgil said. "So who was at the bridge club?"

"Well, let me see, there would have been nine or ten of us . . ."

She listed them; he only recognized one of the names.

WHEN HE WAS DONE with Sweet, he strolled up the hill to the newspaper office. He pushed in, and found Williamson behind the business counter, talking to a woman customer. Williamson looked past the woman and snapped, "What do you want?"

"I have a question, when you're free."

"Wait." Williamson was wearing a T-shirt and had sweat stains under his arms, as though he'd been lifting rocks. "Take just a minute."

The customer was trying to dump her Beanie Baby collection locally—ten years too late, in Virgil's opinion—and wanted the cheapest possible advertisement. She got twenty words for six dollars, looking back and forth between Virgil and Williamson, and after writing a check for the amount, said to Virgil, "I'd love to hear your question."

Virgil looked at her over his sunglasses and grinned: "I'd love to have you, but I'm afraid it's gotta be private, for the moment."

"Shoot." She looked at Williamson, who shrugged, and she said, "Oh, well."

WHEN SHE'D GONE out the door, Williamson said, "I'm working. You can ask me out back."

"You still pissed about the search?"

"Goddamn right. Wouldn't you be?"

Virgil followed him through the shop. Williamson's van was parked in the dirt space behind it, the side doors open. Williamson had been piling bundles of unsold newspapers in the van, and there were still twenty or thirty wrapped bundles inside the shop. Williamson propped the door open, picked up two bundles by the plastic straps, carried them to the van, and asked over his shoulder, "What?"

Virgil grabbed a couple of bundles, carried them out and threw them in the van. "When did you last see Junior?"

"About an hour and a half ago."

"Alive." They were shuttling back and forth with the bundles.

Williamson stopped and cocked his head. "Day before yesterday . . . let's see. Down at Johnnie's, at lunch."

"Did you hear him next door? Yesterday?" Virgil asked, heaving two more bundles into the van.

"No. He wasn't there. I stopped, I wanted to ask him where I should send the money we've got coming in. His office was locked."

"What time was that?"

"First time, about nine o'clock. Right after I got here. Then, when the shooting started out at Feur's—I heard about it from a cop, and I took off, headed down there, to Feur's, but the cops had all the roads blocked. Before I took off, I ran next door, I was going to tell Bill about it."

"Why?"

Williamson shrugged. "I don't know. Big news. Maybe something to do with his old man."

"All right," Virgil said. He threw two more bundles in the van, leaving three in the shop. "So he wasn't here all day yesterday, and wasn't here last night?"

"Nope. And I was here late."

Virgil nodded. If Judd had disappeared some hours before the fight at Feur's, that meant that both Stryker and Feur, or one of Feur's men, could have killed him.

THEN WILLIAMSON STACKED the three remaining bundles, one on top of the other, and stooped to pick them up. As he did it, his T-shirt sleeve hiked up, exposing a tattoo of a crescent moon. The moon with a slash for an eye, and a pointed nose: a man in the moon. The tattoo was rough, with bleeding edges, dark ink from a ballpoint pen.

Virgil blinked. Another man in the moon.

Sonofabitch.

HE LEFT WILLIAMSON with the van, walked back to his truck, got on the phone to Joan: "What're you doing?" he asked.

"Headed over to Worthington to do some federal bureaucratic bullshit about crop insurance. What about you?"

"I'm headed up to the Cities," Virgil said. "Could be overnight . . ."

"I'd love to come," she said, "but this appointment in

Worthington is not optional, if I want to stay in business. I've got everything in quintuplicate, and they want it today."

"Okay. See you tomorrow, then."

She laughed at the tone: "I'll brace myself."

HE CALLED the Laymons, but nobody answered. Called Stryker, and asked if he had Jesse's cell phone. He got the number and said to Stryker, "I'm running up to the Cities. Back tomorrow."

"Anything good?"

"Just some federal bureaucratic bullshit. How's the election looking?"

"Folks are smiling at me," Stryker said. "I'm golden for at least a week; and as long as you're wrong about Feur. If somebody else gets killed, now that Feur's gone, I'm back in the toilet."

VIRGIL CALLED JESSE. She answered after a couple of rings: "Virgil . . ."

"Jesse: listen. I'm going to the Cities. It's really important that you and your mom get someplace safe. Don't get alone with any third person, no matter whether you know him or not. Maybe go over to Worthington or Sioux Falls, check into a motel. Just overnight—I should be back tomorrow."

"You think somebody's looking for us?" she asked.

"It's possible. I don't want to take any chances. Get yourself under cover until tomorrow."

"Mom's at work," she said.

"Pick her up," Virgil said. "Keep her away from the house."

"I was planning to go out tonight . . ."

"Jesse, just for the heck of it . . . let's say you should stay away from Jim Stryker, too."

"Jim?"

"Just for the heck of it. Until I get back."

HE SWUNG BY the motel, picked up a bag, headed out on the highway. As soon as he was clear of town, he turned on the flashers and dropped the hammer. Got settled online, and called Davenport. He wasn't in the office, but he got him on the cell phone. "Can I borrow Sandy or Jenkins or Shrake for a few hours?"

"Jenkins and Shrake are picking a guy up," Davenport said. "Sandy's working on something, but if it's important . . ."

"I'm cracking this thing," Virgil said. "I need some names and some record checks."

"She'll call you back."

VIRGIL REMEMBERED Joan's mother, Laura, talking about grandmothers—about how she wanted to be one, about how she wanted to watch her grandchildren grow up, about how she had time to see great-grand-children.

Laura Stryker wasn't that old—a baby boomer, in fact. A rock 'n' roller. The same age as Williamson's mother.

Williamson's mother might have been dead, but it was possible that his natural grandparents were still alive. And grandparents do take an interest; normal ones, anyway.

So there might be, Virgil thought, somebody in the Cities who'd taken a lifelong interest in Todd Williamson . . .

HAD TO BE Williamson, Virgil thought.

Judd Sr.'s sister-in-law, Betsy Carlson, in wandering in and out of rationality, had mentioned the man in the moon. Virgil had connected that to the man-*on*-the-moon party at Judd's, but Betsy had been right: she said she'd seen the man *in* the moon. She'd talked to Williamson at some point, had seen Judd within him, and had seen the tattoo, which brought everything back.

And Williamson would have no reason to talk to Betsy Carlson, unless he knew that Judd was his father.

NEW FACT: When he and Stryker checked Williamson's police record, they'd found nothing at all. But the tattoo on Williamson's arm hadn't come from a tattoo parlor. It was a prison tattoo, done with a sewing needle and ballpoint-pen ink. Maybe he'd gotten it on the outside, from somebody who'd been inside, knew how to do it. Maybe he chose a crude tattoo for aesthetic reasons. But Virgil was willing to bet that Williamson had been inside, at least for a while.

So why didn't Virgil know that? Why hadn't a record

popped up? He could think of one good reason . . .

He looked down at the speedometer: one-oh-one. He called the Highway Patrol in Marshall again, and cleared the way out front. Got off the phone, then got back on when the cell burped.

Sandy.

"SANDY: I want you to find Todd Williamson's adoptive parents. Search every database you can find. Look at their taxes, find out when they stopped paying them, then check all the surrounding states and Florida, California, and Arizona, see if you can find them. Call old neighbors, if you have to."

"I can do that," she said.

"Then: Check Margaret Lane, died seven-twenty-sixty-nine. See if you can find a birth certificate. Find out if her parents are still alive—this would be Todd Williamson's grandparents. Then, check the NCIC for a Lane, unknown first name, born seven twenty sixty-nine."

"You think he used his mother's name?" Sandy asked.

"If he got a birth certificate, he could use it to get a driver's license, and he could use that to get a Social Security number. He could do the same thing with his adoptive parents' names, have two perfectly good IDs based on official state documents."

"How soon do you need it?"

"I'm on the way up there, hundred miles an hour," Virgil said. "Feed it to me as you get it. If you find people, route me to their locations."

When he got off, he looked down at the speedometer. Hundred and five. He'd always liked speed—but the truck was squealing like a pig.

SANDY CALLED BACK as he was making the turn north on I-35. "The NCIC has a William Lane, seven twenty sixty-nine, showing arrests in eighty-seven and twice in eighty-eight, possession of a small amount of cocaine on the first one, and then two assault charges in eighty-eight, apparently a domestic thing. He spent four months in the Hennepin County jail on the second assault . . . let me look, blah, blah, a Karen Biggs, I'll see if I can find her . . ."

"E-mail it to me . . ."

SHE CALLED fifteen minutes later: "I've got the Biggs woman, she lives in Cottage Grove now, her name is Johannsen, got a bunch of DWIs. I checked William Lane, he shared an address with Todd Williamson in 'eighty-eight and 'eighty-nine . . ."

"Got him," Virgil said.

"Yup. Haven't found his parents yet, they left too long ago," Sandy said.

"Keep looking. How about the grandmother?" Virgil asked.

"Ralph and Helen Lane. Ralph died a long time ago. Helen is still alive, she lives up in Roseville, but I haven't been able to reach her."

"Give me those addresses." He propped his notebook in the center of the steering wheel, kept one eye half-cocked toward the highway, took the addresses down.

TEN MINUTES AFTER THAT, Sandy was back. "The Williamsons are in Arizona. I've got an address but no phone number. I'll try to get one."

"Good. If you have to, check on neighbors, have them go next door and find out the number."

"Okay. I'm looking at license photos on Williamson and Lane and they are indeed the same person, though Lane has some facial hair and an earring," Sandy said.

"E-mail them."

He got off the phone, stayed on the accelerator, took a call from Davenport as he swung onto I-35E south of the Cities. "I talked to Sandy. She says you're rolling on this thing."

"I think so."

"You got anything for a trial?" Davenport asked. "Gotta think about trial."

"Not yet. Gonna have to think of something cute, to get that. Right now, I'm trying to nail down the fact that my guy's a psycho."

"All right. Stay in touch."

HE CAME OFF I-35E, cut east across the south end of the Cities on I-494, and then south on Highway 61, the same one that Bob Dylan revisited, heading into Cottage Grove. Off at 80th Street, he called Sandy, who got on MapQuest and took him straight in to Johannsen's place.

Johannsen's son came to the door, wearing rapper jeans with the crotch at knee level, and a T-shirt that was four sizes too big; he had a GameBoy in his hand. His eyes were at half-mast, and the odor of marijuana floated out of the house when he opened the door.

"She's at work," he said, sullenly.

"Where?"

"Either SuperAmerica or Tom Thumb. She works at both of them," he said. "I don't know where she's working today."

KAREN JOHANNSEN was at the SuperAmerica, throwing expired doughnuts in a dumpster. "I have some questions about William Lane, who was convicted of assaulting you," Virgil said, flashing his ID.

"Shoot. That was twenty years ago, almost." She was a short, broad woman with black hair and watery brown eyes, a pushed-in nose, older-looking than her years.

"I know that," Virgil said. "What we're trying to do is, we're trying get a grip on what kind of a guy he is. The assaults . . . were they heavy-duty, or just sort of . . . routine domestic fighting?"

"He was trying to kill me," Johannsen said, matter-of-factly. She waved her hand in front of her face, like a fan. They were too close to the dumpster, which smelled of spoiled bananas and meat, and sour milk. "He would have,

too, if he'd been stronger. The first time, he was hitting me
with a chair, and he couldn't get a good swing and I was
running around, so he never did hit me square. The neighbors called the cops. There was a car in the neighborhood,
and they got there in time. But he would have killed me."

"What set it off?" Virgil asked.

"Basically, we were drinking, and started arguing," she
said. "I was working and he wasn't and I told him he was a
worthless piece of shit who couldn't even pay the rent,
and he punched my arm and I hit him with my purse, and
knocked him down, and he just went off . . . completely
out of control."

"What about the second time?" Virgil asked. "When he
went to jail?"

"That time, he choked the shit out of me," she said.
Her hand went to her neck, as she remembered. "He came
home, drunk. I was asleep, he woke me up and wanted,
you know, and I didn't want to. He started screaming at
me, and I wised off, and he jumped on me and choked me.
He had some friends with him, out in the living room, and
they heard the fight . . . One of his friends pulled me off,
and then I wasn't breathing so good, so the girlfriend of
the friend called the cops, and they called an ambulance
and they started me breathing again."

"That was all for the two of you?"

"Yeah. When he was in jail, I moved. Changed my
address and got an unlisted phone . . . but I saw him
anyway. We had some of the same friends. But we were all
done, and he didn't come around anymore," Johannsen

said. "Good thing, too. He would have killed me, sooner or later."

"Did he ever mention his parents?" Virgil asked.

"Said his mom was killed in a car wreck," she said. "Didn't say who his dad was."

"What about his adoptive parents . . . some people named Williamson?"

She shook her head. "Oh . . . I thought they were his foster-care people, or something. They adopted him?"

"Yes. When he was a baby."

"Jeez—I didn't know that," she said. "That makes it worse."

"Worse."

"Yeah. I met them two or three times, I guess, going over there with Bill. We used to go over there for beer—he had a key. But. They were like, total assholes."

"Yeah?"

"Yeah. Like they believed in slavery," she said. "They used to tell him about how much he owed them—in money. Bill ran away when he was fourteen; he was living on the street when I met him. He ran away because they wanted him to work in their store all the time. They called it earning his keep, but most kids who are thirteen or fourteen don't have to work sixty hours a week. That's what they wanted. No kidding—they were assholes."

"Did Bill ever call himself Todd Williamson?"

She shook her head: "Nope. He was Lane to all of us guys—the people he hung around with."

"Good guy, bad guy?" Virgil asked. "I mean, when he was sober?"

"Not bad, when he was sober," Johannsen said. She looked at her thumb; it had frosting on it, and she wiped it on the dumpster. "Bad when he was drunk. But that was twenty years ago. He was a teenager. You work in this store, you realize that a lot of teenagers are assholes, and a lot of them change when they get older."

"Think Bill would change?"

She shrugged. "I don't know. He was like a dog that you beat for ten years. Not the dog's fault if he goes crazy."

SANDY CALLED. "I got the grandmother. She's home. I told her to stay there."

"Call her back, tell her I'll be there in half an hour," Virgil said.

HE SAID GOOD-BYE to Johannsen and headed north, twenty minutes to an inner-ring suburban neighborhood, green lawns, cracked driveways, older ranch-style and split-level homes, two long-haired teenagers doing intricate and athletic bike tricks.

Helen Lane, Williamson's natural grandmother, was alone in her living room, watching television when Virgil pulled into the driveway. She came to the door, kept the screen locked: "I don't know where Todd is. I don't want to know. He was in jail for a while. Did he do something else?

"Did he give *you* a hard time?" Virgil asked.

"He'd steal money from me. He'd sneak into the house and steal," she said.

"How'd he find out you were his grandmother?" Virgil asked.

"He was smart. Got his brains from my daughter," she said. "I guess the Williamsons had a paper, maybe his birth certificate."

"Did he ever figure out who his real father was?"

She frowned and said, "None of us knew who it was. I don't think Maggie knew, for sure. She was running wild."

"You never knew?"

"No . . . and after she died, there was no way to find out. Sure as heck weren't no men coming around to ask about it."

"And the baby . . . ?"

"Was adopted. We didn't have any money, my husband was sick all the time—he was a roofer, he hurt his back," she said, sorry for herself. "I was working all the time, so, it seemed like the best thing to do was to let the baby go."

"Yeah?"

"Yeah. You know, to a good family."

22

VIRGIL GRABBED a McDonald's meal on the way back to Bluestem, ten minutes off the highway and back on, the car smelling like Quarter Pounders with Cheese and fries, driving into the dying light; thinking, as he drove, that Williamson's past had not been quite what he'd expected. You could take the mad-dog view of things—that Williamson was nuts, driven that way by parental neglect and, possibly, actual abuse. And that as sorry a tale as that might be, a mad dog is still a mad dog.

You could just as easily take another view: orphaned kid, abused by adoptive parents, pushed onto the streets when he was still a kid—and somehow, he rights himself, goes in the Army, learns a trade, and becomes a respectable citizen.

Virgil, who basically had a kindly heart, preferred the second story. But his cop brain said, a mad dog is still a mad dog, even if it's not the dog's fault.

HE WAS in Bluestem a little before eleven o'clock. Larry Jensen's house was lit up like a Christmas tree, and when he got out of his truck, on the driveway, Virgil could feel an impact through his feet, as though somebody were shooting a big gun in Jensen's basement, but not quite like a gun.

He rang the bell, and a moment later, Jensen's wife came to the door. She was a small woman, sweaty, very pregnant. She turned on the porch light and Virgil felt the impact again, whatever it was. She peered out through the window in the door, then opened it and said, "You're Virgil."

"Yes. Is Larry here?"

"He's down breaking up the basement," she said. "What's going on?"

JENSEN WAS BREAKING UP the basement floor with a sledgehammer, working bare chested. The basement had been finished sometime long before, and now the walls had been stripped of the Sheetrock, showing the bare studs and long streaks of old PL200, with chunks of drywall still stuck to it.

Virgil came down the steps just as Jensen came through a swing, the hammer cracking into the concrete, and then he turned and his eyes narrowed when he saw Virgil. He wiped his head and asked, "What's up?"

"Putting in a toilet, huh?"

"Gonna have one more kid," he said, propping the hammer against the basement wall. "That'll be three girls and a boy, and we sure as shit won't get along with one bathroom . . . So what're you doing?"

"Gotta ask you a question, Larry. If Stryker's popularity takes a fall . . . are you running for sheriff?"

Jensen looked at him for a moment, not answering, then, "Why would you want to know?"

"Larry, believe me . . . Just answer the question, okay?"

Jensen wiped his forehead with the palm of his hand, wiped his hand on his jeans, and said, "Naw. I'm happy like I am. I'll get my twenty-five when I'm forty-five, and then maybe try something new. Double-dip."

"The power doesn't appeal to you," Virgil said.

Jensen shook his head: "What're you up to, Virgil? And no, it doesn't appeal to me."

"Come on. Get your jacket: we gotta make a call."

"It's midnight, Virgil. Does Jim know about this?"

"Get your jacket, Larry. We gotta make a call, and I'm not going alone. I need a witness. And Margo Carr—call her up, too. Jim doesn't know about it, because it would embarrass him to know about it. Officially."

Jensen put his hands on his hips: "Well, shit."

"Larry . . ."

THEY GOT a key from the evidence locker and rode out to the Schmidt house in silence. "This worries me; I really don't like it," Jensen said.

"I don't like it either," Virgil said.

The Schmidt house was dark and silent, an air of gloom gripping it like a glove. They parked under the yard light, and Jensen led the way across the yard, joked, "You're not afraid of ghosts, are you?"

"No. Not that I'd mess around with one, if I had the chance," Virgil said.

INSIDE, THEY BROUGHT the computer up. Virgil went to the in-box, checked Schmidt's e-mail. The letters from the Curlys were gone, as Virgil thought they would be.

"Doesn't necessarily mean a lot," Jensen said.

"No, it doesn't—it can't be entirely innocent, but it might not be entirely guilty, either. Just trying to keep their asses out of the fire," Virgil said.

A set of headlights swept the yard, and a minute later, Margo Carr knocked, then stepped inside. "What've you got?"

"I need you to take this computer to your place—not the office, to your place—and lock it up," Virgil said. "Then, tomorrow, I want you to get in touch with the state crime lab about recovering files on the hard drive. Should be simple enough. Don't have to do it yet, but make the arrangements."

She looked from Virgil to Jensen and back again: "What are we looking for?"

"Roman Schmidt's e-mails," Virgil said. "All of them."

HE MET STRYKER and Jensen again at nine o'clock the next morning, at the sheriff's office, Virgil carrying a cup of coffee. "Where's Merrill?"

"He's on his way," Stryker said. "Larry's filled me in: I think you probably ought to do this somewhere else. You could use a courtroom."

Virgil nodded, then said, "What about the guys from the DEA? They holding on?"

Stryker nodded: "All holding on; I talked to Pirelli this morning. What exactly are you doing, Virgil? You never told Larry exactly what . . ."

"Talk to you in a bit," Virgil said. "Send Merrill over when he shows up." To Jensen: "Let's go nail down that courtroom."

THE COURTROOM WAS EMPTY, and Virgil walked back and turned the latch between the courtroom and the judge's chamber. He asked Jensen, "When are you gonna get that basement finished?" Virgil asked.

"Virgil, I'm not up for any small talk, right now," Jensen said. "These guys are friends of mine."

Virgil said, "Don't worry about it. If they *did* do something wrong, we can always cover it up."

That made Jensen laugh, once. Then he shook his head and said, "I'll remember that. You know, when they have me on the witness stand, and they're puttin' the screws on my thumbs."

"Listen," Virgil said, "does anybody in town teach CPR? You know, where you practice on one of those dummies?"

Jensen was confused: "Yeah. The fire guys do that. They go around to the schools . . . Why?"

"Small talk, just keeping you occupied," Virgil said. They heard footfalls outside the courtroom, and Virgil lowered his voice. "Here comes one, now."

MERRILL CAME IN, looked at Virgil, and said to Jensen, "You called?"

Virgil said, "When you talked to me in the men's room, about Jesse Laymon, and her car not being there, at the Judd fire . . . Where were you? I didn't see you there."

"I was up the hill, trying to keep people from doing an end run to the fire. I saw you go by."

"So, you said you didn't see Jesse's truck. Did you look at all the trucks?"

"No . . ."

"Then why pick on Jesse?" Virgil asked.

Merrill hooked his thumbs over his gun belt, which, in a cop, is defensive: "I heard talk that nobody had seen her. And since *I* hadn't either, I thought you should know."

"Who'd you hear that talk from?" Virgil asked.

Merrill's eye went to Jensen. "What's going on, Larry?"

"Not a big deal," Jensen said. "We're just trying to track down where you might have heard that."

"It's sort of confidential . . ."

"It's not confidential from us," Virgil said. His voice was mild, and quiet, so Merrill had to concentrate on him. "If I need to immunize you, and put you in front of a grand jury to get it, I'll do that. Of course, you'll lose your job. If there are any subsidiary entanglements, you could be going to Stillwater for a few years."

"What are you talking about?" Merrill barked. "I was giving you a tip."

Virgil looked at Jensen. "Better read him his rights. Do we have to do that with police officers? I think maybe we should."

Merrill said, "What the hell?"

Virgil said, "We really need to know where you heard that. That's all. No crime at this point. Could get to be a crime. Depending. So where did you hear it?"

Merrill looked at Jensen, then back at Virgil. "Jesus . . . I mean, it's no big deal, I guess. I heard it from Little Curly."

Virgil smiled. "See? That was easy enough. We thought you probably had. So, take off. Keep this to yourself. And I mean, Deputy, *keep it to yourself.* We're right in the middle of a complicated thing here, and you best keep your head down."

THE CURLYS CAME in together. Jensen had called Little Curly, told him to find his father, bring him in. Little Curly was wearing his uniform, Big Curly was off duty, wearing red shorts and a T-shirt that showed off his gut.

"Sit down," Virgil said.

They sat, and Big Curly asked Jensen, "What's going on, Larry?"

Virgil said, "You're talking to me. Not to Larry. He's more of a witness."

Big Curly looked at his son, then asked Virgil, "What the hell are you talking about?"

"I need to set some quick ground rules," Virgil said. "You don't have to talk to me. If you don't, then the chips fall where they may. One or both of you have done things that helped out the killer of the Gleasons and the Schmidts and the Judds . . ."

"What? That's bullshit," Big Curly said. He looked at his son, shook his head, then said to Jensen, "Larry, are you putting up with this shit?"

Jensen said, "You should listen to him."

Virgil continued: "Whether you knew it or not—but if you bail on me now, like I said, a prosecutor could take a fairly harsh view of it. Or we can handle it privately, and maybe, if I think it was all innocent, we let it go. Though I'll have to talk to Jim about it."

Little Curly: "I still don't know what you're talking about."

VIRGIL ASKED, "Who went into the Schmidts' house and erased e-mails from Roman Schmidt's computer?"

The Curlys looked at each other, then Big Curly, his face gone grim, said, "I did. But it had nothing to do with the killings. It was a personal matter."

"I know—about the election," Virgil said. "We've got the computer sequestered, and we can recover the e-mails if we need to. Keep that in mind. Now, did you walk anybody through the house after the killings?"

Little Curly shook his head. "Not me. Why would I?"

Big Curly said, "Me neither."

"How about the Gleasons' house? After the murder?"

Little Curly shook his head, but Big Curly hung his, groaned, and said, "That fuckin' Williamson."

"Why?" Virgil asked.

"Because of the election," Big Curly said, looking up at Virgil. His eyes were wet, as though he were about to start crying. "I was getting on Todd's good side—the newspaper's about the only way to campaign here, that anybody can afford. His articles can set the whole tone of the election, and you don't even have to pay for them. Jim is getting in trouble with these murders, somebody was going to take the job away from him . . ."

Virgil turned to Little Curly: "You had Merrill suggest to me that Jesse Laymon might have had something to do with the killings—that her truck wasn't at the park the night of the Judd fire. It *was* there, so why'd you suggest that it wasn't?"

Little Curly shook his head: "I didn't see it. I saw her, but not the truck. I was talking with Todd, and he brought it up."

"Did you ever see Todd up there?"

The Curlys looked at each other, then Little Curly said, "Well, not actually. I assumed . . ."

"WHY DIDN'T YOU tell me yourself?" Virgil asked. "About Jesse?"

"Because . . . Ah shit, because I didn't want to get involved with you. I didn't want to talk to you."

"Because of the election? Because Jim was seeing Jesse, and if you tarred Jesse, you'd get Jim, too?"

Little Curly shook his head: "Look. Todd said she wasn't there. I didn't see her. We thought you should know."

"And smearing Jim was just a side benefit?"

"Fuck you," Little Curly said.

"All right," Virgil said. To Big Curly: "When you walked Williamson through, was he ever alone? For even a minute?"

"Well . . . maybe for a few seconds, here and there—he'd be looking at one thing, taking some notes, I might be looking at another."

VIRGIL TURNED to Jensen: "Did Jim give you a hard time about not spotting that book of Revelation?"

Jensen shrugged. "Not a *hard* time. He got me and Margo in his office, said we should have seen it. Said it was embarrassing that you picked it up first. Wasn't the most pleasant five minutes of my life."

"You didn't pick it up, because it wasn't there," Virgil said. "Williamson planted it when Big Curly walked him through. He was trying to point us at Feur. He did the same thing with that Salem cigarette by the Schmidts' stoop. He knew we'd pick it up. I knew that Feur smoked, and I thought they were Salems. I'm sure it would have come up at some point, if there was ever a question. A trial."

"Why? Why would he do all this?" Little Curly asked. "Judd's money?"

Virgil shook his head. "Nope. Basically, he did it because he's nuts. Nuts, but careful, and he thought he was smart enough that he could get away with it. I don't think he could really help himself on the killings—not on the first five, anyway, the Gleasons and the Schmidts, and Judd Senior, Judd Junior might have been a cleaning up.

"But after he killed the Gleasons, I think he decided to try to pin it on Feur. Just in case. And maybe, because his office was right there with the Judds', he knew that Judd Junior and Feur were involved with each other, and he could throw enough suspicion on Feur to create doubt, even if we did tumble to him. So he started by planting the Revelation. Then the Salem. And to tell you the truth, those documents we found in Judd's computer: there wasn't a thing in Judd's own machine, but they were right there in his secretary's."

"Like they were planted?" Jensen asked.

"I don't know," Virgil said. "But when Jim saw them, he drew a line from anhydrous ammonia to ethanol to meth pretty goddamn quick. It like jumped up and bit you on the ass."

"Williamson's office has an internal connection with the Judds'," Big Curly said. "There're equipment and storage spaces behind all three offices, with connecting doors. He could have sat in there as long as he wanted, at night, working on the locks. Maybe they weren't even locked—it was all behind the same security system. He used to work all night, sometimes. Nobody would have thought anything of it, seeing him come out of there in the middle of the night."

"THE THING about framing Feur is . . . it might still work," Jensen said.

"It might," Virgil agreed. "A decent defense attorney will put Judd and Feur on trial, tie them to the Gleasons and the Schmidts. The Gleasons and the Schmidts did help cover up a murder . . ."

Jensen: *"What?"*

"I'm keeping some of it confidential," Virgil said. "But I'll fill you in later."

The three deputies looked at each other. "What are you going to do?" Big Curly asked.

"Nothing, right now. Just keep your eyes open and your heads down."

Little Curly stood up and said, "That's it?"

Virgil nodded: "Yeah. I'm willing to hold this talk privately—I'm not required to file a public report. But I really do think you should drop any election plans. It might even be a good idea to show some public support for Jim Stryker for re-election."

Big Curly said, "Shit."

"Six people dead so far," Virgil said. "Your relationship with Williamson would be a tough thing to come up, during an election year."

Big Curly looked around the courtroom and said, "There are things that ain't right about this place."

Little Curly interrupted: "Shut up, Dad." He said to Virgil, "It's a deal. We're backing Jim." To his father: "Let's go, Dad. C'mon. Let's go."

They trooped out, but a couple of seconds later, Big Curly stuck his head back inside the courtroom. "I'm sorry," he said. Then he was gone.

Jensen said, "Now what? I'm not sure that any of this will get a conviction . . ."

"I gotta run an errand," Virgil said. "I'll be back in the early afternoon."

JESSE LAYMON was sitting at the bar, eating a cheeseburger, talking to a guy with a flat-top and a red face, whose arm was very close to hers. They both had beer glasses in front of them. Her ass looked terrific on a bar stool, Virgil thought, as he pulled up next to her and said, "Hello, darlin'. Am I late?"

The flattop guy gave him a drop-dead stare, and Jesse said, "Hey, Virgil." She pointed to the beefy guy and said, "This is Chuck, uh . . ."

"Marker," the beefy guy said.

"Marker, who is a deputy sheriff with Kandiyohi County," she said. "We have some friends in common, in Willmar. And Chuck, this is Virgil Flowers, of the Bureau of Criminal Apprehension, who is trying to keep me from being murdered."

Marker straightened a little: "What?"

"She's the center of a pretty big . . . Say, you guys known

each other long?" Virgil asked, looking from one to the other.

Marker picked up his glass: "About ten minutes. I better get back to my meeting."

When he was gone, Jesse smiled and patted Virgil on the arm and said, "That wasn't very nice."

"Well, I don't have a lot of time. I'm here to bullshit you into doing something that you won't want to do," Virgil said.

"Do I get to wear a wire?"

"Well, they're not actually wires anymore, but they're sort of like that," Virgil said. "Smaller. But I do want you to have a chat with Todd Williamson."

"He's called me on my cell a couple of times, but I haven't answered," she said.

"Eat your lunch: I'll get a cheeseburger. Then we'll give him a call back. I've got a script for you."

"You think he's the one?"

"Maybe," Virgil said. "Evidence seems to be piling up."

"You think he'll admit it to me?"

"Hard to tell," Virgil said. "Could be putty in the hands of a pretty woman . . ."

"Yeah, right." She held up a finger to the bartender. "Bill, please. Give it to this guy."

23

VIRGIL GOT ON the extension, listened through four rings, and then Williamson picked up.

Jesse said, "Todd—I'm sorry I'm late, but I conked out last night. You called me?"

"Just to tell you that I talked to Judge Solms last night and he said that we both ought to get started on DNA testing. We can get kits from the same lab that the sheriff's office uses, and have them witnessed by a court clerk or a sheriff's deputy, and send them off for testing. That'll clear up our rights to the estate of the Judds. I'm still kind of uncertain— I know that you've pretty much got it nailed down."

"Ah, you're a Judd," Jesse said. "You can see it in you, if you look. You can see it in me, too. So what do they do? Suck some blood or something?"

"No, no, it's just a little kit with a Q-tip on the end of it, and then we scrub in the inside of our cheeks. No blood, nothing like that. Doesn't hurt—it's like brushing your teeth. Solms said the reason for using the same lab is, we can get a better price on comparing the DNA to the two Judds'."

"All right," Jesse said. She was interested. "What do I do, just call the sheriff's department and make a date?"

"Call Solms' clerk," Williamson said. "She'll set it up for you. They might have Margo Carr come over from the sheriff's office to supervise, make sure we do it right. Okay?"

VIRGIL THOUGHT he was about to ring off, and made a rolling motion with his forefinger, and Jess nodded and jumped in: "I'd like to talk to you about Virgil Flowers. I'm really getting confused about this. You know, Mom and I visit Betsy Carlson over in Sioux Falls, at the rest home, every once in a while . . . Do you know Betsy?"

"I know who she is," Williamson said. "Never met her."

"Well, the last time we went over there . . . her mind wanders. We told her some of the things that were going on. We told her that Bill Judd died, we thought maybe she was in a will or something. Anyway, when we told her, she got all excited, and said she'd seen the man in the moon. She was really freaked out about it: she'd seen the man in the moon."

"I'm sorry," Williamson said. "What are you talking about?"

"Well, I noticed, one time, you've got that man-in-the-moon tattoo on your arm. I thought maybe she was talking about that. And Virgil's been asking me about the man in the moon because I've got man-in-the-moon earrings . . . and, well, what's this man-in-the-moon stuff?"

Williamson said, "I don't know. Betsy wasn't talking about me. How could she be? We never met."

"I thought, I don't know," Jesse said. "You look a little like Bill Judd, and if you'd interviewed her or something . . ."

"Nope. Never did," Williamson said. "She was in the home long before I got here."

"All right," Jesse said. "Still. I'd like to talk about Virgil. I'm over in Worthington with my mom, I won't be back until late, 'til the stores close. You think we could hook up somewhere in Bluestem? Like at the Dairy Queen? I'll probably be back at nine-thirty or ten?"

"Let me think . . . What time do they close? The Dairy Queen?"

"Eleven."

"Ah . . . tell you what. Let's hook up at ten. I'm working late tonight, I could walk over."

"See you then," she said.

She rang off and Virgil flopped back on the bed. "Excellent," he said.

"You *really* think he did it?" Margaret Laymon asked. She was sitting on the other bed, had been looking on in bemusement as Virgil and Jesse worked on the phone call.

"Yes. Probably. But not for sure," Virgil said. "If he shows up tonight, he could dig his own grave. Or, he might clear himself. Either way, I get rid of a major suspect."

Margaret looked at her daughter: "Told you. Pure cop."

24

WHEN THE OUT-OF-TOWN COPS had been milling around the salad bar, Virgil had spotted a deputy from Dodge County that he'd done some work with a few months earlier. When they got off the phone with Williams, he took Jesse along and introduced her to the guy, whose name was Steve Jacobs. Jacobs was chatting with another cop, a deputy named Roger Clark from Goodhue County. Virgil told them about the killings in Bluestem and introduced Jesse as one of the people under threat.

"It'd be good if we could get her bodyguarded until this evening," Virgil suggested.

"I'd guard her body as long as she wants," Jacobs said.

"Me, too," Clark said.

Jesse said, "Ha-ha," but she liked the attention.

Virgil: "I'm a little serious, here, Jesse. I don't want you running around outside. Todd's a smart guy and until we figure out how to drag him down, you've got to be careful."

"Mom and I were planning to go shopping, and then come back here and watch some movies," she said.

"Don't get alone," Virgil said. "You should be okay—but just don't get alone. I'll be back by eight o'clock to get you wired up. If you get the smallest little crinkle of thought that something's wrong, find Steve here, or Roger, or one of these other cops, and tell them."

"I'll be okay," she said

Jacobs said, "We'll keep an eye on her."

"Where are you going?" Jesse asked Virgil.

"I've got an appointment at the fire department to learn CPR, and then I'll poke around, see if I can spot Todd without being too obvious about it."

"CPR?"

"It's a lifesaving technique," Virgil said.

She frowned, then shook her head. "Whatever. Don't get alone."

Virgil left her with Jacobs and Clark, headed back to Bluestem, stopped at the fire department. A big man with a handlebar mustache met him, took him back to an equipment locker, opened a door: "There you go," he said.

ON THE WAY back to Bluestem, Virgil called Joan: "Where are you?"

"At the post office," she said.

"Then where're you going?"

"Mmmm. Might go home and watch television," she said. "What're you doing?"

"Trying to contain my animal spirits."

THE GREAT THING about daytime sex, Virgil thought privately, is that you got to watch. Women didn't like to watch so much, which was understandable, because they were watching men, and men having sex wasn't that interesting. At least, not to Virgil. Women having sex was. Which was why he liked daytime sex.

And Joan said, "I gotta give this up and get something regular."

"You had something regular," Virgil said.

"You're right," she said. "Once a year is regular. Just not frequent. I need something regular and frequent. Not all over the goddamn place, morning, noon, and night."

"That would be 'nooner.' "

"You know, people haven't used that term in fifty years," she said. "You are such a small-town guy."

"I've heard it four times since I've been here," he said. "Tends to stick in your mind."

"I'm not positive that you've got enough extra space, to collect small-town sayings," Joan said.

Virgil said, "Bite me."

SHE ROLLED OVER on her stomach: "So what's the big mystery?"

"I've got it worked out that Todd Williamson is going to hang himself tonight. Or, clear himself. I'll take either one."

Her eyebrows went up. "How're you gonna do that?"

"That's complicated and confidential. However, I will take either one. If I clear him . . . Hmm. Never mind."

On the way out to the truck, Virgil noticed a clump of multicolored paper sheets stacked on the kitchen table. "Crop insurance," Joan said. "Everything the federal government touches, turns into quadruplicate or quintuplicate or something, and it takes *days* to fill it all out. And then, they do it all over next time."

Virgil looked over the forms: "Christ, I don't even understand the words."

"I'm the party of the foreplay," she said. "The government's the party of the gang bang. See, it's right there . . ."

VIRGIL LEFT JOAN'S and cruised the back of the newspaper building, in a mood, now.

A mood going sour.

He saw Williamson's truck; so he was probably in. He parked in the Ace Hardware lot for twenty minutes, watched the front of the newspaper, two blocks away, saw nothing. Moved to the McDonald's lot, parked behind the restaurant, and watched the newspaper by looking straight through the building's windows, feeling somewhat invisible.

Forty-five minutes after he began watching, Williamson came out of the newspaper, walking fast, crossed the street in the middle of the block, and went into Johnnie's Pizza. Five minutes later he came out with a pizza box and soft-drink cup, crossed the street back to his office.

So Williamson was working. Virgil called Stryker: "I need to get you and five deputies to work tonight. I'd like to get the Curlys, Jensen, Carr, couple more guys. Hook up tonight at eight o'clock. To whenever."

"What are we doing?"

"Surveillance and maybe an arrest. I'll brief everybody at eight, at the courthouse. Tell everybody to be on time and to keep their mouths shut—I don't want any of the other deputies to know about it."

"You think . . ."

"Something could happen. Or maybe not. Can't take a chance."

WHEN HE GOT OFF the phone, Virgil spent another ten minutes watching the news. Five o'clock. The rest of the day would drag. He'd deliberately set the meeting between Williamson and Jesse Laymon for after dark, because he thought the killer would feel safer. Fewer people around; and if he trailed Jesse afterward, he'd be easier to tag.

Still: a long time to wait. Maybe go back to Joan's? Maybe not. He thought about it, fired up the truck, and headed back to Worthington.

MARGARET AND JESSE were in their room, watching a movie about languid Englishmen and -women who lived in London at the beginning of the twentieth century.

"We're kinda into this movie. Could we do the planning thing afterward? There's only twenty minutes left."

"We got time," Virgil said. He left his sound kit next to the bed, and went out to the lounge. Had a beer, watched the end of a Twins–White Sox game, and walked back to the room at seven o'clock.

TO JESSE: "There is some small risk for you, but not as much as letting him go on. I don't believe there's any chance that he'll attack you at the Dairy Queen. Just in case, we're gonna have a deputy sitting outside eating an ice-cream cone. I'm thinking Margo Carr, with a gun."

Margaret said, "If Todd is a lunatic, how do we know he won't just explode and start killing people?"

"Because if he *is* a lunatic, he's a special kind," Virgil said. "He's a planner. He's meticulous. He'll do it, but he'll lower his odds of getting caught, however he can. He won't just start blasting away."

Jesse asked, "Then what do you think he'll do?"

"He'll meet you. He'll bullshit you. He'll find out what you're planning to do. Then he'll come after you. Might have a long gun, pull up beside you on the road home, after you get off the highway, take a shot. Might dump his car and walk to your house, and then come in after both of you. That's what we're hoping he'll do . . ."

"You're *hoping* he'll do that?" Margaret asked.

"Jim Stryker and I and the Curlys and Larry Jensen will be staking him out. Margo will be at the Dairy Queen.

Two more will actually be inside your house—we'll drop them off early. I'll need a key from you. So Jesse goes and talks to Todd, then she gets in her truck and she takes off— and when she gets out on the highway, she really rolls." He looked at Jesse. "You move just as fast as you're comfortable with."

"I'm pretty comfortable with ninety," she said.

"That's good. You've only got a few miles down to your exit, if you get even a small jump on him, he won't be able to catch you before you get home. We'll have two guys on the highway in front of you. When you get home, you go in the back door and right down the basement. The two guys who are in front of you will keep going, two blocks down the way, and then out on their feet. Then we've got two guys inside if he goes in after Jesse, and two outside, and two more right behind him."

"What am I doing during all this?" Margaret asked.

"I'd like you to stay here," Virgil asked. "Or wait in my room down in Bluestem. We'll keep you right up to date on what's going on . . ."

Virgil picked up his sound kit and unzipped it. The two microphones and transmitter together were no bigger than a matchbox, and the microphones themselves were as thin as pennies. "This is a radio," Virgil said, showing it to them. "There are two microphones; they route separately through the transmitter. Like a cell phone, but the microphones are way better. We'll tape the mikes to your chest—best if you wear a T-shirt—and clip the transmitter inside the waist of your jeans, at the small of your back. We'll both be able to hear you, and record it at the same time.

"When you meet him, you push him about the moon tattoo, the man-in-the-moon thing," Virgil continued. "You push him about how he must've known that Judd was his father—how could a Twin Cities newspaper reporter, with all that curiosity, and all those records right there in St. Paul, not know who his father was? And didn't he have grandparents, and wouldn't they know? He won't want you to ask those questions—he'll be pretty hot about keeping you from asking. I think he'll be right after you."

"What if he doesn't do all that?" Jesse asked. "What if he goes home and goes to bed?"

Virgil said, "Well, shoot. Then we'd have to start over with something else. But he was calling you because he wants to make some kind of move. I think."

"I'd like to get it over with," Jesse said.

"We all would," Virgil said. "So. You want to take your shirt off?"

WHEN HE LEFT Worthington the second time, at seven-thirty, Jesse was ready to roll, the wire tested both for recording fidelity and for direct sound.

At five after eight, Virgil was back at the courthouse.

Daylight was beginning to fade, the shadows long across Main Street, red light reflecting off west-facing windows. Sundown would come a few minutes before nine o'clock.

Stryker was waiting, with the two Curlys, Jensen, Carr, and two guys named Padgett and Brooks.

Virgil leaned on the front edge of Stryker's desk. "I've pulled together evidence that suggests that Todd Williamson might have been capable of doing the Gleason and Schmidt killings, and the two Judds, and might have been inclined to do them. I'm going to feed that evidence back to him, tonight, through Jesse Laymon, and hope that it forces him into an overt act. They're going to meet at ten o'clock at the Dairy Queen. After the meeting, which I'm set up to record, and to monitor, Jesse is going to take off as fast as she can, for home. So fast that Williamson won't be able to ambush her, or run her off the road, on the way.

"Deputies Padgett and Brooks"—he nodded at them— "will already be at her house, waiting. Jim and Larry will try to figure out where Williamson is, before he goes to the meeting, stake him out, and track him toward the Dairy Queen.

"The two Curlys will be down south of the Dairy Queen, in separate cars. Once Jesse takes off, I want you two *in front* of her, heading back to her place . . . The rest of us will follow behind, so we'll have him boxed in if he goes after her."

"What about me?" Carr asked.

"I've got something touchy, if you're willing to do it," Virgil said. "I want you in civvies. But with a gun: this guy is dangerous. You'll be in your own car, and as soon as Larry sees Williamson walk into the Dairy Queen, I want you to pull in and order an ice-cream cone. Sit outside on one of those benches, and lick it down. One hand on your gun."

She smiled: "Sounds good to me."

"Where'll you be?" Stryker asked Virgil.

"I'll be in my truck, parked behind Jane's Nails. I want to stay back in the dark, but I've got to be in radio range, too, so I can monitor the meeting."

"I've got a couple of questions," said Brooks.

"ALL RIGHT," Virgil said. "Let's do the details. But: we've got to be in place an hour before Williamson is due to meet Jesse, by nine o'clock. Williamson is at his office: we don't want to lose him . . ." He stepped to a wall map of Bluestem, on the wall behind Stryker's desk, touched street corners. "I figure Stryker and Jensen will be here and here, covering the front and back doors of the newspaper office."

WHEN HE WAS DONE, Carr asked, "So if Todd doesn't do anything, we just go home?"

"No. We'll be giving him a serious push—he won't want Jesse Laymon to talk to me. I think he'll have to do something. If Jesse takes off, and Williamson goes home, or back to his office, or wherever, we'll tag him. Overnight, anyway. And just in case he figures out a way to sneak off, I want Padgett and Brooks to hang at Jesse's overnight." He nodded at the two men: "If nothing happens, I'll join you out there early tomorrow, and I'll ship Jesse back to her hideout while I try to figure something else."

"All seems a little shaky," Brooks said.

"It's a lot shaky," Virgil said. "But to tell you the truth, with what I've got now, and what I'm likely to get, I don't think we've got a conviction. He'll get away with it, unless he kills somebody else, and trips up. We gotta take the shot."

"Not against that," Brooks said. "I'm just sayin'."

"I hear you," Virgil said. "I'm more worried than you are."

"WHAT IF he really didn't do it?" Jensen asked.

Virgil smiled. He'd been waiting for that question. "That's almost as good. If we clear him, I think I can work out who we're really looking at. We've really got quite a bit of detail, once you sift it out," Virgil said.

"What detail?" Stryker asked.

Virgil shrugged. "I got notes. Small stuff. Show it to you later."

THEY WENT OVER the details one more time, but it wasn't rocket science, and they were done by 8:45. They were all a little hot, eager to get going, and by nine, Virgil was alone in his truck, and called Jesse. "You ready to roll?"

"Yup. I'm a little nervous."

"Good. You should be. We've already got the place staked

out," Virgil said. "Margo Carr will be outside. She'll be close enough to be there instantly if you scream; and she's armed. I'll be five seconds away, on the corner by Sherwin-Williams. Now: remember about the radio check. You call me on your cell when you're coming up to the exit so we can get Margo moving, and then when you're coming into the Dairy Queen, turn on the radio. I'll make sure you're coming in clear. Don't get out of the truck until I give you the okay."

"Okay. I'll leave here right at eight-thirty."

"Stay in touch," Virgil said. "You've got my cell. Call me for anything."

AT TEN AFTER NINE, Virgil was squatting between two plastic recycling bins and the back wall of Jane's Nails and Extensions, a cell-phone bud in one ear, a cop-radio bud in the other. Stryker called: "All right, I got Williamson. He's at the office. Saw his head in the window, clear as day."

"His house is dark," Jensen said. "I'm moving up behind the Judd building, looking down the alley toward the back."

A minute later: "I'm looking down the alley. His van is there."

Another minute, Stryker: "Got him again. He's working."

STRYKER SAW HIM twice more, the clock creeping around to nine-thirty.

Virgil: "All right, everybody, Jesse is on her way. Margo, are you there?"

"At my house, all set, in my car. I am two minutes away," she said.

"Big Curly?"

"Here."

"Little Curly?"

"Looking at the Diary Queen."

"Stay cool, everybody."

Virgil himself was not that cool. He lay behind the two garbage cans, with the shotgun, watching his truck across the street. Nine thirty-two. Nine thirty-five.

LIKE THIS: he thought the odds that the killer was Williamson were about thirty percent, one in three. If he was, then Williamson would meet Jesse in the Dairy Queen, and Jesse would unload a whole bunch of things that Virgil had told her, about his record, about being Lane, about how he must've known he was Judd's son, just to get there . . . about talking again with Betsy, to see if she could identify him. If that happened, then Williamson would follow her home and try to kill her, and they'd get him.

But the Curlys had shown themselves capable of some serious shit. Big Curly had been there the night that Maggie Lane died; might have known that she'd been beaten before she died. They'd tampered with a murder scene, for sure. They said that Todd Williamson had fed them Jesse Laymon as a suspect, and Big Curly said that Williamson had gone through the Gleason house, and may have left the Revelation. But all of that was what the Curlys said . . .

An alternative: one of the Gleasons, knowing about the cover-up surrounding Maggie Lane's death, had gotten religion. Maybe even from Feur. And fearing for their souls, had started talking about coming clean. So the Gleasons had been silenced by someone else involved in the cover-up: Big Curly.

Judd suspected something: so Judd died.

Roman Schmidt began to put things together: and the Schmidts went down.

Thirty percent, Virgil thought.

BUT THE STRYKER FAMILY was deep in this, as well. Had the motive to get rid of the Judds—Judd had killed their father and husband. And when Amy Sweet had told Virgil that she'd mentioned the Judd ethanol plant to her bridge group, the one member of the group whose name Virgil had recognized had been Laura Stryker's. So at least one Stryker had known that Judd was headed back toward ethanol, a scheme that might have looked a lot like the Jerusalem artichoke scam.

It was possible, he thought, that the Strykers, one or all of them, would not want Williamson cleared, as Virgil had suggested he might be. And Stryker did have a streak of violence in him, as Jesse had suggested. He'd killed Feur and the man named John without turning a hair. Twenty percent, one or all.

THERE WAS a possibility, which would never really come clear, if it were true, that *George Feur* was behind it all, as Jim Stryker believed. Good reason to believe that— Stryker wasn't a stupid man. Fifteen percent.

MARGARET LAYMON was another possibility, although he really didn't think she would have left that pistol in Jesse's boot. Or, in any case, he couldn't see why she would do that.

Then there were a few outliers: Jensen and Margo Carr. *Somebody* had planted that Revelation, and that Salem cigarette butt, and had known that Carr would pick it up.

Altogether, another fifteen percent.

FOR A TOTAL OF 110 PERCENT.

VIRGIL NOW HAD them all separated and one of them, maybe, was worried. He'd carefully primed them all with the belief that he had more information, had more ideas about who the killer might be . . .

And one of them, he thought, the crazy one, the man in the moon, might well be coming with a gun to erase the Virgil Flowers problem.

And if nobody did? Well, then, maybe it *was* Feur.
Maybe . . .

VIRGIL LOOKED DOWN at his watch. Nine-forty.

Had to be Williamson, Virgil thought. He was still in his shop, under surveillance.

If it was another one of them, he or she would have already made a move. Maybe it was a bust . . .

Then Moonie came out of the shadows . . .

25

V IRGIL HAD JUST called Stryker: "He moving yet?"

"Not a thing. Lights are still on."

"Have you seen . . . ?"

AT THAT MOMENT, a figure emerged from the hedge at the back of the Sherwin-Williams store, dressed all in black, except for jogging shoes with reflective strips on the back, little white flashes in the night. Hard to see him, though it was a *he*. Couldn't be Williamson, because he was still at the paper.

The killer jogged silently in a combat hunch to the back and then down the side of Virgil's truck. Virgil half stood as the figure lifted the muzzle of a shotgun as he came up to the truck's front door, then stepped back and fired a single shot like thunder and lightning in the night, a flash of exploding glass, through the window on the truck, neatly blowing the head off the CPR dummy that sat behind the wheel.

In the flash, Virgil caught his face.

VIRGIL SHOUTED: "Williamson: lay the gun on the ground."

Williamson had never struck Virgil as an athlete, but he spun and pumped and fired and the last words weren't out of Virgil's mouth when lightning flashed at him, but going wide, and he went flat and squeezed off a shot from his own shotgun, but Williamson had vanished. Virgil had the impression that his shot had gone in close, but he'd learned early that a shotgun was no sure cure in a gunfight.

Fuckin' Williamson!

He could hear Stryker screaming on the radio: he picked it up and shouted, "Williamson's out. Williamson's out. He's got a shotgun and he ran behind Sherwin-Williams. Kick in the door on his office, make sure he's not headed back there. He's got a shotgun and I don't know what else, he's shooting, so everybody take it easy. Everybody stay in your cars, let's see if we can spot him . . ."

"You okay, you okay?" Stryker was still screaming.

"I'm okay, except I'm scared. Everybody stay cool now. Let's round him up. Margo, are you there? Jensen?"

Stryker: "How'd he get out, how'd he get out . . . ?"

THEY CHECKED IN, all cruising.

Little Curly said, "I'm going down the tracks, I'm going down the tracks . . ."

Big Curley: "I'm behind Marvin's, heading toward the elevator."

A few seconds later, the tornado siren went off. The dispatcher called: "I'm waking up everybody in town. I've got the weather-tree going—in five minutes, everybody in town will know that it's Williamson and they'll all be looking out the windows."

Margo Carr: "Do you think he cut back across Poplar? If he's headed down to the river, he'll be hard to spot."

Jensen: "Tommy, get back to the weather-tree, tell people to lock their doors and call if somebody tries to get at a car."

Dispatcher: "Louie Barth says somebody ran down the alley just a minute ago, behind his house . . ."

Carr: "I'm right there, I'm taking the alley . . ."

Virgil had brushed the glass off the seat of his truck, threw the decapitated dummy in the back, and took off, calling, "Careful, careful, Margo, don't let him ambush you. Where am I going, where am I going . . . ?"

Saw flashers, north, turned that way, more flashers coming up behind. Dispatcher called, "I've got everybody coming in, we're coming right in on top of you, Margo . . ."

VIRGIL HEARD the boom of a shotgun, close, no more than a couple of blocks, called, "Got gunfire, got gunfire . . ." saw the lights ahead, cut left, closed, cut left, found a squad car across a street, a body on the ground, Stryker standing, then on the radio, "Margo's down, she's hit, he took her car, he's running east on Clete, he's turning north on Seventy-five . . ."

Virgil was out on the street and Stryker shouted, "She's bad, she's bad . . ."

"Get her in your truck, run it to the hospital." Together, they lifted her into the backseat of the truck. She had shotgun-pellet wounds in her face and neck; she was semiconscious, pumping blood, and Stryker took off and Virgil shouted into the radio, to the dispatcher, "Call the emergency room, they've got a gunshot wound coming in, gonna need a surgeon, gonna need some blood . . ."

"I think I got him, I think I got him," Jensen called. Big Curly: "I got him too, he's running north on Seventy-five . . ." And a third cop, unknown to Virgil: "I'm running south on Seventy-five, I'm just going past Ambers, I don't see him yet."

Virgil took the truck back down the street and cut onto the main drag, saw flashing lights ahead, accelerating out of town. More lights were filing in behind him, every cop in the city, then Jensen called, "He's turned off at the park, he's turned at the park, he's headed up to Judd's . . . He's running out of road."

Virgil: "Dispatch, start breaking people around the perimeter of the hill, we don't want everybody at the same spot up on top. Tell them to put their lights on the hill but get out of the trucks in the dark behind them, watch for him coming down the hill."

VIRGIL WAS two hundred yards behind Big Curly, who was two hundred yards behind Jensen, who was a half mile behind Williamson. Virgil saw Carr's truck, driven by Williamson, climbing the hill toward Judd's, then Jensen's tail-lights flaring as he slowed to turn through the park gates and up the hill, then Big Curly slowing, and then Virgil was slowing, and then Jensen said, "Holy shit! He's turned down the hill toward the bluff, toward the Buffalo Jump. Man, he's headed right toward it . . . Jesus Christ!"

Virgil had turned and was looking up the hill when he saw the lights of the lead car, Williamson, bounding over humps in the turf, once, twice, and then he was gone.

"He went over," Jensen screamed. "Jesus Christ, he went over."

Virgil shouted: "Dispatch, get people down there. Larry. Stop where you are: put your headlights down there, Big Curly, get up by Larry, put your headlights across the slope, I'm coming in, I'll bet he bailed out before the car went over the edge."

Then he was there, pulling past the second cop, pulling past Jensen, playing his lights across the slope; saw no movement, was out of the truck, stepped back to Jensen and Big Curly and said, "Get back out of the light, guys, get back in the dark."

"Don't see anybody. I don't see anybody," Jensen said. He and Big Curly both had shotguns. Virgil popped the back of his truck, unlocked the toolbox, lifted out the semiauto .30-06 and two magazines; opened his duffel, took out a long-sleeved camo shirt that he used for turkey hunting.

"You guys stay here. Watch the light: he'll have to move if he didn't go over the edge." He slapped a magazine into the rifle, worked the bolt one time. "If you see him, yell. I can't use the radio. It'd give me away."

"Where're you going?" Big Curly asked.

"I'm gonna crawl around up the hill. If he's not dead at the bottom, he must've headed uphill. He'd be crawling."

Jensen: "Man, maybe we ought to wait."

Virgil shook his head: "Can't. Once he's off the hill, he's got a hundred miles of cornfields in every direction. We'll get him sooner or later, but not before he kills a couple of farmers for their cars. What we need, Larry, is every cop you can find, throwing a perimeter around this hill . . . It'll take him a while to get off."

"Get some dogs in," Big Curly said.

Virgil snapped his fingers: "Do that. Do that right now. If you can get a couple of dogs, tell the handlers to get them to bark. Get them down below. We want him to think that the dogs are coming."

"They will be," Big Curly said.

"No, no. If he sees people coming, and feels like he's trapped, he'll go down shooting," Virgil said. "If you have a dog walk right up on him, the handler gets shot. We don't want that. Want the dogs barking, but we don't want them trailing in the dark. I'm going. Keep watching the headlights. If you see him . . ."

"Take it easy," Jensen said. "Take it easy."

"If he's down there at the bottom of the hill, just start honking your horns," Virgil said. "I'll be back."

IN THE GOOD OLD DAYS, in fifth, sixth, seventh, and maybe eighth grades, before the whole issue of women came up, Virgil and his male friends would occasionally play war, always on a soft summer evening, when the light was fading to dark. There were apple trees in the neighborhood, to provide the ammo; a golf-ball-sized green apple, thrown at close range, could give you a bruise like a good left hook. Tree lines, fences, hedges, and overgrown bridal-wreath bushes provided the cover.

One thing everybody learned quickly was that in the dark, even with a bright moon—a full moon hung over-head as Virgil slipped into the grass, heading up the hill—was that you were never sure what was human and what was shadow; you learned not to look directly at some-one, because he could *feel* you in the dark. You learned to move slowly, like the moon shadows spreading across the open. If you didn't learn, you'd take a shot behind the ear, just as sure as God made little green apples.

THE WAR GAMES were still in Virgil's blood, refined by years of hunting. He slipped into the thigh-high bluestem, running in a crouch, then duckwalking and crawling, quickly at first, getting away from the lights of the trucks, then more slowly, feeling his way past hard corners of exposed rock, the occasional bit of brush, the prickly wild rose.

Williamson had essentially rolled the car down the hill the same way his mother's had gone down, and over the bluff. If he'd bailed before it went over, he'd have three choices: head sideways and down the hill to the west, head up and across it to the north, or head sideways and uphill to the east. He couldn't go south, because that was sheer bluff.

Virgil didn't think he would go down and west, because that would take him right into the face of the arriving cops, and also force him to cross the approach road. He could have gone north, but that would have cut across the lights from Jensen's and Big Curly's headlights as they came up the hill.

Most likely, Virgil thought, Williamson went east, parallel to the bluff, or slightly northeast, edging away from the bluff. That way, he'd avoid the road altogether, which ended at the ruins of the Judd place. He'd cross below the Judd place, turn more north, across the shoulder of the hill, and after walking down the far side, would step into the ocean of cornfields that spread out below.

The corn was high enough that he'd be able to jog, guided by the rows, without being seen. Someplace along the run, he'd cut into a farmer's place looking for a ride.

IF VIRGIL WAS RIGHT, he should cross paths with Williamson above the Judd place.

If he was wrong, if Williamson had gone straight north,

and he'd made it across the road . . . then Williamson would be behind him, and above him.

That wouldn't be good.

He stopped for ten seconds, listening. Could hear men shouting, a long way away, but no horn honking. Williamson had bailed. Could hear crickets, could hear the crinkle of grass in the breeze, could hear the rasping *szzzikks* of nighthawks. Listened as hard as he could, heard nothing more.

Moved on.

WILLIAMSON RAN AWAY from the car, into the dark, clutching the shotgun, no particular destination in mind. He'd fucked up, and this was what happened when you fucked up.

He'd known that Flowers would be out there on the street, watching the Dairy Queen. What he'd thought was, "How stupid does he think I am?"—that dumb little bitch Jesse Laymon calling him up, laying all that past-history stuff on him, like she thought it up herself. The meeting had to be a setup.

Had to be.

So he'd come up with a counterstroke: it was possible that Flowers had kept his investigation to himself, because Stryker and the others were also suspects. And if the newspaper were under surveillance, and if he showed himself there, and then, if he went over the roof, down the whole block, and came down the fire escape on the back of Hartbry's, and wired it down . . . and if he nailed Flowers as he waited in his truck, and then cut behind Sherwin-Williams and made it down the alley and back up the fire escape . . .

Hell, it was a big risk, but the jig was almost up anyway. Flowers was pushing him, and if he knew about the Williamsons and the way they died . . .

But if he pulled it off—he was good.

Flowers killed, while *he* was under surveillance.

The shotgun was Judd Jr.'s and old enough that they'd probably never trace it to him. He could drop it in the street after he fired it . . .

He'd worked through it, frightened himself, worked through it again, rehearsed it, had, at the last minute, gone to the roof and spotted two watchers—he knew every car in town, certainly knew Stryker's and Jensen's—and convinced himself it would work.

Scared, sweating, pulling on the black turtleneck, hot in the night, the gloves, his regular black slacks.

HE'D RUN the turtleneck and the gloves through the shredder when he got back, he thought, flush them down the toilet . . .

Jesus, what a risk.

Jesus, what a rush.

End it. End it.

HE'D ALMOST DONE IT.

He'd been sure he had Flowers, if nothing else. Had seen the head in the window of the truck, from the back. Had come up just right, had hardly heard the boom of the shotgun, had felt the most intense joy at the impact in the glass, and started to run, and then somebody called his name and he finished turning and saw movement and fired the gun and realized he'd been had . . .

"How stupid does he think I am?"

THE REST of it all passed in a panic flash. He was on foot, he could hear the cop cars all around, then the lights came around a corner, and Carr was coming up the alley. He stepped into a hedge, simply pressed back into it, and when she came up . . .

Boom/Flash.

HE HAD the car; he could hear them screaming on Carr's radio as he dumped her into the street, and then he was around the corner; and then more lights, and a flasher bar behind him. He hadn't thought about where to go, but he happened to be going north. He heard more cars calling in, heard them calling out his location, felt the squeeze.

He wouldn't go far in the car.

A last stand wasn't his style.

He turned without thinking down the county road that led to the park road, then up the park road to the Judd turnoff, radio blasting, lights behind him, more lights on the road below . . . and he turned down the crease in the hill that had taken his mother, and thought to follow her over, get it done with.

No guts.

Bailed at the last moment, grabbing the shotgun as he went.

Found himself rolling across the rocks, in the dark, as Margo Carr's vehicle rolled down the hill and over the bluff, like a GMC Buffalo.

HE CRAWLED, got up, started to run. Fell, hurt himself. Take it slower.

Slower. The car disappeared and he dropped into the knee-high prairie grass and began to crawl, the shotgun clattering over the surface rocks, and he crawled and shuffled and duckwalked and hopped, away from the lights, below the pit of the Judd house, along the bluff, to get away, to get anywhere . . .

And he heard a rock rolling; a footstep. Froze.

Lights down the hill, men shouting, but here, it was as black as a coal bin, and quiet.

Another rock. He wasn't alone. Buffalo? There was a fence, couldn't be a buffalo. Could be a deer . . .

Could be that fuckin' Flowers.

VIRGIL SAT at the corner of the hill, below a clump of plum trees, none more than about six feet high, and all of them armed with sharp spurs: not quite thorns, but they hurt like hell if you jabbed yourself.

He was sitting on a crumbled pile of rock. He hadn't had

the eye to hit major-college pitching, but he had the arm to be a major-college third baseman. He sat and threw rocks into the dark, listening to them hit, listening for reaction.

HEARD WHAT he thought might be a footfall, below, a hundred feet away. Threw a rock out in front of it: the quiet got quieter. Interesting. Threw another rock into the night, and picked up the rifle. Nothing. Threw another rock . . .

WILLIAMSON HAD the movement figured. Somebody moving to his right, kicking an occasional rock. He focused: he had three shells left. Had to be Flowers . . . didn't it? He thought about firing, but didn't. Instead, amazed at himself, he called, "Virgil? You there?"

VIRGIL HEARD HIM clearly, below, to the right of the place he'd been throwing rocks. Eased himself flat, pushed the rifle out in front of him.

"Todd? You okay?"

Williamson: "I'm pretty fuckin' scared, man."

Virgil: "We know you've got that shotgun. Margo's gonna be okay; she's got glass but she's not going to die. Give it up."

Williamson: "You won't shoot me?"

Virgil: "You must've heard about the time I shot at somebody fourteen times, and missed. Everybody else in town has. I don't want any goddamn gunfight."

Williamson: "Judd killed my mom."

Virgil: "I know. I got the same opinion from a medical examiner. Judd beat her with a pool cue. She was already dying when she went over the edge. You really *were* a miracle baby."

WILLIAMSON HAD him spotted. Flowers was no more than thirty or forty feet away, he thought. He was invisible, but then, *he* must be invisible to Flowers, as well. He half stood, pointing the gun in the direction of the voice. "I quit," he said. "What do you want me to do?"

Virgil said, "Toss the shotgun . . ."

Williamson pointed the shotgun and fired and pumped and then . . .

HE WAS on his back, the shotgun clattering away, and he was looking up at the moon, almost full, and he heard Flowers shouting and then a bright light cut his eyes and Flowers was kneeling next to him.

The pain cut in: everything below his waist was on fire. He said to Flowers, "I guess that wasn't too bright."

"NO, IT WASN'T," Virgil said. He patted Williamson on the shoulder, not knowing what else to do. "Hang in there, we'll have you on your way in a minute." He stood up and circled the flash, "Over here, goddamnit, we need to carry him, we need a litter, something to carry him with. Let's go, go . . ."

People were running and Virgil sat down next to Williamson again. "That was you that shot at me and Joanie down in the dell?" Virgil said.

"Ahh," Williamson said. Pain and agreement. But of course, it had been. That's why he hadn't known about a better place to park, and a better approach to the dell: Williamson wasn't a Bluestem native, had never taken his girl up to swim in the dell.

"One more question, before everybody gets here . . ."

Williamson was fading but he answered the question and then Jensen stumbled up, Stryker was there, and more people were yelling and they started moving Williamson.

Too late.

The hornet's nest of .30-caliber slugs had taken out a chunk of his femoral artery, a chunk no bigger than a corn kernel. That was enough.

Halfway down the hill, Todd Williamson bled out and died.

26

VIRGIL AND JOAN took a picnic basket up to the top of the hill above Stryker's Dell, spread a blanket, ate pastrami sandwiches, and found faces in the clouds. Virgil was disturbed. He'd never killed anyone before, though he'd once shot a woman in the foot.

Joan knew that, and prattled on about other things, trying to pry his mind away from it. He knew what she was doing, and it wasn't working.

And she said, ". . . definitely in love. When Jim was married the first time, it was like, you know, they were *obliged* to get married. They dated in high school, and everybody else got taken, so they got married. But they never clicked. There wasn't any heat."

"I hope it works out," Virgil said. "Jesse's a handful. I saw them this morning, and they seemed pretty happy."

"Well, at least Todd . . . it's all done with," Joan said. "Being scared, being worried, being lonely. A lot of things changed in the past couple of weeks." She looked up at him: "You're brooding."

"Sorry."

DAVENPORT HAD CALLED the morning after the shooting and the first thing he'd asked was, "How are *you*?"

"He never touched me," Virgil said.

"That's not what I meant," Davenport said. "I meant, 'How's your head?'"

"Don't know."

"Keep me up on it," Davenport said. "You've always been the sensitive type. It worries me."

"Okay."

Davenport pushed: "Virgil: the guy was like a drunk driver, and you were the wall. It's not the wall's fault when the drunk gets killed."

"Okay."

"When are you coming back? No rush, you're on leave until we have the board."

"I'll be back. Couple of things to pick up here," Virgil said.

"Take it easy. If it really gets on top of you, there are pills," Davenport said. "Believe me: they can help. I know."

"Thanks, man. Talk to ya."

SO VIRGIL AND JOAN looked at the clouds and picked out an elephant and a burning bush and a fat man's ass, complete with a tiny blue anus with a streak of sunshine showing through it, and Joan asked, "How did you get so focused on Todd?"

"The Revelation," Virgil said. "The book of Revelation at the Gleason's. It was planted. It was not in the crime-scene photos. There are at least a couple of hundred photographs inside the Gleason place, and there was no Revelation. The house was sealed up tight—not even family was allowed inside. So it had to be a cop or some-body with a cop. When Big Curly confessed that he'd taken Williamson through, that did it. Although . . . I still con-sidered the possibility that it was one of the Curlys. Or another cop."

After a minute, he added, "Ah, man."

Joan said, "I know you're upset, but I say, thank God it's over."

"Yeah."

"Well, look: the alternative would have been a heck of a lot worse—if it'd been you who got shot."

"On the other hand, Margo Carr *did* get shot," Virgil said. "She's gonna have six different surgeries before she's back. Hospital for a month, physical therapy, gonna have to take some skin off her thigh to make her neck right, never gonna *be* right . . ."

SHE LOOKED HIM over carefully: "You're really frozen up, Virgil. The guy was crazy."

Virgil, lying on his back, his head cupped in the palms of his hands, said, "I had a chance to talk with him before he died. Isn't that just like a cop? Interrogating a dying man?"

"You didn't know he was dying," she said.

"I knew I'd shot him with a .30-06, which wouldn't do
him a hell of a lot of good."

"Well . . ."

THEY PICKED OUT a watermelon, which was just an
oval cloud, and a three-legged dog, or maybe a three-
legged chicken, after the wind blew a beak on it, and Joan
asked, "What'd you ask him?"

Virgil wiggled his butt around on the blanket, and said,
"I asked him about the woman who called and told him
that he was Bill Judd's son. Asked whether it was an old
woman or a young woman."

Long silence. Then, "Oh, shit."

"Yeah. He said young."

They sat in another cloud of silence, until finally she
said, "Who was the other candidate?"

"Your mom. Amy Sweet said she mentioned at her
bridge club, three, four years back, that Judd was getting
into the ethanol business. I asked her who the members of
the club were. Your mom was one of them."

"So how did that . . . ?"

"A whole list of things. I couldn't figure out how
Williamson knew he was Judd's son. I talked to Maggie
Lane's mother, and *she* didn't know. She said *Maggie* might
not have known for sure . . . though I suspect she did. That
might have been what she and Judd were arguing about the
night of the man-on-the-moon party: the pregnancy."

Virgil yanked a long grass stem out of its envelope,

nibbled on the sweet end. "Anyway, if nobody in the Cities knew, then it had to come from here. And who would put Todd Williamson in with the Judds? Had to be somebody with a hard grudge against Judd. Who was that? The Strykers.

"It seemed too subtle to be Jim. And then you told me directly that you'd been too young to be much affected by your father's death—but your mother told me the exact opposite, a couple of times. Said your father's death really tore you up.

"And you've been all those years out here on the farm, trying to pick up the pieces.

"And you got close to me the very first day I was in town, and suggested Williamson as a target . . .

"Then I got that note out of nowhere. That got me looking for a typewriter, and I never found one—but then you had those federal farm crop insurance papers, in several copies, and they were filled out with a typewriter."

"Shit, shit, shit . . ." More silence. "When Williamson showed up and shot the dummy in your car, did you expect it to be Williamson? Or Big Curly? Or me or Jim?"

He shook his head: "Didn't think it was you. We had the evidence of Roman Schmidt's dick to say so."

He had to explain that.

"How'd you track him down?" Virgil asked finally. "How'd you find out he was crazy?"

"I didn't know he was crazy." She sat up and pulled her

legs against her chest, wrapped her arms around them. "I knew Junior was in financial trouble and that Senior had bad health problems. When I heard about the ethanol thing from my mother . . . well, we both thought it was another scam, the whole Jerusalem artichoke deal all over again, with a bunch of farmers getting screwed.

"I didn't know what to do about it," she said. "Then, I was thinking, there'd always been rumors about Lane, that the baby was Judd's, that Judd had killed her. So I wondered, what if another heir showed up? What if the whole Judd fortune had to be taken to court? If the details of the ethanol plant came out? What if somebody sued Senior for wrongful death? All kinds of things could have happened— maybe we'd even find out where the money went from the Jerusalem artichoke business . . . That's what I thought.

"About that time, the Internet was really getting going and they had all these groups that were set up to help adopted kids track their natural parents. I got hooked up, found out how it was done. Ended up with Todd Williamson. Gave him a call. Told him he was heir to a fortune."

"And then?"

"Nothing. For quite a while. Then he just showed up. Never made any claims: just showed up as the editor of the *Record*." She frowned, tossed her hair. "I don't know how he did that, but it freaked me out. And nothing happened. I knew he *knew*, but I couldn't *say* anything. I figured he was waiting for the old man to die; or maybe he'd already talked to the old man, and had made a deal."

"You waited."

"Three years. When the Gleasons got killed, it never crossed my mind that it was Todd. Honest to God. Then old man Judd was murdered, and Jim thought—and you thought—that the two things went together. That worried me."

"You should have said something."

"I should have—I sorta did, to you—but I felt like . . . people would blame me," she said. "And I wasn't sure that it was related. I just wasn't sure."

"So you sent me a note . . ."

"Because nobody was doing anything about the *Judds*. And it seemed to me that the Judds were right at the center of all of this. If they were running another scam, then wouldn't that say something about the murders? When you and Jim checked it out, you found Feur—I didn't know he was in the ethanol plant; I just knew that Judd was. And then, Jim was *sure* that the murders were Feur, or Feur's people. So I kept letting it go, the thing about Todd. You found out pretty quick anyway . . ."

"But you sorta killed the Schmidts, Joanie."

"OH, HORSESHIT," she said. "I thought about that, I really did. And the Gleasons. But you know what? The Gleasons killed the Gleasons. And the Schmidts killed the Schmidts. And the Johnstones would have killed the Johnstones, if they'd been killed. They'd all covered up that awful murder and what they got back was Todd

Williamson. That was the return on the investment."

"Jesus."

"He would probably disapprove."

AFTER A WHILE, Joan asked, "So what are you going to do about it?"

"Nothing," Virgil said. "Go home."

"That's it?" She seemed a little surprised.

"I think you fucked up, Joanie. But I'm not sure you've committed a crime," Virgil said. "If you have, I sure couldn't prove it."

She sighed, and lay back on the blanket. "Ah, gosh, Virgil."

"Yeah."

They picked out more clouds: an atomic-bomb explosion, a semierect and uncircumcised penis, and the hat of the quaker guy on the Quaker Oats label.

Eventually, Joan sat up and stretched and said, "Listen. If you ever come by this way again . . ."

Virgil pulled out another blade of grass, chewed for a second, getting the sweet out, then said, "Bite me."

POCKET
BOOKS

John Sandford

Broken Prey

The first corpse is found on the riverbank. The second in an
isolated farmhouse. Both have been savagely beaten, the skin
flayed from their bodies, their throats cut.

For both victims, there's a DNA match. Charlie Pope, a
convicted sex offender, has cut himself free from his court-
imposed ankle bracelet and disappeared. Now all Davenport
has to do is find him.

But something doesn't smell right. The killings were
calculated and methodical. Pope is of low mental intelligence,
incapable of forethought and planning.

All the evidence points to Pope – but Davenport has his
doubts. To find the answers, he must track down his key
suspect. And to do that, he'll need the help of the Big Three:
three vicious serial killers locked up in the state security
hospital. Three killers as cunning as they are deranged . . .

'An exciting and superbly elegant demonstration of intelligent
crime writing' *Guardian*

ISBN 978-0-7434-8417-6
PRICE £6.99

POCKET
BOOKS

John Sandford

Mind Prey

It was raining when Andi left the parent-teacher meeting with
her two daughters, and she was distracted. She didn't notice
the red van parked beside her, or the van door slide open. The
last thing she did notice was the hand reaching out for her –
and the menacing voice from the past.

When Lucas Davenport hears that psychiatrist Andi Manette
and her daughters have been kidnapped, he knows
instinctively that he's about to tackle one of his worst ever
cases. For this time, Davenport has truly met his match – a
nemesis more intelligent, and more depraved, than any he has
tracked before. A pure, wanton killer who knows more about
mind games than Davenport himself.

'Few do it better than Sandford' *Daily Telegraph*

'Sandford knows all there is to know about detonating the gut-
level shocks of a good thriller' *New York Times*

ISBN 978-1-4165-0232-6

PRICE £6.99

**POCKET
BOOKS**

John Sandford

Winter Prey

The Iceman crept into the house on the edge of the lake. He killed the father first. Then the mother and child. And when his work was done, he set the house on fire.

Lucas Davenport had tracked killers in cities across America. But the woods of rural Wisconsin are as dark and primal as evil itself. The winters are harsher and colder. And in the heart of every mother and father, there is fear . . .

Because tonight, the Iceman cometh.

'Delivers twists to the very last sentence' *Daily Mail*

'Tough, engrossing and engaging, Sandford writes superb thrillers' *Literary Review*

ISBN 978-1-4165-0231-9
PRICE £6.99

POCKET BOOKS

This book and other **Pocket Books** titles are available
from your local bookshop or can be ordered direct
from the publisher.

9781416511434	The Devil's Code	John Sandford	£6.99
9781416502319	Winter Prey	John Sandford	£6.99
9781416502326	Mind Prey	John Sandford	£6.99
9780743484176	Broken Prey	John Sandford	£6.99
9780743484183	Easy Prey	John Sandford	£6.99
9780743484213	Sudden Prey	John Sandford	£6.99
9780743484193	Certain Prey	John Sandford	£6.99
9780743415558	Chosen Prey	John Sandford	£6.99
9780743468695	Naked Prey	John Sandford	£6.99
9780743484206	Secret Prey	John Sandford	£6.99

Please send cheque or postal order for the value of the book,
free postage and packing within the UK, to
SIMON & SCHUSTER CASH SALES
PO Box 29, Douglas Isle of Man, IM99 1BQ
Tel: 01624 677237, Fax: 01624 670923
Email: bookshop@enterprise.net
www.bookpost.co.uk

Please allow 14 days for delivery. Prices and availability
subject to change without notice